LIGHT
OF THE
TWIN
MOONS

TWIN MOONS SAGA: BOOK 6

HUMAN
AUTHORED™
ᴬᴳ The Authors Guild
5012999

BY
HOLLY BARGO

CREDITS
Editing by Cindy Draughon
Cover Design by Elementi.Studio

IMAGE SOURCES
Man's eyes: https://www.freepik.com/premium-photo/serious-man-pointing_415276394.htm

Man's head: https://www.freepik.com/premium-ai-image/serious-man-giving-thumbs-up_416144655.htm

Trees: https://www.freepik.com/premium-psd/3d-rendering-various-kinds-winter-trees_12143619.htm

Moon: https://www.freepik.com/premium-photo/full-moon_1244194.htm

Hand: https://www.freepik.com/free-photo/athletic-man-with-muscled-body-holding-weights_6654593.htm

Clothes: https://www.freepik.com/free-photo/portrait-fashion-young-man_6435939.htm

Body: https://www.freepik.com/free-photo/man-applying-sunscreen-lotion-beach_4967597.htm

For Evelyn Grace

PROLOGUE

"YOU DISAPPOINT ME," THE COOL, DISPASSIONATE voice of the Unseelie King sliced through the chaos and pain of a crumbling fortress.

Marog opened his eyes. Encased in a bubble of darkness with his father, he heard the muted sounds of screams and crashing stone. He closed his eyes again, unable to bear the king's disappointment.

"I suppose I am partially to blame," the Unseelie King murmured, his claw-tipped hand moving in a languid gesture. A pinpoint of light sparked above Marog's head. "But you have long since been responsible for your own actions, and I cannot condone what you have done. You have lost your honor and brought shame upon yourself, the Unseelie Kingdom, and *me*."

Marog tried to squirm; his groin felt like it was on fire. However, he could not move, not so much as to turn his head. *Father keeps me immobilized.*

"Indeed I do," the Unseelie King said. "The oracle warned me you would do this. I had other plans for you. Bathasul may yet have plans for you."

"*The oracle is—*"

"Silence!" the king commanded. "You may yet redeem yourself."

Marog glared at his father, fulminating hatred making his eyes glow red. The Unseelie King had been a distant father showing little interest in his heir, the crown prince of the Unseelie Court. Yet he dared not blast his rebellious, resentful thoughts at his father. Worlds trembled before the ruthless Unseelie King's might, and for good reason. Uberon did not know the meaning of the word *compassion*.

"All of Fé-Ree will believe you dead, as well you should be. But the oracle and I will know differently, and we will tell no one," the Unseelie King said as the point of light expanded. "Perhaps a realm of iron will teach you what I failed to."

Iron? For the first time, fear tingled down Marog's spine.

"If you seek a mate, then perhaps you shall find one here," the Unseelie King added. "Or perhaps this world will kill you. I no longer care, for you are dead to me. I wash my hands of you." The Unseelie King spread his fingers to hold the portal open. "Begone, Marog. Redeem yourself and I may once again call you son, but no more are you heir to the Unseelie Court. I will find my true mate, and our son will be my heir."

With a flick of his fingers, Uberon, the cold and often cruel king of the Unseelie Court, sent his only son through the portal into the realm of ancient Earth. Only after Marog passed through the portal did his body once again move.

Marog screamed until he hit cold, damp earth and the impact knocked the breath from his lungs.

CHAPTER 1

ICY WIND WHIPPED AT THE TANGLED LENGTH OF her hair, white as the sparkling snow that blanketed the vast expanses of the northern wastes. Iselde plunged her pole into the snow in measured beats as she patrolled the perimeter of her tribe's current settlement. With each step, she tested the depth of the fluffy, glittering ice crystals and set wards to alert her to danger. She glanced toward the sheltered valley where her people went about their daily tasks.

Iselde did not fear danger; any fae as ancient as she feared little at all. But time and generations of new blood had thinned the innate power of her people, so she depended on those wards to ensure her tribe survived whatever desperate fool braved the never-ending winter of the northern wastes. Iselde could not always be there to vanquish threats.

Slow, careful progress completed Iselde's circumnavigation of the small collection of tipis. Upon returning to the village, she pulled aside the flap that served as the door to the tipi she shared with the unmated women of her tribe.

"You're back just in time for supper, Matriarch," one of the women greeted, offering her a bowl of savory seal stew.

Iselde let her furs fall from her body and accepted the bowl with a solemn nod. "All is well?"

The woman nodded. "Yes, Matriarch."

Iselde carried her bowl near the small firepit in the center of the tipi and sat on a small rug. She brought a spoonful of stew to her mouth, blew on it to cool it down, and ate, analyzing the flavors. *We are low on salt.*

A restlessness beat at her. She ignored it.

"Something disturbs you, Matriarch?" another of the unmated women asked, hand extended but not quite touching Iselde.

"It is nothing to concern you," Iselde replied between bites. "How goes your courtship?"

The pretty female blushed and averted her gaze while the other four women giggled.

"Guorik gave her a polished gem," one of them said.

"It's blue and very pretty," another volunteered.

"Let me see it," Iselde said.

The young female drew a polished rock from beneath her tunic. Caged in silver wire and threaded on a leather cord, the iridescent stone glowed in the dim firelight. Iselde touched it lightly with a clawed fingertip. The stone pulsed with cool, gentle power, an aura of protection. Guorik had chosen well.

"Pretty indeed," Iselde agreed with a nod. She tilted her head. "He took no liberties?"

The woman's blush deepened as she lifted the necklace and lowered the cord around her head. Rubbing the gemstone between her fingers, she confessed to having paid him for the necklace with a kiss.

Iselde nodded and asked, "And do you accept his suit?"

The woman nodded again. "He is a fierce hunter and will be able to provide for our children."

Iselde nodded again and said, "Aye, he is and he will. But how does he treat *you*?"

"He makes me feel special," came the softly voiced answer.

Iselde took a final bite of the stew and set the bowl aside. "If you consent to this match, then you have my approval."

Although none of the women in the tipi doubted the Matriarch would have forbidden the match, they still gasped in delight.

"Bid him see me tomorrow morning," Iselde said.

"Of course, Matriarch."

One of the young women retrieved the empty bowl and spoon to clean them while another spread out the Matriarch's bedding. Although ancient and powerful, she looked no older than they did, except for the agelessness of her cobalt eyes. None in the tribe was as old as the Matriarch, although some were pureblooded, lesser fae. Most were refugees and counted themselves fortunate to have found sanctuary with the White Witch whom some called the Ice Queen.

Iselde stripped down to her chemise, lay down, and snuggled into the pallet of furs only to wake within the familiar environs of the oracle's dimly illuminated cabin. With the long practice of a skilled warrior, she sprang to her feet, claws unsheathed.

"Peace, Iselde," the oracle said from her rocking chair near the hearth.

Iselde lowered her hands and retracted her claws. "I've asked you not to do that, Mother."

The oracle's shoulders moved in a tiny shrug. One bony hand clasped the white pendant resting against her narrow chest. "It is time."

"No," Iselde said, her voice firm. She'd refused her mother before, the first time resulting in banishment to the northern wastes millennia ago. Banishment hadn't taught her the lesson her mother wished her to learn.

"Your fate draws near," the oracle intoned. She stroked the large white jewel dangling between her withered breasts. The oracle was not only ancient, she *looked* it.

"The fate that *you* would choose for me," Iselde hissed, unhappy to revisit that old argument. "I will choose my own fate."

"Your fate is quickly becoming neither your choice nor mine," the oracle countered, her tone peevish. "I will not have you die when I can prevent it."

"My life is not yours to save or squander, Mother."

The oracle's white eyes narrowed as she glared into her daughter's cobalt gaze. "I do not require your consent, Iselde."

"But you seek it nonetheless."

The oracle sniffed, a haughty sound. She flicked her other hand at her daughter in a shooing motion. "Then go, daughter."

"Gladly," Iselde muttered and headed for the door through which she had not passed to enter the small cabin. Light glowed in the crack between the door and the jamb. Iselde opened the door and stepped into the glare. The door slammed shut behind her.

Her bare foot landed on a hard, warm surface. The air around her was warm, too, positively broiling compared to the icy winds of the northern wastes. The humid and oppressive heat held a foul miasma of noxious odors that assaulted her sensitive nose: rotting food, excrement, unwashed flesh, urine, blood, vomit, and other things that were not natural. As sweat bloomed on her skin, she wracked her brain for the correct term and could not come up with one. The cacophony of odor smelled of desperation, poverty, fear, greed, lust, revelry, and violence. Lively music in the distance floated in the heavy air.

Iselde paused and looked around to get her bearings. Though it had been centuries since she had walked through any city, she recognized a blind alley when she found herself in one. She squared her shoulders and muttered under her breath, "That's the last time I trust you."

Since the first time testing her daughter's will and having lost, the oracle continued to periodically summon Iselde to accept the fate she chose for her, and Iselde refused. Every time, the oracle had returned her home, so Iselde had expected nothing different this time. She cursed herself for becoming complacent.

She stepped forward and bit back another curse as her foot landed on something sharp. *You could at least have pro-*

vided me with boots. She balanced on one foot while she pried a shard of broken glass from the sole of the other. She squeezed the wound to make it bleed and flush the impurities that would cause infection. Though the immortal fae were hardy, they were not immune to all illnesses. Her blood sparkled faintly in the weak ambient light filtering into the alley. She waited, poised and motionless, while the small wound healed.

Iselde stepped forward again, exercising extreme care. Three dark figures paused at the end of the alley, silhouetted against the brighter light that could not enter the dark, narrow space. One of them raised his face and inhaled deeply.

"Do you smell that?" he said, his voice rasping.

Another of the men sniffed and chuckled. "Blood. Sweet, sweet blood."

The third inhaled, exhaled, and inhaled again. "I've not smelled blood like that before. Is it even human?"

The first rubbed his crotch. "Human or not, we've hit the jackpot."

Iselde lowered her newly healed foot and extended her claws.

"Pretty woman ..." the second male coaxed, singing the words. Or perhaps he taunted her. "... the kind I'd like to eat."

"We should keep her for a few nights," the third male suggested as all three of them crept forward into the alley. "Even if she's not human, she *does* smell delicious."

Again, Iselde wracked her ancient memories for the word she needed. This time she found it and whispered, "Vampire."

"She knows what we are," the third vampire hissed in alarm.

"That doesn't matter," the first replied.

"On three," the second whispered.

Iselde did not wait for them to count to three. She drew upon the ancient fae power within her soul and flooded the alley with intense white light and heat to rival the sun. The three vampires shrieked as their undead flesh ignited and bright blue flames quickly consumed them. Glass, asphalt, and steel melted. Bits of wood, paper, and plastic flared and burned. A vagrant lurking behind a dumpster cried out and died, his few possessions vaporized to smoking ashes.

Across the alley, a wooden building burned. Sirens began to wail. From beyond the alley, someone screamed in terror amid shouts and calls for help.

Iselde tiptoed through the alley across the hot surface and skittered away from the crowd assembling before the burning building. She ignored the myriad small scrapes and cuts that scored the soles of her feet as she raced along the hard pavement made of something that was not quite stone. Two more words rose to the forefront of her mind: *concrete* and *sidewalk*.

She rounded a corner and skidded to a halt as an iron gate flung open. She narrowly avoided crashing into the caustic metal. A woman garbed in a colorful dress beckoned.

"Psst! In here, girl!"

Iselde hesitated.

"I been expecting you. Now git in here!"

Iselde cautiously rounded the gate and met the woman's dark eyes. Her dark skin gleamed beneath the street lights.

"You've been expecting me?" she echoed with a frown as the woman's language registered in her mind. She'd not heard it nor needed the knowledge of it for a long, long time.

The woman frowned as her gaze swept over Iselde. "You from Sweden or somethin'? You sure ain't from here."

"You've been expecting me?" Iselde said a second time.

The woman propped her fists on her broad hips and she tilted her head to one side. "Yeah, I been expecting you."

"Who told you I was coming?"

The woman shook her head. "Look, I know y'all ain't gonna believe me, but some lady who looks jus' like you but a whole lot older came to me and said you was comin'. She said you'd need a place to stay."

Suspicion ignited. Iselde's eyes narrowed to slits and her delicate nostrils flared. "That's what she said?"

The woman exhaled a gusty breath and shook her head again. "She said you'd be difficult. *Sanctuary*. She tol' me to offer you sanctuary."

Iselde registered the promise of the term, but remained distrustful. "And what did she offer in recompense?"

"I ain't been paid the full amount yet," the woman snapped. "Now, you can either git in here or you can go on your way. It don't much matter to me."

Iselde pursed her lips, weighing her options: the unknown against the unknown. She stepped toward the woman, eyeing the iron gate with wary distrust as she passed through the opening. The woman harrumphed and slammed the gate behind her guest. The latch clanged then clunked.

"The gate's warded. Ain't nothin' nasty gonna come into *my* territory."

"You ward the iron?" Iselde blurted in surprise. She hadn't known humans had magic. She hadn't realized one *could* ward iron, which repelled fae magic.

"Before midnight, I work a little good. After midnight, I sometimes need to work a little evil," the woman said with a wave of her hand. "Well, come along then."

Wondering whether her hostess considered the wards a work of good or evil and having no better option at that moment, Iselde followed her down a short, narrow corridor between two buildings into a small courtyard paved with bricks. Large pots situated around the courtyard overflowed with greenery, some vining, others more bushlike, and most with flowers in vivid shades of red, yellow, and purple. Lights strung overhead added a festive ambiance to the space.

The woman pulled aside a wrought iron chair and said, "Sit."

Iselde met her gaze and said, "I prefer to stand."

"Suit yerself." The woman pulled out a second chair of the four arranged around an ironwork table. The legs squealed as they scraped across the brick. She settled in the chair with another gusty sigh and rested a plump arm on the table and demanded, "Now, what in the *hell* am I supposed to do with *you*?"

"Why don't you tell me what my mother said to you," Iselde suggested.

"Yo' mama?" The woman shook her head. "Girl, you're too young to be that woman's daughter. Yo' sure she ain't yo' grandma or great-grandma?"

"I'm older than I look," Iselde said without irony. Unlike other fae, the oracle allowed her great age to show. She claimed it incited respect when a youthful visage would not.

"Well, you'd have to be. That white hair run in the family?"

"Yes, it does. Now what did my mother tell you?"

"Only that I'm supposed to give you shelter for three days."

"Three days?"

"Am I not speakin' clearly?" the woman snapped. "Or are you jus' hard of hearin'?"

Iselde bowed her head and murmured, "My apologies. I am not from here."

"You sound like you're from Sweden. Or mebbe Russia. You got a weird accent."

"Regardless—"

"Irregardless."

Iselde blinked at the correction. She knew a thousand or more spoken languages, and "irregardless" wasn't a proper word among them. However, she decided she needed the woman's good will more than she needed to prove herself linguistically correct. She took a breath and said, "Why three days?"

"She didn't say." The woman rummaged in a pocket and pulled out a large nugget of gold. It gleamed in the artificial lights strung overhead and carried a faint whiff of magic. "I'll have to sell this. Pure gold ain't 'xactly easy to spend these days. I s'pose I'll have to git you something to wear, 'lessen you got a stash of clothes somewhere?"

Iselde looked at her soiled chemise and dirty feet. "This is all I have, but I will compensate you for your service."

The woman's eyes gleamed with avarice. "Now we talkin'. You can borrow from my daughter's closet tomorrow, and I'll take you shopping for a few things."

"I appreciate your kindness and hospitality."

"You hungry?"

Iselde's belly rumbled in response. "Apparently, I am."

The woman heaved herself to her feet with a grunt and dropped the gold nugget back into her pocket. "Well, come on in and keep yo' sticky fingers to yo'self. I got some leftover gumbo that I can heat up in the microwave. The bread's more'n a day old, but still good."

"Whatever you have will be fine," Iselde said as she followed the woman into the long, narrow house. "You have my gratitude."

The woman grunted. "I'd rather have your money." She poured herself a glass of brown, sweet smelling liquid and took a long gulp. "Anyway, I got a spare bed for you to rest in tonight."

"I will ensure you are compensated," Iselde promised as the woman spooned something goopy into a bowl and set it inside a strange cabinet. She paused, watching as her hostess pressed her fingertips to a number and the cabinet's window lit up. As the cabinet hummed, she asked, "What is your name?"

"Hah! I *knew* I forgot somethin'. I'm Zarafille, the best damn voodoo priestess in the French Quarter."

"French Quarter?"

Zarafille sighed in exasperation. "Ain't you never heard of N'awlins?"

Bemused, Iselde couldn't remember if she had heard of this city which stank of mold, fish, and vomit. She discovered a few minutes later that she'd never had food that tasted quite like gumbo either. The spicy, fragrant stew made a welcome change from the monotony of her diet in the northern wastes.

CHAPTER 2

ZARAFILLE'S DAUGHTER PROVED TO BE ALMOST as tall as Iselde and built like a warrior with thick, strong thighs and broad shoulders. The sixteen-year-old girl reluctantly parted with one of her older dresses, a lightweight cotton peasant dress in a bright floral pattern. Even though she'd outgrown the dress and it was out of style—pencil skirts being back in vogue—it remained a sentimental favorite and comfortable in New Orleans' sweltering climate. Zarafille also persuaded her daughter to part with a cheap pair of flimsy flip-flops for her guest's feet.

As Zarafille watched Iselde slide the rubber sandals onto her feet, her expression tightened. Meeting her guest's unblinking gaze, she whispered, "What are you?"

Iselde met the woman's gaze and decided on candor rather than expend the energy on a glamour or to erase the woman's mind. "I am fae."

"F-fae? You mean you're a fairy?"

"Oh, I'm much more than a fairy," Iselde replied, her voice soft and quiet. "I have no butterfly wings; I have claws."

"And yo mama?"

"She is fae."

"I heard the gentry was immortal."

Iselde shrugged. There was a limit to her candor, and she felt she'd given enough information away. She wondered what she was supposed to do for the three days Zarafille had agreed to host her.

Zarafille gestured vaguely at her. "Can you, you know, make yourself look normal?"

"I do look normal," Iselde muttered.

"Normal meanin' *human*," Zarafille clarified, her acid tone dripping annoyance. "Y'all can keep that white hair, but them eyes, ears, and claws got to be hid, or we gonna draw a *lotta* unwanted attention." Her gaze narrowed and she jutted her head toward Iselde. "And I don' think you want *that*."

No, she did not. With no further talk, Iselde obliged her hostess by drawing a glamour over herself to conceal the physical features that instantly distinguished her from human beings: the clawed toes and fingers, the pointed ears, the cobalt cat's eyes with vertical pupils.

Zarafille circled her and harrumphed in satisfaction. "Good enough. You'll do."

Iselde nodded.

"Marnie'll watch the shop while I take you shopping," Zarafille said. "We got to at least get you some underwear. Anyway, I know of a thrift store in the Seventh Ward that usually has good stuff. There's a discount store nearby where we'll pick up some underwear for you, too. You won't want to wear secondhand panties."

No, Iselde was sure she didn't, even if she'd never worn panties in her lifetime and had no idea what they were. Regardless, she fell into step alongside her hostess who maintained a running commentary on the famous city's fascinating history as they walked block after block after block after Iselde refused to climb into a bus: "I cannot enter a steel carriage."

Zarafille huffed and muttered under her breath that she ought to have known the pesky fairy-girl would be a nuisance.

"Huh. I guess them legends 'bout fairies and iron is correct. That's why you wouldn't touch my patio furniture."

Iselde did not respond. Zarafille huffed again and resumed walking at a brisk pace as though the oppressive heat and humidity did not affect her, despite the beads of perspiration on her face and neck and the wetness darkening the cloth of her dress wherever it pressed against her flesh.

As they walked, Iselde examined passersby and what they were wearing. She ignored the chafing of the thong between her toes and the annoying slap of rubber soles against the hot concrete sidewalks. The strange sandals which Marnie called flip-flops at least protected her newly healed soles from broken glass and other sharp debris.

"We'll get you something better for your feet," Zarafille whispered before they entered the thrift store.

She said nothing as Zarafille guided her to racks of clothing and began to riffle through them. She pulled out several outfits, holding them up to estimate whether they'd fit her guest. Most went back to the rack. Iselde listened as customers conducted loud conversations with each other or spoke into rectangular devices they held next to their heads.

Zarafille tugged on her arm and drew her to a counter where a bored clerk rang up their purchases. The voodoo priestess paid the amount and said, "Let's stop for lunch."

"Thank you," Iselde said, remembering her manners. "What are those devices?"

"Devices?" Zarafille echoed. Her eyes widened as she understood what Iselde referred to. With a chuckle, she replied, "Oh, them's cell phones. I s'pose you ain't never seen them before."

"No."

"The younger generation's addicted to 'em and don't hardly know how to conduct a face-to-face conversation these days." Zarafille shook her head. "But I shouldn't badmouth them, 'cause I got one, too, and I use it."

"Is it a weapon?"

Zarafille snorted. "Not hardly. It's more like a drug."

"Then I do not want one." Iselde looked around. "But I do want a weapon."

"You got I.D.?"

"What's that?"

"Hah. You can't get no gun without no I.D.—not legally." She shook her head. "And I ain't gonna burn my cred by findin' you an *illegal* gun."

"I'd prefer a dagger."

Zarafille's eyes narrowed. "I thought fairies—er—*your kind* couldn't touch iron."

"We cannot," Iselde admitted. "But the hilt will not be iron, and I am skilled enough to avoid cutting myself on the blade."

"And where you gonna carry a dagger?"

"I could strap one to my leg underneath the skirt."

Zarafille sighed. "Look, I don't know the laws about weapons like knives, but I don't want no trouble comin' to my house."

"And if trouble comes anyway, despite your preferences?" Iselde countered.

"I sure ain't gettin' paid enough to die for you."

Iselde smiled, baring teeth the voodoo priestess realized just then were pointed. A tremor of fear trickled down her spine. No, this tall, skinny woman was no Tinkerbell-like fairy from Neverland; she was a lethal *fae*.

"What are you gonna do?" Zarafille whispered and wondered if her wards really, truly could repel evil from entering her home.

"I'll protect you for as long as I impose upon your hospitality," Iselde promised. "A sharp dagger will make protecting you and Marnie easier."

"You may have to make do with my kitchen knife. It's got a wooden handle, and I keep it sharp."

Iselde nodded. At least she knew where that blade was kept.

Zarafille led her guest into a small restaurant where she commandeered a small table and ordered for both of them. She handed Iselde the shopping bag she carried and said, "There's a restroom at the back of the building. Change them flip-flops out for the shoes. You don't wanna attract the wrong attention."

Iselde found the small room and changed her footwear as bidden. She released the small portion of the glamour that concealed her toes. When she returned to the table, she discovered their meals had already been served. She seated herself and looked at the strange food.

"It's a muffaletta," Zarafille said. "If you're only gonna be here for a few days, you might as well experience the local cuisine like any other tourist."

Iselde picked up the sandwich and bit into it. She chewed quietly, analyzing the flavors and textures of the chewy bread, the salty ham and salami, the pungent cheese, and the tangy olive tapenade. After swallowing, she favored her hostess with a close-mouthed smile then said, "It's very good."

"Meh," Zarafille replied. "I'd rather have a meatball sandwich."

They ate in companionable quiet as the city bustled about them, tourists sampling the local wares and office workers on lunch break escaping their sedentary drudgery to eat and gossip for an hour. Iselde listened to the conversations around them, her keen hearing catching and cataloging the myriad accents and unfamiliar terms. She found the infinite variety of humanity marvelous and mind-boggling.

"Did my mother leave you with any instructions?" Iselde asked her hostess when they finished their meal and resumed walking.

"Nope," Zarafille replied, popping the *P*. "She jus' said I was to give you sanctuary for three days."

"Will you work your magic tonight then?"

Zarafille cast her a suspicious glance. "Why you ask?"

"I will accompany you and ensure your safety."

Zarafille snorted. "As if! Ain't no one gonna bother me when I'm workin' my voodoo."

"Not even the vampires like those I defeated last night?" Iselde prodded.

"Vampires?" Zarafille snorted again, then burst out in a loud guffaw. "Girl, you cain't be serious!"

"I know a vampire when I smell one," she replied. "Are they so rare here?"

The woman snickered. "Hollywood would have you think we're overrun with such things, but, my skinny fairy, vampires ain't real."

Iselde frowned. She did not understand the reference to Hollywood, but she knew vampires existed. Rather than assume her hostess thought she spoke a falsehood, she decided that Zarafille was simply mistaken. "I could prove to you they exist."

"Pshaw!"

"Did you believe in the fae before you met my mother?"

That question made Zarafille pause. She cast a considering glance at Iselde, cataloging the now-hidden physical differences distinguishing her from human: the tips of sharp claws that curved over her fingertips and now-concealed toes, the delicately pointed ears, the cobalt cat's eyes, the serrated smile. She took a deep breath and replied, "Okay, you got me there."

Iselde nodded. "I will capture a vampire and bring one to you."

"Are you sure you can control it?"

"After I show you such evil exists, I'll kill it."

Zarafille shuddered.

"How can you work magic and not know such things as fae and vampires exist?" Iselde asked.

"My wards keep out human nasties," Zarafille answered. "And bad spirits. I don't need that bad juju."

Iselde nodded, accepting the explanation and walked in silence the rest of the way back to Zarafille's house.

"You go up to your room, Iselde," the priestess ordered as the iron gate clanged shut behind Iselde. "I'm gonna check on Marnie."

"All right," Iselde replied and watched the voodoo priestess head toward the small shop where she sold charms, spells, and memorabilia. Her nostrils flared as she inhaled. She recognized that musty scent.

Iselde dropped the shopping bags to the bricked courtyard and raced after Zarafille. She unlatched the gate and wrenched it open, hissing as the iron burned her flesh. She raced through the portal, took a sniff, and followed her nose.

Luckily, the storefront was but a few doors down. The door was closed. Iselde opened it, glad the doorknob was brass instead of steel or wrought iron. If her instincts and nose had not failed her, the vampire inside the shop would hear her enter, so she discarded the idea of a stealthy entrance and flung the door open. The glass window in the door shattered as the door slammed against the wall and Iselde darted inside, glamour dropped, claws unsheathed, and lips peeled back from pointed teeth.

The reek of fresh blood assaulted her sensitive nose. Again, Iselde followed the scent trail which led her to the back of the shop. Marnie lay crumpled on the floor, her dark skin having taken on an ashen hue. Iselde kneeled beside the girl and rolled her over. She pressed her palm against Marnie's fleshy chest and did not feel a pulse. She sent her senses downward in a hasty search for power. Iselde almost laughed when she found a powerful ley line pulsing close to the surface. She tapped into it and connected the power to the girl's still heart, the shock jolting the muscle into beating again. Iselde fixed the connection, ensuring the power of the ley line fed into Marnie's body, then she headed off in search of Zarafille.

Again she followed the scent trail, but this time the trail smelled of fear, rage, and salt. *Ah, tears.* She burst through a door only to enter into another small, shady courtyard shared with two more buildings. Zarafille held out a crucifix attached to a delicate chain around her neck. Sweat poured down her face which was set in a rictus of horror.

"I suppose I don't have to capture one of these abominations to convince you they exist," Iselde commented in a conversational tone as she sidled around the vampire held at bay by the crucifix.

The vampire glanced at her, back to Zarafille, then turned to face the fae. His thin, bloodstained lips split in a fearsome smile. "You are the prize, not the priestess."

"Did you come here to fetch me or to snack on children?" Iselde taunted.

The vampire licked his lips. "She was delicious. But the king wants you."

"King?" Iselde echoed.

"King?" Zarafille echoed.

"Koriolis is waiting for you," the vampire crowed, "and I shall receive the reward for having been the one to capture you."

"And if I refuse to accompany you?" Iselde asked, ignoring the way Zarafille shook her head.

"You'll go, dead or alive. It doesn't much matter to me."

Iselde tilted her head to one side. "Leave now and tell your king to wait upon me where I am staying and I'll listen to him." She paused. "Or you will die."

The vampire sneered at the tall, slender female. "I'll have fun eating you."

Iselde's lips peeled back from her pointed teeth. She lunged forward, claws extended. Her limbs whipped around and her body swayed, a blur of movement and lethal grace. Less than two seconds later the vampire's body collapsed to the courtyard's brick floor. His head, torn from his neck, rolled to a stop a few feet away, just inches from Zarafille's sandals.

"Go to your daughter," Iselde ordered as Zarafille wheezed.

Zarafille glanced at her guest, then at the decapitated vampire. "What are you gonna do?"

"I will dispose of the vampire." She met the priestess' shocked gaze. "Marnie lives."

"D-d-dispose?"

"Fire."

Zarafille looked at the wooden buildings enclosing the courtyard. "Y-you'll be careful not to set the city on fire?"

"I'll be careful. You do not want to see this."

Zarafille took a deep breath and shook her head. "No. No, I do not want to see this."

As soon as the voodoo priestess disappeared into the shop and the door closed behind her, Iselde summoned power from the nearby ley line and directed a white hot beam of light onto the vampire's body and head. Seconds later the extreme heat turned the monster's body and head into small piles of gray ash. Iselde summoned a current of moisture laden air to scatter the ash. Except for a couple of small scorch marks on a nearby wall, nothing remained of the vampire to indicate he had ever existed.

She returned to the shop and found Zarafille cradling her daughter in her arms, heedless of the sticky blood smeared on her or the floor.

"What happened?" the girl asked, her words slurred and her eyes groggy.

"Get her home," Iselde ordered. "Feed her red meat as raw as she'll eat it."

Zarafille's eyes widened, but she nodded and drew Marnie to her feet. The girl leaned heavily against her mother, her rubbery legs unable to hold her weight.

"Hello?" an unknown voice called out, followed by the patter of footsteps inside the shop.

"I'll take care of it," Iselde said.

She made her way back to the store's front to encounter a small group of tourists. Adopting the vocabulary and accents of the conversations she'd heard throughout the day, she said, "There's been an emergency with the shop's owner. We're closing early today."

"Oh, when?" one of the tourists responded with a pout of disappointment.

"Now. I hope you will return tomorrow."

The tourists nodded and sighed. They turned to leave. One called over his shoulder, "I hope everything's all right."

"It will be," Iselde assured him. When the door closed behind them, Iselde noticed the sign in the shop's main window. She turned it from OPEN to CLOSED. With a flicker of power, she swept the shattered glass and blood from the floor and with another flicker of power put the glass back into the empty pane. The shards rippled and melted together, restored to a single sheet, but now it appeared faceted. Rays of sunshine refracted as they passed through the glass, spraying small rainbows throughout the shop.

Iselde inhaled and tracked Zarafille and Marnie to the tiny courtyard behind the shop. Zarafille sat on the brick floor with her daughter cradled in her arms. Tears ran down her plump cheeks.

"Give her to me," the female fae ordered.

Zarafille released her beloved daughter to Iselde who lifted the large girl as though she weighed nothing at all. The voodoo priestess' eyes bulged in disbelief, but she said nothing as she followed Iselde. She gasped when the brick wall separating that courtyard from the one she shared with other neighbors opened like a curtain. She stuck close to the tall, white-haired woman just in case the suddenly fluid brick decided to close and solidify without warning. She followed Iselde who carried Marnie across their courtyard into her house and up to her room.

Iselde turned to her and simply said, "Meat."

Zarafille nodded and hurried to the kitchen where she had some ground beef thawed in the refrigerator. Marnie would just have to eat her burger medium rare.

When Zarafille returned to the bedroom, Iselde said, "I must find another vampire to convey my invitation to this king of theirs."

"You can't!" Zarafille protested.

Iselde sought to reassure the distressed woman. "I will not willingly enter a vampire's nest. I am powerful, but that would be foolish."

"Just … just don't meet with him!"

"This vampire king wants something from me. He knows I am here, although I killed his minions I encountered. I must discover what he wants of me."

"He wants to eat you, girl!"

"He is welcome to try," Iselde said, baring her own fangs. "Do not fear. I will keep you safe."

Finished with the conversation even if her hostess was not, Iselde turned on her heel and left to find another vampire and coerce it into carrying a message from her to its king.

CHAPTER 3

FINDING ANOTHER VAMPIRE IN THE CITY OF NEW Orleans was not difficult. As she roamed the streets, she quickly discerned the scents of human beings from many other less savory odors. Vampires had a musty smell hinting of decay despite the power that kept them animated. One needed only to present oneself as a hapless victim.

As she prowled the city, the very antithesis of a hapless victim, she watched no fewer than three humans captured and drained. She observed their behavior carefully, noting that the predators took care not to kill their prey. She reasoned they exerted such care because they did not wish to attract notice and they feared being discovered. *What do these predators fear?* The answer to that question piqued her curiosity.

Iselde knew any attempt to portray herself as easy prey would fail. These vampires, she thought, were more discerning than the inebriated humans who thronged the city's narrow streets. Growing louder as day eased into evening, music pumped through doors and windows. Currents of air carried delicious scents of spicy food on the waves of cheerful sound. People laughed and conversed in loud voices. They staggered and stumbled and giggled with drunken glee as waiters and bartenders bustled, hospitable smiles gleaming on their sweaty faces.

Truly, the heat and humidity of this place is oppressive.

A likely human caught her eye. Lurking in the shadows, Iselde observed the two women who thought there was safety in numbers. They tottered on high, spiked heels totally impractical for the uneven pavement. They clung to each other, drinking from large cups containing something that smelled sweet and fruity, although Iselde's nose caught the underlying sharpness of alcohol. She watched as two handsome young men approached the women and struck up an acquaintance. Iselde inhaled and her nostrils flared. Those two men were not human. She could not hear their conversation over the cacophony of noise and music.

The two women succumbed to the vampires' blandishments, the males turning on the charm to lure their victims down a dark alley. They steadied the drunken girls, preventing them from tripping and falling. Iselde rather thought the vampires exercised a gentlemanly care with their victims, a solicitousness that appeared to keep their prey safe from their own instability and poor judgment.

The loud music, fragrance of cooking food, and stench of trash and vomit combined with the vampires' concentration on their victims to make them oblivious to the alien predator stalking them. As each vampire held a woman close and tilted her head to expose the tender, sweaty skin of a slender neck, Iselde drew power from the ley lines far beneath the surface. Before either could sink his fangs into a juicy vein, Iselde wrapped them in ropes of pure power.

"Hey!" one of the vampires shouted, but he did not release his victim.

"Damn it, I knew we should have taken the fat girls earlier," the other vampire griped.

His companion shot him an annoyed glance.

Iselde approached them, letting the power she siphoned from the ley lines crackle around her.

"What the hell are you?" the first vampire demanded, red eyes wide with fear, an emotion to which he was not accustomed, as his lips peeled back from his teeth in a snarl.

Iselde bared her own serrated smile.

"What do you want?" the second asked, his voice thrumming with menace.

"Tell Koriolis I received his message," she said.

"I'm not your messenger boy," the first vampire snapped. He hissed and trembled as the ropes of power spat electricity into his flesh. His companion glanced at him and pursed his lips.

"Tonight you are," she corrected, her tone mild and conversational. "Tell your king that Zarafille and her daughter Marnie are under my protection. I will exact retribution for any further action against them."

"And who are you to give orders to Koriolis?" the second vampire demanded, his red eyes narrowing.

"I am what he has been seeking." Iselde let a surge of power flare, limning her in eerie blue light. "Tell him to meet me tomorrow evening."

"Where?" the second vampire asked.

"I will leave a note with Zarafille. He may retrieve it at sundown," Iselde said. She glared at him in warning. "Should so much as an eyelash be harmed on either Zarafille or Marnie, I will lay waste to your entire nest."

"Do you really think she can do that?" the first vampire asked aloud, head swiveling to look at his buddy.

Iselde's smile widened as power crackled around her. "I never make idle threats."

The second vampire, perhaps older and less impulsive, nodded. "We will deliver your message. Will you allow us our meal?"

"Do not harm them," she warned with a nod at the women they held.

"Koriolis commands that we do not," the vampire murmured in a sullen tone.

"And those who disobey his command?" she queried.

"Koriolis seldom gives second chances," the vampire said, and the other one nodded in agreement.

Again, Iselde wondered what the vampire king feared. She released her hold on the ley line's power then took her leave, returning to Zararfille's home. The voodoo priestess had waited for her, but fell asleep in an overstuffed armchair.

"I am returned," Iselde said quietly.

Zarafille wakened with a startled snort. She pressed her hand over her heart and looked up and down at her guest, visually checking for any obvious damage. "Y'all ain't hurt?"

"I am unharmed," Iselde replied, "and would rest."

Zarafille heaved herself upright with a grunt. She glanced at the analog clock on the wall. "It'll be dawn in a coupla hours."

"You go about your day as though I were never here," Iselde instructed. "I need you to write a message for me, a note that you are to give to Koriolis."

Zarafille's eyes grew wide and round. "You dared to summon the vampire king hisself? Girl, are you *trying* to get yo'self killed?"

"I was sent here to meet with him, but I'll do it on my terms," Iselde said. *Not my mother's terms, for she is surely the architect of this encounter.* "I sent a warning that neither you nor Marnie are to be harmed. You are under my protection."

As Zarafille slowly turned to head to her bedroom, she muttered, "Fat lot of good that'll do when he eats you."

"He can't eat me," Iselde called softly.

Zarafille stopped and looked over her shoulder. "What do you mean, can't?"

"Fae blood is poisonous to vampires," she explained. If Koriolis did not know that, then a single sip would quickly inform him.

"Poisonous? How?"

Iselde gave her a small, enigmatic smile then said, "Demonkind always delude themselves into believing they are the ultimate predators."

"So, you fae are?" Zarafille's chin jutted in challenge.

"No," Iselde replied with bald candor. "The ultimate predator cannot be killed."

"Don't tell me … dragons," Zarafille scoffed. "I'll write that note for you after the sun comes up."

Iselde turned around and walked toward the staircase to the second floor without responding. Reaching her room, she removed her new clothes and indulged in a steamy shower. After drying off her body with a fluffy towel the likes of which she'd never seen in Fé-Ree, she combed out her long white hair and wove it into a single plait to keep it from tangling as it dried while she slept.

She slept deeply through breakfast and past lunch. Marnie gave her a small, subdued smile when she made her way to the kitchen.

"Where is Zarafille?" Iselde asked.

"Mama's mindin' the shop," Marnie answered. "She's gotta make a livin', you know."

"I need her to write a note for me."

Marnie gaped in astonishment. "Don't you know how to write?"

Iselde offered her honesty. "Not your language."

"English. My language is English. An' I'm takin' Spanish in school. Mama says I need a foreign language to get accepted to college, but I ain't sure I wanna go to college." Marnie pursed her lips then rolled them between her teeth. Iselde's stomach rumbled. "You hungry? I can make you a sandwich."

Iselde accepted. Marnie quickly cobbled together meat, sliced cheese, lettuce, and bread. She cut the sandwich diagonally and set the halves on a red plate which she slid across the table to her mother's strange guest. She turned around, picked up a can, and opened it. Iselde's eyebrows rose when the can hissed. Marnie poured its contents into a glass tumbler and dropped a handful of ice cubes into the liquid. She slid that across the table, too.

"What's this?" Iselde asked as the liquid fizzed.

"It's Coke," came the astonished reply. "Ain't you never had Coke before?"

"No." Iselde sniffed at the cup's contents and wrinkled her nose.

"Oh." Marnie looked at her for a moment, then lifted the tumbler and brought it to her mouth. She took a sip then set it down. "It's good. It won't hurt you."

"I would prefer to have water."

Marnie shrugged. She turned around to pluck another glass from the cupboard and filled it from the tap. She dropped a couple ice cubes into the cup and set it next to the plated sandwich.

"Mama says I'm to thank you," the girl blurted, averting her eyes. "She says you saved my life yesterday."

"Do you remember what happened?" Iselde asked before taking a bite of the sandwich. It wasn't as good as the muffaletta she had the day before, but she had better manners than to insult her hostess by saying so.

Marnie shook her head and took a long gulp of the Coke. "I waited on some customers, tourists mostly. Then this guy came in. He gave off creepy vibes, you know. He tol' me I was pretty and …" She sighed. "And I don't remember nothin' after that until I woke up in my bed."

"He nearly killed you," Iselde said, avoiding the truth of just how lucky the girl was to be alive.

"But?" Marnie rubbed her arms up and down to soothe herself. "I mean, I'm a little tired today, but I didn't see no injuries on me when I showered this morning."

Iselde felt no obligation to explain. Instead she finished the sandwich and drained the glass of water, wrinkling her nose at the chemical aftertaste. *The sooner I return home the better. I do not like this place, despite its marvelous conveniences.*

"Marnie, where is a good place to meet someone privately?"

The girl frowned in thought. "Well, there's always the courtyard. I mean it's private property and all."

Iselde shook her head. "No, I prefer a place away from here."

"Oh." Marnie pursed her lips as she considered the best options. "Well, I'd say one of the cemeteries, but they're closed at night. You cain't go in there."

Iselde was sure she could, but let the girl ramble on. "If I was you, I'd go to City Park. There's always somethin' going on there, usually a performance or somethin' for the rich folk. All ya gotta do is slip away from whatever fancy concert's goin' on and wander off somewhere private."

"A park?" Iselde echoed thoughtfully.

"Yeah. Just 'cause N'Awlins is a big city don't mean we ain't got nice parks 'n' all. I like to go there after school sometimes and look at the sculptures. They're really cool."

"A sculpture garden? That might work."

"Well, the park's real big."

"Does it have walls around it?"

Marnie frowned as she considered the question. "No, I don't think so. It's got a fence at the entrance and around some parts of it. But totally enclosed? I don't think so. Why d'ya need walls?"

"Privacy." Iselde stepped away from the table. "What's the best outdoor space with walls?"

"Prolly one of the old cemeteries," Marnie answered with a sigh. She anticipated the next question and said, "St. Louis Cemetery on St. Louis Street's the closest to here. But like I said, the cemeteries are closed at night."

"Thank you, Marnie. You've been quite helpful. Please fetch parchment and something to write with."

Marnie shrugged and said, "I'll get you pen and paper. Hold on."

Iselde waited while the girl fetched a pen and sheet of paper so white it made the fae female blink in astonishment. She fingered the sheet of paper, so thin and crisp and fragile, not at all like the soft, thick parchment she was used to. Marnie handed her a short stick.

"What do I do with this?"

"Jeez, don't you know anything? It's a pen," Marnie explained.

Iselde looked around for an inkwell and did not see one. "Show me."

Marie pulled off one end of the slender wand, an end which Iselde realized was a cap covering an oddly shaped nib. The girl handed it back to her.

"Now start writin.'"

"Where is the ink?"

Marnie sighed. "The ink's inside the pen. Jeez."

Iselde lightly pressed the pointed tip of the nib to the paper and gently dragged it across the pristine white surface. It left behind a blue line. Amazed, she lifted the pen to examine it more carefully, but she could not see how the ink had been loaded into the wand. Rather than ask the girl how the pen worked—mainly because she suspected Marnie neither knew nor cared and would mock *her* for not knowing—Iselde handed the pen to her and reminded her, "I speak your language, but I do not write it. Will you write for me?"

Marnie sighed as though uncommonly burdened and held the pen poised above the paper. "My handwriting ain't the best, you know. If you wanna leave a note for Mama, I could just text her."

"The note is for your mother to give to someone else, someone powerful and dangerous. It is best to keep things simple."

Marnie's expression told her that a physical note was not keeping things simple, but she only said, "Okay, go on."

"I await you in the cemetery on St. Louis Street at midnight," Iselde dictated.

Marnie frowned as she carefully wrote the short note. She looked up at the white-haired fae, her expression quizzical. "Is that all? Ain't you gonna sign your name to it?"

"That is all. Thank you, Marnie."

The girl folded the paper and handed it to her. "Do you want me to take the note to Mama, too?"

Iselde plucked the folded paper from the girl's hand. "I'll do that. You rest. You are still recovering from yesterday. I would see you fully recuperated."

The girl looked abashed at the woman's solicitousness. "Um ... yeah ... well, thank you."

Iselde gave her a small, closed-mouth smile and departed to deliver the note to Zarafille. She took no insult from the girl's less than conciliatory and cooperative attitude. Adolescents of every species were overly dramatic and begrudging of kindness. Maturity would, she hoped, soften the girl's rough edges.

It took only a moment to find Zarafille in her shop. Iselde waited patiently while she waited on a customer who purchased a bracelet of pretty crystals and what Zarafille called a voodoo doll.

"Now, you'll have to get some hair or somethin' real personal to link the doll to the person," the priestess said. "Don' go sticking pins in the doll to make whoever hurt; voodoo ain't s'pposed to be used for evil."

The customer giggled. "Then what good is it?"

"You bless it," Zarafille said, her tone firm. "Now will there be anythin' else?"

The customer completed her purchase. After the transaction, Zarafille stepped into the shop's back room where Iselde waited.

"Foolish woman," Zarafille muttered. "At least that doll's got no power."

"You sell false charms?" Iselde queried. "Why?"

"People is stoopid. They'll do more harm than good if given the chance." Zarafille shrugged. "But the voodoo dolls sell real well. So, I make blanks as it were. They got no magic in 'em—no blessings, no curses. I won't have dummies doin' evil with *my* voodoo dolls."

"Wise of you," Iselde approved. She held up the folded sheet of paper. "Please give this note to Koriolis or his agent."

The priestess took the note from her fingers. "You sure *this* is wise?"

"I will not meet with him within your territory, but I will have privacy. It's best you know as little as possible, so do not read the note."

"I won't tell him nothin', but I got to know where you'll be."

Iselde shook her head. "If I have not returned tomorrow morning, then I will not return at all. Either way, you remain protected."

"How's that gonna work if you ain't here?"

Iselde smiled. "That's how I'm going to spend the rest of the afternoon—making sure you and Marnie remain safe whether I am here or not."

Zarafille's eyes widened. "Do you need anything? Any supplies? Herbs? Crystals?"

"No, thank you," Iselde replied. "Just a strand of your hair will do."

Zarafille plucked a strand of hair from her scalp and handed it to her guest. "And Marnie's, too."

"And Marnie's, too," Iselde agreed as she took the black, curling strand from the woman's fingers. She turned on her heel and soon returned to her hostess' sheltered courtyard where Marnie sat reading a book. The girl looked up at her approach.

"You talk to Mama?"

"I did. I need a strand of your hair."

Marnie frowned. "Why?"

"You know your mother is a voodoo priestess?"

"Yeah, why?"

"Well, I'm a kind of witch, too. I promised your mother I'd work a spell to keep you safe. To do that, I need a strand of your hair."

Frowning, Marnie obliged by plucking a strand of hair from her scalp. She winced. Handing it to Iselde, she asked, "Can I watch?"

Iselde shrugged and removed her shoes to put her flesh in direct contact with the ground. Both strands held in her hand, she walked across the courtyard to a sunny spot. The brick was hot beneath the soles of her bare feet. She raised both hands toward the pale sky and chanted in the fae High Tongue. The two strands dissolved in a curl of smoke as she called upon the power of the sun above and the power of the ley lines below to set strong wards around the property and to protect the women themselves. The last word ringing loudly, she clapped her hands.

A flash of golden light surrounded Marnie. The girl yelped and jumped from the chair in which she lounged. "What the *hell*?"

"It is done," Iselde said.

Marnie shook her hands as though they'd been stung. "That was weird, but I don't feel nothin."

Iselde fixed her attention with a hard look. "You are protected. Any vampire you encounter will smell sunshine on you. Anything else intending you harm will be stung by the protection I have placed upon you."

"Stung?"

"Stabbed perhaps."

"Huh."

"Now I will anchor the wards for the property."

"Mama's already set wards."

"Mine will supplement hers."

"Oh, well, that's okay then, I s'ppose."

CHAPTER 4

GARBED IN A LIGHTWEIGHT, FLOWING DRESS THAT caught the slight breeze rolling off the enormous river she'd learned the natives called the Mississippi, Iselde quickly traversed this city that never seemed to rest. People in the city worked and shopped during the day, and at night they indulged in raucous parties and revelry. Music, heat, and humidity saturated the air. The eternal bustle of business and gaiety reminded her of the Seelie Court.

She'd preferred the calm of the Unseelie Court until the crown prince, Marog, had turned irredeemably dark while his father, King Uberon, puttered away in his laboratory and library. The last time she'd seen the all-too-handsome prince happened long before the Seelie Court deposed the Unseelie king, the prince was killed, and the Unseelie Court's fortress crumbled. But even in the northern wastes, snippets of con tinental news reached her. Uberon had carved out a new kingdom; her uncle, the mighty and enigmatic Archivist, had mated the moon-born's daughter; and the Erlking's oldest son had usurped the throne of Fyrgia, a human kingdom within the fae realm. Even in the stale world of the fae, change came.

Who is this male who dares to think to take me for his own?

Arriving well before midnight, Iselde paused before the tall stone wall surrounding the cemetery. She kicked off her sandals then scaled its height, the claws tipping her fingers and toes digging into the rotted mortar to give her purchase. With an agility no human could match, she flung herself over the tombs lining the wall and landed lightly. In the distance she heard the growls and whines of passing vehicles.

With lithe grace, she prowled between the tombs until she reached the grandiose vault Marnie had informed her was practically a national monument. The girl had used her wondrous device to display a map of the cemetery so Iselde could study its layout. She gazed at the vault's magnificence and how it clashed with the more stately tombs surrounding it. Again having used her handheld device, Marnie had identified the vault and informed Iselde of its famous owner. Like some fae, some humans enjoyed outsized delusions of their own importance and grandeur.

She selected a likely place and took a seat, leaning against the still-warm marble wall of a tomb. Perhaps doing so was disrespectful to those of that family who had gone to their eternal rest, but Iselde didn't particularly care. With idle curiosity, she raised her hand and exerted her will to open a portal back to her own world and time, wondering why she hadn't already attempted to do so.

Nothing happened.

Iselde sighed, not so much with disappointment, but with resignation at this recent inability. Her mother's interference did not surprise her. Only a fool underestimated the oracle's influence and the reach of her power.

So, she waited. She watched as a trio of foolish young humans clambered over the wall and sneaked through the cemetery with the intent to wreak havoc and defile the sacred resting places of their ancestors. Before they got very far in their depredations, Iselde sent a swarm of angry sparks on a current of air to sting them. Like hornets, the sparks followed the shrieking young men who fled from the cemetery, then dissolved into nothingness after the boys passed the cemetery's boundaries.

She watched the waning crescent moon rise and move across the night sky in its eternal arc. Smog and city lights obliterated the twinkle of stars. Despite the tasty food and rollicking music, Iselde disliked the city and longed for the quiet, windswept expanses of the northern wastes. Though her homeland was harsh, she found peace there.

A disturbance in the air brought her to her feet. She unsheathed her claws, yet let her arms dangle loosely at her sides, showing herself as neither threat nor easy prey.

"You summoned?" came a velvety baritone from the deepest of shadows.

"Koriolis?"

"Aye." After a pause, the voice continued. "You have audacity."

"Your minions attacked first."

"And how can you be sure they are mine?" he argued, though his tone remained light and conversational, a cat toying with a mouse.

"You are the vampire king of New Orleans," she said. "In this territory they are all yours."

She saw a shift in the darkness, perhaps a nod.

"What is your business with me?" she asked, wrinkling her nose as she took a delicate sniff.

"I smell your power. I ... collect ... powerful things."

"I am not for *collection.*"

"I cannot let you wander my city freely, much less leave it."

"I don't see that you have much choice." She took another subtle inhale, tasting the sultry air on the back of her tongue, analyzing the subtle scent of him. "Step from the shadow, Koriolis, so I may see you."

"Why should I? Perhaps you should join me here."

Iselde snorted. "Do you know who I am?"

A shift of darkness. The slight rustle of fabric. A quiet rush of air. Perhaps he shrugged in response to her question. She knew he sniffed to catch her scent as she did to catch his.

"I know *what* you are. I don't care *who* you are," he replied after a moment, scorn coating each syllable.

"More than one ambitious fool has made that mistake."

"And many have underestimated me, too."

Finally, the oddity she scented on the air made sense. Eyebrows rising, she exclaimed in quiet surprise, "You're no vampire."

The darkness shifted again. Perhaps he nodded. "Very good, Mistress Fae."

"Ah, you do know what I am."

"And you know only that I am not truly vampire."

She pursed her lips, rather than smile and bare her gleaming white teeth. "Nor are you demonkind, but close, very close."

No response was forthcoming.

"I have scented your kind before, Koriolis."

"Do tell."

"You were once fae."

"Once," he admitted. A sliver of darkness shifted again. "Now I am even more powerful."

"And yet you are stuck in this realm with its polluted air and this city that stinks of vomit and debauchery."

"You're rather judgmental, aren't you, especially as you're stuck here, too."

His observation stung her pride. "What makes you think that?"

"The last fae to shift through the veil was Ishjarta Ornstal. I felt his presence ripple through the ether, although only briefly. Before him, the Unseelie King himself visited briefly, and before him, the captain of the Seelie Palace Guard. None of them invaded *my* city as you do, so I ignored their presence."

"Ah, but you do not know me," Iselde deduced. "And you do not know why I am here."

"It matters not. I'll know you soon enough, if only because I have declared you belong to me."

"No one owns me," Iselde retorted.

"I came here long ago, Mistress Fae, and made this realm my own. I content myself with ruling the underworld of this fascinating city, although I could have established myself as this continent's king."

"You are bored," came the flatly stated accusation.

A low, velvety chuckle floated in the air, then the vampire king replied in words, "Yes, I am bored. But I cannot return to Fé-Ree, so I keep my eternal existence here comfortable and ensure that none dare defy me."

"You are a petty king in a petty realm."

"Are we slinging insults now? Isn't that beneath one such as you?"

"And what do you know of one such as I?"

"I know you cannot tolerate the taint of iron, for you are purely fae such as I have not laid eyes on since being exiled from Fé-Ree. I *know* this realm will poison you unless you accept me and my … let's call it *patronage*. You will weaken and become a cold shadow of yourself—perhaps even die— so why not embrace the darkness and me and not only retain your power, but increase it?"

"Why did you not confront Uberon or Ishjarta or Thelan?" Iselde asked, rather than address his question.

He exhaled a small sigh of annoyance. "I shall play your game, mistress, for a moment longer." He paused. "Only the veriest fool would confront either Uberon or Ishjarta or Thelan. Besides, none of them entered *my* kingdom." He paused again and shifted, a flicker of shadow within darkness. "But you did … and in spectacular fashion."

Iselde sniffed, an expression of icy hauteur.

Koriolis stepped from the blackness of night shadow into the dimness of the crescent moon's weak illumination. Iselde's breath caught in her throat, for he was *beautiful*. Hair black as a raven's wing flowed back from a sharp widow's peak high on his forehead. Pale skin stretched over high, prominent cheek- bones and a sharp, square jaw. A long, aquiline nose cast a small shadow over full, ruddy lips. Hooded eyes glinted from deep within their sockets. The strong column of his neck was rooted between broad shoulders encased in black fabric which did nothing to hide the bulge of muscle or the trimness of his waist.

He also towered over her.

In her second of reluctant admiration, he moved with blinding speed to stand a hair's breadth from her, her breasts nearly touching him with every inhalation. He raised a hand as though to skim the white silk of her hair, but she took a quick step backward.

"I have no wish to harm you," he said as he inhaled her scent of pine and ice. Recognition of what she was to him sent tingles up and down his spine and made his blood effervesce.

"I have no wish to be owned," she replied.

"You are mine. I have decreed it."

"I am not your subject," she objected and took a quick step to the side so as not to find herself trapped against the tomb's wall.

"But you are mine nonetheless." He inhaled again and smiled, fangs flashing white in the moonlight. "We are *fated*."

He reached for her hand, but she caught the movement and struck instead, leaving bleeding welts across his palm. His lips pressed together in a thin line of disapproval, perhaps tightly controlled rage, yet he remained icily calm and controlled. He slowly brought his hand to his mouth and licked his palm. The wounds healed right away.

Lowering his hand, he said, "The next time you draw my blood, I will draw yours, and we will share a blood bond."

"I will not bind myself to one such as you," she hissed in sudden fear, for she sensed his strength in this iron-tainted world, a strength much greater than hers. "I will bind myself to no one ever again."

He took a step forward and pondered her last two words and what they implied. He inhaled again, sifting her scent from the others lingering in the hot, heavy air. After a moment's tense silence, he spoke.

"You need me," he said, the words hardly more than a breathy exhalation. "I *know* you, know *who* you are now, know *what* you are. This realm will destroy you in short order unless you give yourself to *me*. I will give you the strength you need."

Realizing she had entirely lost control of the conversation—which had not gone the way she intended at all—Iselde fled. Her bare feet skimmed over concrete and narrow bits of grass as she hurled herself across the cemetery and over the back wall where she stooped to collect her sandals and race back to the safety of Zarafille's warded home.

"Well?" Zarafille asked when she entered the woman's house. The voodoo priestess poured hot water from a kettle into a mug and dropped in a teabag. She handed the other woman the mug and said, "Let it steep a moment. I have sugar or honey if you want it."

"He's not a vampire," Iselde blurted, staring at the mug's contents with unseeing eyes as the implications of her meeting with the vampire king sank in.

Zarafille blinked in surprise. She returned to her seat. "The vampire king isn't a vampire?" She shook her head. "Then what is he?"

Iselde took a deep breath and tried not to reveal how perturbed she was. "He *used* to be fae."

"Fae? You mean like you?"

She nodded. "Yes."

Zarafille pursed her lips. After a few seconds, she exhaled, then said, "Your wards won't do us no good against such as him, will they?"

"I'll adjust them," Iselde promised, but wasn't sure if she could prevent him from trespassing upon the woman's property. She'd sensed his power, a dark, simmering power beneath the veneer of urbane conversation and tainted fae beauty. She looked inward and checked on her link to the ley line. It remained strong and steady, but she knew a constant connection would quickly turn into an addiction. The ley line would, sooner or later, overwhelm her control and command and suck her into itself. It would burn her alive from the inside out, rendering her nothing but a memory without even physical ashes to testify to her existence. Yet, with or without the link and the constant draw to the earth's natural power, this realm and its prevalence of iron would corrupt her flesh and mind and corrode her magic. When it came to ferrous corruption, the strong and ancient proved more susceptible than the young and weak—and Iselde was both ancient and powerful.

She knew the vampire king spoke the truth: she either had to somehow adapt as he had—and quickly—or surrender to corruption … if addiction to the ley line didn't kill her first.

"*That's* what he sensed," she murmured to herself and lifted the mug of hot tea to her lips. "He sensed my draw on the ley line."

"What are you talkin' about?" Zarafille demanded. "What ley line?"

Iselde shook her head. "I'm faced with a dilemma."

"You need help makin' a decision, girl?"

She looked at the human woman's dark eyes and slowly said, "I believe I do."

"Well, spit it out." Zarafille lifted a transparent bottle shaped like a bear. "Honey?"

Iselde shook her head. Zarafille set the bottle of honey on the counter then seated herself at the small kitchen table.

Iselde took a breath and explained, "There is power beneath the earth, far below the surface. I can tap into this power. In fact, I am connected to it now. But I cannot sustain this connection, for it will … it will *assume* me and I will lose myself to it."

"You mean it'll suck you in and kill you?"

Iselde dunked the tea bag as she'd seen Zarafille do and nodded. "In essence, yes. But if I do not remain connected to it, then this realm" —she gestured with an airy wave— "will weaken me. When I am sufficiently weakened, it will corrupt me and turn me into something dark and vile deserving of execution if it does not kill me first."

"Like the vampire king who ain't a real vampire?"

Iselde nodded again. *Except he is not weak.*

"Then what is he?"

"Demon, or nearly so."

Zarafille pursed her lips and pondered that for a moment. She took a long sip from her own mug of tea. Setting the mug on the table, she suggested, "Why not just tap into the ley line only when you feel yo'self weakening and disconnect when you've recharged?"

"That might work for a short time," Iselde replied, choosing her words carefully. "That's what I've already begun doing, as setting the wards around your property took more of my own strength than I anticipated." She pulled the teabag from the water and squeezed it gently. Setting the damp teabag on the table, she added, "But the ley line is addicting—a taste fast becomes dependency. I have witnessed it. It will soon consume me until nothing is left."

"We got drugs like that," Zarafille muttered in a worldly analogy. "Let me think on it. How much longer do you got?"

Iselde contemplated a response. She released her connection to the ley line and felt the pinch of pain and the whining reluctance to let go of such bright, steady power. She blanched, recognizing just how fast that dependency had manifested. "Not long."

"Nothing like bein' specific." The woman huffed in annoyance at the lack of detail. "Okay, I'll see what I can come up with, 'cause this is my world and I don't think you belong in it."

"I don't," Iselde agreed. "I don't want to either."

"You say that like we live in a cesspit." Zarafille sniffed.

Iselde realized she'd offended her hostess. "I miss my home."

"Ah." Zarafille nodded, mollified. She frowned. "What's your home like?"

"Most refer to it as the northern wastes. Even so, it has no country name, though some call me its queen. It's a vast expanse of ice and snow with rocks and mountains swept clean by the constant wind. It's a harsh place of bleak beauty and stunning fragility."

"Huh. Sounds like the North Pole to me." Zarafille licked her full lips. "No cities where you live?"

"No."

"So, d'you think if y'all go to where there ain't no civilization, a place that's all wilderness, you'll have more time to do whatever it is you came here to do without gettin' consumed by a ley line?"

Iselde speared her with a sharp look. "Are there such places in this realm?"

"Honey, you got no idea." Zarefille chuckled. "If you were the tropical type—which I can tell you ain't—I'd suggest you spend some time in the bayou. But you like the ice and cold, so I'd suggest you get yerself to Alaska or maybe even Norway or Siberia."

"Do you have a map?"

"Honey, I got an atlas, a keepsake from my mama. I'll break it out for you tomorrow." She glanced at the clock on the wall. "Well, that'd be today." She yawned. "I'm ready for bed. Y'all ought to get some rest, too."

Iselde drained the mug and set it on the counter next to the sink. "Yes, rest will be good for us both. I'll see you again in a few hours."

CHAPTER 5

ISELDE LAY ON THE SOFT MATTRESS AND SHIVERED, appalled at her reaction—her attraction—to the vampire king. Feeling desperate, she focused her will to create a portal. Once again, the effort failed.

"Mother, let me go home," she whispered, hating the way her voice shook.

She received no response.

"What do you want me to do?"

Again she received no answer, although she hadn't really expected she would. She sighed and closed her eyes, her mind racing over the unexpected turn her encounter with the vampire king had taken. Her thoughts circled until, exhausted, her mind eventually lapsed into slumber as the pearly light of dawn oozed over the eastern horizon.

Secluded in his quarters after dismissing his servants, Koriolis Valchik syn Acul looked at the black claws sprouting from the ends of his fingers. His fingertips and palms itched to touch the white-haired fae's smooth, luminous skin to see if it was as silken as it appeared. A painful twinge in his chest made him grimace. His nostrils flared as if trying to catch the female's elusive fragrance, but she was nowhere near, and the slice of her claws across his right palm left no trace of her scent. His body thrummed with anticipation, eagerness, and *need*.

He had never felt such need.

He wanted to wallow in the female's scent.

He wanted to wrap himself around her and never let go.

He wanted to sink inside her body and plunder the ecstasy of her depths.

He wanted to …

"No, it cannot be," he rasped into the silence of the dimly lit room. "It's impossible."

Demons did not have mates.

He reviewed their conversation, what he had said. Nothing he said was untrue. This world of aggressive science and cold iron would soon corrupt her, turn her from the pure fae who had captured his obsession into a tainted parody, a demon such as he had become.

Koriolis remembered, if faintly, the early years of his glory when he had strutted about his homeland, secure in his place as a highborn fae and in the company of the mightiest of his race. He had enjoyed the privileges of his First House lineage and his family's wealth and status. His exile to this caustic realm, which resulted from selfish reasons he preferred neither to recall nor explore, had shocked him.

If the fae realm was cruel, this realm was pure hell for one such as he had been. He rather thought that some of those humans he'd encountered in the early decades of his exile—very few of whom survived those encounters—had it right: this realm was their God's purgatory, a place of suffering and penance through which the benighted souls condemned to live there might earn redemption and their eternal reward. Or not.

"I must save her from this world's corruption," he groaned, unfamiliar with the concept of being someone's salvation rather than their doom. However, he was stuck. He had no escape from this iron-saturated world where silver quickly tarnished. His lovely fae female would soon tarnish, too. Her hair would turn black, and her magic would sour and become corrosive. And if she drank the blood of her victims—drank them dry and killed them as he once had—eventually those victims' souls would have their revenge. Her metamorphosis would come full circle. She would transform from fae to demon as he nearly had and be condemned to eternal damnation.

Koriolis licked his dry lips and wondered how he had managed over the millennia to avoid killing his victims as the unholy hunger grew stronger. He credited his iron will—oh, the irony of that term!—for the strength to refrain from drinking his victims dry and swallowing that last tiny drop of lifeblood that would complete the terrible metamorphosis. Would she have that strength of will?

I fear that loss of control. Does that mean I still believe in redemption for myself?

He scoffed wordlessly for even thinking the question. The vampires over which he ruled believed him one of them, merely incredibly ancient, a goal to which they aspired. They believed if they endured for millennia as he had, then they, too, would acquire the power—both physical and magical—that he commanded.

He had no intention of informing them he'd killed more of their kind than had any human or group of humans. He secured their fear and obeisance by drinking from *them*, though the taste of their corruption was sour on his tongue.

"I control the pestilence," he whispered. "I cannot eliminate them."

He considered those he ruled much like rats. They spread beyond any one person's ability to wipe them from the earth, yet their population and their depredations could be managed.

Without the control imposed by his rule, New Orleans would be gutted of human occupation. Vampires, in their arrogance, greed, and predatory nature, had little self-restraint and would kill the herd upon which they fed.

"I must see her again."

"Your Majesty?" a muffled voice filtered through the closed door. "Is someone in there with you?"

He blinked, surprised to realize he'd spoken aloud. "No, Serena. I am alone."

"To whom do you speak?"

"Do you doubt my word?" he flung back.

"No, Your Majesty. I heard your voice and wondered if you had a visitor or needed service."

He pressed his lips together in a thin line of anger. They both knew what she meant by "service." For nearly a decade she had serviced him well, but she'd grown clingy and demanding, appointing herself as his queen. Honesty compelled him to admit he'd done nothing to dissuade her delusion of grandeur.

"Not tonight," he replied.

"Are you certain, Your Majesty? You seemed ... tense when you returned from your ... meeting."

Serena knew practically as much as he did about what happened in the city, so he did not lie to her. He rose and walked to the door. Opening it, he said, "I met with the fae."

Serena stepped inside, glancing and subtly sniffing to detect the presence of another person. With a disappointed moue, she said, "She lives?"

"For now."

He felt more than heard the shudder of her greedy anticipation. "When you capture her, I would *love* to taste her."

"Fae blood taken without consent is poisonous," he said.

"Bah! Then what good is she?" Serena paused, then tilted her head and smiled, revealing sharp white fangs. "Can one such as she be compelled to consent?"

"I do not know if vampire compulsion works on the fae mind," he replied honestly. He'd never had the opportunity to try compelling a fae, as none venturing into this realm was stupid enough to seek out the vampire king of New Orleans.

"Well, there's nothing like trying," Serena quipped brightly. Her expression turned sly. She raised a hand and slid it down the plane of his face. "I could bring her to you."

Fury clogged Koriolis' throat. He swallowed it before speaking in a cool, dispassionate tone, "The fae is *mine*. None but I shall touch her."

Serena heard the adamantine refusal in his voice and sighed her disappointment. "It would be marvelous to imbibe that kind of power, even just a taste of it."

"Heady indeed," he agreed mildly, despite the urge to wrap his hand around Serena's delicate throat and squeeze until her head popped off. "But taken without her consent, that taste of her blood would kill either of us."

"So, you intend to seduce her?" Serena's eyes narrowed in jealousy at that conclusion.

"Yes."

The female vampire's eyes glittered red with rage, but she kept her expression and voice mild. "Let me know if you wish for assistance … or if you'd rather have someone less like Tinkerbell in your bed."

"Tinkerbell?"

She smiled and did not explain. "You know where to find me, Koriolis."

"I do," he replied. "Now I would like to be left in privacy."

"Of course, Your Majesty," she replied and bowed. With a provocative sway to her hips, she departed, leaving him once again alone with his thoughts.

When the door closed behind her, Koriolis exhaled in relief. The comparison to Tinkerbell meant Serena had not caught sight of Iselde, or she would never have likened that sharp, silver blade of a fae to a sprite from a children's book. Iselde was as unlike the cartoonish Tinkerbell as he was to a choirboy.

Struck by an idea, he moved to his desk and pulled out paper and a pen, ignoring the sleek laptop computer plugged into the outlet. He began scribbling in the ancient written language of the fae, a language no other in this realm but his fated mate could read, crossing out and rewriting until he had a plan that made him anticipate a very satisfying triumph.

"I will have her *and* my redemption," he vowed, his voice a sibilant whisper.

CHAPTER 6

"THIS ARRIVED FOR YOU," ZARAFILLE ANNOUNCED, holding out an envelope sealed the old fashioned way with a wax seal. She sighed and added, "I ain't a post office, you know."

Iselde took the envelope from her hostess' hand and ignored the complaint. She knew very well that her time as Zarafille's guest was coming to a quick end. She unsheathed a claw and pried off the seal to extract the letter, noting the luxurious quality of the heavy stationery as she unfolded it. Tucked inside the letter was a small card with information that made no sense to Iselde.

"What's it say?" Zarafille asked after a moment's silence.

Iselde looked up from the letter, her cobalt eyes meeting the other woman's dark gaze. She held the letter up for her hostess to see, knowing Zarafille could not read the language, and tucked the business card into a pocket. "It's an invitation."

"Invitation? To what?"

"A ball."

Zarafille frowned. "I don't know of no fancy balls bein' held 'round here."

The woman plucked the letter from Iselde's fingers and scanned the fine calligraphy. After squinting her eyes then blinking several times, she sighed and handed it back.

"I cain't read it. What language is that? Cyrillic? Farsi?"

"Fae," Iselde murmured, looking at the black ink pressed into the heavy paper. She retrieved the business card and held it up for Zarafille to read. "Not only fae, but the High Tongue. It's been ages since I've dealt with anyone who knew how to speak—much less read and write—in the fae High Tongue."

"What's that mean?"

Iselde sighed. "It means what I suspected: Koriolis is First House ... or he *was* First House. He's powerful and quite old."

Zarafille took the business card, read it, and huffed. "We already knew he was powerful. Ain't no one commands the *vampires*" —she shook her head in astonishment that vampires actually existed— "in a city without bein' powerful."

"You have a point," Iselde conceded, taking the card back. "But now I have a very good idea as to how powerful he is."

"And that means?"

Iselde met her gaze once again. "You had better hope *I'm* even more powerful."

Zarafille frowned. "Or?"

Iselde just shook her head. Taking a deep breath, she squared her shoulders, stiffening her already erect posture. "Where shall I find suitable attire?"

Zarafille pursed her lips as she considered viable options. "There's a place called Red Carpet Formalwear. Ain't nothing there gonna be cheap, though."

"I shall see you reimbursed," Iselde said. "Let's go."

"I gotta take care of my shop!"

Annoyed, Iselde turned on her heel and left.

"Hey! Wait!"

Zarafille's words fell on deaf ears.

Iselde walked a few blocks then paused to summon an aerial sprite. She whispered to it, asking it to guide her to the shop. Drawing upon the power of the ley line surging far below, she sped along sidewalks and across streets, a nearly invisible blur that had passing humans blinking in bewilderment and wondering what had just passed them. Iselde came to a halt, breathing heavily in the hot, oppressively humid air. She wiped her forearm across her forehead, smearing the sweat beading on her skin. With another pull on the icy power below, she tidied herself then stepped inside the boutique.

After wandering for a few minutes and peering at the many gowns hanging on racks, Iselde turned to face the sales clerk who offered to assist and ignored the woman's politely skeptical expression.

"I have been invited to a ball. It's tonight," she said. "I require appropriate attire."

"With whom?"

Iselde raised an eyebrow at being questioned.

"Which ball?" the sales clerk asked. "I can better direct you to a suitable evening gown if I know which event you're attending."

"Koriolis."

"*You're* our local billionaire's guest?" The woman's eyes widened in surprise. "I know the elite of New Orleans by sight, and you're not one of them."

"No, I am not one of them," Iselde agreed, her voice soft and cool. "Do you intend to assist me or not?"

The woman realized she'd been inexcusably rude. She coughed and blushed and spluttered, "Will that be cash or card?"

"Put the expense on Koriolis' account," Iselde replied.

"B-b-but Mr. Koriolis Valchik doesn't have an account here."

"And he never will if you don't accommodate me. I'm his bride," Iselde argued with a cold smile even as she wanted to cringe at what she'd claimed. Saying she was the demon's bride should not have felt so ... so ... *satisfying*. She took a deep breath to control the trembling that threatened to overwhelm her. *I do not need a mate, Mother. I do not want a mate.*

"I'll need assurance, ma'am, that the expense will be paid."

Almost, Iselde admired the clerk for standing her ground. "Contact him."

The clerk's eyes widened. "Do you have his phone number?"

"Will this do?" Iselde asked, drawing the business card from her pocket.

The clerk's fingers trembled as she accepted the card. She swallowed, licked her lips, then turned away to pull out her cell phone and dial the number on the card.

"Acul Enterprises. How may I assist you?"

"Uh … um … I'm calling from Red Carpet Formalwear to verify an account for …" the clerk looked at Iselde in panic.

"Iselde Brúðurkonung," Iselde supplied, suppressing a sly smile.

The clerk's tongue stumbled as she repeated the name given to her. There was a pause while the receptionist put the clerk on hold. A moment later, a rich, velvety baritone that was nonetheless crisp and sharp came on the line.

"This is Koriolis Valchik syn Acul. Is my bride there?"

"Um … yes?"

"She is tall with long, white hair, and brilliant blue eyes, yes?"

The clerk looked at Iselde, her eyes wide and her expression filled with the realization that she'd gravely offended someone very, very important and powerful. "Um, yes, sir."

"Then she is my bride. Send the invoices to me."

"Of course, sir."

The connection terminated with a click. The clerk swallowed her consternation as she slid the phone back into her pocket. She took a breath to steady herself. "My apologies, ma'am. I didn't know …"

"Silence," Iselde ordered.

The woman's jaw snapped shut, her teeth clicking.

"I need something appropriate to wear *tonight*."

"Of course, ma'am." The clerk blinked her eyes as she mentally sorted through the boutique's selection of designer elegance, taking into account her new customer's slender figure, dramatic coloring, and height. The white-haired woman was tall, but she was sure the reclusive, mysterious billionaire was taller. She'd seen photos of him standing next to an NBA star. There hadn't been much difference in their heights, the lanky basketball player being a smidgen taller.

Within several minutes, she had plucked a handful of dresses from the racks. Carrying them to a dressing room so her new customer could try them on, she said, "These are manufactured extra-long so they can be altered to the wearer's preferred length. I don't think we'll need to raise the hems on any of these for you."

Iselde followed her into the small room and looked around.

"Um, ma'am, if you need help trying on the dresses …"

"No."

"All right then." The woman cleared her throat. "I'll just wait outside until you call me in or you've decided which one you like best."

Iselde nodded, a regal gesture, and said, "I shall need shoes."

The clerk looked at the cheap flip-flops on Iselde's feet and nearly repressed a shudder of distaste. Gauging her customer's shoe size, she asked, "Do you have stockings? A thong? You won't want panty lines. Some of the gowns won't work with a bra, either."

Iselde knew what stockings were, but she didn't understand the reference to a thong—why would she wear a leather string?—or a bra, whatever that was. "No."

The clerk sighed and nodded to herself as though silently saying, *Of course, she doesn't.* Aloud she said, "Let's see what I can find."

The dressing room door closed behind her as she departed on her quest to find suitable shoes, stockings, and other undergarments. Iselde's lips peeled back from her teeth as her sensitive ears caught the woman muttering under her breath, "Oh my God, she'll have to have a manicure and her hair done, too."

Iselde wasn't sure her glamour would withstand such close work. Also, she had no intention of allowing anyone to file down the sharp points of her claws.

She took a deep breath and raised a hand, using her index finger to draw a circle in the air. She pulled power from the ley line, feeling its icy energy surge through her, and focused her will to create a portal. The circle lit up with crackling blue light then fizzled into harmless sparks. Iselde ground her molars in exasperation. The oracle yet again denied her escape. *I do not want this fate.*

This fate is yours. Embrace it, daughter.

Iselde's breath hissed through her bared teeth as she trembled with the effort to quell the rage that whipped through her. Her nostrils flared with a huff of exhaled breath.

"Are you all right in there, ma'am?"

"Yes, thank you," Iselde forced herself to reply politely in a mild tone.

With careful delicacy, she stripped then tried on each of the five gowns in turn, taking a few minutes with each to ensure she did not inadvertently tear delicate fabric, snag a thread of lace, or jam that strange fastening she soon learned was called a zipper.

When she made her decision, she donned the dress in which she'd arrived and stepped from the dressing room. The clerk waited with three boxes in her arms.

"I have some shoes for you to try on."

Iselde held out her hands. The clerk handed her a box which she opened. It contained tall stiletto heels with a line of sparkling crystals running down the back of each heel.

"No." Iselde put the lid back on the box and handed it to the clerk who handed her the second box. The second box contained a pair of sandals also with tall, slender heels. Again, she said, "No." She looked at the third box and refused those shoes, too.

"What are you looking for?" the clerk asked, exasperated.

"I cannot run in those," Iselde said, her upper lip curling in disgust.

"Run?" the woman echoed in confusion. "Why—" She shook her head and collected herself. "No matter. I'll find you some elegant flats."

"Good."

The clerk collected the shoe boxes and disappeared into the back room where she rummaged for something more practical than the fashionably high-heeled footwear the finest ladies in New Orleans and every other major city in the world wore to formal events.

"I can't believe this," she muttered under her breath, not realizing Iselde could hear her. "We've actually got something that might work."

She returned to her customer bearing a box with a pair of silver ballet flats with ankle straps. With a polite smile, she opened the box to display them for the customer's approval.

"I will try them on," Iselde said.

"Great! Have a seat over there and—"

"I'll do it myself," Iselde insisted, her voice cool and adamant.

"I'll just fetch you some footies to use for trying them on," the clerk said, dashing behind a counter to grab a pair of mismatched nylon socks. She handed them to Iselde.

Iselde took them and looked at them with curiosity. After a few seconds, she figured out what they were for and drew one over her bare foot, careful not to snag or puncture the thin, stretchy brown fabric on the glamoured claws tipping her toes. She pulled on one of the slippers and tied the shiny silver ribbon around her ankle.

"It looks like it fits!" the clerk exclaimed with ill-disguised relief.

"It will do," Iselde agreed and removed the flimsy shoe which was, in fact, slightly too small.

"Will you need anything else? Jewelry, perhaps?"

"No." Iselde looked toward the dressing room. "I'll take the lavender gown."

"A lovely choice! I'll just get everything boxed up for you," the clerk said as she busied herself with closing the sale. She glanced at Iselde, cleared her throat again, and said, "Would you like me to make you an appointment with a stylist to do your hair and face?"

"No."

"All right then." The clerk tallied the sale and said, "The total comes to eleven thousand and fifty-six dollars and fourteen cents."

Iselde shrugged. The amount meant nothing to her.

"I'll just generate an invoice and ... there! It's been sent."

"I'm sure it will be paid promptly," Iselde said.

"I'm sure it will," the clerk agreed with an uncertain smile. Two seconds later, she smiled broadly in relief. "Wait! Oh, the payment's already come through. Perfect!"

She looked up, but her customer had already collected her purchases and departed.

"How'd she do that?" She shuddered. "What an awful bitch."

CHAPTER 7

THE VAMPIRE KING OF NEW ORLEANS—WHO WASN'T actually a vampire—waited with well-concealed impatience as the decadent opulence of the ball proceeded without his active participation. Willing human blood donors fascinated by the mystery of vampires and unknowing humans of wealth and power mingled among actual vampires who were on their very best behavior. Glittering evening gowns, shiny tuxedos, and sparkling jewelry provided a sophisticated veneer of civility among the conniving, scheming horde of those addicted to pleasure, blood, and power.

Koriolis felt a fingertip run lightly over his upper arm and shoulder. Serena bent her lovely blonde head near his and whispered, "Is she coming?"

"She replied that she would," he responded, his keen gaze focused on the tall doors at the other end of the long ballroom. "She's not the sort to break her word."

"You know her so well already?" Serena asked, jealousy seeping into her voice.

"I know her kind." That was certainly true. Stiff-with-honor fae like the captain of the Seelie Court's palace guard, the

Erlking, and the Ice Queen of the northern wastes would burn down worlds to keep their word. *The Erlking probably had.*

The mansion's doors opened. Koriolis' breath caught in his throat as his mate stepped into the vast, gleaming ballroom. She was tall for a woman, although she would have rejected the title of "woman." She was fae and female, not a mere human woman. She stood tall, her shoulders square, the lean, lithe muscles of her bared arms hinting at her greater-than-human physical strength. She nodded at the human minion who greeted her, a regal gesture of acknowledgment that was more gracious than any vampire would have delivered for all that it invited no friendship. Her long, silvery white hair cascaded down her back in twisting, shining curls. Koriolis wondered if the voodoo priestess who hosted her had dressed her hair. The gentle sheen of her lavender silk dress contrasted beautifully with her olive skin and cobalt eyes. That he could discern the color of her dress, eyes, and skin made his cold heart pound. *Was that sweat beading on his forehead?* He discreetly dabbed his brow with a folded handkerchief.

"Tolerable," Serena murmured. "She's elegant, but skinny."

Koriolis bit back a sharp snort of derision. His erstwhile mistress had no appreciation for the slender, sharp-edged beauty so opposite her own lush curves. Instead, he merely replied, "She's fae."

"Are they all like that?" Serena inquired, the intense interest in her eyes belying the idle curiosity of her voice. "I thought she'd be more ... impressive."

"The females, yes, tend to be slender, elegant, and graceful."

"And the males?"

"Taller."

"A race of stick figures," Serena remarked with derision. "She looks like she'd blow away in a stiff breeze."

Koriolis said nothing, almost hoping that Serena, in her jealousy, would cause a scene. The vampire woman was fast, strong, and vicious, more than able to slice and dice many of the vampire men in his court, yet he could not help but feel that the fae female garbed in flowing lavender would easily prove more than a match for her.

As his mate walked across the ballroom floor toward him, he noticed how alert she was, how her movements were economical and smooth. She did not merely walk, she *prowled* … like a great cat. This female was no one's victim; she was an apex predator among a crowd of predators.

He also realized that, as she grew closer, color began to bleed into his vision. He hadn't seen color for thousands of years. He blinked twice, thrice, momentarily stunned by the physical confirmation that the female who had cheekily given herself the surname "Brúðurkonung" was indeed his true, fated mate.

"What's wrong, Koriolis?" Serena whispered, hearing the soft intake of his breath. "You look … disturbed."

Koriolis shook his head, accompanying the gesture with a small wave of his hand to dismiss her question. He rose to his feet to greet his honored guest, extending his hand to her.

To his surprise, she actually grasped it. He wanted to moan at the pleasure of the touch of her palm against his. His blood heated and his libido surged. The subtle scent of her—sharp fir and clean ice—made his nostrils flare and took residence in the depths of his brain. He would recognize and be able to track that scent anywhere. His keen gaze pierced the glamour concealing her claws from everyone else's vision. That same glamour rounded the tops of her ears, gave her white scleras, round pupils, and made her appear human. Regardless of the glamour, appreciative and curious gazes followed her.

"Thank you for coming, Iselde," he greeted her with a polite smile. "I'm gratified."

"I'm not one to shirk unpleasant duties." Ire flashed in her eyes.

"Unpleasant?" he echoed with a small smile as his cock thickened and pressed against the fabric of his clothing. He gestured at the revelry with his free hand. "This is hardly unpleasant. Some of the most powerful people in the nation are here tonight."

"I'm not one for parties."

"Ah." He tilted his head to one side. "Then why did you come?"

Not caring who overheard her, as Serena most certainly could and did, she met his gaze and answered, "Because the voodoo priestess' protection ends tonight, and I would speak with you before that hour."

"You seek my protection?"

"Hardly."

"You seek *her* protection then."

"She and her daughter are under *my* protection," Iselde informed him, her tone cold and haughty. "You and your minions will discover that quickly enough should any of them attempt to harm them."

Koriolis leaned back and released her hand as his lust withered beneath the bitter odor of her disgust. "*I* control my 'minions,' as you call them. If I forbid them the priestess and her daughter, forbidden they shall remain."

"But you haven't," Iselde pointed out.

"Should their protection be my bonding gift to you?"

"Bonding?" Serena hissed. Her hand on his shoulder clenched, fingers digging into the flesh below the layers of fabric. "You offered her a blood bond?"

They looked at her, having quite forgotten her presence, so insignificant compared to the overwhelming emotions surging through them and belied by their quiet verbal sparring.

Frost rimed his voice: "Didn't I tell you, my dear? The fae female is *mine*."

Serena frowned and bared her teeth. "You said she was yours, not that you were *bonding* with her."

"I do not have to explain myself to you." Ice coated each syllable. "I told you she was mine. What did you think I meant?"

"Your Majesty, we are all yours—" Serena began.

"But that does not mean he shares a blood bond with any of you," Iselde continued, cutting her off. Her expression of cold distaste amused Koriolis. "To do so would reveal too much of him."

"What does *that* mean?" Serena demanded, her voice turning shrill.

Heads turned and curiosity flared. The buzz of conversation on the ballroom floor turned speculative and pointed.

"This discussion is over," Koriolis snapped. He gave his mate a cold, vicious smile and drew her closer to him. "Dance with me."

Because he had not released her hand—perhaps Iselde did not want him to release it because she had not tried to pull free of his light grasp—she followed him onto the dance floor where they joined other couples swirling around in graceful loops.

"I do not know this dance," she said.

Koriolis rested his free hand on her waist and drew her even closer to his body, careful not to snag the delicate fabric of her dress on his glamoured claws. "Place your hand on my shoulder and follow my lead."

He smoothly moved into a graceful waltz, cuing his partner through the hand at her waist and his intense gaze. Lithe and sensitive to every nuance, she soon picked up the simple rhythm and glided across the gleaming wooden floor with him.

"We do not dance like this in my tribe," she confessed as she relaxed into the rhythm.

"Your tribe? I do not recall the fae being divided into tribes, just the Seelie and Unseelie Courts."

"I was never a part of the courts," she said. "I live in the northern wastes."

"I never visited there when I still had access to that side of the veil."

"No one really visits there," she said with a small smile. "It's an inhospitable place, bleak and beautiful. I love it."

"And you eked out a life there alone?"

"For a long time, yes. Eventually, I built a tribe, mostly of rescues and refugees. I gave them my protection and loved them in my own way. In turn, they became my family."

"And you became the Ice Queen of lore," he murmured.
She shrugged.

"What will it take to thaw your icy heart, Iselde?"

"Why do you care?" she countered, eyes narrowing to slits.

"Because you bring color to my sight."

Iselde's eyes widened and her sudden, indrawn breath hissed at the implication of his words. Then she cursed, quietly muttering profanities in several dozen languages, none of them spoken on Earth.

Koriolis smiled, displaying glamoured teeth as flat and blunt as any human's. "Not expecting that, were you?"

"Such a bald admission? No."

He shrugged, the gesture Gallic and elegantly expressive. "I see no reason to deny it. No fae male—even one nearly turned demon as I—denies finding his true, fated mate. This is cause for celebration and—" he leaned forward to whisper in her ear "—claiming is the best way to save what's left of my dark soul from complete damnation and you from being corrupted by this tainted world."

"I don't accept that," Iselde said, her tone flat. "I don't *want* that."

He drew back, then leaned forward to brush his lips over the sharp slant of her cheekbone. His lips stretched in a smile as a delicate shiver rippled through her. "You will. Our mating, blood bond and all, will be our redemption as well as our shared pleasure."

"I need no redemption."

"My beloved, we all need redemption, some of us just a bit more than others." They twirled. He leveled a perceptive stare at her. "And you *will* need redemption if you stay here for much longer."

Iselde leaned back and met his eyes, her own gaze unflinching. "I do not want this. I wish to keep my freedom."

"You think I have intentions of keeping you imprisoned?" He chuckled, the sound dark and rich.

"Mated fae males are unreasonably possessive and protective. I do not need your protection and do not want to be possessed."

Saying nothing about the habits of demonkind, he gave her hand a light squeeze. "You will possess me as much as I will possess you. That is the way of soul bonds."

"And what do you know of soul bonds?"

"I was once true fae and have always been fully male. This is engraved upon our hearts."

Iselde snorted in disbelief.

"You doubt me? I'm wounded."

She snorted again. "I think you see the opportunity to save your own damned soul and pass through the veil to return to Fé-Ree, and I'm the means to make that opportunity happen."

He squeezed her hand again, this time not releasing the firm pressure. "Think what you wish, but you are my true, fated mate and we *will* be bonded, blood to blood, soul to soul."

"Not if I have anything to say about it."

Fire flashed in Koriolis' black eyes. "You don't."

Iselde pressed her lips together in an angry line. The music ceased, the band's leader announcing they would take a short break. She yanked her hand from Koriolis' grip with a strength he'd underestimated.

His velvety baritone wafted over her ears. "Don't make a scene, beloved."

"And what if I do?" she challenged, then turned on her heel.

In a flash he was beside her as she headed toward the exit. He grabbed her hand in his and held it in a firm, unbreakable grip. She would not pull free so easily this time.

"Then I will be forced to kill every human in this building."

She said nothing. Her expression revealed no horror at his bloodthirsty threat. Blood and violence held no horror for this ancient fae.

He found that insight interesting, if not surprising. He probed that insight: "You would not protest the slaughter of innocents?"

She snorted, the sound a haughty derision of a superior being for lesser life forms. "I doubt many of the humans here are innocent in any sense of the word."

"But many are," he assured her, his voice remaining as smooth and soft as velvet. "I have no reason to lie to you. I will not speak falsely to my mate." He gestured with the jut of his dimpled chin. "The servants are innocent. They merely think they are catering the food and drink for a fancy gathering of politicians and celebrities. They do not know what darker beings walk these floors, what dark revelries go on behind closed doors."

"And you would hold their lives hostage to my compliance?"

"Of course."

She bared her teeth at him in a saccharine facsimile of a smile, knowing he saw through her glamour to the pointed teeth shown in silent threat. "Then introduce me to your guests, darling."

He smiled back at her, revealing his own serrated smile, though his oozed satisfaction and triumph rather than fury. He tucked her hand into the crook of his arm in a most gentlemanly fashion and said, "It would be my pleasure."

"Right up until the point I kill you," she promised with another smile while speaking in her native language.

"You'll soon be too satiated with pleasure to entertain such bloodthirsty thoughts," he replied in the same language, his sultry tone indicating he fully intended to keep her mind and body lust-drunk.

"You realize I hate you." *Almost as much as I hate my mother right now.*

"A temporary condition, my dear." Iselde opened her mouth to retort, but he spoke again when they paused in front of a businessman in a designer tuxedo. "Good evening, Simon. My love, this is Simon Belvedere, a real estate mogul from California who has some properties I'm interested in acquiring."

The tall, well-built man with graying hair smiled a politely empty smile, although his eyes glinted with interest as he shook Koriolis' free hand. "Have you been keeping secrets, Kori?"

"Almost as many as you, Simon," Koriolis replied. He released the man's hand and gestured toward his unwilling mate. "Simon, this is my fiancée, Iselde Brúðurkonung, who has only tonight agreed to accept my proposal."

The man's polite smile widened, displaying many white teeth. "You lucky dog! Congratulations! Iselde, every woman in society will be heartbroken to hear Kori's been taken off the market."

"Thank you," Iselde replied with a small smile and a gracious nod even as her glamoured claws pricked through the fabric of Koriolis' sleeve and dug into his skin. The glamour held fast, none of the humans or vampires in the room realizing what she was doing.

As he led her away to greet the next guest, Koriolis tilted his head toward hers and murmured in the ancient fae tongue, "If you draw blood, every predator in here will notice, and all of them are hungry."

"You just don't want them drinking from you."

"They are not easy to control. The scent of my blood will incite a feeding frenzy that will end badly for everyone, especially those innocent humans."

The sharp tips of her claws retracted, although the press of her fingertips did not.

"Now, allow me to introduce you to Mayor Emmaline Dubois and her worthy husband, Gerald."

CHAPTER 8

STREAKS OF PINK AND ORANGE SPREAD ACROSS the sky, heralding dawn when the last guests finally departed. Iselde's feet hurt. Her cheeks ached from the polite smile she forced herself to maintain throughout the long night. Her molars hurt from constantly clenching her jaw to hide her fury.

After closing the door behind their yawning guests, Koriolis turned to her and said in the fae tongue so as not to be overheard or understood by any vampires, "You'll sleep in my bedroom."

Cognizant of the nosy vampires nearby, Iselde raised an eyebrow in silent inquiry as he led her across the empty ball-room floor.

"It's the safest place for you."

She bared her pointed teeth at him again, another ersatz smile he did not mistake for gladness or pleasure. Cognizant of the privacy using their native language afforded them, she replied in kind, "I am well able to take care of myself. I've been doing so for millennia."

"I'm sure," he agreed and wrapped a hand around her upper arm in a gentle grip. "But I find myself feeling strangely protective of you and would prefer to rest reassured of your well-being."

Iselde snorted and wrenched her arm from his light grasp. "There's no need to hold me as if I were going to bolt."

"Aren't you?" he shot back. Koriolis rolled his shoulders, enjoying the stretch of tight muscles that had stiffened over the long hours of polite socializing. He continued walking. "You did before."

She shrugged, falling into step beside him. "I'm proficient with weapons and power. Your minions would be smart to fear *me*."

He grunted. "While I've many intelligent vampires among my minions, as you call them, they tend to be governed by their appetites. Fear is not something many of them would heed when their hunger rages. And even you would be over-whelmed by a feeding frenzy."

Iselde shrugged again, confident in her ability to unleash lethal power and decimate any and all who attacked her, then gave voice to her curiosity, "How do you keep them from eating the city's population?"

"Compulsion."

"Fae do not compel."

"As you've intimated, I am more demon than fae, and vampires are basically lesser demons converted from humans rather than fae."

The base material matters. She snorted, having overheard the vampires' supercilious comments among themselves and observed their predatory behavior during the gala. The vampires exhibited a foolish arrogance that failed to recognize a superior predator in their midst. "Better not let them hear you say that. They'll be insulted."

Koriolis chuckled. "They would, at that. They like to believe they are the apex predator in this world."

Koriolis opened a door and ushered his mate through. He flipped the switches on the panel beside the door. The ball-room behind them plunged into darkness, unrelieved by the brightening dawn. Iselde glanced at the heavy velvet draperies shielding each window, then at him. He closed the door behind them and made sure it was latched and the lock engaged.

"Do you fear the sun, too?"

"Not at all," he replied and resumed walking. She fell into step beside him. He led her into an elevator. "High caste demons have no aversion to sunlight. The sun is little more than an immense ball of fire, and we demons do love our fire."

"But the vampires …"

The elevator doors closed.

"Ah, yes. That." He chuckled, pressed a button, and the elevator descended. "Vampires are quite flammable. They sizzle in the sunlight. For a newly turned vampire, immolation is nearly spontaneous. After a few centuries, they develop a slight resistance. I've never seen one so aged as to be able to walk in full afternoon sunshine."

"So, they strengthen as they age."

"They do," he confirmed. The elevator stopped moving and the doors opened. As he led her from the carriage into the corridor, he explained, "Immortality is difficult for an unprepared mind. Humans are never prepared, regardless of how fervently they insist they want to be turned and how firmly they believe they are strong enough to withstand centuries or even millennia of existence. Immortality turns many of them mad. I've known some vampires to willingly seek the sun after a thousand years."

Iselde listened to what he did not say and wondered about those vampires who unwillingly met the sun. She wondered if Koriolis had "helped" them. It would be to his advantage not to allow any vampires to acquire the age and strength necessary to resist his control.

Koriolis halted before a door and opened it. "After you."

Iselde peered inside and took a delicate sniff. Mingled with the ever-present, if faint, odors of earth, damp, and mildew were the scents of bergamot and citrus. "This is your room."

"It is."

"I prefer a room to myself."

"You will stay with me," Koriolis said, repeating his earlier command that she stay in his room.

Her expression turned mutinous. "I did not agree to sleep in your bed."

He gave her a look of contempt. "I have no need to rape an unwilling female."

No, she thought, with his dark beauty, he had beautiful females like Serena throwing themselves at him and begging him to take them to his bed. Or their beds. They probably didn't care whether a bed was involved at all. The spark of jealousy those thoughts germinated took her by surprise and raised her ire.

"You won't find me willing," she said, her tone frosty.

He gave her a small smile displaying the tips of his fangs. "I could persuade you."

Defiant, she lifted her chin. "You could try ... and you would fail."

He chuckled, a low, rich sound that reverberated through her. Iselde liked it more than she should have, more than she wanted to. Outwardly she maintained her icy demeanor.

"I could kill you," she hissed.

He laughed, then threw her words back at her, "You could try ... and you would fail."

Iselde wanted to grind her molars, but satisfied herself with clenching her jaw. She swept past him to enter the room. It was larger than she would have guessed, palatial in proportion. Her entire tipi and plus a couple more would have fit inside the room. An enormous bed occupied the far wall. An ornate chandelier dangled above it. A large fireplace that looked like an enormous geode cut in half commanded an adjacent wall. The gleaming stone floor sent its damp chill through the thin leather soles of her slippers. A carpet, something rich and woolen and woven in an intricate pattern with lots of red, stretched beneath an intimate seating area where two over-stuffed armchairs flanked a small table. The dark wood of the chairs, table, headboard, and other furniture gleamed with the rich glow imparted through centuries of carefully applied and buffed beeswax. It was a room of sublime comfort and deep sensuality, wonderfully conducive to seduction.

Iselde's shoulders stiffened as the door closed behind her and the latch engaged. She swiveled about when she heard the soft *click* of a lock. Eyes narrowing, she said, "Why did you lock the door?"

"So we are not disturbed," he replied and shrugged off his tuxedo jacket.

"We will not be doing anything to be 'disturbed,'" she snapped.

He pulled off his tie. "So, you wouldn't mind if Serena barged in and we fucked in front of you?"

Iselde acknowledged privately that she would definitely mind, but she had no intention of letting him know that. Rather than trust her voice, she simply shrugged and held his gaze.

Koriolis flashed her another small smile as he began unbuttoning his shirt. "Actually, my beloved, I'm tired and would prefer to sleep." He gestured toward a door. "The bathroom is through there. If you'll allow me to wash up first, you may then indulge in a long, hot bath." He gestured with a jut of his dimpled chin, "There's a robe you may use over there."

He finished unbuttoning his shirt, pried the diamond and onyx cuff links from his cuffs, and let the shirt fall off his shoulders to the floor where it joined his jacket and tie. Iselde could not peel her gaze off the exquisite physique displayed before her as he turned and walked to the bathroom. She knew this game; she knew *his* game: he was trying to seduce her.

When the bathroom door closed behind him, she waited until she heard the sound of running water before she released her grip on the power siphoned from the ley lines. The cord of power snapped away from her, and the recoil of exhaustion descended with heavy force. Iselde's knees buckled and she staggered to one of the armchairs where she collapsed in perspiring exhaustion. Breathing heavily, she let loose with a low groan. All around her she felt the chilly damp of being underground where sunshine could not penetrate. At least the walls and floor were not sheathed or ribbed with iron.

She shook her head and wiped her brow with a trembling hand. This city had so much iron! The city seemed to celebrate the caustic metal, working it into fanciful and decorative forms, using it everywhere. She worried at how rapidly this realm drained her. She trembled with the effort not to reach down to grasp the power of the ley line and let it fill her. *I am addicted already.*

Iselde shivered in the cool room and chastised herself for such unwarranted delicacy. She was the ruler of the northern wastes, the matriarch of the only clan that had survived the icy desert's brutal cold, the powerful and feared Ice Queen. This damp chill could not compare. *I am made of sterner stuff.*

Yet she wished she had the strength to ignite the logs so carefully stacked on the hearth. Again, she acknowledged that this realm was draining her—fast. How the Unseelie Queen's family had managed to hold onto their magic for generations in this toxic environment defied her imagination. Iselde knew she could not rely entirely upon the ley lines to fuel her magic and her strength, even though the ley lines themselves had already seduced her into craving their power and powerless to resist their lure. She'd witnessed that same addiction in the former Champion of the Seelie Court and already acknowledged the nearly overwhelming hunger to reconnect to the ley lines—and the young fae had lasted years before succumbing. She rubbed the back of her neck and whispered aloud, "I need food. Real food."

Like any living creature, she needed a proper diet. Power required fuel. The hors d'oeuvres served at the ball did not constitute a meal, and her body had been starved of proper nutrition for nearly an entire day. She rubbed the back of her neck again and felt another wave of exhaustion shudder through her, making her skin mist again with perspiration, which seemed to deepen the discomfiting feeling of being chilled. No, she admitted to herself, she needed more than mere food. She needed to return to the fae realm before this one killed her or she succumbed to the other alternative: following the same

dark path as the male she recognized but refused to acknowledge as her true mate.

At this rate, I'll be as weak and helpless as any human female.

"I do not want this, Mother," she whispered.

You have been rescuing the lost for ages.

Iselde frowned at her mother's words spoken directly into
her mind. She replied in kind, *Let me return, else I'll fade to
nothing here.*

You have not accepted your fate.

I will determine my fate, not you.

But her mother did not reply. Iselde lifted a hand, index
finger extended, with the intent to draw another portal. Her
arm trembled. With a sigh of defeat, she let her hand fall to her
lap. Expending the energy to create a portal now, especially
when she was positive the oracle would not allow her return to
the fae realm, would accomplish nothing more than to further
drain her rapidly dwindling energy stores.

"I hate this realm."

"You get used to it," Koriolis replied.

Startled because she had not noticed the cessation of water
or the opening of the bathroom door, Iselde could hardly mus-
ter the energy to turn to face him. She watched wordlessly as
he padded naked to the enormous bed and crawled beneath
the covers.

"The bathroom's yours. I'll trust you not to kill me while
I sleep," he said, meeting her gaze. She nodded. He closed his
eyes and rolled over, giving her his back.

By sheer will, Iselde rose to her feet and walked, keeping every step both fluid and firm, her back straight, and her
shoulders square. She dared not show weakness. She ignored
the robe he'd indicated she could use. When the bathroom
door closed behind her, she leaned against the countertop and
loosed a long exhale of relief. The bathroom's steamy interior
felt delicious after the damp chill of the bedroom. She turned
on the water, testing its temperature and setting it to as high as
she could tolerate, then divested herself of the elegant gown,

undergarments, and silver slippers. She stepped into the deep bathtub and let the water continue to run until she was most submerged. It was the humbling work of a few minutes for her tired eyes and brain to discern what was soap, shampoo, and conditioner, products she'd quickly learned while staying with Zarafille. All the products were imbued with Koriolis' distinctive scent of citrus and bergamot. Iselde disliked spreading that scent on her skin, but had no legitimate reason for objection. She needed a thorough washing.

The hot water eased her aching muscles. The simple action of bathing relaxed her mind. Clean and lethargic, she left the bath's liquid embrace before she succumbed to the oblivion of exhaustion. Unlike the Daimónio Refstófae, she had but one form, and that form did not breathe water.

The thick, soft towel she used to dry her body was, thus far, her favorite part of this realm. Idly, she wondered if she'd be able to take some back home with her. *Probably not.* Perhaps she could figure out how the cloth was woven and teach some of the artisans in her tribe that craft. Looking at the cloth more closely, she decided that such a marvelous fabric required a loom too large and unwieldy for a nomadic tribe.

She hung the damp towel over an empty bar. Opening the bathroom door, she walked into the bedroom and paused beside the overstuffed armchair. She considered pulling them closer together and somehow using the combined chairs as a bed. She'd have to sleep in a fetal position.

"Come to bed, beloved," came the drowsy command.

She blinked, startled again.

"You are safe with me," he assured her.

She glanced at the locked door and calculated her odds of killing him without the entire nest of vampires descending upon her to kill her in retaliation. In her current state of exhaustion, she'd lose that fight. Or perhaps she could escape, fleeing to fight another day.

"The handle and lock are iron. You won't be able to manipulate it." Koriolis rolled over to face her. "And I know how to draw on the ley lines, too. You won't overpower me."

She clenched her jaw and wondered how he knew what she had been contemplating.

"I know you're tired," he said and patted the mattress. "And I know you're uncomfortable. I will not harm you. Trust me." He imagined killing her and his muscles seized. *I cannot harm you.* The mental image dissolved.

"I trust no one," she growled.

"Beloved." His muscles relaxed.

She closed her eyes and willed the moisture welling up to recede. "I do not want this."

"We are true mates. This is fated."

She scoffed. "You know *nothing* of fate."

He rolled over, raised himself to his elbows, and fixed her gaze with his own. "And you do?"

Iselde's lips stretched in a bitter smile. "More than anyone."

"What do you mean?"

"What do you know of the oracle?"

He shrugged. "As much as anyone, I suppose, if you mean the oracle at Delphi. She was a haughty bitch."

"No, the fae oracle."

"The Archivist's sister?" He blinked. "No one, except perhaps the Archivist, knows anything about her. I never met her and never knew anyone who had met her while I still lived in the fae realm." He said nothing about learning his father had discussed him with the oracle when the Unseelie King had banished him to this iron-tainted world.

"Wrong. I know about her."

"And why would you know about her?"

"She's my mother."

CHAPTER 9

"EXPLAIN," HE ORDERED.

Rather than stand naked beside the bed, Iselde climbed under the covers. She positioned herself to face Koriolis, but carefully avoided touching him. He did not reach for her.

"My mother is the oracle."

Although his expression remained stern, surprise glinted in his dark eyes. "Who knows this?"

"The Archivist, the Erlking and Unseelie King, perhaps the Seelie King, and now you. No one else."

A low whistle escaped through his teeth. He leaned his head back. "That has got to be the best kept secret among all the fae." He paused, then asked, "Is either the Erlking or Unseelie King your father?"

"No."

"Then who?"

She shrugged one shoulder, the one she wasn't lying upon. "I don't know. Mother never deigned to tell me, and he has never come forth. It really doesn't matter, you know."

"Actually, it might."

"After all this time?" she scoffed. "I know *your* family."

He sighed. "They're dead."

"Dead?"

"Dead to me," he clarified. "I was exiled here."

She paused, rummaging through ancient memory to news concerning a powerful fae male who'd been exiled to this iron-tainted realm. She probed for more information. "Why?"

He shrugged. *Surely she knows this story.* "I sought the wrong mate. She came from this iron-saturated world. I was informed that if I so sought a mate from this world, then I should live here."

Iselde exhaled. "This realm reeks of iron."

Although he said nothing in response, he agreed.

"Did you not draw upon the ley lines?" she asked.

"I did, just as you have. I turned cold, dependent upon that power. When it was no longer sufficient, I turned to blood."

"And the female whom you attempted to claim?"

He shrugged again. "I assume she is in good health. I have neither seen nor heard of her since my exile."

"So, how did you survive?"

He pointed to himself, a clawed fingertip touching his breastbone. "Demon, remember?"

Her eyes widened in horror. "Surely, you have not forsaken all that is fae?"

Up to and draining humans dry and eating their souls. He nodded, not knowing why he'd yet to lose that last tiny spark of light to the darkness of pure evil. He doubted he would have missed that infinitesimal shard of what remained of his soul. "Now you know the depths of my evil."

"You are despicable."

"I never pretended otherwise." He looked away from her, his eyes focusing on the patterned ceiling above them. "I had honor once as a prince among the fae." He paused, not mentioning that his hair and soul had turned as black as a raven's wing long before his exile, the very portrait of power corrupted. "This realm corrupts. It corrupted me and it will corrupt you."

Iselde licked her dry lips.

"Already you crave the cold power of the ley lines."

She inhaled slowly and did not want to admit the truth of his words.

"In this realm, that power is filtered through iron. It is tainted. It will corrode your soul, your flesh, and your mind unless you act to save yourself." He paused. "Strangely enough, it is the most powerful and ancient of us who succumb faster to iron than do those who have lived mere centuries."

She exhaled slowly, understanding what he implied. *He is right—the older we are, the faster we fail—and I am very old indeed.* Unwilling to concede, she said, "Unlike you, Koriolis, I still have honor. I will not turn to blood."

He blinked in the darkness, reveling in the vast spectrum of color newly restored to his eyes. His true mate's presence gave him that gift. His voice was dispassionate as he replied, "Then you will die."

Iselde rolled over. "I'm going to sleep. Touch me and I'll gut you."

Koriolis closed his eyes and let himself drift off to sleep, secure in the knowledge that his honorable mate would not slaughter him while he lay defenseless.

Except he was never truly defenseless.

No demon was.

Iselde took a long time to relax, but she eventually recognized that Koriolis, for all that he had trapped her in that room with him, meant her no harm. *Only confinement.*

In the subterranean room, cool, dry air gently whooshed and swirled through the vents, carrying the city's faint but prevalent odor of mildew, damp, and rot. She could practically feel the sun's passage across the sky, blasting the city with its scorching heat. The city, surrounded by a river, a lake, a swamp, and an ocean, sweltered in a sticky heat that defied her description. Why, she wondered, would anyone willingly live in this oppressive climate? Had the Quol managed to plant a tendril in this verdant land? She shuddered to think of the ramifications. Without the great power commanded by the most ancient fae to restrain its savage hunger, the Quol would quickly devour this continent and its inhabitants.

Lying in the cool, dark room, Iselde missed the icy wind and drifting snow of the northern wastes. She released her glamour and dreamed of the bleak beauty of home.

When she woke, Iselde was mildly surprised to open her eyes and realize she had slept. The pillow next to hers was empty, the pillowcase creased. Only a couple strands of black hair remained of Koriolis' presence. She picked up one and ran her fingers down its curling length. It was fine and strong and shining, resembling silk. She wound the strand around her fingertip and brought it to her nose. It held a faint trace of his scent. She gnawed on the inside of her cheek as she privately acknowledged that she liked it.

Disgusted with herself, she shook her hand to free her finger from the strand of hair. Iselde rose from the bed and explored the confines of Koriolis' private quarters. Now familiar with the realm's modern conveniences, she availed herself of them. Declining to wear the evening gown, she rummaged through Koriolis' enormous closet and donned one of his shirts. She rolled up the sleeves which dangled past her fingertips. The shirt's hem descended nearly to her knees. The size of his shirt reminded her how much larger he was compared to her: a physically ideal male among the fae, and a giant among humankind.

So garbed, she crept toward the door and looked at the handle for a long moment. She unrolled a sleeve, deciding the fabric would serve as a thin buffer between her delicate fae flesh and the burn of iron. She pressed her lips together and took a deep breath, girding herself against the anticipated pain. Nothing hurt quite as much as fire.

As she reached for the handle, the door swung open. She danced backward to avoid being hit.

"Ah, you're awake," Koriolis remarked as he swept into the room. "And you're … dressed."

She narrowed her eyes. "Why wouldn't I be?"

"You're suspicious," he observed with a small smirk. A servant entered the room bearing a wooden tray. "I've brought you breakfast."

Iselde declined to point out that *he* had not brought her breakfast. Instead she remarked, "I'm surprised you have food."

"You're not the only guest we host here."

She blinked in surprise, for she had assumed she was the only guest—at least the only one who required sustenance that didn't consist of blood. Then she supposed that any blood donors staying overnight in the nest did require food, so perhaps the edible bounty wasn't such an aberration after all. Her lips curled in a sardonic smile as she silently remonstrated with herself for having assumed anything at all.

"Thank you," she replied, remembering her manners.

"I'll leave you to eat," Koriolis said as the servant placed the tray on a side table. "Then we'll head out."

"Where are we going?"

"Into the swamp."

The servant scurried from the room, taking care not to brush against Koriolis.

She raised an eyebrow. "And what's out there that you want me to see?"

"Something ancient."

Intrigued, Iselde lifted a plastic cover to see what was on the porcelain plate beneath. She sniffed. Whatever had been cooked for her smelled delicious, even if she didn't recognize everything on the plate. She looked up. Koriolis was gone and the door was closed, the latch engaged.

Deciding to bide her time, Iselde tested a small bite of each item on her plate to ensure nothing had been poisoned or drugged before devouring it all. A few minutes after she had finished eating, the door opened again. Koriolis entered bearing several shopping bags.

"You can't go about in nothing but my shirt," he explained. He flashed her a grin. "I enjoy the sight, but I won't tolerate other males also enjoying it."

Iselde rolled her eyes.

"I've purchased clothing more appropriate for a visit into the swamp, including footwear."

"Thank you," she said and made no mention that surely there could be nothing in the swamp more dangerous than she. In this realm, she was learning, the pervasive presence of iron weakened her more than she liked to admit, even though she felt much restored by food and rest.

Iselde kept an eye on Koriolis as he changed from his dapper suit to loose, lightweight clothes and sturdy boots much the same as he had purchased for her. She wondered about his lineage and admired the ripple and roll of hard muscle beneath his skin as he shed his clothes. She knew who his father was, but not his mother.

She drew on the clothes he provided as well as her glamour to conceal her fae nature and asked, "How do you survive here?"

"I drink blood." He flashed her a quick smile and did not mention the part about eating souls. "I can eat and drink such as humans do, but it doesn't sustain me."

She met the dark flicker of his black gaze and did not flinch. "You cannot be the only fae to survive this realm. I know others were exiled here, but I cannot recall any who were exiled. Some fled here to escape the Quol."

He shrugged. "It does not matter."

Exasperated, she demanded, "Did you know them?"

"Some."

She rifled through her memories again, recalling the lands the fae had ceded to the Quol so very long ago. Only recently had the combined efforts of the former Unseelie King and the former Champion of the Seelie Court enabled the fae to beat back the ravenous Quol's relentless advance and reclaim long lost territory.

"I remember one First House family whose lands were consumed by the Quol. They were part of the Lahn Ursai." She frowned, trying to recall them. "The Quol ate their estate millennia ago."

He shrugged. "The borderlands like Lahn Ursai were always at risk. That family's exile helped ensure its demise."

"I do not remember why they were exiled or if they chose to come here." She looked around again and saw nothing more than the luxuriously appointed room. "Why would they have chosen to come here?"

He shrugged again, not confiding his suspicions as to the origin of certain human bloodlines said to thrum with arcane power. "It no longer matters. Now, are you ready to go?"

She nodded. Koriolis extended his hand, and she took it without thinking about the wisdom of doing so. He led her through the old mansion into the heavy night air. They stopped at a concrete structure beside one of the realm's motorized horseless carriages, which stank of iron.

"I can't get in there," Iselde protested.

"This is an Aston Martin and has a carbon fiber body. Beyond the engine, there's really very little actual iron in this machine," he assured her.

She paused and searched his face for falsehood.

"I have not lied to you, and I will not," he stated and opened the passenger side door. "I will not speak falsely to my mate."

She nodded and slid into the bucket seat. She ran a fingertip over the buttery leather. It was more comfortable than she had expected.

Koriolis installed himself into the driver's seat. With a muted purr, the powerful engine came to life. He pulled on thin leather gloves, gripped the stick shift, turned on the lights, turned on the air conditioner, and put the car into forward motion. He drove the powerful vehicle without drama, feeling no need to push the engine to its limits or to race other vehicles. The pleasure of driving the sleek, powerful machine was sufficient to satisfy him.

Curious, Iselde asked, "Is it difficult to drive one of these machines?"

"No. It just takes practice," he replied. "When automobiles first came out, their steel bodies made driving them an exercise in pain, even for one such as I."

"Even as a demon you fear iron?"

"When I first turned, iron still burned my flesh. I prefer to exercise caution rather than test my resistance to its taint."

She nodded. That made sense.

The next several miles passed in companionable silence, neither driver nor passenger feeling the need to fill the quiet with aimless chatter. Iselde inhaled deeply of the cool air flowing from the vents and wrinkled her nose, disliking the smell of air having passed through the compressor.

"The cool air is comfortable, but I do not like its scent," she said.

Koriolis understood her unvoiced question. Without comment, he pressed a button and the passenger side window rolled down. Iselde's eyes widened in surprise. She took a deep breath of the hot, humid air and smiled. "Much better, thank you."

"I am surprised," he commented as he slowed the car and turned onto a hard-packed dirt road. "I thought you would appreciate the cool air."

"I did. It was considerate of you to create it for my comfort."

He smiled. "You will find that I have little consideration for any but myself—and now you."

Iselde's lips curled in a small smile, recognizing the glimmer of a fae male's possessive and possibly protective devotion to his mate. Looking out the open window into the sun-dappled tangle of green redolent of squeaks, chirps, belches, growls, and many other sounds, she said, "I appreciate that. But do not forget: I am no helpless female."

Koriolis glanced at his mate. "No, you are not helpless, yet my strength is yours."

"Why are you so quick to declare your devotion to me?" she asked, tilting her head in curiosity.

"You are my true mate," he replied without ire. "We were made for each other."

"I don't believe that."

He turned another corner onto another dirt road. "In your presence, I see color. I need no further proof."

Her eyes widened, then narrowed in suspicion. She knew him to be old, although discerning whether he was younger or older than she was impossible to determine, as well as irrelevant. Time between realms and dimensions was fluid. Few fae—she knew of two, the Erlking and the Unseelie King—could move smoothly between realms and worlds without being lost to time or circumstance. How they achieved that feat she had no idea, even though she, too, had the rare skill to create portals between places. Before being thrust into this realm she'd had the rare skill to create portals to travel instantaneously from place to place, but traveling between realms and dimensions … no, she'd not been granted the power to control the ebb and flow of time and hold it steady between destinations.

Iselde also knew a fae male lost his ability to see color well before his first millennium unless he found his mate. From what she'd learned, assuming it wasn't all a lie, Koriolis had aged well past his first millennium before he'd been exiled to this realm contaminated with iron. *He might even be nearly as old as I.*

She looked at him, then glanced away again. "What color are my eyes?"

"The most vivid of blue," he answered without hesitation, for he had not seen color for longer than he could remember. "Cobalt. They are beautiful."

Iselde pressed her lips together, determined to test him further once they reached a place where light would reveal the colors of the world around them beyond the unceasing variations of green and brown. Suddenly impatient and breathless, she said, "Stop!"

"Why?"

"I need to get out of this vehicle."

"This is not a good place to stop and wander about."

"Then make sure I am not harmed."

He sighed and brought the car to a gentle halt. "Do not wander far. Snakes and alligators won't care whether you're fae."

She nodded, fumbled for the door handle, and opened the door. She climbed from the vehicle and stepped around the car until she stood behind it. She plunged her senses into earth and sent her questing mind deep below to the most powerful ley line available. She flung her hands up and concentrated. Silvery light limned her body. Power pulsed around her and within her.

"What are you doing?" Koriolis cried as he hastened toward her, but the force of the power she wielded repelled him.

In a low, guttural voice, she chanted the words in the High Tongue to force open a portal. Above her power swirled and undulated. An unwary insect hit it and exploded in a bright shower of sparks. Her throat soon turned raw as she channeled the power and bent it to her will.

"Stop, daughter."

The power surrounding Iselde abruptly vanished. Although his mate stood erect and defiant, a fine tremor ran through her. Sweat beaded on her skin. Koriolis looked beyond his mate and gaped.

Silvery white and deepest black, two unicorns stood side by side. Their twisting spiral horns were pointed at them, the white swift's horn at Iselde and the black swift's horn at Koriolis.

Iselde turned her head to look at him. "Is *this* what you brought me into the swamp to see?"

Koriolis shook his head. "No. I have never seen the dawn and midnight swifts before."

The black beast lowered its horn. "And you likely will not again, demon, unless I decide to kill you."

The white swift shook its heavy neck, tossing the thick, gleaming mane. "Daughter, you shall not avoid your destiny."

"Do you mean that?"

"Mean what?" Koriolis murmured in confusion.

"You called me daughter. Are you truly my sire?" she demanded, raising her chin and looking down her nose at the magnificent beast of fable.

"How ..." Koriolis whispered.

"Of course not," the dawn swift replied. "But you are my daughter nonetheless. Your mother has seen your fate, and you shall not be permitted to deny it."

"So, I *can* deny it!" she crowed.

The midnight swift tapped Koriolis on the shoulder with the tip of his horn. The demon was startled, for he'd neither seen nor heard the beast move, much less maneuver so closely to him. "Take her to mate, Dra'Acul."

"That is not my name," Koriolis replied, keeping his voice cool and even.

"Henceforth it will be," the unicorn answered.

"I am not Vladimir Tepes," he snapped. "Nor will I allow you to make a mockery of me."

"You are not Vladimir Tepes," the unicorn agreed. "You are king of his line."

"Because I control the New Orleans nest of vampires?" Koriolis scoffed.

"Because you will control the evil that spreads in Fé-Ree," the unicorn replied, enunciating the words so each syllable stood on its own and carried a deeper meaning.

"Don't you mean vanquish?" Iselde interjected, swiveling on her heel to face him.

The black unicorn turned its large head toward her. "No, daughter. Evil cannot be vanquished; it must be controlled. You and Dra'Acul are fated to this task."

"I will not be manipulated or coerced!" she cried.

"Then you will die here," the midnight swift replied. "Do not attempt another portal, daughter."

"Is *that* what you were doing?" Koriolis blurted.

The midnight swift jabbed him with the point of his horn and drew blood. "And you—"

Koriolis glared at the unicorn, but held his tongue.

"—you *will* take her to mate, else your doom will be most ... unpleasant."

Now Koriolis spoke, "And if I do not wish to contain some nameless evil in a realm that no longer accepts me because of what I have become, what I am now, and what I embrace?"

"Then you will die here, too," came the dispassionate reply.

The dawn swift minced closer to the midnight swift. The two unicorns crossed horns and a blinding light flashed the instant the beasts connected. Koriolis and Iselde's eyelids slammed closed lest they be blinded. Frigid cold blasted around them, an arctic wind that flash-froze everything for hundreds of feet around them, except for the demon and the fae. The unicorns had vanished.

Brushing his hair out of his face, Koriolis rasped, "Just what the hell was that?"

Iselde's breath caught in her throat as her legs buckled. Leaves and debris crunched beneath her as she sat on the temporarily frozen ground. She huffed and said, "I can't blame my mother for meddling this time."

Her eyes rolled back and she slumped. Koriolis darted forward and gathered her into his arms. With a gentleness none of the vampires under his authority would have believed, he placed her into the passenger seat of the Aston Martin and buckled her in. Then he got into the car and resumed driving.

"They hold no authority in *this* realm," he muttered as though to convince himself.

The fae had their oracle. The primordial swamp of Louisiana had something different, but possibly no less powerful and certainly something even the newly named Dra'Acul respected. He called her by the Russian name of Baba Yaga, although the ancient sorceress was not nor had ever been Russian.

CHAPTER 10

"WHAT BRINGS YOU HERE, DRA'ACUL?" THE WIZENED old woman asked as she emerged from her shack, which squatted on its grotesquely gigantic chicken legs. Despite her decrepit appearance, power radiated off her in slow, heavy pulses.

Recoiling from the old woman's malignant power, Iselde positioned herself slightly behind Koriolis and to his left, fingers curling around the hilt of a silver athame he had pressed into her hand before they exited the vehicle a second time and climbed into a pirogue. Koriolis had deftly maneuvered the shallow watercraft through the swamp's black water, quietly pointing out predatory creatures lurking in concealment. The heat and humidity and the pervasive smell of decay made Iselde long again for the clean, cold, windswept expanses of the northern wastes.

"Why do you call me that?" Koriolis countered with his own question. "Did you receive a visit from Fé-Rec?"

The woman nodded, her stringy gray hair lying limp and tangled over her shoulders. She folded her skinny arms over her sagging breasts. "I did. Arrogant beasts."

Iselde repressed a snort.

"So, what brings you here?" the old woman repeated.

"Returning to Fé-Ree," he answered.

The woman's eyebrows rose in surprise. "I did not expect that. In all the time I have known you, you never once considered returning to your homeland."

"I never considered it possible," he corrected. "Demons are not welcome there."

"And this world thrives on monsters, eh?" she cackled, spittle flying from her thin lips. She tucked a lank lock of hair behind her ear then shook her head. "No, I cannot pass through the veil to Fé-Ree."

"We do not require escort," Iselde said with icy hauteur.

The old sorceress' eyes flickered with dark light. "I know who you are, Ice Queen."

"I am no queen," Iselde denied.

"But you are ice, cold and sharp." The old woman cackled again and gestured to the verdant swamp surrounding them. "But you will melt in this place. It will conquer you."

"Baba Yaga," Koriolis recalled the old woman's attention, "can you return us to Fé-Ree?"

"I will not."

His eyes narrowed and power thrummed through his body. "But you *can.*"

The old woman shrugged. "Your fae beasts cannot defeat me on my own turf."

"You wield iron," Iselde muttered.

The old woman laughed. "Of course, I wield iron!" She pointed at Koriolis. "As does your mate!"

Annoyed, Iselde glanced at him and muttered, "Does *everyone* know?"

Still chuckling to herself, the sorceress gestured toward her shack. "Take the Ice Queen to mate, Dra'Acul. Bind her by blood and the elements, for you'll need all of it to secure her to you."

"No," Iselde said, her tone brooking no argument.

"Then die," the old woman retorted with a shrug of her bony shoulders. "I care not."

"Fae cannot survive in this realm for long," Koriolis said, his voice soft but not pleading. "If you do not want to die, you have but two choices: turn demon as I did or accept my bond. My bond will at least give you more time."

Iselde turned her arctic gaze on him.

"This world is no place for the fae," he said. "You do not belong here, but every particle of my being knows that you belong with me."

She shook her head. "And you, demon, do not belong in Fé-Ree."

Her musical pronunciation mimicked the unicorn's and imbued the word with a wealth of meaning.

"Stubborn to the end, aren't you, Ice Queen?" the old woman said with a derisive snort. "Already I can see you crave the earth's cold power. Already, you sustain yourself with it, but you forget that such power is filtered through iron. It's tainted, you fool, and will kill you just as surely as any steel blade."

"Do not call me that," Iselde commanded.

"Take the pigheaded girl to mate, Dra'Acul." Then she glared at Iselde. "Accept your destiny."

"I am Koriolis," he insisted, "not Tepes."

"I *knew* Vlad Tepes," the old woman snapped. "But my tongue will not speak your other name. Damned pretty unicorns must have cursed it."

Iselde pursed her lips, considering this small display of power the unicorns had exercised upon the sorceress. *Perhaps they are not so powerful here as in Fé-Ree, but they are still formidable.* She glanced at the beautifully fashioned male beside her, muscled like a warrior of old, tall and commanding, a dangerous male with dark, dark proclivities.

She remembered that some once claimed Uberon, the Unseelie King, a demon. Some still did. It didn't seem to bother him. She'd witness him take advantage of such superstition and wield it to great effect.

I could do worse than learn from him.

But what would a mate bond with this tainted, beautiful creature do to her? Not knowing disturbed her. She privately admitted that not knowing frightened her. It had been so long since she had not known what to do, not foreseen the consequences of her decisions and actions.

She glanced at him again. Her blood stirred with interest, and heat pooled low in her core. Her flesh wanted this male as much as her soul had begun to crave the cold power of the ley lines. Would she find herself as addicted to him as others who succumbed to the lure of drugs, gold, and power? She felt her resolve to resist him weaken and stiffened her spine. Her mouth opened and words that horrified her rushed forth: "I fear losing myself to you."

Profound relief rushed through Koriolis: *It is not me she hates, but erasure.* He reassured her, his voice gentle, "You will not, beloved."

Her eyes widened at the endearment, although it certainly wasn't the first time he'd used it. Perhaps she finally accepted he meant it.

The sorceress' cackle disturbed the tender moment. "You'll find the necessary accouterments inside." She gestured again toward her shack.

"Why are you so eager to see us mated?" Koriolis asked.

The old woman pointed a gnarled, bony finger at him. "*You* do not belong here."

"I haven't belonged here for millennia," he pointed out, his tone dry as old bone. "Yet here I remain."

The pointing finger moved to aim at Iselde.

"And *she* brings doom upon this world should she remain unbonded and uncontrolled. Power like hers must be harnessed, controlled, and directed."

Iselde's nostrils flared and her lips thinned in offense. Fury at the sorceress' words resonate within the tall, white-haired fae. As though knowing her icy rate, Koriolis risked injury and raised his hand to stroke the back of one finger down her smooth cheek. The gentle touch distracted her.

"Come, beloved," he said as the lust in his body rose to feverish intensity. "I would share this joy with you."

"Joy?" she hissed.

"Aye, the joy of a true mating, a soul bond. My strength, my power will be yours."

She blinked. "You do not fear losing yourself to the mate bond?"

He gave her a small, sad smile. "I was lost ages ago and am eager for this opportunity to find myself again and perhaps be restored."

Iselde looked away, shoulders sagging. She did not quite trust this male, although he had yet to exhibit any genuine unkindness toward her. Trust, she knew, did not come easily to her. She knew he wanted something from her. She knew they were true mates, for how else would he have known the color of her eyes? Their mating would bind them, boost their power, and irrevocably link them together for all eternity.

For most immortals, the concept of eternity did not inspire dread; however, Iselde had lived longer than most of her kind. She'd grown used to herself, comfortable in her own skin and with her own thoughts. The idea of sharing the very essence that made her *her*, perturbed her.

Yet, she wanted to return home.

She heartily disliked this stinking land of oppressive heat and humidity where she met iron at every turn.

"If I agree, you will send us to Fé-Ree?" she asked, turning her attention back to the sorceress.

The old woman smiled, revealing dark gaps where teeth once were.

"I would have your word," Iselde insisted, because she knew words spoken with power bound the speaker as much as they bound the object or person spoken of.

"If you agree *and complete the mate bond*, then I will send you back to Fé-Ree," the woman said with a nod of respect.

"Before the next moonrise," Iselde added, knowing that leaving the timing up to the sorceress might leave them stranded in this terrible, corrosive realm for centuries or even millennia.

"Before the next moonrise after your mate bond is sealed," the old woman enunciated. Then her expression turned sly. "And what do you give me in exchange? Everything has a price, particularly favors."

"What do you want?" Koriolis asked. He gestured broadly with a hand. "If it is gold or jewels you want, I will give them to you."

Baba Yaga snorted. "What use have I for gold or jewels out here?" Her expression turned cold. "No, what I want from you is blood, blood from you both."

"No," Iselde replied. "You shall not have my blood. Koriolis may indulge you, but I shall not."

"What do you intend to do with this blood?" Koriolis inquired.

"What does it matter to you, demon?" the sorceress retorted. "You will be back in Fé-Ree."

"If she binds herself to us with a blood bond, she can recall us here at her whim," Iselde pointed out in a quiet voice. "We will be subject to her command."

"No blood," Koriolis stated, his voice cold and hard.

"Then no deal," the sorceress said. With a shrug, she turned to walk back inside her hut.

Koriolis opened his mouth to demand the sorceress come back, but Iselde touched his sleeve and shook her head.

"What?" he asked, puzzled.

"She placed no condition upon her vow until after she spoke the words. She is bound by her words, but we are not bound to pay her in blood."

Koriolis felt his lips stretch into a sharp smile of triumph. The rules of commitment in this realm did not work the same as in Fé-Ree, and that would appear to work in their favor. He extended his hand. "Will you accompany me back to the city?"

She tilted her head and said nothing more about their failure to secure the old sorceress' cooperation.

"I would prefer to initiate and seal our mate bond in the comfort of my own bed, not hers," he explained with a glance of distaste at the sorceress' shack. "We will return before moonrise."

She nodded. "Have your minions gather the elements."

"Come, my lady, let us defeat those who would manipulate me and control you."

The ride back to New Orleans was tense. Driver and passenger stole glances at each other when they thought the other wasn't looking. A few times their gazes met and held for a moment before breaking to pay attention to the drive.

Iselde admitted Koriolis Valchik Dra'Acul—the "syn" exchanged for the new designation "Dra," meaning "king" in the old tongue. It amused her to reflect on the etymology of his given name, Koriolis, which also alluded to "king." *King of kings. This king of kings is not my king, nor will I be his subject.*

She noted his large hands and long fingers, masculine and strong without being bulky. She observed the bunch and roll of taut muscle under smooth skin that disappeared beneath the short sleeves of his shirt. She was not familiar with the soft, stretchy fabric. Intrigued by the fabric, she wondered if her mate's skin was as soft.

The sultry light of dusk spread across the western horizon as Koriolis parked the car. He glanced with worry at the darkening sky vivid red, orange, pink, and purple, but said nothing as he got out of the vehicle and walked around the car to open the passenger door while Iselde studied the door to figure out how to open it. He touched the handle and murmured, "Pull up this lever here," and showed her how to open it.

"Ah." She locked away that tidbit of information so she need not depend upon him the next time.

Koriolis held out his arm, and Iselde lightly rested her fingers on it, allowing him the chivalry of escorting her into the mansion via a different route than they took earlier. He carefully navigated the enclosed courtyard, lifting his face to the rising moon as she had often done to soak in sunshine. The combination of moonlight and electric lights highlighted the planes and angles of his chiseled face. Iselde stared at him and wondered if he'd lied to her.

"I miss the sun," he admitted. At her frown, he explained, "Moonlight is as close as I can get to sunshine without my vampires suspecting something untoward."

"Do you think the sunshine of Fé-Ree will affect you?" she asked. "I thought you were not affected by sunlight."

"I said I did not fear sunlight, not that it had no effect on me. Because of my position, I seldom go out during the day. I must rest, and daytime is best for that." he pointed out, then added, "As for whether the sunshine in Fé-Ree will affect me, I don't know. There's only one way to find out."

Iselde assumed demons to be creatures consigned to darkness and wondered if, by mating her, the soul bond would spare him from his depravity or drag her down into those murky depths with him.

"Are you hungry?" Koriolis asked her as they passed by the commercial kitchen used for cooking food for guests and those who served as resident blood donors for those in Koriolis' coven.

"Perhaps later," she said, feeling nervous, awkward, and hungry, but unwilling to admit it. It had been a long, long time since she'd found any male worthy of intimacy. Holding herself apart from her own clan reinforced feelings of isolation.

Koriolis must have sensed her unease as they entered his bedchamber. Drawing her close to him, he ran the back of his index finger down her cheek. "Are you afraid?"

Iselde's eyes narrowed. "I do not fear you."

"Ah, I misspoke," he said and stroked his hand over her head and down the shining length of her hair.

Iselde's eyes fluttered shut and she said, "I am ... uneasy."

"Are you a virgin?"

"No." At his sigh of relief, she added, "But it has been a long time."

"And you were never promiscuous, were you?"

She shook her head again. "The oracle's daughter cannot afford promiscuity."

"There is too much power to risk," he murmured.

She nodded, grateful for his insight. "My mother wants this."

"And so you resist because this is what *she* wants? Do you not want this? Us?"

She leaned her head against his shoulder and said nothing.

"Do you find me repulsive, Iselde?"

"No," she replied, her voice muffled against his shirt. She examined the sensations running through her body, her own observations of his physical beauty. "No, you do not repulse me."

Koriolis' lips curled in a small smile as he continued to stroke her, letting the soothing action relax her defenses. "I find you beautiful, the most beautiful female I have ever seen."

She sighed, her breath warm and moist through the thin fabric of his shirt.

"Your beauty makes my blood sing."

She sighed again, allowing herself to be seduced. She had agreed to follow through with mating him, and she would not break her word, but neither did she see any reason to make the experience unpleasant. Iselde raised her hands and placed them on his shoulders. She leaned back and whispered, "Kiss me."

Koriolis obeyed. He lowered his mouth to her soft lips in a kiss so gentle Serena would have scoffed in derisive mockery. Where the vampire craved forceful domination, the fae would resent it. This female needed to be an equal partner, so first, she needed to be lured into trust.

He kissed her gently again, the press of his lips light upon her skin. He continued stroking her, his hands moving slowly, surely, and firmly. He felt her muscles relax beneath his touch as her body grew accustomed to this gentle pleasure. Iselde's trust was a fragile thing, precious and easily destroyed. Her fury at being betrayed could kill him.

Literally.

Koriolis wanted her power allied and aligned with his own, quite possibly more than he wanted to slake his ardor with her flesh.

As Iselde's skin prickled and was soothed, as her muscles warmed and relaxed, as her wariness melted, she felt her clothes slip away from her body. She let her glamour slip away, too. Soon she was naked in his arms, but she felt no shame. Shame was a foreign emotion associated with dishonor, and she had done nothing dishonorable.

Iselde dug her claws into the thin fabric of Koriolis' shirt and tore it with a sharp pull. The scent of his heated skin filled her nose, and she bent her head to the exposed flesh to taste it. She stroked him, and he sighed at her willing and enthusiastic touch. The power he sought, the vengeance he craved, was nearly within his grasp.

"Allow me," he murmured as he skimmed a hand across her flat belly. With a smooth, subtle touch, he quickly divested her of what remained of her reluctance, every touch, every caress, every kiss, lick, and nibble designed to stoke her passion. When his hand slid between her thighs, he smiled against the skin of her neck: she dripped for him. He did not not allow himself to do more than catalog the absence of a filigree collar emblazoned upon her fine, smooth skin.

At Koriolis' most intimate touch, Iselde released the cautious restraint she'd imposed upon herself and began to take as well as give. Her claws tore at his clothes, and she pulled off the shreds of fabric and flung them away. Soon, he, too, was naked, his fine skin pebbling beneath the stroke of her hands and flicks of her tongue. She drew back to allow herself a moment to admire the wide, intricate band of black engraved into his skin in a drape across his chest from shoulder to shoulder, over his shoulders, and across his back from shoulder blade to shoulder blade, a sure sign of a powerful First House male had it been silver. But he *had* been fae, she realized.

At her sound of dismay, he drew back and asked, "What is wrong, beloved?"

She drew a finger across the black tattoo, noting the subtle difference in texture. "Your House mark. It is tarnished."

"Ah," he sighed and drew her close, wondering why she hadn't mentioned it before. He gently pressed her head against his shoulder. "A consequence of living here for so long."

"Ah," she echoed, accepting the explanation. She pressed a kiss to the black filigree engraved in his skin.

He maneuvered her to the bed. She allowed him to lower her to the soft, springy mattress, more comfortable than any bed of forest moss, if not so fragrant with the scents of a verdant forest, the last place where she'd given her body to a worthy male.

Koriolis crawled over her and kneeled between her spread legs. Her gaze latched onto the proud jut of his cock rising long, thick, and ruddy with eagerness. A glimmering pearl of fluid seeped from its tip and dribbled down the turgid length. Iselde reached for his cock, stroking the liquid path with her fingertips and gathering the lubricant in her hand for the upstroke. Koriolis groaned at the sublime pleasure of her intimate touch.

He felt the tightness of his balls and the tingle at the base of his spine signal the readiness of his climax. He took a deep breath and drew back, pulling himself from the pleasure of her grasp.

"Not yet," he growled.

Iselde smiled a wicked, knowing smile which turned into a gasp of pleasure as he dove between her legs and swiped his tongue along her slit. Her hands clutched at his hair as he feasted upon her, showing her with lips, teeth, and tongue pleasures she'd somehow neglected to savor in far too many years. Heat and pressure built up low in her abdomen as she chased the climax that would surely explode with all the brilliance of a thousand shattering stars. She felt the intensity swell and expand, heard herself gasp and sob as she ground her soaked pussy into her mate's face, chasing an orgasm that felt millennia in the making.

Koriolis drew back, his face shiny with her juices. He drew a hand over his face and smeared the wetness across her lower belly.

"No," she keened. "I need more!"

"And you'll get it," he promised, his voice rasping. He surged up her body and notched the tip of his pulsing cock at the entrance of her body. Iselde keened, her blazing blue eyes locked on his dark gaze, as he slowly pushed inside her body and lowered his mouth to hers, sharing the taste of her with her. He trembled with the effort not to surge into her, for her channel was tight and resisted his intrusion.

However, he encountered no maiden's barrier when he sank as deeply into her as physically possible. Iselde groaned at the fullness within her, a rightness that no other male had delivered, not even the ones who'd sired her children long since grown, mated, and dead. That son and his family had formed the core of her tribe, explaining the cobalt eyes common among so many of them.

Koriolis drew back, making her gasp at the wet friction. Her body clung to his, so he thrust again, beginning an ancient rhythm of physical magic ensuring the perpetuation of the species. The tingles renewed at the base of his spine and his balls drew tight as he felt his essence boil up the length of his cock embedded within his mate's body. He cried out as the vow was pulled from him, "I pledge myself to thee as written on the wind, witnessed by the sun, remembered by the earth, and sung by the rivers!"

When the words left his lips, he bit down upon the tender junction where Iselde's neck and shoulder joined. Her blood filled his mouth as she screamed in a startled mixture of pain and pleasure as another orgasm exploded. He drank deeply from her, sating the sudden rise of bloodlust, until her heartbeat fluttered and her eyes rolled back in their sockets.

Unwilling and unable to cause her permanent harm, he gently withdrew his fangs from her flesh and lapped at the wounds, letting his saliva close them before her fae physiology could heal them. Easing his spent cock from her body, Koriolis gathered her close and held her within the shelter of his body as the power of his vow and the ingestion of her blood bound their souls for eternity.

CHAPTER 11

FIERY PAIN CATAPULTED BOTH OF THEM TO WAKE-fulness with a shared outcry as a wide, intricate pattern of silver erupted around Iselde's throat. Curling tendrils of silver extended to her collar bones and upper chest. The collar blazed with light and heat. She felt her skin sizzle and smelled the stench of burned flesh as the mate bond took hold and anchored her soul to Koriolis'. When the smoke cleared, another surge of intense heat swept over her as cobalt and black jewels erupted, gracing the elaborate silver filigree steaming in her skin.

Unable to tend to his mate as she cried out due to his own agony, Koriolis clutched at his chest, digging in his claws, as his own First House brand manifested cobalt and black gemstones that signaled a true mating of fated mates. Forever now he would see color—at least within the proximity of his mate—and be granted the blessing of the finer emotions through her heart and soul. No longer would he be cold and calculating, closed off to the repercussions of heart and conscience.

"Damn it," Iselde muttered through panted breaths as her fingertips traced the glittering brand emblazoned upon her flesh. "That *hurt*."

Angling himself up his arm, Koriolis winced. "I did not wish to say anything earlier about your lack of a House mark."

She snorted, fingertips still tracing the intricate pattern, running over the bumps of gemstones embedded in her skin. "I was born before the fae split into Houses."

"Huh," he exhaled. "I knew you to be highborn because of your power and who your mother is, but this I did not expect."

Iselde pushed herself up into a sitting position and examined his House mark. She frowned. "I know that pattern."

He sighed. "I'm sure you do." He pressed his hand against a section of wide band running over a bulging pectoral muscle. "And you recognize the House color, too."

She extended her hand and ran her fingertips lightly over the stretch of his House mark running from collar bone to nipple. "Unseelie black mixed with my blue." She frowned. "Only the Unseelie King's House manifests black gemstones." Her eyes narrowed. "Koriolis is not your true name. Who are you? Whom have I mated?"

Koriolis exhaled a gusty sigh and let himself flop back down, his head landing on the pillow. He did not wish to confess, but the demand in her voice compelled his candor: "I was once Marog, prince of the Unseelie Court."

"You were *banished*," Iselde whispered. "Not dead."

"Folk believed me dead, crushed by the castle," he admitted, closing his eyes against the memory of his dishonor. "Father would not grant me that boon."

"You acted with grave dishonor," Iselde said, unable to hide her disgust. Although she'd heard what happened via secondhand and thirdhand source, she'd gleaned the basics: Marog had abducted the moon-born female mated to Thelan, captain of the Seelie Court's palace guard, *and* he'd attempted to break the captain's mate bond by forcing his own upon her.

"I did," he agreed. "King Uberon spared my life, then banished me to this realm."

"Uberon does nothing without reason."

"No, he does not," Koriolis said. "But neither does he make a habit of divulging his reasons."

Iselde sighed. "That's true. Folk think my uncle, Enders, is mysterious, but really, it's Uberon who defies explanation." She glanced at her mate. "He's mated now, you know—and a doting father."

Iselde opened her mind to allow him access to her few memories of the Unseelie King and his family. He saw more than that, though. He glimpsed her activities over the millennia, rescue missions to liberate slaves from Djaria, Corta, and even Fyrgia that left many dead humans and djinns in her wake. The need for freedom burned in her.

"I knew my mother was not his true mate," he said, thinking of his father's lack of interest in him while setting aside what he'd seen for later rumination. Uberon was not entirely to blame for the estrangement between sire and get, for he'd not had the emotional wherewithal to love his mate or his first born son. The Unseelie King only had his honor which wasn't, perhaps, as robust as it might have been.

Iselde spoke again. "You were once called Marog. Why did you not keep the name? It meant nothing here."

"I abandoned that name," he replied, "but not my hope that I will return to Fé-Ree." *Perhaps it is that hope that keeps that last spark of my soul alive.*

She snorted. "Good thing, because *Marog* will not be welcome back home."

"And do you truly believe you'll ever go back to Fé-Ree?"

"I hope so. I do not like this realm."

"Despite places of beauty here, it's a miserable place overall," he agreed.

"It's the iron," she said.

"Indeed."

Iselde ran her hand over the bejeweled House mark engraved into her skin. It no longer hurt. The silver and gemstones felt cool to the touch. She yawned. "I would sleep."

Koriolis pressed a gentle kiss to her brow and said, "Then sleep, beloved."

"Do not leave me." The order came out almost as a whine. The ache of his pending absence clawed at her as she closed her eyes.

"Never," he promised, ignoring the hunger that began to throb.

A moment passed. She inhaled a slow, deep breath and exhaled. In a sleepy voice, Iselde said as she raised her arm, "I can feel your hunger. Feed and be gratified."

Her consent overwhelmed him. Gratitude the likes of which he had never experienced nearly brought Koriolis to tears. He gently grasped the arm she offered and kissed the delicate underside of her wrist.

"Thank you, beloved."

"Do not make me regret this," she warned.

"Never," he vowed then pressed his fangs to the thin skin and bit down.

He inhaled as heat, blood, and power flowed into him. The immensity of her innate power awed him even as it hummed with an unspoken warning not to misuse what she gifted him. He was ancient, she even more so, and with the incredible power only the eldest of the fae possessed. Little separated her and the fae gods. The power in her blood made him wonder what his father commanded, being among the oldest generation of fae. He'd always been in awe of the Unseelie King, but this taste indicated that his father's strength and power exceeded even his own guess.

True mating occurred between equals. He'd always assumed that meant equals of status, not necessarily equals of power. His fruitless pursuit of the moon-born long ago would have been a terrible mismatch, for her power did not match his. It did not complement his. But this female? He shuddered in pure pleasure as he took a final gulp and licked the wounds closed. She sighed and lapsed more deeply into slumber.

The knowledge that Iselde held greater power than he took him by surprise. She was stronger by nearly every measure of fae magic and honor. Millennia living in the northern wastes had honed her into a weapon too sharp, strong, and dangerous for him to wield. It also explained the rapidity with which the mortal realm affected her.

"I could never compel you," he whispered, for forcing her to abandon her honor would destroy her or turn her into an evil he doubted even the dawn and midnight swifts could conquer. *I cannot compel you, but perhaps I might persuade you.* "You are so strong. Why would the oracle force you to mate one such as I?"

It takes a demon to fight a demon.

The words chimed loud and clear in his mind, but they did not originate from his sleeping mate. Koriolis gently disentangled himself from Iselde's embrace and rolled out of bed. Standing, he lifted his chin and whispered, "Who speaks?"

You must bring iron to Fé-Ree.

"Fé-Ree has iron," he pointed out. "Just not in the concentration found here."

Bring the iron doom to Fé-Ree.

"And Iselde?"

She will supply the power you need.

"You would have me use her."

Is that not what you intended?

"I will not harm her. I *cannot* harm her."

Almost I think better of you, Marog.

"Who are you to speak to me like this?"

Who do you think I am?

"You are not my father."

Derisive laughter ensued, filling his mind with a feminine cackle. *No, not even I dare to command the Unseelie King.*

"Yet you dare command me."

You are not Uberon.

Koriolis shook his head. There was no point in debating who was who any further. He would discover who spoke to him soon enough. "What iron should I bring? Raw ore? Steel bars?"

The sword.

"What sword?"

Asi, the sword of Rudra.

Koriolis took a second to rummage through his memories to find the reference. He frowned. "There is no such thing. It's entirely mythological, just like Excalibur."

Asi exists, though humanity has lost it.

Rather than debate the existence of a mythological sword with an incorporeal entity speaking directly into his mind, Koriolis changed tactics. "Why Asi?"

Asi was forged to destroy demons.

"I'm a demon, remember? Why would I wish to carry my own doom with me?"

Wouldn't a demon wielding a sword to kill demons be considered invincible? A sly tone beckoned to a yearning for power and control.

"Foolish, more like," Koriolis retorted with a nearly inaudible scoff. "And whom am I supposed to vanquish with this legendary weapon?"

Not vanquish. Conquer.

The wheedling undertone appealed to a greed he had long since abandoned. Mountains of administrative work and an infinite number of niggling little details had long since crushed an early desire to conquer the world and rule it. He replied with bald candor, "I no longer desire a crown."

Whoever spoke did not believe him. *You are the king of New Orleans. You rule the city's underworld.*

"And that's quite sufficient. I do not want or need more."

Yet you are fated for more.

Koriolis sighed. "Whom am I supposed to conquer then?"

Those against whom my daughter has little defense.

Koriolis' upper lift lifted in a sneer. "Ah, you're the oracle. And who would be stronger than Iselde and also wish her harm?" He doubted the Unseelie King, the Erlking, or the Archivist wished her ill.

The djinn. They wield magic and iron, and they've a grudge against Iselde.

Koriolis could agree that was a bad, bad combination. Djinns were powerful and worked magic the fae had never bothered to understand. "All right. Where do I find Asi, the sword of Rudra?"

However, the oracle had retreated, vanished as it were, leaving him without answer and only the conviction that it might be a long, long time before the oracle allowed her daughter to return to Fé-Ree and set him on a course to kill demons and conquer the djinns. He wondered if she'd considered the corruption of her daughter that would inevitably occur—and sooner rather than later—if she did not permit Iselde to return home.

He sighed and glanced at the female sleeping beside him. His cock twitched. *Not now.* Pursing his lips as he thought, Koriolis lay back and curled his body around Iselde. He did not look forward to telling her of their imminent travel plans.

Perhaps she would like India. Certainly the spices would intrigue her: cinnamon, turmeric, cumin … fae cuisine lacked such bright, piquant flavors. Fae tastes tended toward the subtle—bland, one might even say—such that some fae made a hobby of distinguishing the slightest differences in flavor. The bold flavors found in this realm shocked the sophisticated fae palate attuned to subtle nuances and overwhelmed delicate fae senses.

As he drifted off to sleep, he wondered what Iselde thought of the spicy food her voodoo hostess had served.

CHAPTER 12

"WE'RE GOING WHERE TO DO WHAT?" ISELDE RAISED her eyebrows as she sipped at thick, hot coffee cut with chicory. She'd soothed the bitterness with a heavy dose of cream and a touch of refined sugar to make it palatable and wondered if it were possible to import this heady brew to Fé-Ree. *Perhaps coffee beans could be grown there.*

"You heard me the first time," Koriolis replied.

"Where are you going?" Serena asked as she entered the kitchen and poured herself a cup of coffee and stirred in some B-negative. She perched on a stool and took an appreciative gulp.

"This doesn't concern you," Koriolis replied.

"Oh, if you're going somewhere, it most certainly does," she countered, giving Iselde the side-eye. "Whom will you leave in charge while you're gone?"

"I won't be gone that long."

"Who says?" Iselde interjected. She took a sip and grimaced, but did not look ready to relinquish the mug. "She's sending us on a wild goose chase."

"So, where are you going?" Serena repeated. "We deserve to know."

Koriolis pinched the bridge of his nose. "Summon Aristide."

Serena frowned. "Why him?"

"Because he's my second in command, not you."

"He's a dick."

Koriolis shrugged. "Serena, sharing my bed in the past does not increase your importance."

Serena's mug thumped on the table. "That was cruel."

He shrugged, not really caring. Iselde's amusement flickered in the back of his mind.

"Serena," Iselde said, her voice a lazy drawl, "if you want to challenge me, go right ahead."

Serena eyed the whipcord-lean, razor-sharp female who was not a vampire and yet exuded a predatory air that any vampire could recognize and respect. "He seems fond of you. I'd hate to earn Koriolis' wrath by killing you."

"You're welcome to try." Iselde extended a claw and drew a line in the granite countertop. She flicked off the stone dust, smirking at Serena's narrowed gaze.

"If you're finished baiting my consort," Koriolis drawled, "fetch Aristide."

"Consort?" Serena hissed in surprise. Her glare flickered from Koriolis to Iselde and back. Koriolis said nothing. Serena pursed her lips and shot another fulminating glare at Iselde who ignored it. She set her cup down with exaggerated care and stalked off to do her lord and master's bidding.

"You've made an enemy of her," Iselde mentioned, ignoring that she had, too. Serena would take advantage of any chance to eliminate her, but she was confident in her ability to defeat the fulminating vampire.

Koriolis shrugged. "We won't be coming back here."

She focused a narrow-eyed glare at him. "She spoke to you."

He raised an eyebrow.

"My mother. The oracle."

He nodded.

Iselde's upper lip lifted in a sneer, then she said, "And what does she have you doing?"

"She offered me and you the opportunity to return to Fé-Ree."

"In exchange for what?" she demanded.

"We have to find a sword."

"A sword?"

"A particular sword."

"So, we find this sword my mother covets and she'll bring us back to Fé-Ree?"

"That's the deal."

Iselde snorted. "No, it's not. If she is directing you to this sword, then she'll want you to wield it as she wills. If you refuse, she'll choose for you the worst of all possible fates you could imagine."

"Choose?"

Iselde leaned back in the chair and set the mug down. She put her hands together, index finger steepled. "Each being is born with infinite future possibilities. The choices we make narrow those possibilities. Mostly, Mother does not interfere; however, when she does, she alters one's future to her choice."

"Is that what she did with you?"

Iselde nodded. "Once. She mated me to a male who was not my choice. I was very young, still naive and obedient to my mother's will."

Koriolis intuited what happened. "It turned out poorly, didn't it?"

Her expression shuttered. "It did. I killed him."

"If she knew …"

"She knew the potential futures awaiting depending on what each of us chose."

"Ah."

"She chose estrangement." Iselde rested her clasped hands on the tabletop. "I vowed to kill her if she manipulated me like that again."

"Isn't she manipulating you now?"

"She's manipulating *you*," Iselde corrected him. Her eyes glimmered with tightly restrained fury. "But when—not if—I return to Fé-Ree, I intend to kill her, and she knows it."

"Can she not prevent her own demise?"

Iselde smiled, revealing those sharp, pointed teeth. "Not even the oracle can prevent a blood oath from manifesting its destined conclusion."

Koriolis blinked in surprise. "You vowed to kill your own mother?"

"On the blood of my first mate, my daughters, and myself."

Disgust filled him. "You slaughtered your own children?"

Iselde drew back, her cobalt eyes darkening to midnight with rage. "If that is what you think of me, then you should fear for your own continued existence."

Koriolis exhaled and murmured an apology, knowing she would indeed slaughter him, too, mate bond notwithstanding, if he did not tread carefully. She'd endured that pain once and knew what to expect. It would not kill her, but merely harden her even further.

Accepting his apology at face value, she explained, "The male to whom my mother mated me killed our daughter. Then I killed him and used her blood, his, and mine to seal my oath."

"Did she not manipulate you into doing that?"

Iselde snorted. "At the time, I was little more than an inconvenience to her. My future held so many possibilities that she never considered I might choose the one that would lead to her annihilation."

He nodded. "And you intend to follow through.'"

She bared her pointed teeth again. "One cannot break a blood oath."

However, Koriolis wondered about that. She had killed her first mate, and the mate bond required a blood oath. He pondered as to how she had broken that oath. After a long moment during which she finished sipping her coffee, he said, "You did. How?"

Those icy cobalt eyes had never looked harder when she replied, "Don't cross me and you'll never have to know."

He fully understood the implied threat and knew that, were she at full strength in Fé-Ree, she'd have the power to crush him. Leaning back in his chair as though lounging at ease, he asked, "Will fulfilling your vow kill you, too?"

"I don't know." She shrugged and rose, ending the conversation as a vampire entered the kitchen. "Until now, I never cared." Iselde paused again, running her fingertips over the bejeweled House mark peeking above the neckline of her dress. "Nope, I still don't care. Given the opportunity, I will kill the oracle for what she has done to me."

"My lord," a new voice intoned. Iselde looked at him over the rim of her coffee mug as she took another sip.

"Aristide," Koriolis acknowledged.

Tall, burly, and roughly handsome, the vampire's dark gaze flickered over Iselde as he replied, "You summoned me, my lord?"

Koriolis stood. "I'm leaving. You're in charge."

Aristide nodded. "When shall you return, my lord?"

Koriolis' thin smile was not reassuring. "I don't know. Keep things under control, will you? I do dislike chaos—and killing off the herd that feeds you isn't good husbandry."

Aristide nodded, his expression grave. He understood the unvoiced goodbye. "And Serena?"

"What about her?"

"Will she be accompanying you?"

Koriolis leveled a hard look at his second-in-command. "I will say this once." He gestured toward the slender fae female who seemed made of marble and shards of glass. "I have mated Iselde—"

"Mated?" Aristide echoed in surprise and bewilderment.

Koriolis' eyes narrowed. "You, of everyone in this coven, know exactly what I am."

Aristide nodded, a single curt dip of his chin. "I do, my lord."

"Iselde is from my homeland."

Aristide raised his eyebrows. "She's one of your kind?" His expression turned cunning. "Interesting."

Koriolis snapped his fingers, reclaiming his second-in-command's attention from scheming and said, "We leave momentarily."

"And Serena?" Aristide repeated.

"She is yours. Do with her as you will."

Aristide nodded again, his expression inscrutable.

"Do you have another question?"

"No, my lord."

Koriolis held out his hand. Iselde placed her palm in his and allowed him to lead her from the room. She opened her mouth to ask about Serena's fate, but said nothing, deciding she didn't really care.

CHAPTER 13

THE SUN BURNED LOW OVER THE EASTERN HORIZON as Koriolis and Iselde disembarked from the aircraft. Iselde looked about Delhi's teeming airport with wide eyes, taking everything in as they passed through what her mate called customs and exerted his will to compel petty government functionaries to believe they carried the proper identification. The idea of needing documents to pass from one place to another astounded her. She thought it absurd, but did not protest when he explained the necessity of such mental manipulation. He knew this world and its practices better than she.

At least being enclosed in the aircraft hadn't been as painful as she expected. The fuselage was constructed of something Koriolis called carbon fiber—the same as his favorite automobile—and was filled with other materials with which she also had no familiarity, like plastic and foam rubber. What little metal was exposed was aluminum. In a realm that relied so heavily on iron, the lack of the caustic element in the aircraft surprised her.

Exiting the airport brought a cacophony of noise: horns honking, engines rumbling and sputtering, vendors hawking their wares, and the general din of throngs of humanity going about their business. Iselde wrinkled her nose at the pungent mix of odors, strengthened by the oppressive heat and humidity, that bludgeoned her olfactory senses. She detected spices, smoke, vehicle exhaust, body odor, and dung mixed among the stench of waste and industrial pollution. The sensory assault made her long for the clean, windswept spaces of the northern wastes.

"Is everywhere in this realm so hot and sticky?" she grumbled as Koriolis led her toward a shiny vehicle looking like a large cat lounging amid a crowd of vermin.

"No," he replied and glanced at the rising sun.

"You are protected," she murmured, reminding him of the blood she had allowed him to take from her during the flight. Her wrist still throbbed, as did the sensitive flesh between her thighs.

He gave her a faint smile of acknowledgement and turned to the man who stood beside the large vehicle.

"You are Koriolis Valchik?" the man asked in a lilting accent.

"Yes, and Mrs. Valchik," Koriolis replied.

The driver raised his hands, palms pressed together, and bowed. "*Namaste.*"

Koriolis inclined his head in almost polite acknowledgement. The driver opened the vehicle's back door.

"I have instructions to take you to the Shangri-La Eros, *sahib*?"

"Yes."

The driver looked at the small suitcases his customers had brought with them. "I shall load these, yes, *sahib*?"

"Thank you," Koriolis replied and gestured toward Iselde to get into the car.

She gracefully entered the car's cool, air conditioned interior and slid across the smooth leather upholstery to make room for her mate. As he eased his long, muscular length into the vehicle, she looked at him and repeated sotto voce, "Mrs. Valchik?"

"That would be this realm's common nomenclature for your status as my mate," he explained. "In human parlance, we are *married*."

Iselde blinked and said nothing further on the matter. The driver finished stowing their luggage in the trunk of the car and took his seat behind the steering wheel. A moment later, the driver eased the vehicle into the city's congested traffic.

Iselde had long grown bored of looking out the car's tinted window at the ebb and flow of humanity—and the occasional cow—they passed on the drive to their temporary destination. She pressed a hand against her belly and sniffed at realizing how quickly she'd grown used to eating regularly. Food was abundant in the mortal realm, at least more so than the northern wastes.

"Hungry?" Koriolis murmured in the ancient fae tongue to ensure the driver repeated none of their conversation.

Replying in the same tongue but without the accent imposed by millennia away from Fé-Ree, Iselde replied as she looked out the window at the filthy brown water of the Yamuna River, "Yes, and thirsty. The water here is horrid."

"You'll find the cuisine in India beyond anything you could imagine," he promised with a smile.

"Do you intend to eat?"

"I do."

She raised an eyebrow.

"Anyone who witnesses me eat will not be a vampire." He rapped a knuckle against the window. "Sunlight, remember? Vampires won't be out."

She nodded. "And your need for blood?"

He gave her a close-mouthed smile then said, "I only need yours."

She raised the other eyebrow.

"I do not need much. Your blood is more … *satisfying* than human blood."

"As long as I consent," she said.

He nodded. "As long as you consent." He leaned his head back against the headrest and sighed. "I have missed the sunshine. Whatever happens, I am grateful that you have restored the sun to me. Keeping vampire hours becomes wearisome."

She smiled, enjoying the idea of a demon being in her debt.

The car rolled smoothly to a stop in front of a towering building.

"Welcome to the Shangri-La Eros," the driver said. He got out of the vehicle and scurried around to open the passenger door, then the trunk. As his wealthy passengers exited the car, he hefted their luggage from the trunk and set it on the curb.

"Enjoy your visit to New Delhi, *sahib, memsahib. Namaste,*" the driver said, pressing his palms together and bowing. He closed the car's passenger door, rushed around to the driver's seat, and drove away.

Koriolis and Iselde turned to face the doorman who had approached to greet them. The man snapped his fingers, and a bellman approached to take their luggage.

"Welcome to the Shangri-La Eros, Mr. and Mrs. Valchik," the doorman greeted them. He smiled broadly, white teeth brilliant against his swarthy skin. "*Namaste.*"

Again, Koriolis nodded with the aloof arrogance one expected from a king. The attitude appeared to satisfy the doorman's expectations as he hurried forward to open the hotel's front door.

Iselde followed her mate into an expansive lobby complete with gleaming tile floors, fresh bouquets of exotic flowers, and a hushed ambiance. The bellman followed as they crossed the expanse toward the front desk where obsequious personnel greeted them and checked them in.

"You and Mrs. Valchik will be staying with us for three nights, Mr. Valchik?" the front desk clerk said in a crisp British accent made musical by the lilt of his native tongue.

"At least," Koriolis replied.

"Very good, Mr. Valchik." The clerk handed over two key cards and murmured their room numbers. "Please let us know if there is anything we can do to enhance your stay with us."

"Thank you," Koriolis replied.

"Sir, madam, if you will follow me?" the uniformed bellman said.

They followed him to the elevator bank and entered the first car that opened.

Speaking in the fae tongue, Koriolis murmured, "Had we given them more advance notice, they would have already taken our luggage to our room and unpacked it for us."

"The servants are most efficient," Iselde commented.

"Do not call them servants."

"Their purpose is to serve, is it not?"

"It is," Koriolis said, "but the term 'servant' is no longer commonly used these days in this realm."

Iselde pursed her lips as she considered the implications of his words. After a moment, she asked, "Then what shall I call them?"

"It's best you leave the speaking to me."

She frowned. "Do not attempt to isolate me and control me, Dra'Acul."

"Iselde, for the purpose of our visit here, we are a wealthy businessman and his spoiled wife, nothing more."

She glanced at her glamoured self. She detected no magic overlaying her own. "You have disguised us?."

"We are hiding in plain sight," he confirmed. "Please remember that India is, for the most part, still quite patriarchal. You will fit their expectations and become unmemorable if you act the part of an entitled noblewoman."

She flashed him a serrated smile masked behind the glamour of her human appearance. "I can do that."

The elevator stopped its ascent and the doors opened.

"Please follow me, *sahib, memsahib*," the bellman said.

They fell into step behind the bellman who stopped a moment later in front of a door. Koriolis waved the keycard in front of the lock and opened the door. Iselde swept through the doorway into a lavishly appointed room. Koriolis followed, with the bellman trailing closely behind.

Iselde crossed the room to the large window and peered out. In awe, she said in the fae tongue, "This must be how your gods see the city."

Speaking in English, Koriolis said to the bellman, "Mrs. Valchik understands more English than she speaks."

The bellman nodded. "We speak many languages here at the Shangri-La Eros. Let me know, sir, what language she is most comfortable with and I will see that we have the appropriate personnel to accommodate her."

"English is sufficient. I doubt you will find someone in all of India who speaks Sarsi," Koriolis replied.

The bellman's eyes widened, not recognizing the tongue. He nodded and said, "Very well, *sahib*."

The bellman left. After the door closed behind him, Iselde turned away from the window, a smile curling her lips. "Sarsi? What is that?"

"It's one of the rarest languages in the world and spoken only by a handful of indigenous people in Calgary."

She snorted. "And who are you to know this?"

"Several centuries ago I lived among them for a decade or so."

Iselde nodded, realizing that her mate had lived a full and adventurous life of which she knew nothing. Then again, she'd lived a long life of which he knew little. "Someday you will tell me about your life here."

He shrugged. "Let's unpack. I detest living out of a suitcase."

They worked in companionable silence. Iselde examined the luxury lotions and toiletries available in the spacious bathroom. Feeling grimy after more than thirty hours of travel, she turned on the taps to fill the tub. Hearing the water run, Koriolis peeked into the bathroom as his mate began to undress. Eyes gleaming, he asked, "Would you like some help?"

An answering heat in her gaze accompanied her sultry smile. "I would enjoy the company."

Libido surging, Koriolis stripped and a moment later joined her in the rapidly filling tub. She shuddered as creamy, floral-scented lather foamed in his hands and he massaged it into her skin. He softly moaned with pleasure as she did the same to him. By the time they'd washed each other's bodies, her core dripped with passion and semen dribbled down his erection. He turned her around and positioned her hands against the wall. Thus braced, she moaned when he gripped her hips and pressed into her body.

He paused, luxuriating in the delicious sensation of simply being inside his mate's body.

"Move," she demanded in a throaty voice.

He complied, the wet slap of their bodies echoing off the bathroom's hard walls. When he felt her channel tighten around him and begin to ripple, he withdrew. She whined in protest. He turned her around and lifted her, pressing her back against the wall. She slid down, impaling herself on his cock as his mouth slanted over hers and he tangled their tongues. His hips snapped with a punishing rhythm, and they ate at each other's mouths. Soon, Iselde's breath caught in her throat, and she tore her lips from his as she crested the height of passion. Koriolis lowered his head to feast upon her breasts, nipping her pebbled nipples even as his fingers dug into the firm flesh of her buttocks and upper thighs. Soon he shouted as his body strained against hers in the instinctual effort to plunge his seed as deeply into her womb as physically possible.

Their chests heaved as they panted for breath in the aftermath of explosive passion. Koriolis' arms and legs trembled as he disengaged from his mate's body and gently lowered her back into the water. He sank down beside her and leaned against the tub's side.

Iselde closed her eyes for a moment, then slowly opened them. She looked around at the suds and water splattered about, and a small smile curled her kiss-swollen lips. "We made a mess."

His gaze followed hers to take in the aftermath of their passion and grinned. "So it seems."

"The servants will clean it up."

"That's my queen," he murmured, leaning his head back with a smile.

CHAPTER 14

THROUGH A DELICATE COMBINATION OF BRIBES AND compulsion, Koriolis managed to secure them an audience with a well-known Sanskrit scholar at one of the city's few Institutes of Eminence. Tufts of white hair poked from beneath his turban, merging with a full, bushy, white beard confined by a long braid.

Koriolis knocked lightly on the open door to the professor's office. The scholar looked up from the old manuscript he was perusing and blinked to transfer his focus from the cramped writing on the tanned vellum to the elegantly garbed westerners waiting politely for his permission to enter. After gesturing at them to enter his office, he brought his palms together and slowly nodded as he murmured, "*Namaste.*"

The westerners copied his solemn greeting with the appropriate level of reverence.

"Dr. Bhatia," the tall man began, his voice a velvety baritone lilting with an accent the professor could not quite place, "thank you for agreeing to meet with us."

In a rapid, sing-song intonation of English, the professor nodded and replied, "Yes, yes. I am to express my gratitude for the generous donation you have made to our esteemed institution of higher learning. Consider it said."

One corner of the man's lip curled in cynical amusement. "We are here to research the Asi."

The professor's nostrils flared. "It is Asi, not 'the' Asi. It is claimed Asi is a sentient entity and cannot be compelled to harm the innocent."

"Of course, forgive my ignorance," the man said with a small conciliatory gesture of his hand. The platinum-haired, blue-eyed woman at his side remained silent while somehow appearing predatory. Dr. Bhatia's guest added, "We are searching for it."

The professor snorted. "Many people have searched for it, and all have failed. Why do you believe you will succeed? Why would the gods favor your pursuit of a sacred Indian artifact?"

Koriolis met the old man's gaze without flinching and replied, "I would kill a demon with it."

"You think you are Ashwatthama?"

"Indeed not," Koriolis replied. "I have no such delusions of grandeur. However, I am a warrior with a need for a divine sword to vanquish a demon."

The professor snorted. "I don't believe you. Asi is a *sacred* artifact belonging to *India*."

"Of course, you don't," Koriolis replied and held the man's challenging gaze with his own. Exerting his will, he said, "But you will tell me where I might find Asi."

Dr. Bhatia's eyes lost focus, and his expression turned slack as he succumbed to the overpowering will of the man standing in front of his cluttered desk.

"Direct me to Asi," Koriolis ordered.

"No one knows where it is," the professor replied after a moment's sluggish thought.

"Where do you think it rests?"

"Ashwatthama is said to live in the Arabian peninsula."

"I found that information on the internet," Koriolis snapped, having discovered through that same internet-based research that Ashwatthama was the last known person to have possessed the legendary sword. "Do not lie to me."

"I do not lie."

"Then where do you think he is?"

"Kapil Adwait claims to have met him in the foothills of the Himalayas during his journeys."

"Thank you," Koriolis replied and released his hold on the professor's mind. "Do you know where in those foothills?"

The professor shook his head. "Pilot Baba, for that is what Kapil Adwait is commonly called, will not divulge the information. He may not even still be alive. He's quite elderly, you know."

Koriolis looked over his shoulder at the tall woman standing near him, her expression inscrutable. She gave him a tiny, nearly imperceptible nod. He commanded, "Tell me what you know about Pilot Baba."

"He has four ashrams in India. Considering his age, he probably does not travel extensively any more. Perhaps you will find him at one of those ashrams," Dr. Bhatia said. "There is also a rumor Ashwatthama was seen in the jungles of Navsari in Gujarat."

"So, basically, he could be anywhere."

The professor grinned and nodded. With a shrug, he raised his hands and said, "It is not for us to question the gods' decisions and wanderings."

"We'll learn nothing more from him," Iselde murmured, taking care to use the fae tongue. "If this Kapil Adwait is still alive, let's find him and question him."

Koriolis nodded in agreement and released his mental hold over the scholar. He turned back to Dr. Bhatia and bowed. "Thank you, Dr. Bhatia, for your time. *Namaste.*"

Rubbing his temples and wondering at the slight headache that suddenly came over him, the professor nodded and muttered a polite reply. He returned his gaze to the vellum on his desk, dismissing them from his office and from his mind.

Iselde looped her hand around her mate's arm and fell into step beside him as he headed toward the building's main entrance. "Where are these ashrams of Kapil Adwait?"

"We can look it up on the internet," he replied.

"Did you say Kapil Adwait?" a passerby echoed in surprise as he halted. "You mean Pilot Baba?"

"Yes, Pilot Baba," Koriolis replied and remembered to stretch his lips in a friendly smile glamoured to conceal his pointed teeth.

"Ah, you seek enlightenment!" the man said, eyes brightening with enthusiasm. He gave them a broad, gap-toothed smile. "You could choose no better guru than Pilot Baba to lead you."

"Yes, that is our hope," Koriolis said. "Do you know where we might find him?"

The man's expression fell. "Alas, no, I do not. He takes no new students these days, but the masters who studied under him are very skilled! You will do well with any of them." He brought his hands together in front of him in a prayerful gesture. "I myself make a point of going to the ashram in Uttarkashi every year. I leave rejuvenated and peaceful. It is a most marvelous experience."

"Thank you for being so informative," Koriolis said and bowed. "*Namaste.*"

The helpful stranger smiled again and returned the ritual salutation. "*Namaste.*"

"So, do we go to Gujarat or Uttarakhand? They're on opposite sides of the country," Koriolis asked his mate.

"Which are we closest to?" Iselde did not know this realm's geography.

"Uttarakhand."

She lifted one shoulder in a shrug. "Then let's go there first."

They returned to the hotel and availed themselves of the property's business center, complimentary to guests, to research the legendary sword. Iselde stood behind Koriolis as his nimble fingers danced across the keyboard and information and images flashed across the monitor. Although curious about the fascinating technology, she withheld her questions until a more appropriate time.

"It says here that Asi is connected to Agni, the Indian fire god; Rudra, the storm god; and Surya, the sun god," Koriolis said as he looked up references via the internet. "There are more gods mentioned, but those are the three major deities associated with Asi."

"Who is the last god to be associated with the sword?"

"Krishna, but that's more because he cursed Ashwatthama." He pinched the bridge of his nose. "The more I read, the less I understand. Indian mythology is seriously convoluted."

"How long have you been in this realm?" Iselde asked.

"Too long, but obviously not long enough." He shook his head as though to clear his mind. "I toured the subcontinent for a decade or so in the nineteenth century, but never made a study of Indian mythology or history." He shrugged his shoulders. "I spent millennia settling in various places for a decade or so then moving, but ..." He sighed, disappointed in himself. "I obviously neglected my education by not spending more time here. I probably ought to have delved into Chinese culture, too."

"Chinese?"

"Never mind," he said, his fingers tapping the keys. "Perhaps we might appeal to Krishna to lead us to Ashwatthama."

"Was Krishna prone to forgiveness?"

"Probably not." He sighed. Gods were notoriously fickle and tended to hold grudges. "Perhaps we ought to focus more on who *created* Asi than on who had it last."

Iselde nodded in approval. "Ah, when the sword was new and bright with promise."

"The literature here says Brahma, who created the uni verse, also created Asi." He did not quote the passage from the Mahabharata announcing the creation of the legendary sword which spoke of a dreadful, blue-skinned creature that Brahma transformed into a sword destined to destroy the enemies of the Indian gods and restore order to the world.

"Agni is its deity," Koriolis murmured. "Rohini is its gotra, and Rudra is its high preceptor."

"Perhaps its deity, Agni, is the one with whom we should speak," Iselde suggested. "Let's go to the nearest temple dedicated to Agni. We will speak with the priest there. Perhaps he will consent to help us."

Again his fingers danced upon the keyboard, then paused while Koriolis scanned the information displayed. "I can't find any significant temples dedicated to Agni." He searched further and paused on a web page. Pointing to a passage, he added, "This says Agni is worshiped in fire, not in a temple. Agni, it says, is a 'personality' of God, and the two primary avatars or personalities of God are Surya and Ganesha."

He sighed and rubbed his forehead. "This is so convoluted."

"History always is," Iselde agreed. "Should we look for a minor temple then, if there are no significant temples dedicated to Agni?"

"I don't think so. In my experience, deities prefer the grandiose."

Iselde shrugged. In her experience, First House fae and human royalty preferred the grandiose, but they were not deities however much they might have liked to pretend.

Koriolis continued, "All right, the four major temples to Surya are the Modhera Sun Temple in Gujarat, the Konark Sun Temple in Odisha, the Sun Temple in Martand, and the Dakshinaarka Temple in Bihar."

"Where is the closest temple to Surya?"

"The one in Uttarakhand."

Iselde snorted. "That's not one of the four options." She paused, thinking, then offered her insight, "In Fé-Ree, the holiest of shrines tend to be the oldest. Which of those four temples is the oldest? We'll go there first and speak to the god."

"The Sun Temple in Martand. It's in ruins, though. The most visited one is in Bihar."

"Ruins or not, it is likely to be the most favored of its deity. If Surya does not speak to us there, then we'll go to the one in Bihar. When age does not factor in a god's favor, then popularity will."

"And gods do enjoy their popularity," Koriolis agreed. He approved of her certainty that the Indian god would answer their summons and talk with them. "I doubt Surya will allow this sword to leave his people's realm."

Iselde raised an eyebrow. "Then we'll just have to convince him."

"How do you propose to do that?"

"I am the daughter of the oracle of Fé-Ree and powerful in my own right. You are Marog, the firstborn son of the Unseelie King and once the crown prince of the Unseelie Court."

"But I am no longer fae," he corrected.

"No, you are demon. Your power as demon complements mine as fae. Together we are stronger than any god of this iron-tainted realm." She tucked a lock of hair behind her ear. "Together we will convince him."

"Surely, it won't be that easy."

"Probably not," she agreed and flashed him a quick, predatory smile telling him without further explanation that she was accustomed to difficulty. A hardscrabble life of living in the northern wastes had forged her into a sharp blade, indestructible and true. "Nothing worth having ever is."

CHAPTER 15

"I COULD OPEN A PORTAL TO TAKE US TO KASHMIR," Iselde muttered. She picked up a slick brochure and examined its colorful pages before looking out the window to the tangle of vehicular and pedestrian traffic far below.

"I'd rather not apparate within a stone wall or, more likely, amid a crowd of people," Koriolis replied. "That way lies torches and pitchforks."

She gave him a confused look.

"People on Earth react poorly to what they do not understand. They seek to destroy it, not understand it."

"Perhaps they might merely assume we, too, are gods."

"I'd prefer not to chance it." He looked up at the brilliantly blue sky which shimmered in the sultry heat. "Whatever happens, know that I am grateful to walk in the sun again. Keeping 'vampire hours' gets dreary."

Iselde nodded. "In the northern wastes, we live in darkness during the depths of winter. The return of the sun is welcomed with song and festivities among my tribe." She pursed her lips, then exhaled a gusty breath through her nostrils. "Is all of this realm so hot and sweltering?"

Koriolis shook his head at her repeated dislike of heat and humidity and dug out a handkerchief from his pocket, an old fashioned affectation he considered practical enough not to relinquish in an era of disposable paper products. He handed her the square of linen which she used to pat against her skin to soak up the perspiration. "No, actually there are places on Earth which are eternally bound in ice."

"I miss my homeland," she admitted, her voice low and aching with loss. "I miss my people."

"The sooner we succeed, the sooner we will return to Fé-Ree."

She cast him a sour glance. "You do not fool me, Koriolis. The oracle has a purpose for Asi, and we are bound to that purpose. There will be no easy return home for either of us."

"At least you will not be exiled here as long as I have been," he shot back.

Iselde ducked her head in acknowledgement of the hit. "Aye. I expect the oracle does not wish me to follow your path."

Koriolis sent her a penetrating look. "If we do not succeed, you will. This world will poison you. It already affects you and blackens your magic and your soul."

She shook her head, refusing to accept a corrupt destiny for herself. "When I was a child, my mother called me Ljós."

"*Fos,*" he translated to Greek, then again in Latin, "*Lux.*" He wondered at the non sequitur and waited for her explanation.

She shrugged, remembering how her true uncle, the enigmatic Archivist, had once called her *Lumi*. "I paid little attention to that pet name then, until I realized she referred to a destiny. What she called me—light—did not arise from affection, but from a fate she'd chosen for me. If I am to be a light, then I shall not succumb—at least not entirely—to the taint of this afflicted realm."

Koriolis considered her words and what he knew of the oracle. "Does the oracle truly choose? Or does she merely see what will happen?"

Iselde scoffed. "For those whose fates she chooses to meddle with, she sees the infinite possibilities and eliminates those she does not want to happen. Sometimes her choice is a fate that benefits others; sometimes it's a fate that benefits the victim; sometimes she decides what benefits her."

It was Koriolis' turn to purse his lips in thought. After a moment, he commented, "Then it's good she does not see fit to meddle that often."

Iselde scoffed again. "Despite what she may choose, she cannot force someone to act as *she* wills. We at least retain freedom of will."

He nodded, not voicing his suspicion that the oracle understood an individual's nature well and seldom guessed wrongly, thereby deftly steering one's fate as she wished. *She will do the oracle's will to avoid being condemned by corruption and to return home.* Instead he returned to the subject of their quest: "I will book us transportation to the temple."

Iselde shrugged, not caring how they got there, since he had dismissed her offer to create a portal. She briefly wondered why he did not create his own portal, then wondered if he even knew how or if he had the ability. Perhaps his transformation to demon had cut him off from such fae abilities. She did not know and was not sufficiently curious to ask.

Momentarily distracted, she wondered at her lack of curiosity, at the coldness of her nature. She'd never been overly demonstrative, but the warmth with which she'd always regarded her tribe had faded into cool dispassion. Would it soon fade even further to mere disinterest? If so, this icing of her emotions ought to concern her. Perhaps the mate bond would serve as the barrier to such emotional degradation, the link preventing her from distancing herself utterly from the concerns of the living.

With wry detachment, she hoped so. She skimmed her fingertips over the glamoured jewels embedded in her skin. They felt cool to the touch, not warm from her body.

Well, Mother, you put my well-being in the hands of this demon. I hope you are satisfied.

Ah, Ljós, you will either be the light of Fé-Ree or its doom.

I never wanted this.

Some things are not for the wanting, daughter. You will either accept this destiny or condemn your world to darkness.

Iselde blinked. *You mean your machinations were not merely to see me mated?*

Do you think me so petty?

To Iselde's shame, yes, she had thought her mother so petty.

I seek the ultimate good of our world and many others. I am not so petty as you have long assumed, else I would have left you to your icy desert.

I did not ask for this.

No one ever does.

Iselde blinked again, the sensation of her mother's presence having vanished as abruptly as it manifested. Well, she thought, it appears as though the oracle's ambitions were grander than even the Ice Queen had considered.

Realizing she still held Koriolis' handkerchief in her hand, she wiped the cloth over her face and neck and handed it back to him with a murmured word of thanks. He brought the damp cloth to his nose and inhaled the scent of her sweat before crumpling it in his hand and shoving it deep into his pocket.

"Come," he said, grasping her hand, "let's eat."

She did not resist as he tugged her along. He drew her into a restaurant where spicy fragrances competed with the overwhelming humidity and heat. A smiling proprietor greeted them and ushered them to a table, promising all manner of culinary delights and the most perfect of service. He waved at an aproned waiter who smiled and nodded and offered to bring them lassi to refresh them.

As they ate, myriad flavors—cumin, coriander, turmeric, cardamom, mustard, clove, cilantro, ginger, and more—exploded on Iselde's tongue. Several of the dishes she tasted and rejected as too spicy for her palate, but she appreciated the plentiful servings of yogurt and sour cream to cool down the chemical heat.

"Is all food in the mortal world so … piquant?" she asked as she set down her fork. She'd liked the jambalaya and gumbo Zarafille had served: full of bold flavors but not so spicy as to burn her mouth.

Koriolis shook his head and took a drink of kefir. "It seems the hotter the country, the hotter its cuisine."

The corner of her mouth curling, she asked, "Where would you say has the blandest cuisine?"

To her surprise, Koriolis laughed.

"I don't understand."

He explained, "There's an old joke that England conquered the world for spices and used none of them."

She frowned.

"It's a global condemnation of their reputation for bland, tasteless food."

"Ah."

"You'd probably like it."

"I do not like food that burns my mouth."

"And you probably eat your meat raw."

She bared sharp teeth. "Not always."

Koriolis chuckled and rose to his feet. He extended his hand. Iselde took it and stood. He dropped money on the table and led her away from the restaurant. They wandered through an open market and ignored the vendors hawking their wares, hoping to snag some of the wealthy foreigners' currency.

"You'd look lovely in a sari," Koriolis murmured as a gaggle of women passed, the skirts of their saris swinging gracefully.

"No."

"Why not?"

Iselde shrugged and blurted, "It looks too complicated. I prefer my clothing simple."

"Ah."

"Why do you not dress as the men here?" she challenged. "It would become you."

"Do you think so?"

She nodded. "You know it would."

He grinned and said, "Then you ought to have seen me in a toga."

"What's a toga?"

Koriolis laughed. Spying a museum, he drew her into the building's cool environs. "Since we're here, we might as well explore the local history and culture."

Iselde breathed a sigh of relief as she looked around. She did not know how air conditioning worked, but she was grateful for it. "When do we go to Kashmir?"

"Tomorrow."

"You have made arrangements for our travel already then?"

Koriolis held up a cell phone, having already booked a flight to transport them to the Sheikh ul-Alam International Airport in Srinagar, the closest airport to the Markand Sun Temple. "Yes. This realm's technology is truly marvelous."

Iselde shrugged, not caring how the arrangements were made, only that they were. "And it requires none of your power?"

"This is a marvel of *science*; it's not magic. This realm has little faith in magic and much in science."

"I could have—"

"Yes, I know, and I already explained why it was not feasible."

She pursed her lips as he dropped the phone into a pocket.

"Beloved, trust me to lead you well in this realm. I have been here for a very long time."

With a sigh, she nodded. "I will trust you."

He took her hand and gave it a light squeeze. "You are my true mate. I will not fail you or us. We will find Asi and take it to Fé-Ree to fulfill whatever destiny the oracle has decided for us."

"Assuming we can wrest it from whatever god holds it."

He nodded. "Assuming that." He leaned down to press a kiss to her cheek. "Now let's explore what this museum has to offer."

CHAPTER 16

FAMILIARITY BRED CONTEMPT. BY THE TIME ISELDE and Koriolis disembarked the aircraft in Kashmir, she had lost all enchantment with air travel. She welcomed the subcontinent's summertime humidity and heat after the aircraft's dry, artificially cooled air and the airline's dry, tepid, tasteless snacks.

Iselde peered out the car's window at Kashmir's stunning vistas as the vehicle Koriolis rented rattled down country highways. The rickety automobile could not compare to the luxurious vehicles she'd ridden in thus far. She laughed at herself to think of how she'd already grown accustomed to such comfort and how quickly she missed it. A thought occurred to her and she voiced it: "You know where we're going."

The corner of his mouth lifted in a faint smirk. "I do."

"You've been here before."

"Yes."

"When? Why?"

One shoulder lifted in a shrug as he remembered marching along with red-coated English soldiers. Traveling with Great Britain's military had served as an innocuous way to tour the subcontinent, blending in as he had with the other soldiers who often went where European tourists never ventured. "It was a long time ago. It no longer matters."

"It does if you angered Surya."

He sighed. "I did not anger the sun god. I have never met him."

"You're sure?"

"I'm sure."

Iselde made an inarticulate noise in her throat that conveyed her doubt in his ability to traverse a country without annoying its people's deities. Koriolis glanced at her, but she had once again turned away from him and was staring at the countryside.

Not quite two hours passed before he pulled off the highway and parked the car. "We're here."

Iselde nodded, just a quick dip of her sharp chin, and got out of the car with lithe grace. The summer sunshine set her platinum hair ablaze and made her pale skin glitter as though burnished with diamond dust. Koriolis' breath caught in his throat. Like a goddess herself, Iselde passed through the thick brush serving as a barrier between the historical site and the highway. Following close behind her, Koriolis watched as branches and leaves parted to make way for her passage.

"You know there's a parking lot on the other side of the temple to accommodate tourists," he mentioned. "There's no need to clamber through the weeds."

She shrugged and continued walking.

"In ancient times," Koriolis said, when they climbed the outer perimeter of stone, "a colonnade surrounded the temple. Between the colonnade and the temple were pools of water. It was quite a serene and lovely place."

"Water surrounding a sun god's temple seems disingenuous or at least ironic," Iselde commented as she looked around the ruins.

They entered the ancient stone building. Sunlight penetrated the structure which had long since lost its roof. Tall stone walls cast deep shadows. Iselde paused and lifted her face to the sky. Closing her eyes, she took a deep breath and absorbed the ambiance empty of deities.

"He's not here," she said with utter certainty.

"Then we'll go to Dakshinaarka Temple in Bihar," Koriolis said as a tourist peered around a corner and stared at them. He reached into his pocket to retrieve his cell phone. "I'll book another flight."

Iselde locked gazes with the tourist and felt an unfamiliar hunger kindle. Holding still, she listened and heard the man's heartbeat and the surge of his blood. Her mouth watered. *This is odd.* Her eyes locked on to the man, and her body grew still in the way every elite predator did in preparation for the kill. The sudden desire to hunt the man, to see a human as prey, disturbed her.

Swallowing and forcing herself to look away from the human, she closed her eyes and said, "I'm not getting into one of those contraptions again."

"Unless you wish to spend several days on the road, we'll have to."

Iselde snorted and opened her eyes. "No. I will open a portal."

"Beloved, that's not wise."

Her upper lip lifted in a sneer. "This tainted world is killing me. I doubt I have 'several days' remaining before I, too, turn demon."

He gave her a long, intense stare then murmured, "Why do you say this?"

She averted her gaze for a moment to stare into the bright sky before lowering her eyes and meeting his gaze. She answered him baldly: "I'm beginning to crave blood."

Her admission gave Koriolis pause. "I assumed we had more time."

She shook her head and glared at the tourist who lingered nearby and watched them. The man's eyes widened, and he glared back at her.

"Begone," she hissed in her native tongue.

He shouted something at her in his own language. Koriolis stiffened and slowly turned toward the man. Speaking to him in rusty Hindi, he said, "Insult my wife again and I will kill you."

The man's eyes narrowed at the unexpected experience of hearing Hindi, however faltering, spew from the mouth of what appeared to be a pale-skinned European. "You do not belong here. Your presence desecrates Surya's temple."

"Surya's not here," Koriolis replied.

"And how would you know?" the man demanded.

"Indra told me," Koriolis lied.

A handsome, well-built man approached the tourist from behind and raised his eyebrows at Koriolis. His long black hair was pulled back in a low ponytail and the deep yellow tee shirt stretching across his muscular chest was emblazoned with the screen printed image of a white elephant with its trunk raised in a triumphant trumpet. The man's dark, fathomless eyes met Koriolis' and he said, "No, actually, I didn't. I told her."

Iselde concealed her surprise at the newcomer's sudden appearance and his lie—for he had not told her anything—and said nothing. Startled, the tourist squealed and swiveled to face the stranger. His eyes bugged. He trembled and began to gibber.

"Surya doesn't come here anymore," the stranger said.

Iselde slowly turned to face him and, senses open, recognized him as a god. Only a god would have that strong an energy signature. "You know why we're here."

"I do." Indra, once worshipped as the king of the Indian gods and long since downgraded to a mere god of rain, thunder, and lightning, nodded. "I may be a laughingstock among the ancients, but that doesn't mean I'm stupid."

"You're keeping tabs on them," Koriolis murmured, then glared at the tourist who continued to mutter incoherently under his breath as he stared at Indra.

Indra grinned, although the expression was anything but happy. The ancient god's bitterness and ferocity shined through what would normally have been a pleasant expression. "I don't like Surya."

"That doesn't mean you like us," Iselde remarked, assuming Indra had revealed himself to offer his assistance. She raised a hand and pointed at the spluttering tourist. "Please send him away."

Indra shrugged and fixed the man's gaze with his own. "Go home and never speak of this."

A squeak of terror spewed from the man's mouth, then he ran.

"You have my appreciation," Iselde said.

"But not your thanks?"

Her lips lifted in the glimmer of a smile. "I would not owe you my obligation."

Indra nodded. "So that old tale is true then."

She shrugged. "Where is Surya?"

Indra responded to her earlier comment: "No, my dislike of Surya doesn't mean I like you." He tilted his head to one side. "However, I'll admit that your Unseelie king isn't all that bad." He grinned, that time an expression of malicious amusement. "He unnerves Vishnu, which amuses me."

"Uberon has that effect on most," Iselde agreed, her tone bland.

"Will you help us?" Koriolis inquired.

"What do you offer in exchange?" Indra asked. "The fae give nothing away, so why should I assist you without compensation?"

"What do you want?" Koriolis asked.

"I want the respect due to me!"

"I cannot displace Vishnu," Koriolis replied.

Indra's expression turned speculative as he continued to look at the platinum-haired fae. He inhaled, nostrils flaring at the tingle of her power. "I want a son, a *powerful* son."

Koriolis held himself still as cold fury whipped through him. "No. You'll not touch my mate."

The god's expression again changed, this time to disgust. "My people have lost their power. I would have a son and him be a king! *That* is my price."

"There are a paucity of princesses in this world, and none of their husbands will become a king," Koriolis pointed out.

Indra ground his molars in exasperation.

Koriolis continued, "You'd do better to wed the daughter of a billionaire and get a son upon her. He would be more powerful than any royal figurehead."

"Then find me the eligible daughters of the world's richest men that I might choose the most worthy among them."

"Done," Koriolis replied. "But whichever woman you choose will retain the right of refusal."

Indra waved his hand. "Whatever."

"I will have your oath."

"And I'll have yours, demon."

Indra produced a knife. The blade flashed, catching a sliver of sunlight. The god drew the sharp edge across his palm. Blood welled from the thin slice. He held out the knife to Koriolis who took it and deftly sliced his own palm. The two males clasped hands, pressing their bleeding palms together. The temple began to tremble, the grinding of stone producing a thick, choking dust. With a wave of her hand, Iselde summoned a breeze to blow the dust away.

"Take us to Asi," she said.

"Better yet," Indra replied, his expression turning crafty, "I'll bring it to you. Wait here."

He vanished, and Iselde turned to her mate. "That was stupid."

CHAPTER 17

"IT WILL BE FASTER FOR INDRA TO BRING ASI TO US than for us to track it down," Koriolis replied, imperturbed by her insult. "You do not have time."

Her eyes narrowed in suspicion.

"You forget, beloved, that we are *mated*. I am in your mind even as you are in mine. I know your worries."

She affected a cool tone, "I am not worried."

"No, your severance is nearly complete. You do not have the rage and bitterness I did to hold you to your true nature; therefore, it is easier for the taint of this world to consume you. I will not tolerate your degradation."

"What? To become like you?"

"Yes, to become like me, a demon." Koriolis shook his head. "Aye, you are powerful, more powerful than I among fae, but I have long since relinquished my fae nature. I am *demon*, and that gives me power beyond your ken."

She snorted. "And what makes you think I, among the most powerful of fae, will not also be among the most powerful of demonkind?"

"The transformation does not work quite like that," he said. "It is your connection to this world's iron-tainted ley lines that maintains your power even as it corrodes your nature. Do you not find yourself expending greater energy to maintain that connection?"

Iselde blinked in surprise. She took a moment to look inward at her connection to the lines of power crisscrossing beneath the earth's surface and the effort required to maintain that connection. She was astonished to realize that the constant draw over the past several days had grown stronger, becoming a steadily and consistently more concerted effort that she had not noticed. The realization perturbed her.

"It is like an addiction," Koriolis explained, his voice soft with sympathy. "I had no one to help me navigate the process, no one to tell me that when the conversion was complete I would have to learn to endure—even enjoy—the bitter sting of iron and rebuild my ability to see, touch, and use the power of the ley lines." He took a breath. "It was a humbling experience."

She gaped. "You mean to say …"

"You will lose your strength." He shook his head. "I cannot permit that."

"Cannot permit what?" Indra inquired as he materialized beside them.

"That was quick," Koriolis commented.

A small, sly smile stretched Indra's mouth as he held the double-edged sword aloft. "Take it and find me my bride."

Koriolis accepted the khanda, noting its poor condition. "It needs a good polishing and sharpening."

"Ashwatthama must have gotten complacent," Iselde commented in mild disapproval.

Indra pursed his lips and shrugged. "I did not kill him. One cannot kill what is already dead."

"He's undead then?" Koriolis mused.

"Not one of your European vampires, if that's what you're thinking of," Indra sneered. "Now fulfill your promise."

Koriolis looked at the ancient Indian god once revered for making and unmaking the world and in the current yuga relegated to being a mere god of rain and thunder. *A laughing-*

stock indeed to have come down so far. Koriolis concentrated and exerted his will, drawing heavily upon the power blazing beneath the earth's surface to manifest his command. He held the power, felt its pulse in the depths of his being, and slowly released it to avoid a catastrophic recoil.

"It is done."

"What is done?" Indra demanded.

Koriolis let his gaze rove over the god who materialized as a handsome specimen of ideal Indian masculinity and nodded in approval. "You'll want to wear a tuxedo."

Indra raised an eyebrow and waited.

"And put on a few inches."

Indra raised the other eyebrow.

"You're on the short side, Indra. The ladies prefer tall men." Koriolis grinned as Indra absorbed the words and grew until he was a smidgen taller than the demon. His clothing magically expanded to accommodate his new height and breadth. The god's new size did not intimidate him one bit. Koriolis continued, "The world's most eligible women will be at the Grand Ball of Monaco. The Prince of Monaco has invited the unwed men and women of the world's elite to this ball for a true Cinderella experience. You'll have your pick of lovely, wealthy women there, some powerful in their own right."

"A ball?"

"Not just *a ball*, but the Grand Ball. No other country on the planet has such a gathering anymore of hereditary royalty, political power, and global wealth. The only thing that comes close is the Monaco Yacht Show, but that would have you searching multiple sites rather than collecting candidates for your hand in one place."

"A ball?" Indra repeated incredulously.

"I suggest you learn to dance."

"You agreed to find me a bride."

"And I have. Those women who meet your criteria will be at the ball. They cannot do otherwise. You pick the one whom you like best and she'll fall into your hands like a ripe plum."

"I do not like this manipulation," Iselde murmured.

"Oh, Indra will treat his bride well," Koriolis said in an arch tone, "will he not?"

Indra bowed, gesturing with a flourish. When he straightened, he said, "My bride will lack for nothing."

Koriolis raised his eyebrows, shrugged, and said, "See, she'll be well taken care of."

Iselde glared at both males. "Hurt the woman, and I'll return to this cursed realm to annihilate you myself. She is an innocent."

"Don't you trust me?" Indra asked, affronted. He drew himself to his full height which was equal to hers.

"Gods are not to be trusted," she answered flatly.

"And what makes you say that?"

"Yes, beloved, why do you doubt him?" Koriolis asked, his tone conveying nothing more than mild curiosity.

"I've met more than one god in my time," she said. "I wasn't impressed."

"And who did impress you?" Koriolis asked.

"Enders."

"The Archivist?"

"Uncle Gus, too."

"Ah, good old Uncle Gus." Koriolis nodded. "I suppose I was lucky he wasn't summoned to serve me justice."

Iselde's upper lip lifted in a silent sneer. If all of the fae realm had not believed him dead, crushed by his father's castle, then Thelan likely would have called upon the Erlking to exact justice. "I've always liked Uberon, too."

"No 'uncle?'"

Deadpan, she replied, "I suppose I may call him 'Papa' now."

Laughter burst from Koriolis' mouth in a loud bark. "Oh, I bet he'll just *love* that."

"I do not know these gods of whom you speak," Indra complained.

"They are not gods," Iselde explained, turning her flinty gaze to him. "They are *fae*, the most powerful fae all the worlds have ever seen, the Archivist, the Unseelie King, and the Erlking."

"Ah." Indra turned a speculative gaze upon Koriolis. "And you are the Unseelie King's son, are you not?"

"Figured that out, have you?"

"I've been around for longer than one yuga, demon-fae."

Iselde shook her head. "He is no longer fae."

Indra lay a finger alongside his nose. "Yes, he is a demon, but he never quite lost his fae nature. Even now, his bond to you strengthens what remains of his original nature." He redirected his attention to Koriolis. "When is this ball?"

"April," Koriolis replied. "You've got two weeks to get ready."

Iselde blinked. "It is not summer?"

Koriolis laughed. "Oh, beloved, New Orleans in late March is balmy compared to summer."

She lifted her face toward the sky. "This place is hot, too."

"Well, most of the subcontinent is tropical," he explained, hefting the ancient sword. "Indra, do you have the scabbard for this thing?"

"Speak of Asi with respect, demon-fae," the ancient god warned. "It is sentient."

"Of course, my mistake," Koriolis replied with smooth courtesy. "Do you have its scabbard?"

"I do not. I suspect that has long since disintegrated."

Koriolis shrugged. Lifting the sword, he ran the fingers and thumb of his hand down both sides of the long blade. In the wake of his touch spread dense black, shiny like lacquer, until it encased the entire blade.

"Nicely done," Indra praised. With a grin and a snap of his fingers, the hard shell cracked, and the cracks filled with gold and colored enamel to create swirling patterns like peacock feathers. Near the hilt bloomed a white elephant with its trunk raised. Glittering rubies clustered to form a red juhl over the elephant's back. "That's more like it."

"Thank you. This is indeed a scabbard worthy of Asi."

"We must be going," Iselde said.

"Of course, beloved." Koriolis nodded to Indra in a rare gesture of mutual respect. "Enjoy the ball, Prince Charming."

Indra tossed his head backward and laughed. Somewhere in the distance, thunder rumbled.

Iselde took her mate's free hand and led him beyond the temple walls into the glare of full sun. She looked around, but the site appeared deserted except for the three of them—and she wasn't so sure Indra had lingered. She reasoned the tourist from earlier had departed along with any other visitors to the site.

She raised her free hand above her head and flicked her fingers in a summoning gesture. "Mother!" Her voice rang across the valley. "We have Asi."

The fabric of reality ripped with an unearthly shriek. Silver light sparked along the ragged edges of the rip in the fabric of time and space.

"Come," Iselde urged.

Koriolis stared into it but did not move.

"Come! She will not hold it open indefinitely," Iselde urged, giving his hand a sharp yank.

He blinked, the keen edge of her tone and the hard jerk on his arm recalling him to himself. He followed her through the portal and would have rather died by torture than admit his knees trembled with fear upon his return to Fé-Ree.

He did not look forward to his reunion with his father, the fearsome and mighty Unseelie King.

CHAPTER 18

THE VEIL BETWEEN THE FAE REALM AND TWENTY-first century Earth sizzled as Koriolis and Iselde passed through its torn fabric. With a steamy hiss redolent of cauterization, the tear's ragged edges came together, re-merged again into an interrupted whole, and severed Iselde's connection with the ley lines of Earth. Iselde gasped and her eyes rolled back as sudden pain arced like lightning through her body. Koriolis dropped the sword of Rudra as he lunged to catch his mate when she stumbled. Her body arched and her hands spasmed. He ignored the clang as the sword hit flagstone.

"It is good to see where your loyalty lies," a thin feminine voice remarked as he grappled with the convulsing female in his grasp. "Lay her here, boy."

A shrill keening sound escaped Iselde's lips as he turned toward whoever spoke to him. An ancient female with opalescent eyes and hands like claws gestured toward a cot draped in woolen blankets. She raised her eyebrows, a small gesture of impatience. Iselde wailed again as she thrashed.

"She is your daughter. Help her," he demanded as he took the few steps necessary to cross the small space and set her down on the cot.

A fire burned low on the hearth beside the cot. The entirety of the space reminded him of a medieval artisan's home, a single room occupied by a work table that also served as a dining table, a hearth for cooking and heat, a couple of wooden chairs, and three trunks which undoubtedly held what few treasures and luxuries the oracle had decided to keep. It certainly bore no resemblance to the vast spaces and many luxuries of the castle where he'd spent millennia as the crown prince of the Unseelie Court.

"Ah, Marog, you are returned here on my sufferance. You will make no demands of *me*."

Kneeling beside the cot, he lifted his upper lip in a vicious snarl. "Do you bring her back just for her to die?"

"Of course not, stupid boy. She stayed too long away and must be purified of her sin."

"Sin?" he echoed in confusion as his own body began tingling from the separation from the mortal realm. "What sin?"

"Another day, perhaps two, in the mortal realm, and my daughter's degradation would have been complete."

"And that justifies your letting her suffer now?" he sneered. "No wonder she resents you." He spared a hard glance at the sword on the floor as he gathered his trembling mate into his arms. Rising smoothly despite the uncomfortable twinges reverberating through his body, he snapped, "We have no need of your interference, oracle."

"If you leave now, you will not again pass through my door," the oracle warned.

"So be it. We are well rid of you," he snapped with all the aristocratic arrogance of the prince he used to be. Cradling his mate against his chest, he lurched toward the door. "I'll find someone who *will* help her."

The oracle's opalescent eyes narrowed to an angry squint as the door to her small cabin flew open. With one hand, she clutched the white crystal dangling from a leather cord around her neck and whispered, "Your obligation to me is due *now*."

"Keep the damned sword," he snarled and stepped through the doorway.

The door slammed shut behind him. Koriolis blinked, having expected to be thrust back into the iron-tainted world he'd just left. But this cool, verdant forest smelling of moist loam and conifers bore little resemblance to the lush forests of Kashmir. He looked around but did not spy a path. Murmuring a soft reassurance to the female in his arms, he strode forward and ignored the tingling in his own blood.

He walked a winding path between towering trees, avoiding places where the underbrush grew too thick to allow easy passage. He walked and walked and walked. When he came upon a shallow stream, he carefully lay his mate on the ground long enough to drink from its cold, sweet water and tear a strip of cloth from his shirt, which he dunked in the water and wrung out. First he wiped the cool, wet rag over his mate's face then rinsed it, wrung it out, and wiped his own sweaty face and neck. He cupped water in his hands and dribbled it into Iselde's mouth. She swallowed reflexively and cried out as her flesh absorbed the pure liquid.

Iselde coughed and convulsed as she gagged. Koriolis rolled her over so she would not choke on the foul black substance she spewed. When she again breathed without gagging, he carefully poured more of the clean water down her gullet. Again she coughed and retched a thick, sticky ooze that reeked of corruption. Though he was loath to cause his mate additional discomfort, he realized the water from the stream was helping her body purge itself of the taint of the mortal realm.

Hours passed beside that cold stream. Six times he moved her so she would not lie in the foulness of the putrid infection spewed from her body. Finally, as the two moons rose, their bloated forms emanating silver light, Iselde managed to swallow water from the stream without vomiting. Instead she shivered, not the violent tremors of earlier, but a bone-chattering indication of cold.

Koriolis gathered his bride in his arms and hugged her close, though he desperately wished to succumb to the fire burning through his veins. Clasping his bride to his chest, he bowed his head over hers and sang a plaintive tune that had been all the rage in early Renaissance Austria.

"You forgot something," a deep voice, rich as velvet and clear as a church bell, intoned from across the shallow, gravel-bottomed stream.

Startled, Koriolis lifted his head and stared at the fabled unicorn. A low thud behind him had him swiveling to see who else had managed to creep so close without him noticing. Darkness congealed into the shape of the midnight swift, gleaming spiral horn held all too close to him for comfort.

"Your sword," the black unicorn said, the lethal tip of that horn dipping to point at the fabled weapon on the ground.

"It's not mine," Koriolis said.

"Well, it's certainly not mine," the swift retorted. The large beast minced backward a few steps and tossed his chiseled head. "Pick it up and follow me."

"I cannot carry my mate and the sword," Koriolis said, tightening his arms around Iselde.

"And I suppose you think *I'm* going to carry that iron abomination?"

"You brought it here," he pointed out. "You can carry it wherever else it's supposed to be."

"It is *your* sword, Dra'Acul. *You* brought it to this realm."

"As the oracle ordered," he said, each word bitten off. "Give it back to her."

The stamp of a cloven hoof caught his attention. He looked around to see the dawn swift had crossed the stream, although he'd not heard the telltale splash of water.

"Place Iselde on my back," the dawn swift said. "I will carry her, and you will carry Asi."

"You know this sword?"

The white unicorn snorted. "Are you really surprised at that?"

The back of Koriolis' neck burned. No, he wasn't really surprised. The highest, most powerful beings in all the fae realm were mysterious. Even the ancients walked and spoke carefully around them—something his powerful, ruthless father was unlikely to do around anyone. He looked at the unconscious, shivering female in his arms and said, "She cannot ride on her own."

The unicorn sighed and repeated, "Place her on my back."

The light poke of a sharp point emphasized the prudence of obedience.

Koriolis leaned away from the midnight swift's deadly horn and said, "All right."

He rose with lithe strength that gave no hint of the pain sweeping through his body. He lifted his mate and settled her on the white unicorn's broad back.

"Press her hands to my mane."

He did as the mystical beast bade him and watched in interest as the long white locks of the unicorn's mane wrapped around Iselde's hands and tightened around her wrists.

"Pick up Asi and follow, foolish boy," the midnight swift commanded.

Pressing his lips together to prevent a foolhardy retort from escaping, Koriolis obeyed again. The white unicorn took the lead, its swift walk gliding smoothly across the stream and through the forest. Koriolis followed, fighting the agony that burned in every cell and exploded in every joint with every movement.

Again, he walked and walked and walked. Slowing down resulted in a sharp poke from the black unicorn ensuring he did not fall too far behind or stumble too far from the invisible path. However, his pace did slow as weariness and pain coalesced into a dizzying weakness that finally pulled him to his knees. With a gasp, he toppled forward.

"Get up, boy," the black unicorn snapped.

Koriolis struggled to rise, but his knees and ankles buckled. Spitting out a mouthful of forest debris, he rasped, "I cannot."

"Puny weakling," the black unicorn berated him.

Koriolis managed a shrug. "Do as you will with me, but spare my mate."

"Almost I think better of you," the unicorn muttered.

"Will he go no further?" the clarion voice of the white unicorn called from ahead.

"No."

"We're too far from the Deepwood."

"He won't get there tonight under his own power."

"So—"

"No!" the black unicorn snarled. "I will *not* bear him on *my* back."

"Will you bear the female then?"

The black unicorn pondered the offer then sidled next to the dawn swift. Panting heavily, his head too heavy to lift, Koriolis did not witness Iselde's transfer from the white unicorn's back to the black unicorn's. He gasped with sudden agony as an obsidian horn speared him through the gut and lifted him off the ground. With a gruesome sucking sound, the horn withdrew from his flesh as he slid off it onto the white unicorn's back. Venom from the horn filled the fresh cavity, and Koriolis shuddered with excruciating pain and cold where once pain and heat ravaged his body. He collapsed forward and clutched at the long white mane. The silvery locks entwined around his hands and wrists and locked him into place.

"The sun will rise soon," the midnight swift commented, its tone dispassionate as though Koriolis' survival meant nothing. "He won't survive it."

"Make haste," the dawn swift said. The large, finely chiseled head dipped to pick up the sword in its mouth, then the mythical beast leaped forward.

Burdened with an unconscious rider, the midnight swift followed suit, its steps silky smooth so as not to jar the passenger. Soon both beasts disappeared into the innermost depths of the Great Forest, the seat of their power, the Deepwood.

CHAPTER 19

THE LOCKS OF SILVERY WHITE MANE UNWOUND from Koriolis' hands and wrists, allowing him to topple from the unicorn's back. He landed with a thud and a low grunt of pain on thick, cool grass. Through slitted, bleary eyes, he watched as the dawn swift dropped the sword and took a mouthful of Iselde's clothing to pull her off the midnight swift's back and lower her to the earth in a gentler, more controlled dismount. Koriolis opened his mouth to speak, but a full body shudder locked his voice within his throat. Gasping, he watched helplessly as the dawn swift rolled Iselde over to her back then plunged the razor tip of its horn into the soft flesh below her collar bone.

"Spare her," he finally managed, the two words uttered in a guttural croak.

The midnight swift nudged him with a front hoof with enough force to make Koriolis grunt again. "Silence, Dra'Acul."

He closed his eyes against the dark spots that clouded his vision and repeated in a nearly soundless exhale, "Spare her."

The dawn swift extracted the tip of his spiral horn from Iselde's flesh and shook it free of the drops of blood clinging to it. With a final swish of his mighty head, the unicorn sprayed a gust of venom over her. Iselde's eyes flew open. Her body arched and her mouth gaped open in a soundless scream.

"Rest, daughter," the unicorn ordered.

Compelled by the beast's command, she relaxed. Her eyes closed once again, and she slept in the soft warmth of dappled sunshine.

The white unicorn minced across the glade to stand over Koriolis. "I supposed I'll have to heal him."

"Or not," the midnight swift said, his dispassionate tone grating against Koriolis' survival instincts.

"The oracle will be displeased if we allow him to die."

"The oracle does not command *us*." The black unicorn stomped a hoof in emphasis.

"The oracle is not to be trifled with," the dawn swift rebutted. The silver horn dipped to point at Koriolis. "He is the only one who can wield Asi in this realm."

"He is tainted."

"Indeed, but that taint is what allows him to wield the sword."

"He is *demon*."

"He is not *fully* demon, but I will ensure he does not lapse entirely into the dark," the white unicorn said. It glanced back toward Iselde. "And, tainted as she now is, she is no longer completely fae."

The white unicorn lowered its silver spiral horn to the bloody wound in Koriolis' gut and dipped the tip into his body. The beast closed its large eyes and exhaled. The horn pulsed with light, and Koriolis screamed as he had never screamed before. Scalding light beamed from his open eyes and gaping mouth.

"Well that'll do it," the black unicorn commented. It nudged Koriolis with a front hoof, but the male had slumped into unconsciousness.

The white unicorn pulled its horn free of Koriolis' belly, leaving behind a silver scar permanently embedded within his pale flesh. With a shake of its head and neck tossing the heavy mane, it said, "The soul of the oracle's daughter shines brightly.

It needs a touch of your darkness. True mates must complement each other."

The midnight swift bared its teeth which were, unlike any equine's, pointed. It walked with delicate, mincing steps around Koriolis and across the glade, stopping beside Iselde's sleeping form. The finely chiseled head lowered and positioned the pointed tip of the ebony horn over her mouth. A viscous drop of venom gathered at the point and fell onto her lips. Instinct had Iselde's tongue gathering the venom and swallowing it.

Her eyes flashed open and she gasped as the black unicorn's venom hit her bloodstream. Before she was fully conscious, she'd roused into a defensive crouch, teeth bared, hissing, claws extended.

"Peace, daughter," the white unicorn said, raising its head. A pearly beam of sunlight refracted off its silvery spiral horn.

Iselde's gaze darted between the two mythical beings. She licked her lips again then asked, "What have you done to me?"

The black unicorn snorted. "We saved you, girl."

"Why?" she asked, knowing there would be a price to pay. "What do you need from me?"

"He" —the white unicorn answered with a toss of its head toward Koriolis who yet remained prone and unconscious on the ground— "must be the one to wield Asi. *You* are required to control him."

She scoffed, a harsh sound spurting from her throat. "I cannot *control* him."

"Without your gentle restraint and guidance, he will wreak havoc on this world," the black unicorn explained. "You are the only one who can control him."

She raised an eyebrow in silent expression of cynical disbelief.

"He will restrain himself for you, but for no one else," the white unicorn said.

Iselde narrowed her eyes. "So, that's why I was practically compelled to mate with him—to serve as an ameliorating force."

"You are the light to his darkness," the white unicorn said.

Iselde looked at the sword which lay on the ground next to the dawn swift's cloven hooves and winced. She could feel its corrosive iron taint from where she yet crouched and cringed. "I cannot wield it."

"No, you cannot, but *he* can and will. You must direct him, lead him to war, and inspire him to victory."

"Against what?" she spat, annoyed by the high-handed arrangement of her life yet again.

"Demons, of course," the midnight swift replied. "It takes one to kill one."

"Fé-Ree does not have demons."

"Fé-Ree *does*, and their spawn corrupt this realm," the dawn swift corrected.

"Let me rephrase that. Fé-Ree did not have demons when my mother sent me to the mortal realm," Iselde said.

"Ah, yes, well the balance must be maintained."

"And what does that mean?" she demanded as she rose to her feet. Standing proudly, she would have died before admitting her knees and ankles felt rubbery.

The dawn swift ignored her question. "Collect yourself and release your glamour."

Iselde blinked, surprised to realize that the glamour she'd affected in the mortal realm yet held. With a sigh, she let it go and gasped at the tingle of power that swept over her skin. It felt clean and natural, unlike the cold, iron-tainted power from the ley lines in the mortal realm. She took a deep breath and ran her fingertips over the silver filigree and the jewels embedded in her skin.

The midnight swift noticed her reaction. "The glamour does more than conceal your true form from others, it also muffles your magic."

Iselde loosed a long, low breath. She'd known that. Of course, she'd known that. But having never needed or wanted to affect a glamour until this last … *excursion* … to the mortal realm, she'd not remembered how it felt to truly release it. She fisted her tingling hands then unclenched them.

Koriolis groaned. His leg twitched. Eyes widening, Iselde hastened to his side and kneeled on the cool grass beside him. "Koriolis?"

"Call him by his true name, daughter," the white unicorn ordered.

She frowned. "Marog?"

Impatient, the black unicorn corrected her, "Dra'Acul."

"That is not a fae name," she said.

"No, it is a demon name."

Koriolis' eyes opened. Iselde clenched her jaw and said nothing in response to seeing the shining pools of blackness where once he'd sported silvered eyes like his father.

"Demon indeed," she murmured as his hand reached for hers and clasped it.

With a grunt, he shifted to his feet, allowing Iselde to lend him her strength. His knees wobbled then locked into place to bear his weight. His skin prickled with a fresh, clean power he had not felt in far too long. Old habits long forgotten surged to the forefront, and he reached out to gather it to himself, but the power of Fé-Ree slipped through his grasp as though he were attempting to hook his claws into quicksilver.

He glared at the unicorns. "What have you done to me?"

The white unicorn replied, "You must wield Asi; Iselde cannot."

Koriolis bared his teeth. "Why?"

The black unicorn snorted. "Surely you do not think we permit you to break Uberon's banishment without purpose?"

"No, everything fae has a price," he replied, upper lip curling in a sneer.

"No, everything fae demands *balance*," the black unicorn corrected him. "To use the dark power of the mortal realm to fulfill your destiny here, you must relinquish the fae power you once commanded."

"I have no destiny in Fé-Ree," he protested.

"Oh, but you do, Dra'Acul."

"Do not call me that." He stiffened his spine and squared his broad shoulders, the very image of regal threat. "I am Koriolis Valchik syn Acul or Marog, son of Uberon, prince of the Unseelie Court."

"Not anymore. Not here," came the dawn swift's dry response. The magical beast shook its head and heavy mane. "If you wish to remain in Fé-Ree, then you must redeem yourself." The beast stamped a silver hoof. "Your transgressions against *our* moon-born are not easily forgiven."

Koriolis' nostrils flared. "She's not been yours for some time, has she? She was mated to Thelan, captain of the Seelie Court's palace guard. She belongs to him. Remember? I certainly do."

"The boy always was stubborn," the black unicorn muttered.

Iselde extended her hand and touched his shoulder. His head whipped around to face her.

"Koriolis, do you wish to remain in Fé-Ree?" she asked, her voice soft. "That is what matters. That is what we must focus on."

The proud male's fierce expression softened. He held out a trembling hand and she clasped it, twining her fingers through his. With a sigh, he bowed his head to think. Looking up again, his expression determined, he said softly, "You cannot survive uncorrupted in the mortal realm, and I would see you remain unharmed."

She gave him a small smile conveying both approval … and, perhaps, affection.

Koriolis returned his gaze to the unicorns. "What would you have me do?"

The dawn swift explained, "The humans transported into this realm brought with them their native beliefs. The ambient power of Fé-Ree has manifested many of those beliefs. Some are benign, others malicious. Most are short-lived and pose no real danger to the balance here."

"Humans brought the demons," Koriolis said, making the connection.

"Humans *manifested* the demons," the black unicorn corrected. "That evil born of native power had the strength to endure and propagate."

"The Quol?" Iselde queried. "Chastian almost single-handedly depopulated the Quol."

"No, the Quol is indigenous to this realm," the midnight swift answered. "The Quoli, although you may describe them as demonic, are not truly demons. They belong here. Demons do not."

Iselde tilted her head and wondered what served as a counterbalance to the human incursion, even as she realized the truth of the ravenous jungle's existence. "It is the balance of the courts."

"Aye, partially," the dawn swift replied. "The Quol balances the Seelie and Unseelie Courts, the canidae and felidae, and others."

"Then what about Fyrgia, Djaria, and the other non-fae nations in Fé-Ree?" she asked, silently wondering how the Erlking's demesne factored into that balance.

"The demons manifested in balance to them," the midnight swift answered, "but the nature of humans, djinns, goblins, and such aligns too readily with those demons. The balance tips too far toward darkness."

"So, you want me to go to Djaria, Fyrgia, and other places and slaughter the populaces there?" Koriolis asked. He shook his head. "I've never been particularly compassionate, but not even I condone the wholesale slaughter of entire populations."

"Almost I think better of you," the midnight swift murmured.

Koriolis sneered at the black beast.

"You would have us root out the demons in these places where the fae are unwelcome and slaughter them?" Iselde asked.

"Aye," the white unicorn said.

"Then why Asi?"

"Asi was created to kill demons," came the answer.

Iselde took a breath, then asked with a wistfulness that surprised her mate, "Will I be able to return home to my tribe?"

"No, daughter."

She frowned. "They are my kin, blood of my blood. I will not spend my life chasing and killing demons for you."

"Your children are long grown. They have learned to thrive without you. They no longer need you."

"Your *children*?" Koriolis whispered in surprise as the white unicorn answered her.

She looked at him. "I did not come to your bed an unsullied virgin. You know I was previously mated." She sighed and paused, then decided to come clean. "I have had more than one mate—though none of them true mates. I once took a human male to mate and bore him three children. Some of those in my tribe are descended from that union."

He blinked in astonishment and not a small amount of distaste. "You took a *human* to mate?"

"It was *not* a soul bond, *not* a true mate bond." *Besides, he died long, long ago.*

Jealous fury swept through Koriolis. His hand tightened around hers. His voice low and fierce, he growled, "Henceforth, you shall have no male but me."

Knowing he'd not remained chaste during his millennia of existence—either before or after his exile from Fé-Ree—Iselde met his gaze without flinching and ran the fingertips of her free hand over the silver and jewels embossed into her skin. In a dispassionate, even tone, she stated, "We are bonded, soul to soul, Koriolis. As you have my devotion and fidelity, so I have yours."

He exhaled, nodded, and looked away in an effort to master his irrational rage, the possessive wrath of a mated fae male. After another long breath, he said, "I would be happy to visit your people with you, to make their acquaintance, and to know their fae ancestress more deeply."

Iselde guessed what that offer cost him, a most possessive and protective mate, and gave him a gentle smile of approval and gratitude. "And I would be happy to introduce you to them."

The dull thud of a stamped hoof recalled their attention to the unicorns.

"Pick up the sword, Dra'Acul," the dawn swift ordered.

Rolling his eyes, Koriolis did as the unicorn bade him.

Using its spiral horn like a pointer, the midnight swift directed its focus. "Head south for two days, then east. You will come upon the burning sands of Djaria. You will find demons there. Kill them."

"Why can't you kill them?" Koriolis asked.

"We cannot step foot in territory ruled by demons," the unicorn admitted.

"You left it too late," Iselde whispered, realizing that either the unicorns had failed to act in time to maintain the balance themselves or they and the oracle had delayed too long in sending her to the mortal realm.

The black unicorn sighed. "We did."

The white unicorn snorted. "The oracle could have—should have—informed us of such a future."

"Perhaps the oracle did not wish us to know," the midnight swift mused.

Iselde's lips twisted in a bitter smile. "No, because if she had, I would not have mated Koriolis—and *that* is what she wished."

I wonder why?

CHAPTER 20

"WE ARE DRESSED INAPPROPRIATELY FOR A TREK through the Great Forest," Koriolis griped as he stepped over a fallen sapling.

Iselde nodded and pushed a grapevine out of her way. "Have you any coin?"

"Coin? I always keep cash in my pockets." He doubted American currency, even the debased coinage, would be accepted by the merchants of the fae realm. "The bills and credit cards in my wallet are worthless here."

"We shall purchase more suitable clothing at the first village we find. I'll force the earth to bring up gold or silver with which to trade if I must."

"Do you think we'll find civilization yet this day?" he mused, his tone conveying doubt.

"I hope so. I need boots."

Koriolis silently admitted that she was worse off than he. Although the smooth leather soles of his handmade Italian shoes were entirely unsuited for a forest hike, he doubted Iselde had traipsed about the northern wastes barefoot. The pretty shoes coordinating with the once-elegant couture she wore had long since been abandoned, leaving the delicate skin and tender soles of her bare feet to bear the brunt of the debris-covered forest floor. Even with accelerated healing, her feet had to hurt.

"I'm hungry, too," he added with an odd sense of wonder. It was not a craving for blood that cramped his belly, but an honest hunger.

"For food or blood?"

"Food," he replied. "How unusual."

"I'd consider it a good sign," Iselde remarked as she ducked under a low-hanging branch. "You'd think they could set us on an actual path." A huff of discontent puffed her cheeks before exiting her lips. "Will you still need blood, do you think?"

"I don't know," he admitted. "Perhaps." He willed his fangs to drop, and the sharp cuspids descended in readiness to bite. "Regardless, I still have my fangs."

She made a noncommittal sound in her throat and continued to prowl ahead of him. She ducked aside to avoid a spider's web. He used the sheathed sword to break through it.

"There is too much about this that I do not know," he muttered.

Iselde snorted and continued walking.

They trekked through the Great Forest for what felt like days, though they never witnessed the sun set or rise. The light within the forest remained dim, constantly dim. Iselde's feet felt both abraded and bruised, though any small cuts and punctures from forest debris quickly healed. Grasping branches, vines that rasped against their clothing, and other myriad annoyances of a wilderness hike quickly reduced their clothing to dirty rags. Reluctant to abandon his impractical shoes, even though his thin dress socks soon wore through so that his feet rubbed against the ill-treated leather, Koriolis ignored the blisters which quickly erupted and healed as they hiked.

"I begin to empathize with Chastian," she muttered under her breath, remembering his years spent roaming the Quol and hunting its denizens. He'd been little more than a savage beast when she first encountered him. More loudly, she said, "Let's rest a moment."

"I could use a break, too," Koriolis admitted. They squatted next to each other, Iselde leaning against the rough bark of a tree trunk. In the silence of their pause, Koriolis listened. A moment later, he whispered, "Water."

Iselde raised her eyebrows and focused, listening. Her cobalt eyes gleamed. "You're right."

"Where water runs we'll find civilization," Koriolis said.

"Besides, I'm thirsty."

Koriolis grinned at her and stood. He extended his hand to her which she clasped, although she did not need his assistance to rise. Side by side, they raced toward the sound of water to find a small stream winding a shallow path through the Great Forest. Iselde squatted and dipped a hand into the cold stream. Cupping her palm, she brought the water to her mouth and tasted it. She smiled. "It is clean."

Koriolis dropped to his knees and, scooping water into his cupped hands, drank. Iselde did the same. After quenching their thirst, they splashed themselves, rinsing their sweaty, filthy skin.

By unspoken agreement after the rudimentary cleaning, they headed downstream. The small stream joined another, forming a larger stream. A third then a fourth tributary emptied into the river, which grew wider and deeper with rough currents and vicious rapids. The path beside the rushing water grew more treacherous and difficult to navigate as the river cut ever more deeply into the terrain. Eventually, they climbed to walk parallel to the steeply walled gorge. Thirsty, they persevered until they finally emerged from the forest onto a wide plain.

"Where are we?" Koriolis asked without expecting an answer.

Iselde looked around, blinking at the bright sunshine, and shrugged because she had no answer to give. "I have no idea, but at least we won't be dodging foliage and spider webs."

He nodded in agreement and lifted his face to the light breeze blowing across the plain, refreshing after the humid stillness of the Great Forest. They resumed walking, following the river as it bent and turned. They drank from other creeks and smaller rivers that joined the churning water, cascading over jagged rocks in spectacular waterfalls and deepening the gorge and the river. They edged the perimeter of a boiling rapids that carved a pool of water like an anteroom. The water there swirled gently, and fish swam in its clear depths.

"We'll stop here," Iselde said, peering over the edge. She silently noted her mate's drawn face. He was exhausted and, she assumed, too proud or too stubborn to admit it to her. "I'll catch us fish for supper."

Koriolis nodded, agreeing without demur. Carefully, gingerly, they headed down the steep, rocky hill leading to the pool. Iselde led the way. She dug the claws of her hands into the trees and the claws of feet into the dirt to prevent herself from sliding and tumbling down. Koriolis followed suit. When they arrived at the bottom, exhausted, sweaty, and coated in dirt and debris, Koriolis set off to gather wood for a fire. There was plenty.

Iselde dived into the pool. The fish scattered. She floated, appearing harmless. A fish grew brave and swam near to investigate this intruder. Ragged claws extended, she grabbed the fish and shot to the surface. Breaching the water, she threw the fish onto shore where it flopped in a futile effort to return to the water. Taking a breath, Iselde sank back down to lurk for more prey. By the time she had four fish to cook, Koriolis had built a fire. For the first time since returning to Fe-Ree, he felt he had an advantage: fire. No one, except perhaps a djinn, wielded fire quite deftly as a demon. Though the wood he gathered was often damp, his fire burned bright and hot.

"I haven't eaten so roughly in … well … forever," Koriolis commented as he flung the bones of a second fish into the fire.

"It's a change from what I normally eat," Iselde said as she picked the last shreds of flesh from the skeleton. "Not bad, just different."

Koriolis looked up at the tall walls of the gorge. "We'll have to climb."

She nodded and wiped her hands on what remained of her torn and dirty skirt. "Yes. We'll not find a village or town down here." She yawned and stretched. "But I am weary and would rest."

"As would I," he said and moved closer to her. He wrapped an arm around her shoulders. Iselde sighed and leaned into the solid strength of his body. "I'll take first watch."

"Mmm," she replied, closed her eyes, and, trusting him, let herself sleep.

Eyes open and ears pricked, Koriolis kept a wary watch for danger as his mate slept in his arms. The day's heat quickly dissipated, leaving his mate damp and too exhausted to shiver. He called upon his power with a demon's affinity for fire and sent heated air rushing over them both to warm their bodies and dry their tattered clothing.

He watched as the two moons crested the high walls of the river gorge and slowly crossed the visible sky. With reluctance, he awakened his mate, knowing he also needed to rest if he were not to fail her and his duty to care for her.

"Rest, beloved," she said as her eyelids fluttered open. "I will guard us."

Trusting in her vigilance and competence and warmed by her use of "beloved," Koriolis lay back, curled an arm under his head, and slept. Iselde's lips curled in a wry smile. An unguarded moment of softness had allowed the endearment to slip from her tongue. She sighed, realizing that her mate really did trust her with his well-being.

That was good to know.

While he slept and when she judged them adequately safe, Iselde risked distraction. She sent her consciousness deep into the earth and learned their location. She frowned with displeasure. Pulling her focus back to the situation at hand, she scanned the immediate area, all senses alert to the approach of danger. The soft crack of debris under foot caught her sensitive ears. Iselde tilted her head to one side, aiming a delicately pointed ear in that direction. Her hand curled around Asi's hilt. The quiet hiss of steel seemed to echo as Iselde pulled the sword free from its scabbard. The corrosive heat and stench of iron emanating from the blade made her clench her jaws as it burned the hand grasping the hilt. She was too close to it and the sentient blade rebuked her for daring to handle it. With a silent oath, she set the blade down, intending to ask Koriolis to sheathe it later.

Claws extended, Iselde stood in one smooth, lithe move and waited. Her patience was rewarded. A dark figure, obscured by the night shadows, approached.

"Stop," she hissed. "Come no closer."

The approaching figure paused. After a second, golden light limned the tall masculine shape: broad shoulders, trim waist, muscled thighs. Iselde sniffed the air. *Nothing.* The lack of scent worried her. She also wondered why Koriolis hadn't awakened. A predator such as he should have detected an intruder's presence regardless of his exhaustion. She opened her senses further and detected the tingle of magic, an unfamiliar magic draped like a blanket over her mate. Her gut clenched in dread. *It's a spell. Someone has put him under a spell.*

"Who are you?" she demanded, keeping her voice low and quiet so as not to disturb her slumbering mate. She reached over and grasped the sword of Rudra, clenching her jaw against the pain of the iron burning her palm. She lifted the weapon and held it ready.

A soft exhalation preceded the reply: "Your benefactor, you ungrateful fae."

Eyebrows shooting upward, Iselde said, "Indra?"

He approached the small fire and stood for her visual inspection a second before sitting down.

"How did you get here?"

"Really?" he replied. "I unmake and make worlds, and you ask me that?"

"You're a rain god."

He shook his head. "I'm a good bit more than that, despite what the fools of this yuga believe."

"Why are you here?"

"I've developed a recent interest in hunting demons." He glanced at Koriolis, waved his hand, then met her gaze across the low flames.

Iselde edged closer to Koriolis and nudged him with her toe. He didn't move. "Why didn't *you* come here with Asi then?"

He shrugged, the heavy pectoral and abdominal muscles rippling above the loose dhoti wrapped about his loins and thighs. An elaborate, embroidered sash circled his waist, and bejeweled gold armbands glittered in the firelight.

"You couldn't," she accused.

Again he shrugged.

His refusal to answer annoyed her. She shot another question at him: "And why here?"

He grinned then said, "Because you intrigue me."

Iselde frowned and muttered, "Gods always think they can have whatever they want whenever they want it."

"I've not requested anything," Indra pointed out.

"But you will," she rebutted.

He shrugged. "Perhaps. I asked for no payment for giving you Asi."

"You did, and Koriolis paid it," she corrected, referring to the god's desire to find a wife and sire powerful sons upon her. "You handed Asi to us to inconvenience Surya."

His teeth flashed in another quick smile. "That was a bonus."

"And did you not find a suitable bride at the ball?" she asked, unsure whether the fluid ebb and flow of time between realms meant he'd even attended the ball.

Indra shrugged. "Koriolis fulfilled his end of the bargain."

Iselde held his gaze while she thought, veering her focus from *why* he'd come to the fae realm to *how*. The sword in her hand twitched, drawing her attention. *He followed the sword. He was able to cross* because *of the sword. That was the* true *payment he desired: access to Fé-Ree.* The realization settled in her gut and felt right: a god-wrought artefact from the mortal realm set the beacon he could trace and follow. His presence, though, posed another issue.

"The gods of the mortal realm have no place here," she said.

"As you've noted, I've rather fallen from prominence in my home realm—"

"And you seek to restore it."

He shook his head as he slowly moved closer. "No, I cannot overcome Vishnu. And if I wanted to rise to prominence elsewhere on Earth, I'd have to dislodge the entrenched deity of some other faith. What a bother. Rather, I think I'd prefer to rise to prominence here in *your* realm."

"I thought your plan was to take a human woman and get an heir upon her," she pointed out and lowered herself back to the earth, taking a seat beside her mate. She felt reasonably sure the displaced god had no immediate intention to harm them, although she disliked his magical interference.

He shrugged. "It was worth a shot. I went to the ball— great food, lots of lovely champagne, and exquisite music—but none of the eligible women there appealed to me. Humans … so dull. Not a spark of magic among them, and I … well, I want *more*. I want a bride whose power consists of more than mere wealth. I can conjure gold any time I wish. I do not want a mere human. So, I thought I'd seek my fortune in your realm."

"You can try," she said, thinking the unicorns would skewer him without a second thought, much less any remorse. If they didn't do the job, then either the Unseelie King or the Erlking would annihilate the displaced god and take great pleasure in doing so. They did not tolerate threats to their sovereignty.

Indra chuckled, a low, deep, sensuous sound. "Oh, I certainly intend to." She gestured toward him in an invitation to sit. As he did so, he said, "I shall want a queen to rule beside me."

"But not a goddess?" Iselde countered.

"Perhaps."

"I am mated and have no interest in binding my soul to another."

"I didn't say I wanted you," he pointed out. "We already determined you were not eligible."

"That's not what you said earlier." Iselde felt the heat of embarrassment and silently acknowledged the hit. Instead of apologizing for her assumption, she shrugged and asked, "Whom do you have in mind?"

"I've not been here long enough to determine that."

"Fair enough," she said. Gesturing with one hand toward Koriolis, she added, "Remove your spell from him."

He nodded. "In the morning. Let him rest. He looks knackered."

She couldn't disagree with that observation. "Will you aid us on our quest?"

"I'd be happy to accompany you and Dra'Acul."

Iselde's eyes narrowed to slits of suspicion. "How do you know that name?"

Indra touched his fingertips to his bare chest, broad and well-muscled. "I'm a god, remember?"

Iselde snorted and fell silent, keeping watch until dawn. Indra stretched his arms, declared himself a smidgen tired, and lay down across the campfire from her. In moments, he was snoring. Iselde debated waking Koriolis, but decided against it. Dawn would arrive soon enough.

CHAPTER 21

KORIOLIS BLINKED AGAINST THE BRIGHTENING SKY, noticed Indra bathing in the pool, and muttered to his mate, "What's *he* doing here?"

Iselde shrugged and said, "He wants to reclaim his status."

"He's an Indian rain god."

"He says he was much more important a thousand years or so ago."

Koriolis shrugged, dismissing Indra's crisis. He opened his mouth to ask how Indra had come to the fae realm, then decided the *how* wasn't important. The god's motive was. "That doesn't really answer my question. Why is he here?"

"He says he wants a bride with true power, not a mere human."

"Greedy bastard," Koriolis muttered as he scanned the gorge's wall, calculating how they were going to scale the steep incline. "I'm going to wash."

Iselde nodded and kicked dirt over the ashes of their small campfire.

Koriolis stripped and waded into the water. Using silt from the bottom of the pool, he scrubbed his body. When he was as clean as he could get, he waded back to shore and pondered whether to rinse out his filthy, tattered clothes or just put them back on. The idea of donning the dirty garments offended him, but the hard climb back up the steep walls would only grind more dirt into the fabric. He detested exercises in futility. *Perhaps Indra could fly them to the top?* Koriolis looked at Indra and raised an eyebrow in silent inquiry.

Indra approached, slicking his wet hair back. He followed Koriolis' gaze. "I'm not a helicopter, and I'm certainly not going to transport passengers. Can either of you fly?"

"No."

"Then we climb," Iselde said, flexing her fingers and toes to extend her claws. Koriolis used the remains of his shirt to manufacture a sash which he tied snugly around his waist. He stuck Asi, sheathed, beneath the sash to carry it while retaining full use of his clawed hands.

Koriolis followed Iselde up the steep incline, scrabbling over rocks, through brush, and around spindly trees. After slipping for the fourth time, Koriolis kicked off his shoes, pulled off his ragged socks, and dug in his claws. His traction improved, he drew even with Iselde. She looked at him, nodded, and continued scrambling up the gorge wall. The sun hung high overhead and sweat drenched their bodies by the time they reached the top heaved themselves back onto flat ground.

"Let's not do that again," Koriolis muttered between panted breaths as he glared at Indra, who stood several feet away, having somehow gotten to the top without expending physical effort.

Indra walked to the edge and peered over it. "I hope this levels out soon."

Iselde said nothing. She rose to her feet and began walking, picking a careful path after stepping on a prickly weed and needing to pause to remove the small stickers from the sole of her right foot. She chalked it up to one more reason why she preferred the frozen wastelands far north of the Djarian territory with its venomous snakes and lizards, scorching heat, and dangerous plants. It was an inhospitable, predatory environment.

"This place is like the Quol, except dry instead of humid," she commented.

"The northern wastes are like the Quol, except icy instead of tropical," Koriolis pointed out.

Stung, she asked him, "Have you been to the northern wastes?"

He raised an eyebrow. "Once. A long time ago. I never had any desire to go back."

Iselde sniffed, a haughty sound.

Indra caught his eye, grinned, and said, "This rather reminds me of home."

"It would," Iselde muttered sourly.

They lapsed into silence, continuing to walk along the edge of the gorge. Hungry and thirsty when the sun set, they made a cold, uncomfortable camp that evening, splitting the watch between them.

"Can't you at least conjure water for us to drink?" Iselde asked.

"Rain god," he reminded her with a smirk. "And there's not a cloud in the sky I can use."

Iselde and Koriolis' bellies rumbled when they resumed their journey the next morning. To their relief, however, the land began to flatten, the descent to the dwindling river easing to a gentle roll that spread into an insect-infested marsh. They paused at the end of the day to drink from the brackish water which Iselde purified in her hands, as a demon's method of purification required fire.

"What is that?" Koriolis murmured as he gently drew Iselde back from the water's edge.

"It looks like a crocodile," Indra said as he peered across the rippling water. "But bigger. And uglier."

Iselde flexed her claws. "It looks like meat."

"Your cat's claws won't penetrate that beast's armored hide," Indra noted.

"*Deinosuchus*," Koriolis whispered. The other two looked at him. "It's an ancestor of alligators and crocodiles and means 'terror crocodile.'"

Indra loosed a "harrumph," scratched his head, then remarked, "Dabbled in paleontology, did you?"

Koriolis pursed his lips. After a moment, he said peevishly, "I found Earth's history interesting."

Iselde caught a fleeting thought through the mate bond and chuckled.

"What's so funny?" Indra asked.

"He is recognized as a scholar in Earth's ancient history."

Indra's eyebrows rose. "You have a degree in paleontology?"

With great dignity, Koriolis replied, "A doctorate. I am educated in many subjects."

Indra sighed and shook his head. Looking at Iselde, he commented, "Are you sure you'd rather not take me as your mate? After all, *I* am a god."

Koriolis glowered at him. Indra ignored it and offered Iselde his most charming grin.

She rolled her eyes and said, "The presence of that beast means there is either fish or other prey in this festering marsh."

Indra sighed in mock disgust at her returning to the subject of supper. "I'll take care of it."

He raised his hand as though hefting a javelin or spear, aimed, and threw. Although he held nothing in his fist, a bolt of lightning flew through the air to strike the great lizard lurking in the water. The beast roared with pain and thrashed for several seconds before sinking. Blood swirled up through the water, carried away by the current.

"Well, who's going to get it?" Indra demanded. "I did the hard work."

Koriolis exchanged glances with Iselde and shrugged. He stepped forward, peered into the river, then launched himself into its depths. A few minutes later, his head bobbed above the water's surface, his face showing the strain of immense physical effort. Iselde dashed forward to help him drag the heavy carcass to shore. Indra watched, dark eyes glittering with amusement.

Eventually, the fae and the demon dragged their catch from the water. Panting from exertion, they flopped to the ground.

"I don't suppose you have a knife?" Iselde called out.

"Why, yes, as a matter of fact, I do," Indra replied, drawing a dagger from the scabbard anchored beneath his sash and holding it aloft. "Would you like to borrow it?"

Iselde narrowed her eyes. "I would, yes."

"What's the magic word?"

Iselde bared her teeth. "Don't push me."

The Indian god's lips pursed in a sulky moue.

"Hand me the knife or I'll use Asi on that thing."

Indra's eyes widened in offense. "You wouldn't dare."

"Oh, yes, she would," Koriolis replied with a grin because he knew she wouldn't. She couldn't wield the sword without harming herself—although he thought she just might to prove a point. *That dagger is steel, beloved.*

"Fine." Indra handed the dagger to Iselde who snatched it from his hand and bowed over the dead lizard, eyeing the carcass to decide what part would yield the best meat. Determined not to show weakness, she ignored the way her palm burned despite the dagger's steel hilt being wrapped in leather.

"The tail," Koriolis said.

She glanced at him.

"If it's like the alligators of the Louisiana bayou, then the tail's the only part of the animal worth eating."

She nodded and figured his guess was probably accurate. Jabbing the point of the blade into the base of the lizard's tail, she began to saw.

"Hey, you'll ruin my knife using it like that!" Indra protested.

Iselde released the dagger and sat back on her heels. She opened and closed her hand several times to work the pain from her reddened palm. "Then you do it. You butcher this beast."

With a disgruntled harrumph, Indra yanked the knife from the carcass, plunged it in a different place, and tried to slice through the beast's armored hide. It resisted the blade's fine edge. With a grunt, he plunged the knife into the flesh, drew it out, and plunged it in again, creating a series of connected punctures to cut through the tough hide and muscle.

Eventually, via that series of accurately aimed stabs, he managed to open a deep cut in the flesh. At that point, the blade's edge had dulled considerably, a result that had Indra muttering to himself.

"Allow me," Koriolis offered. With a complicated gesture and a few words muttered under his breath to focus his will and power, a round blade of darkness sliced through the carcass, severing the long, thick tail from the rest of the beast.

"Well, why didn't you say you could do that?" Indra demanded.

"You didn't ask."

The corners of Iselde's mouth curled in a faint smile. *You could have spared me a burned palm.*

And assume you could not accomplish the task? I would not disparage you so.

Next time, offer. Maybe I'll surprise you and take you up on it.

Indra gaped then recognized the humor in the situation and began to chuckle. Shortly thereafter, he and Koriolis skinned the tail, separated the flesh from the bones, and skewered slices of tough muscle on sharpened sticks. They angled the sticks over a small fire Iselde had built.

Evening had fallen by the time the meat finished cooking and they ate supper. The leftover meat served as their breakfast the next morning. It was greasy and tough and had a fishy, muddy flavor that didn't complement the taste of the smoke from the campfire. The gristle stuck between their teeth, too.

"Better than nothing," Iselde muttered as she wiped her fingers on the rags of her clothing. Surviving in the northern wastes, she'd eaten worse.

Koriolis looked at the sun clearing the horizon and said, "Let's go."

Continuing to follow the unicorns' compulsion to head south, Iselde and Koriolis, accompanied by Indra, embarked upon a long day's trek skirting the marsh and leaving it behind. The terrain changed again, becoming drier. The wind blew hot by midafternoon. Damp clay transitioned to shallow, hard-packed soil where grasses undulated beneath the ever-present wind. They made camp, slept poorly, and walked three more days in search of potable water. Where none was forthcoming, Iselde tapped into her power and drew forth a thin, clear trickle from deep within the earth. They'd drink their fill, then Iselde would release the trickle back into the earth. Koriolis and Indra hunted, and they dined on the greasy, stringy flesh of marmot-like creatures, rabbits, and grouse. The savannah soon succumbed to the relentless heat and dry weather, turning into desert.

"Why are we doing this?" Indra asked as he shielded his eyes with a hand and peered into the cloudless sky.

"Apparently, we're on a quest," Koriolis replied in a tone no less dry than the hot desert air.

He and Iselde exchanged a look. She shrugged her sun-burned shoulders. They continued their slow trek beneath the blazing sun in companionable silence until Iselde cried out, "Look!"

Koriolis and Indra aimed their eyes in the direction Iselde pointed.

"It's a djinni settlement," she said.

"Do we approach?" Indra asked.

"Do we have any choice?" Koriolis retorted. "We need proper garb, footwear, and a real meal."

"Ah, but they'll want payment," Indra pointed out, hand resting protectively on the jeweled hilt of his now dull-bladed dagger.

"Leave that to me," Iselde replied and dropped to the ground. She placed both palms flat on the earth in front of her and sank her consciousness deep beneath the surface.

"What's she doing?" Indra whispered, but Koriolis did not answer.

A few minutes passed, then the dirt began to seethe and bubble beneath her palms.

"What's she *doing*?" Indra repeated.

Koriolis again did not answer. The dirt beneath Iselde's palms sprayed as though displaced by a small geyser. Her fists clenched and she exhaled long and slowly. With a murmur of gratitude, she rose to her feet and turned over her hands, opening her fists to reveal thick nuggets of purest gold.

"Well, that's a handy skill to have," Indra remarked, not mentioning that—at least in the mortal realm—he could have manifested all the gold they needed with a mere thought. He wondered if he could do so here in the fae realm, but felt no obligation to test himself. "I thought you could just draw water."

"It should more than pay for what we need," Iselde replied, ignoring his comment as she handed one of the heavy nuggets to Koriolis.

"Don't I get one?" Indra asked. "After all, I did kill the lizard for our dinner a few days ago. And I've hunted, too."

Iselde sighed and handed him the other nugget.

Indra grinned. He held up the nugget to admire the sunshine glinting off the shiny yellow metal. "Are you *sure* you don't want to leave him behind and be my most favored wife?"

"I'm sure."

He reached out to skim his fingertips along the long tangled locks of her white hair. He whispered, "So beautiful and exotic."

Iselde reacted with greater speed than he anticipated, wrapping her hand around the front of his throat. Her extended claws pricked the skin. "Don't touch me."

Indra's eyes widened in surprise as blood welled and dribbled down his neck, but he said nothing. He lowered his hand with exaggerated care. Iselde retracted her claws and lowered her hand and took a step backward to put distance between them.

Standing immediately behind the god, Koriolis leaned forward and murmured into his ear, "Never touch a mated fae. That way lies death."

"So, I gather," Indra replied as he wiped away the blood, the pricked skin already healed. He swiped his palm across his thigh, smearing blood over the finely woven fabric.

"If you importune her again, I'll kill you myself."

Indra slowly turned to face the demon. His eyes flashed with power and arrogance, every inch of him an ancient god, a king of gods. "You could try."

"Let's go," Iselde snapped and resumed walking toward the settlement.

The two males fell into step behind her, both keeping a watchful eye out for danger.

CHAPTER 22

THEIR PATH DESCENDED TO A SHALLOW OASIS, marshy at the edge of the water. A short distance beyond, the large reptilian beasts of burden used by djinni caravans lounged in the dirt amid the scrub. Tents of felted wool and canvas and of various sizes were scattered among mud brick huts. Smoke rose from cookfires. From somewhere the hollow notes of a wooden flute resounded, thin and sweet.

"Is it a caravan stopping over for a rest? Or is it a community?" Koriolis wondered aloud.

"A bit of both, I think," Iselde replied, looking at the differing cloths draped over the backs of beasts of burden and the scattering of weathered mud brick structures that stood testament to the permanence of the settlement. Her keen ears picked up at least three different dialects spoken in the small-but-busy marketplace, as well as the chink of coins exchanged for goods and services.

Djinns garbed in flowing robes that caught the desert wind bustled about, several followed by slaves bearing caskets, waterskins, or other material items. Every slave wore thick, heavy chains around the ankles and a metal collar around the neck. Many were deeply tanned, their shapeless, knee-length garb bereft of sleeves and exposing their skin to the brutal sun. Slaves and djinns alike paused in their tracks as the foreigners walked amid them, tall and proud as though the natives did not consider them lesser beings. Iselde caught their whispered comments, speculation as to what price she would bring and whether she and Koriolis, described as "the other fae," could be taken captive rather than purchased from the otherworldly male who most closely resembled them.

Iselde murmured a warning: "Hold your power close."

Koriolis met her gaze, his black eyes glittering with both rage and power.

"I'll take care of this," Indra said and adopted a broad smile as he approached a merchant. "Good sir! I wish to examine your wares."

With an expansive gesture, the merchant invited them into his tent. "I have nothing but the finest cloth for you, master." With another wave of his arm, he directed Indra's attention to the back of the tent. "And there, good master, is the most desirable porcelain!"

Indra nodded. "Be so good as to keep watch over my servants, would you? They're quite valuable, and I wouldn't want them to wander off."

The merchant's eyes gleamed with avarice. "Of course, good master."

The merchant moved to stand in front of Koriolis and Iselde, barring their entrance into the tent. He glared at them in disgust and reached out to touch Iselde. She bared her pointed teeth at him and hissed like a cat. He snatched his hand back and said, "Your servant is feral, good master!"

"Ah, it's been difficult work to tame her," Indra replied from where he was fingering bolts of cloth. "I don't wish to break her spirit; they're no fun if you do that."

"Fun?" the merchant echoed, eyes bugging at the concept.

"Why, yes, good sir," Indra replied. "A cowed servant is obedient but not loyal. Loyalty requires spirit."

The merchant nodded, adopting a thoughtful expression.

"Servant?" Koriolis muttered under his breath in the fae tongue. "How does he know the local tongue already?"

"Bide a moment, beloved," Iselde replied, also speaking fae. "He's up to something, and I want to see how it plays out." She paused then, speculated, "He's a god, an ancient one at that. I'm sure he has a few tricks for picking up languages."

Koriolis snorted and gestured to dismiss the subject of Indra's linguistic prowess. "If that worm touches you, he'll feel my claws."

Iselde sniffed. "If he touches me, he'll feel *my* claws." She met his gaze and held it. "I'm quite capable of defending myself."

"I know, beloved, but I would share in ensuring your safety and well-being." He glanced at the merchant. "Besides, I'm getting thirsty."

Looking at his face, she noticed the tightness of his skin over those sharp, jutting cheekbones. "Craving blood?"

"Aye." He dipped his chin in a shallow, curt nod.

"I thought you'd been relieved of that." Iselde wondered if this thirst for blood was due to the unicorns' meddling or if it was an effect of a demon being brought into Fé-Ree.

"I don't know," he murmured, having caught the thought across the mate bond. He inhaled, taking in the merchant's scent. Nothing. He inhaled deeply and his bloodthirst spiked. Red sparks flared in his all-black eyes, and a low growl rumbled deep in his throat as he exerted the will to master the overweening impulse to hunt and drink and kill. "This must be how my vampires felt."

She came to a decision. "Let me know when your thirst becomes desperate."

He raised an eyebrow in query. "You want me to feed upon you?"

Iselde waved her hand at a flying insect to shoo it away. "I'm your best option, unless you'd like to suck on Indra's neck."

He shuddered in distaste.

"That's what I thought. Or you could just slaughter every djinn here and drink from their dying bodies."

The gleam in her eyes tipped him off. "You dislike the djinn."

"I loathe them. I've taken into my tribe many refugees from Djaria, escaped slaves and whatnot who suffered from djinni greed and brutality." She paused, then added, "Corta is little better. Fyrgia's improved since Ishjarta took the throne."

"Fyrgia and Corta?"

"Ah, you've been gone. Over the last couple of millennia, humans crossed over into Fé-Ree and established their own kingdoms. Fyrgia did not actively engage in slavery, but they did not ban it either—at least not until Ishjarta took the throne. Corta *does* buy and sell slaves."

Koriolis shrugged. "That's not much different from fae society, and you know it. Third House fae are powerless compared to First and Second House fae: they do the menial labor higher caste fae will not."

"They do," she acknowledged, "but they are not, themselves, chattel."

"Stop talking! Silence!" the merchant shouted. He darted uneasy glances at his exotic customer.

Iselde and Koriolis shot him glances of contempt, then resumed their conversation while Indra continued to peruse the merchant's wares. Their conversation soon paused as an anguished cry caught their attention. They looked around to see a djinn take a whip to a slave. The slave crouched, shoulders hunched and head bowed, whimpering as the coiled length of the whip struck her about the head and shoulders. Iselde tensed with outrage.

"Don't interfere," Koriolis warned.

Then blood bloomed bright against the dusty cloth of the slave's garment as the woman collapsed to the ground and cried out. The blows continued to rain down upon her, then stopped long enough for the slave's master to kick her in the ribs. The agonized grunt spewed from her mouth in a spray of blood. Koriolis licked his lips.

"This is one reason why I hate the djinns," Iselde snarled and unleashed her power.

The air cracked. A frigid gale wind swept across the settlement, leveling tents not constructed to withstand the force. Sand rose and swirled in the harsh wind as the ground beneath them heaved and bucked. Beasts of burden lumbered to their feet and bawled in distress. Those not tethered fled for stable ground. The merchant cried out and darted into the dubious safety of his swaying tent. Iselde strode forward, hair whipping about in the wind, but the sand never touched her pale skin and the earth calmed beneath her stride. Claws extended, she grabbed the nearest djinn by the flapping folds of his robe and yanked him around. With the other hand, she slashed his throat.

The scent of the djin's blood dissolved what remained of Koriolis' control. Beside his mate, Koriolis advanced. He drew Asi and tackled the man who launched himself at the enraged fae. He wielded the sword with ancient mastery to disable opponent after opponent, gorging on their blood then letting each fall to the ground after he drained them in loud, sloppy gulps.

Ululating cries joined the scream of the howling wind and the rumble of the earthquake as the djinns quickly mustered a defense. They rushed toward the fae and the demon whose claws and sword left mangled carnage in their wake. Under the djinns' own magic, fire spurted. Iselde's wind whipped the flames into unpredictable blazes that lit the tents on fire.

"Oh, this is much more fun," Indra shouted as he flung lightning bolts and called down the rain from a cloudless sky. Startled by the downpour, the djinns panicked. Their fires sputtered and died. Blood mixed with water and mud.

"Spare the children!" Koriolis shouted. He wiped the blood from his lips and chin with the back of a forearm and returned to the fray.

"And the slaves!" Iselde added as she dodged the vicious swing of a blade and raked her claws across the swordsman's belly. Bright red bloomed where those lethal claws tore through fabric and flesh.

When the furor died down, only Iselde, Koriolis, Indra, and a few dozen people remained alive. A cluster of slaves, children, and those remaining adult djinns who preferred to live huddled together, heads bowed, shivering in terror. Iselde approached them and reached for one slave's leg. The slave sobbed and trembled, but did not pull away. Her clawed fingertips which still dripped blood and bits of gore stopped inches away from the thick chain encircling his ankle.

"Iron," she growled.

Koriolis joined her, saying, "I'll take care of this."

He squatted and touched the chain with a fingertip. Iselde felt the ripple of power as he exerted his will. The link he touched quickly turned scabrous with orange spots, then the rust spread quickly through the metal. After a moment, Koriolis crushed the rusted-through link in his fist, and the chain fell away from the slave's ankle, revealing scabbed, scarred flesh.

Indra's rain ebbed, soon turning into a rainbow-filled mist that quickly morphed into water vapor beneath the brutal sun and filled the oasis with a dense fog. Koriolis went from slave to slave, forcing their iron collars and chains to rust through and crumble until all were freed of their iron shackles.

As the visible accoutrements of their bondage fell away, the slaves picked themselves up from the ground. Some muttered among themselves. One attempted to attack Koriolis who quickly slew him. When he finished, he returned to his mate's side and said, "There were no demons here."

Iselde scanned the carnage and said, "No, just the demonic."

"What are we going to do with them?" Indra asked, gesturing toward the survivors, many of whom were either human or human-djinn hybrids. The handful of children huddled among the slaves and djinni survivors, taking comfort where they could from the horror. The ever-present desert wind soughed past, filled with the sounds of grief and the smells of blood, fear, and tears.

"Give them their freedom," Iselde said.

"Do you think they'll survive on their own?" Indra shook his head. "And what about the djinns who surrendered?"

"Why wouldn't they? They know this land better than we do," she said.

Indra shook his head again at her callousness. "No. No, I will not leave them to be enslaved again." His eyes glowed with renewed purpose as he scanned the subdued crowd. "These people are now *my* people and under *my* protection. This is why I came here."

"You came to Fé-Ree to be worshiped again as a mighty god and to sire a son upon a powerful female," Koriolis reminded him in a dry tone as Iselde walked away to rummage among the toppled tents and merchandise strewn about.

"I'm starting small," Indra retorted with a manic grin. "You don't think India started off as a mighty civilization, do you? It took time and a lot of direction to develop a magnificent culture."

"So magnificent it crumbled under a small European island's military might," Koriolis pointed out.

Indra refused to be deterred. "I will begin a new yuga here in Djaria, a new civilization."

"If you're planning on recreating India's golden age here, I don't recommend it," Koriolis said.

Indra bared his teeth and his eyes glowed with power as the steamy smells of wet dirt, blood, and offal rose around them. "I've learned a few things over the millennia. I won't make those mistakes again."

"Then it looks like we're in business," Koriolis said. His gaze landed on Iselde. "And it looks like my beloved has found us some proper clothing and supplies."

Indra approached the cluster of survivors. "Follow me and you shall never wear chains again. Follow me and you shall be *free*."

They muttered among themselves, several weeping, although Koriolis did not know whether from fright or grief. He wasn't sure he cared, either. His belly gurgled, overfull. He watched with mildly curious dispassion as some of the survivors embraced the frightened children, although whether from instinctive protectiveness or genuine affection neither he nor Iselde knew or cared.

"And if we do not follow you?" one woman dared ask Indra, her voice cracking and her expression resigned to violent misfortune.

"Then you take your chances," he replied in a flippant tone. "I won't be here to save you or protect you from those who would enslave you again." Looking at the group and meeting their collective gaze, he asked, "Will you follow me?"

One by one, former slaves and once-proud djinns prostrated themselves in the mud, although some of the older djinni children remained standing in defiance of the foreigner who dared put himself above them. Indra smiled with satisfaction, not noticing the demon and the fae wander off to loot the wreckage.

"I am pleased to call you mine. Rise and embark upon a new life!"

The manumitted group rose.

"Equip yourselves. Take only what you and the beasts of burden can carry, for we begin a quest to conquer Djaria in the name of freedom under the auspices of your new king and god, Indra!"

"Indra!" the former slaves cheered in lackluster fashion. "Indra!"

The conquered djinns remained stubbornly silent.

"Ah, they'll eventually figure out I'm the better option." Indra turned to face Iselde, ignoring Koriolis. In a quiet tone, he asked, "By the way, if I'm going to bring this nation under my benevolent rule—and I will—where should we go first?"

"Arigoz," she replied. "The capital of Djaria and the emperor's seat."

"Arigoz?" he repeated, tasting the word on his tongue. "Do you know where it is?"

She shrugged. "It's more or less central to Djaria and serves as the crossroads for trade. Anything and everything that passes through Djaria goes through Arigoz. Assuming little has changed since I was here last, that's where the Djarian emperor spends most of his time. It's easier to supply his vices there."

"Ah." Indra nodded and assumed a wise expression. "A quick takeover, nice and direct. I like it."

Iselde did not reply. Quick or not, Indra's establishment of himself as the new emperor of Djaria would be violent and bloody. She popped a dried date into her mouth and savored the sweet chewy fruit. She spat out the pit, looked at Koriolis, and asked, "Did you get enough to drink?"

Koriolis' black eyes somehow pulsed red. His skin, which had looked pale and drawn, was now flushed and ruddy with good health. He nodded and wiped his mouth again with the back of his hand, smearing the blood rather than cleaning it from his skin. "For now."

"Your bloodthirst does not bode well."

He paused, going utterly still as his attention turned inward. After a moment he said, "I do not feel the taint of vampirism in my body." He looked at the cloudless sky. "And I can still tolerate the sun as vampires cannot."

"Hm, perhaps you are some strange amalgamation of fae, demon, and vampire now?"

He shrugged. "Does it matter?"

"Only if you try to eat me."

His smile turned blatantly lecherous. "Oh, I fully intend to do that."

Iselde returned his smile with a sultry one of her own then said, "After we bathe."

He agreed. He'd had enough of feeling grimy and wearing rags. The former crown prince of the Unseelie Court deserved and demanded better.

As did his princess.

CHAPTER 23

"THIS ISN'T QUITE HOW I ANTICIPATED MY RETURN to Fé-Ree would go," Iselde commented as she swayed in rhythm with the stride of the beast she rode. She looked toward the self-styled conqueror of Djaria, who rode at the front of a long column of people trekking across the desert. The last three djinni villages had quickly folded beneath Indra's advance, those natives who surrendered and survived being offered the same opportunity to follow him or take their chances in the desert. Most opted to follow their benevolent new god-king, with some fleeing at night to alert their countrymen of the conqueror's inexorable advance. "I thought we'd be killing demons."

Koriolis shrugged from atop his own riding beast. His hand brushed the hilt of Asi sheathed at his hip. "So did I. Perhaps …"

"Perhaps?" she prompted.

"Perhaps demons prefer more populated areas where the hunting is easier." He gave her a sidelong glance. "I did."

"And now?"

He wiped the back of his hand across his sweating forehead. "And now I'm interested in seeing if the northern wastes are as terrible as this godforsaken desert."

Iselde shrugged. "Here, it's dry and hot and miserable. Home is dry and freezing and miserable."

"Why did you choose to live in the northern wastes anyway?"

She shrugged. "I once attempted to establish a home here, but the natives were ..." she paused to find the right word "... hostile. I wandered the continent for a few millennia before finally settling where no one else wished to live. There I bore my son and raised him."

"You mentioned blood kin before," Koriolis blurted. "I would know more."

"Aye. I've been mated, too," she said, fully realizing she'd already informed him of that. "My first mate was fae, my mother's choice. We had no issue before he was killed." Iselde frowned, her lips pursing in distaste at the sour memory. "My second mate was human—*my* choice. I was lonely and disinclined to allow my mother to choose again for me. He was a good man, brave and kind and one of the first men to fall through the veil and enter Fé-Ree." A small, sad smile curled her lips. "It was Einar who first taught me how to fight. Until then, I'd been the model fae female: demure, gentle, softly spoken, and skilled at needlework. Bah."

"But neither was a fated mate." Rage erupted in Koriolis' gut. It urged him to find her long lost mate and annihilate him. He took a deep breath of the hot, dusty air to calm himself.

"No," she replied, casting him a quick glance, indicating she'd sensed his fiery wrath.

"Tell me about them."

She sighed and her expression turned melancholy. "Einar died before I settled in the northern wastes. Our son died centuries later. Our two daughters were abducted by djinns and died at their hands. They left no offspring."

Relief swept through Koriolis: *I won't have to kill the male she loved.* But there was more to the story. Badgering her wouldn't draw the story from her as he wanted. So, like the predator he was, Koriolis waited. After a long moment, Iselde rewarded his silent patience.

"Torsten, my son, grew up, strong and proud, a fierce warrior like his father. Too proud. Reckless."

Burning curiosity mingled with the smoldering ashes of his rage. His voice guttural, he asked, "What happened?"

"He thought to conquer the Quol, to become a king of his own demesne." Koriolis did not pry further, but Iselde's tongue had loosened. "Even the most doughty of fae warriors tread with supreme caution inside the Quol's boundaries. Torsten was not cautious enough."

Brushing a tear from her cheek, she said nothing of the only fae warrior she'd known to enter the Quol and tame it. She said nothing of the fae king who contained the deadly jungle's spread and kept it from consuming the continent. Neither of those two males had held her heart.

"I am sorry," Koriolis said, knowing the platitude offered insufficient comfort. "The pain of losing a child never fades."

"No, it doesn't," she agreed in a somber tone. "But one learns to find joy beyond the grief. My son left behind a son of his own, Murita. He found a mate, and I adopted others into our tribe. I built a family. Many of my tribe are my own descendants through him."

"And you miss them." Cool determination swept away the ashes of rage and left fertile ground for a new purpose to sprout. *I would give you more children and build a new family.* The thought startled him.

She nodded and looked away. "I do."

"Then when we have finished our quest here, we shall go north."

Iselde sighed and shook her head. "There are too few people in the northern wastes to satisfy your thirst." She said nothing about the unicorns' statement that she could not return to the northern wastes. She *wanted* to return to the fragile peace she'd found in that bleak territory of ice and wind. *I've defied fate before, and I will do so again, unicorns be damned.*

He shrugged. "I do not know if gorging myself at every village we conquer will make it worse or if overindulgence will give me a disgust of blood."

"But you hope for the latter."

"I do."

Another thought popped up. She asked, "What differentiates demon from vampire? Aren't they basically the same?"

Koriolis' lips curled in a small smile. "DNA, basically."

"DNA? What's that?"

He pursed his lips to consider a concise, clear answer then said, "DNA—deoxyribonucleic acid—is your essence, the physicality of what makes you you."

"So, blood."

He nodded, deciding that was accurate enough. "Humans who are bitten, whose essence is corrupted, and who drink blood to survive become vampires. Beings of power, such as fae, whose essence is corrupted and who drink blood to survive become demons."

"But you were never fully demon," Iselde prompted.

"For a corrupted fae, that final step to becoming entirely and irrevocably demon is killing by drinking a victim dry and consuming his or her soul—we just don't know which victim. That last cruelty seals the corruption, the fall from grace, if you will. I was lucky enough to retain the strength of will to not kill my victims, at least not for the past several centuries." He wondered, as ancient as she was, how she did not know that. Rather than annoy her with the question, he said nothing further.

"And what do you think will happen if you starve yourself?" she asked after a moment's pondering.

Koriolis gave her honesty: "I think I'll need to seek my father or the unicorns and beg for their help."

Iselde nodded and did not voice her doubt that neither Uberon nor the unicorns would acquiesce to any such request for help. An idea struck her. "What if ..."

"Yes?"

"What if you were to gorge yourself on *demon* blood instead of djinni or human blood?" Her expression turned curious. "Demon blood is—"

"Powerful," he interjected and rubbed his chin. "It's *powerful*. That might be what I need to break free of this terrible thirst."

"It's worth experimenting."

"First we have to find some demons."

Iselde's nostrils flared. She raised her head and focused her eyes on the eastern horizon where a djinni city loomed in the distance, distinctive spires piercing the sky. "If there are demons in Djaria, we'll find them there."

Koriolis turned his attention in the same direction. He smiled, pointed teeth gleaming in the sunshine. "Arigoz."

"Djaria's city of sin." A cloud of dust swirled between them and the distant city. Iselde murmured, "They have sent an army to greet us."

"Shall we meet them?"

Iselde glanced back at the horde of freed slaves and conquered djinns following them, then returned her gaze to the dust cloud announcing the advance of Arigoz's army. She thumped her heels against the riding beast's sides, cuing it into a rocking run. Koriolis followed closely behind. They stopped beside Indra who led the nomadic procession.

"You see them, too?" he said, eagerness making his voice vibrate.

"This will be your true test," Iselde said.

Indra grinned, the expression more than a little manic. "I am Indra, builder and destroyer of worlds! They shall not prevail against me!"

Koriolis blandly responded, "Leave the demons to me."

Indra's gaze touched upon the hilt of Asi sheathed at his hip. "As you wish, Dra'Acul."

Koriolis' expression soured.

"Why don't we stop here and conserve our strength?" Iselde suggested. "Make Arigoz's army weary themselves by coming to us?"

Indra pursed his lips as he considered her suggestion. It made sense, but the bleak landscape offered no respite for either his conquered people or their livestock.

"I'll summon water for your horde," she offered.

He grinned again. "Good idea." He glanced about, seeking a prime place to pause their advance. Pointing his finger, he said, "Over there. Flat, high ground is perfect."

"I'll accompany you," Koriolis offered as Iselde turned her riding beast to move ahead of the horde.

"No need," she replied. "Someone needs to keep a watchful eye on *him*."

Indra laughed, not at all offended by her dig. "Watch and learn, Dra'Acul."

"You do realize I'm older than you?" Koriolis retorted in an acidic tone.

"Perhaps. Time between realms is a relative thing, you know." Indra's expression switched from amused to commanding. He turned his riding beast around to face the horde following him and ordered a change in direction to the plateau where they would stop and engage in battle.

"Those who fight for me will be rewarded!" he called out. "Those who fight against me will be executed!"

"Well, at least he realizes not everyone in his horde is a loyal subject," Iselde murmured.

Sotto voce, Indra replied, "They'll learn to love me. Right now I'll settle for fear and obedience."

Following the direction he pointed, the horde turned, trudging a wide path through the rolling dunes. When the stragglers passed him, he cued his riding beast to a rocking gallop to resume the lead position at the head of the nomadic crowd. Iselde and Koriolis followed at a more moderate pace.

"He makes for a dramatic figure," she commented.

Koriolis agreed. "Drama inspires."

Iselde made a noncommittal noise in her throat.

Her riding beast soon closed the distance between the stragglers and the front line. When they reached the plateau, she dismounted and took off her shoes. Handing the reins of her beast to a nearby refugee, she began to slowly walk, settling each foot firmly on the ground as she sank her consciousness beneath the dusty, scrub-littered surface. She did not notice Koriolis dismount and position himself protectively behind her, ready to catch her if she fell or steady her if she stumbled. He opened his mouth to speak, then thought the better of it and remained silent.

Finally, she paused and focused. The earth beneath her and around her began to shift and tremble. Grains of sand, then particles of dirt, slid away from her and Koriolis until they stood at the bottom of a wide and shallow bowl. The earth beneath their feet grew damp and dark as she called forth water from deep below the surface.

"Step away," she murmured as the patch of dampness spread.

"I'll not leave you," he replied.

"Then hold on to me." She raised her arms.

Koriolis wrapped his arms around her. Wind began to swirl around them as water bubbled to the surface. He held her tightly as they slowly rose, their clothes flapping in the invisible tornado that lifted them. The upward draw of the tornado and the pull of Iselde's power called forth more water, gallons upon thousands of gallons until the wide, shallow bowl was filled. The wind swept them across the newly formed pond and gently deposited them at its shore. Iselde's knees buckled from the sudden expenditure of energy. Koriolis wrapped an arm around her torso and drew her body against his, offering her his strength and stability while she took a moment to recover.

"Drink your fill," Indra commanded, "and refresh yourselves for battle!"

The horde surged forward to partake of the cool, clear water that Iselde continued to draw from far beneath the surface. She knew that once she released her hold on it, the water would quickly seep away through the porous sand, leaving behind a muddy hole in the ground. Were the area conducive to an oasis, the water would have already been present and available.

Within a few hours, all the people and animals had quenched their thirst. Waterskins and amphorae were refilled. They struck camp, arranging themselves per Indra's instructions with women and children and livestock contained behind a protective ring of able-bodied men, including former slaves, armed with staves, knives, and, for the lucky few, swords.

"They're poorly armed and won't fare well against the army headed for us," Indra observed with disappointment.

"I can't conjure weapons for everyone," Iselde said.

"I can't conjure weapons for them at all," Koriolis added.

They looked at Indra.

"You're the builder and destroyer of worlds," Koriolis said. "Surely you can manufacture weapons from thin air?"

"I could," Indra admitted, "but can this rabble wield them? I think most are likely to do themselves injury."

Iselde admitted to herself that he had a point, a good one. For the most part, these people were not trained warriors.

"Golems," Koriolis said. "Indra, can you create golems?"

"Good idea," the god replied. "However, if I'm creating golems, maintaining their forms, and directing their actions, who will keep an eye on my people?"

Iselde raised her eyebrows at his quick switch from "rabble" to "my people." She raised a hand, claws unsheathed, and said, "I'll do that."

"You're female," Indra objected.

"So I've noticed," came the dry reply.

"And so have the djinns noticed. They'll not take kindly to a female's commands."

Iselde bared her teeth. Neither Indra nor Koriolis was stupid enough to mistake the expression for a smile. "They won't have a choice."

Perturbed, Koriolis asked, "You would rob them of their will?"

"They won't run off," she promised. She turned around and examined the plateau. "Call your fighting men to you. Koriolis will lead them while I safeguard those unable to fight."

"I hope you know what you're doing," Indra said.

"Trust me."

Indra hesitated a second before nodding. He called forth his soldiers, such as they were. Soon they arranged themselves in an anxious crowd behind the trio.

"Hold them there. I'll create a barrier to protect the rest," Iselde said.

They watched her as she walked away and paced a wide circle around the women, children, and livestock. Still barefoot, she paced a circle around them. The air shimmered as it solidified into a thick glass dome.

"You cannot prevent a djinn from apparating into the dome," Indra pointed out. "Besides, anything under the dome will soon cook in this heat."

Iselde responded with a haughty sniff, and the dome turned black. She looked at him, one eyebrow raised.

"That won't work for long," Indra said.

"The djinns won't apparate where they cannot see," she explained.

"The heat trapped inside the dome will kill them all, so the djinn need not do anything," he pointed out.

With a resigned sigh, she focused her will again. At irregular intervals, small holes exploded from the ground, spewing sand and hot air and drops of cool water. A whooshing sound soughed across the plateau, then softened to a low sigh as air circulated through the newly formed ventilation system that delved deep into the earth to blow cool air into the dome.

"Clever," Koriolis murmured.

Indra rubbed his chin. "What's to prevent them from digging out from underneath the dome?"

"It's not a dome; it's more like a sphere," she explained.

"And the bottom of the sphere is open to the water you pulled," Koriolis said.

"It is porous," she clarified.

"How will my people get out of there?" Indra asked.

"Trust me."

"I hate when you say that."

A small smile curled the corners of her mouth.

CHAPTER 24

INDRA RALLIED HIS RAGTAG ARMY, IF SUCH A disappointing collection of ill-equipped, ill-trained people could be named as such. Standing before the army, Iselde said, "I need a blade."

Indra raised his eyebrows. "You know how to wield a sword?"

Ignoring his incredulity, she said, "I do—and you need every skilled sword you can get."

Indra looked at the quickly approaching opposition and pursed his lips. "You cannot wield steel."

"No."

He thought for a moment then exclaimed, "Ah ha!" He held out his hands and concentrated, wrinkling his nose as he did so. He exhaled, drew in another breath, and refocused his will. With a *crack* of displaced air, a copper sword gleamed in his hand.

"Copper is too soft to serve as a blade," Koriolis said.

"I know. This is an alloy made with four percent beryllium. It's as strong as carbon steel and holds a fine, sharp edge."

"Clever," Koriolis said with a nod of approval.

Before their eyes, a strip of blue leather manifested and wound around the copper sword's hilt. With great dignity, Indra presented the weapon to Iselde. "Will this suffice?"

Iselde took it from his hands and brandished it with a few experimental swipes through the hot desert air. "It's well balanced." She swung it again then tested the blade against the hem of her tunic. The fabric parted. "It's sharp." She bared her pointed teeth in a vicious smile and nodded. "Now let's see how well it holds up in battle."

"Because they're here," Koriolis added before he turned to face the oncoming horde. Hefting Asi, he raced forward with a battle cry. Behind him came Indra, his iconic thunderbolt raised and ready for slaughter in one hand a battleaxe in the other, and Iselde, wielding her new copper sword in one hand and her other hand open, claws unsheathed. Behind them, Indra's conquered people attempted the same ferocity, but few had any passion for the battle. They simply wanted to survive.

The armed might of Arigoz swarmed around them. Swords rose and fell in ceaseless, uneven rhythm amid shrill war cries, grunts, and screams of pain. A hailstorm of arrows took flight and were incinerated before they landed. The desert wind picked up and swirled, throwing sand in the enemy's eyes and scouring any exposed skin. Djinni warriors teleported in and out, close and far, some escaping before an invader's blade drew blood. The djinni horde from Arigoz surrounded the three immortal warriors as they attempted to protect the few men remaining of Indra's force.

"Enough!" Indra shouted. "This is ridiculous."

And everything went still, except for the three immortals.

"I will not countenance such slaughter, or there will be none left to rule," he snapped.

"Then let's get this over with," Koriolis said.

"Isn't this taking undue advantage?" Iselde asked.

Indra snorted, then quipped, "All's fair in love and war."

Koriolis rolled his eyes at the cliché. "Ugh."

Iselde shrugged and stabbed her blade between the ribs of a soldier frozen next to her. The djinn's eyes widened in horror. Awareness slowly faded from them as his blood drained away. A low gurgle rattled from his lungs and open mouth, then his body collapsed.

"Too easy," Iselde muttered under her breath. "This is not honorable."

Regardless of the dubious honor of slaughter, the three immortals methodically prowled through the frozen army, lopping off heads and piercing hearts as they went from soldier to soldier.

"Keep two alive!" Indra ordered.

Iselde paused, shrugged, and decapitated the soldier in front of her.

"This one looks like an officer," Koriolis said, scanning the man's gold sash and other accoutrements denoting high rank.

"Spare him," Indra ordered. "I need one more."

Koriolis knocked the incapacitated officer to the ground and hogtied him with the sash from his own uniform. He tore a strip of cloth from the officer's lavishly embroidered tunic and used that to gag him.

Iselde selected a lanky soldier. "He looks like a good runner."

"He'll serve as my courier," Indra said. He grinned. "Someone will have to go into Arigoz and inform the emperor of his army's crushing defeat."

"The Djarian emperor will probably kill him for bringing the bad news," Koriolis commented.

Indra shrugged and lopped off another soldier's head. The carcass crumpled to the ground. "That's not my problem."

"You're rather cavalier about this."

"I prefer the term *efficient*."

Indra glanced over his shoulder at the pitiful remainder of his ragtag army huddling against the dome. "I should have realized they'd be worthless in a war."

"They're a newly conquered people, mainly villagers, slaves, farmers, and merchants," Koriolis pointed out. "It's not like they have been trained for battle. They certainly have no great love for you."

Indra threw him a look of confidence or arrogance: Koriolis wasn't certain which it was. "They will. I'll make their lives better than what they had before."

"What they had before was the drudgery of slavery or the luxury of slave owners." Koriolis watched another soldier's body collapse and moved on to the next. "No matter how much improved some of those people's lives will be, they'll resent you for imposing new circumstances upon them. It'll take a generation, maybe two, to become something more legitimate than a foreign usurper in their eyes."

"Have experience with that, do you?" Indra retorted as he withdrew his blade from a soldier's chest. He glanced at Iselde who moved with speedy efficiency, leaving a wake of bodies behind her. "She's beating us."

"And not to be underestimated," Koriolis murmured.

Pressing his lips together in a firm line of concentration, Indra redoubled his efforts to catch up with and surpass Iselde's lethal progress. By the time Arigoz's army had been dispatched, the three of them were sweating, filthy, and tired. Flies buzzed in ferocious swarms over the carcasses. The putrid stench of blood and loosened sphincters hovered in the hot air.

Indra and Koriolis collected the two prisoners and dragged them to the dome where Iselde waited for them. She raised her hand in a languid move. The surface of the black glass rippled. "Do you want to go inside, or shall I dismantle it?"

Indra considered the options for a couple of seconds. "Leave it up for now. It will keep my people safe while we go into Arigoz."

"I thought you were going to send him" —Koriolis gestured toward the skinny soldier— "as your courier."

Indra rubbed his nose. "I changed my mind. I'll ride into the city in a show of force."

"A show of force?" Iselde echoed. "There are three of us, plus your two captives."

Indra swept his dripping sword across the would-be courier's throat. The djinn gurgled then crumpled to the ground like the rest. "Nope, just one captive." He ran his gaze over the djinn's clothing. "And judging by what he's wearing, he's highly ranked."

That djinn, intuiting that the conqueror spoke of him, growled in fury. Indra looked at him then returned his gaze to the fae. "Well, I don't truly *need* him. I *am* a god."

"He looks like he'll be more trouble than he's worth," Iselde commented.

"Decision made!" the god chirped with a vicious grin. Turning to Koriolis, he said, "He's all yours."

Koriolis lunged, pulling the highly ranked djinn to him and burying his fangs into the officer's neck. He drank deeply, reveling in the djinn's powerful blood as his own flesh absorbed it. When the djinn's heartbeat slowed, he pulled away then decapitated him. He let the body fall and wiped his mouth on his sleeve.

Iselde looked at him, eyebrows raised in silent query.

He explained, "I didn't kill him by draining him of his life-blood or eating his soul."

"Semantics," she said. "He would have died from blood loss."

"Sometimes technicalities make all the difference. What matters is that I did not kill him *while* drinking his blood."

Iselde shook her head and averted her gaze.

As though the conversation had taken no tangent, Indra said, "I do think we ought to look the part, however."

"The part?" Iselde raised her eyebrows again, turning to meet his manic gaze.

"Yes, of conquering royalty." Indra made a sweeping gesture with his arm in a motion meant to encompass the three of them. "We look like vagabonds, not royals."

"I have no desire to rule over the djinn," Iselde said.

"*You* won't be. But a king cannot be accompanied by peasants."

"Iselde and I are here for a purpose, and that purpose is not to conquer Djaria," Koriolis reminded him. He looked at Iselde and fixed her gaze with his. "We'll accompany Indra into the city and hunt down the demons. We'll let him deal with taking over the local government."

Iselde shrugged, not particularly caring. She would not mind if they killed every last djinn in the entire realm.

Koriolis disliked her apathy, but that was not the time to address it. With a light mental touch, he realized how weary she was. Having summoned water and holding it, having formed the glass sphere and holding it, and sustaining ventilation and temperature for those trapped inside the sphere drained her. "Indra."

"Yes?"

"Can you clean us up and apparate us to the city gates?"

The god's teeth flashed in a bright smile. "Ask and you shall receive!"

Koriolis rolled his eyes. "Ugh."

Indra disappeared. After a long moment, he rematerialized in the exact spot he'd left. "I've located just the place."

"And—"

"Makeovers for everyone!" Indra crowed. He waved his arms in a complicated gesture that Koriolis assumed was merely distracting and meaningless showmanship. A moment later his skin felt refreshed. Seconds after that, bright, finely woven cotton and supple leather enveloped his body. Low boots encased his feet.

Indra's costume consisted of a long-sleeved brocaded tunic belted at the waist. Elaborate earrings dangled from each lobe, an anklet with small bells encircled one ankle, and a heavy ruby pendant dangled from a thick chain which hung from his neck. His long black hair hung in orderly coils that looked to have been oiled, and a vermillion headband held those coiffed locks in place. Koriolis realized he was garbed in much the same fashion, although the predominant color of his outfit was deep blue.

"What do you think?" Indra asked, eyes bright as he grinned.

"This is ridiculous," Iselde replied as she looked at the white tunic that flowed over a full, gathered skirt of bright blue. Both items were made of fine muslin. Gold and ivory jewelry decorated her from head to toe. Low boots encased her feet, too.

"Ah, I loved the Gupta period," Indra said. "No other nation could rival India at that time" —he paused— "although China came close."

"The Chinese would beg to differ," Koriolis said.

"These clothes are not in the least practical," Iselde complained. "I can hardly fight like this."

Indra turned a pained expression upon her. "*Ladies* aren't supposed to fight. Your clothing is suitable for the most aristocratic of ladies."

She bared her pointed teeth at him. "I'm no helpless lady."

Indra looked at Koriolis who shrugged and said as he adjusted the belt from which Asi hung, "She's not helpless."

"Well, later period styles are more restrictive," Indra waved his hand. "Lots of elegant drapery, lots of jewelry."

Iselde huffed. "Fine."

Indra raised his eyebrows. "You don't think I'm going to dress you in something Greek or Roman? That's even worse suited to you. Traditional Chinese and Japanese clothes for women are elegant but not exactly amenable to an active lifestyle."

Iselde frowned at him, unsure as to what he meant by "active lifestyle."

He continued speaking. "And forget about dressing you like Boudica. No elegance there. Those people were uncouth savages." He paused. "Come to think of it, the East India Tea Company were all savages, too."

Iselde blinked and wondered, *Who's Boudica?* She raised her hand to forestall any further justification for the way he'd dressed her. "Enough. I'll make do."

"Good," he said with a curt nod. "Take my hands. It's easier this way now that I know where I'm going."

They obliged, each grasping one of his hands. The air cracked behind them as it snapped into the vacuum they left behind. A moment later they materialized in the center of an empty, sun-drenched room. Dressed stone walls and a floor tiled in a bright mosaic reflected the day's heat.

"Odd," Koriolis muttered under his breath at the absence of any furniture.

Iselde merely looked around and said nothing, wondering why Indra hadn't suggested apparating them from the river gorge to Arigoz at the outset. She decided against asking him, figuring it wasn't worth the effort or the annoyance because she guessed the Indian god had wanted to conquer Djaria in grand style with vast armies and lots of pomp and glory. *Vain creature.*

"This way," said Indra as he crossed the small room and put his palm against the wooden door.

Iselde and Koriolis exchanged looks and fell into step behind him as he pushed the door open and marched into a corridor.

CHAPTER 25

"INTRUDER!"

"Well, that didn't take long," Koriolis remarked.

"Don't fret," Indra said, throwing up a hand. The palace guard who sounded the alarm froze in place.

"Shall I kill him?" Iselde asked.

"Not necessary," he replied and continued walking.

As they proceeded, servants and guards sounded the alarm. Each in turn found themselves frozen and helpless to prevent the intruders from passing through. Within a few minutes, the trio found themselves standing in front of a pair of tall doors. A pair of armed guards barred the way, aiming their steel-tipped spears at the intruders.

"Let us through," Indra ordered.

"No one enters, except by the emperor's command," one of the guards replied.

Hearing the thud of boots headed their way, Iselde looked over her shoulder and hissed, "We have no time to spare."

"Let us through or die," Koriolis said, his cold voice sibilant and his serrated smile chilling.

"Fae!" snarled one guard.

"Demon!" gasped the other.

"Close enough," Koriolis said. He lunged toward the djinn closest to him, snatching the spear from his hands and tossing it aside. He hauled the man to him and bit down, fangs piercing his carotid artery. The man cried out and thrashed but could not break Koriolis' hold.

As Koriolis took action, so did Iselde. In a blur of speed, she tore the spear from the djinn's hands, knocked it aside, and swiped the copper blade across his throat.

Indra pushed the doors open. "Fun time's over. Let's not tarry, you two."

Koriolis let the dying djinn fall to the floor. Iselde wiped her blade on the dead guard's clothing. They followed Indra into the throne room where the Djarian emperor held audience.

"Stop them!" the emperor shouted.

Again, Indra exerted his power and froze everyone in the room, except the emperor. Koriolis closed the doors and barred them shut.

"Bring him to me," Indra ordered.

Iselde, seeing Koriolis otherwise occupied with securing the entrances to the throne room, stalked across the expanse and approached the emperor. She gestured toward Indra and said, "I suggest you do as he commands."

"Never!" the Djarian emperor shouted, drawing the ceremonial dagger sheathed at his hip.

Iselde punched him in the gut with one fist and knocked the dagger from his hand with the other. "Don't be stupid."

He wheezed and jabbed a fist at her, catching a glancing blow. She hissed and punched him again. Koriolis returned to Indra's side.

"Try that again and I'll gut you with my claws."

"You might as well," Indra said. "He's not going to live much longer anyway."

"Then what are you waiting for?" she asked as she grabbed the emperor's arm, her claws pricking through the rich fabric and drawing blood. With a grunt, she began to drag him toward Indra, preventing him from apparating. He shouted and struggled against her hold, breathing heavily, but he could not out-muscle a fae, even a female. Pulling both the emperor's upper arms behind him, claws digging in, Iselde said, "Your turn."

Indra touched the tip of his index finger against the emperor's chest. The djinn's breath seized and his eyes widened in terror. Exhausted, Iselde did not notice her grip relax.

"I'll ask this once. Do you cede your throne to me?"

The emperor's lips peeled back from his teeth in a vicious snarl of rage as he wrenched himself from Iselde's loosened grasp and lurched forward in an effort to collide with the Indian god and, perhaps, topple him. Indra took a step backward, out of the infuriated emperor's reach. Koriolis darted forward to take him in hand and restrain him. Feeling the pull of exhaustion, Iselde stepped aside. *You hold the bloated fool.*

"I'll take that as a no," Indra said and shrugged. He lifted his head and leveled a sweeping gaze at all those within the room, people frozen and unable to voice protest or concern yet aware of everything that was happening. "This self-indulgent fool—" he poked the emperor's bulging belly "—is no longer your emperor. By right of might, I, Indra, am now your sovereign king. You will bow before me, swear your fealty to me, and obey me. My word will be your law." His eyes narrowed. "And I do not tolerate mutiny or sedition."

"Not a fan of free speech?" Koriolis murmured.

"This isn't your United States of America," Indra replied.

"Fair point."

"Would you like to do the honors?" the usurper offered.

Koriolis pressed a finger to a wet spot on the emperor's sleeve where Iselde's claws had pierced through the fabric and blood welled. He brought his fingertip to his tongue and tasted the emperor's blood. He shook his head. "No, you must kill him. Besides, his blood is weak."

Indra pulled a knife from his belt and pressed the tip to the emperor's chest. "Djaria is *mine.*"

With a brutal punch, he thrust the knife through the emperor's rib cage and into his heart. The djinn gasped, then gurgled, then sagged in Koriolis' tight grip. He let the carcass drop to the floor.

"I will release you one at a time. You will swear fealty to me and leave in peace. Or you will die," Indra announced.

"Are we finished here?" Koriolis asked.

"I've got this," Indra replied with a deranged smile. Turning his attention to Iselde, he said, "If you don't mind, hold my people safe for a while longer. I'll free them tomorrow after I've got things settled here in the palace."

"Until dawn," she replied.

Koriolis held out his hand. "Let's go hunting, beloved. We have demons to kill."

She placed her hand in his and nodded, then trembled as he sent energy coursing across the mate bond to revive her flagging strength. Together they left Indra to finish usurping the throne and crown of Djaria.

CHAPTER 26

THE LAST RAYS OF THE SETTING SUN DISSOLVED AS Iselde and Koriolis exited the palace.

"We'll not blend in dressed like this," Iselde commented.

Although Koriolis agreed, he did not believe their garb mattered in the execution of their duty. Lifting his face, he inhaled deeply. As the air rushed into his lungs, he dissected the scents: sweat, oils, perfumes, dirt, dung, cooking, and more. Faint, so faint, were the tiniest of particles that sparked a hot, focused hunger in him. A growl rumbled deep in his chest. Turning slowly, he took delicate sniffs, scenting the air and running it over the back of his tongue to taste the spoor of his prey and determine a direction.

Iselde felt her mate's body go rigid beside her. He stepped forward, focusing as he prowled. She followed, noticing how the ordinary citizens of Djaria and slaves alike stepped aside to give him wide berth. Though infused with their own fiery magic, the djinns recognized an apex predator when they saw one, despite his outlandish garb.

Koriolis paused, sniffed, adjusted his direction, and resumed following the trail of his prey's scent as it strengthened. After several blocks, he had locked on the scent and strode with assured purpose. Despite her growing exhaustion, Iselde stepped lightly like the skilled predator she was, following closely, her pale hair gleaming like a beacon in the twilight.

"There," she whispered, catching a flicker of movement in the deepening shadows in the periphery of her vision. "Demons."

Koriolis paused again and sniffed. His lips peeled back from his pointed teeth. "There's a nest of them inside that building."

"Sounds like a good start," Iselde replied.

He glanced at her copper sword. "That might not kill the demons."

She raised an eyebrow. "No, but it will incapacitate them long enough for you to finish them off."

He looked offended as though she'd questioned his prowess.

"Or I could just decapitate them. That's usually effective."

He looked at her. "Burn both the head and heart—*that's* what you need to do to destroy a demon."

"And you know this how?"

He shrugged and quietly drew Asi from its scabbard. "I just know."

Iselde suspected the unicorns had implanted the knowledge within him, but said nothing. Koriolis had already begun creeping forward, sticking to the darkest shadows as he headed toward the building's back door. She followed close behind him. Sensing someone's approach, he went still, blending in with the darkness. Keeping to the shadows close to the building, Iselde froze, too.

"Who's there?" came a sibilant voice. "I can smell you hiding."

Iselde inhaled and took in the scent of a demon, committing it to memory.

"I can see you, fae."

He doesn't scent me, Koriolis thought, sending the comment across the mate bond. *Or he thinks I'm fae.*

But he does smell me. Iselde walked toward the demon whose black eyes focused on the white fall of her hair. "And I see you, demon."

"What a lovely victim," the demon purred as it slinked forward.

Iselde sighed and paused, strategically placing herself. "Don't be predictable."

The demon reared back, offended. "Predictable? That's insulting."

"It's true."

Hissing in outrage, the demon shot forward, never seeing Asi sweep down to part his head from his body. The demon's head landed with a wet, meaty *thud* on the brick pavers. The sickly sweet reek of decay erupted from the body. Both the severed head and body quickly combusted and disintegrated into piles of greasy ash.

"Effective," Iselde commented. "I thought you had to burn the head and heart."

"Very," Koriolis agreed. "And that's always the way it's worked before." He raised Asi and looked at the blade. "Maybe Asi is taking care of that detail." He shrugged. "That's inconvenient if I'm going to assuage my hunger."

"There is that. Those you don't kill with Asi I'll incapacitate with my sword so you can drink."

The door opened. "Uruk? Uruk are you there?"

Koriolis and Iselde heard whimpers from inside the building. They held still as the demon peering out the door squinted against the darkness. They heard an indrawn breath.

"What's that I smell?"

Koriolis stepped forward into the puddle of light spilling through the open door. "Me."

The demon drew back and attempted to slam the door shut, but Koriolis rushed forward. The door slammed back against the wall. Whimpers inside the building curdled into a quickly stifled scream followed by a gurgle, then the wet, sloppy sounds of feasting. Iselde followed Koriolis through the doorway to witness through another open door a demon feeding frenzy. The gorge rose in her throat even as Koriolis impaled the demon on his sword.

In their ravening frenzy, the demons took no notice of the killing just beyond the room in which they devoured the twitching flesh of their prey. The quickly released stench of rot freed Koriolis and Iselde to charge deeper into the building: they now knew the demon's carcass would burn, destroying it completely.

With preternatural speed and precision, Iselde and Koriolis struck. Four more demons fell to Asi before the other demons broke from their feeding frenzy to realize they were in mortal danger.

With bloody hands and fangs, they engaged in battle. Roars and hisses and screams clashed as claws and teeth and blades exacted terrible vengeance for the demons' unknown victim. Weariness causing her to move more slowly and clumsily than usual, Iselde cried out as a demon's filthy claw gouged her upper arm. She switched the sword to her opposite hand and redoubled her efforts to exterminate the infestation. With a roar of outrage at his mate's injury, Koriolis sliced deeply into that demon's thigh. He shoved Iselde back against a wall and positioned himself in front of her, defending his mate with everything he had.

The demon who suffered the laceration leaped backward to regroup, then bellowed a moment later when his flesh erupted in greedy flames. Another moment later, he raced from the building, screaming as fire fully engulfed him. The burning demon collapsed in the street to burn to ashes before anyone even thought to rescue him. Instead, shutters closed and locks engaged in an instinctive effort to keep the danger outside.

After the short but intense battle, nine piles of ash smoldered on the clay tile floor amid viscous puddles of thickening blood, gobbets of flesh, splinters of bone, strands of hair, and scraps of cloth which were all that remained of the demons' main course. Iselde eyed the sword clutched in her mate's right hand. Blood dripped down the fuller groove to the guard. She narrowed her gaze, looking at it more closely.

"The sword is changing."

Lowering Asi, Koriolis blinked as the sound of her voice recalled him from his battle fury. "What?"

"Asi did not have a fuller when Indra gave it to you, but it does now."

Koriolis lifted the blade and peered at it. "Huh. I hadn't noticed." He shrugged. "As long as it works, I don't really care whether it's an Indian khanda, a Roman gladius, a Japanese katana, or an English longsword."

"Fair enough," she murmured. "But the way it's changing gives credence to the legend that Asi is at least somewhat sentient. You'd do well to be careful."

He tilted his head, still looking at the gleaming metal. "I think it will adapt to however it's used."

"Perhaps." She exhaled and took another deep breath. Opening her mouth to speak, another muffled whimper caught her ears. She glanced at the filthy, despoiled table and said, "Our job here isn't finished."

"No," Koriolis agreed.

Together they swept through the building until they found a room where a human and two human-djinn hybrids, all wearing slave collars, quivered in terror as they waited behind a locked door for their turn at the demons' feast. Koriolis directed his power at the iron lock, causing it to rust through and break. After he removed the lock, Iselde opened the door.

"Fae!" the human gasped in horror while cringing against the far wall. The hybrids shivered in another corner of the room.

Iselde stepped aside and gestured toward the open door. "Go."

The three captives scurried out, one of the hybrids pausing to whisper a thank-you before disappearing into the city's tangled streets. Koriolis found a scrap of cloth and wiped Asi's blade clean with it, taking care not to allow the keen edge to touch his skin, lest the sword taste his blood and turn him to ash, too. Settling the sword in its scabbard, he directed Iselde to the kitchen where he hoped to find a bucket of clean water and perhaps some soap. They had no such luck. While Iselde's wound bled and her blood dripped down her arm onto the floor, they gawked at the demons' untidy habits.

"Filthy. Just disgusting," Iselde muttered, thinking of the cold, clean spaces of the northern wastes where she'd simply use snow to clean her arm. But here in the hot, dusty desert of the Djarian empire, there was no snow. She knew of no rivers of clean water flowing near the city either.

"I must sit," she admitted, dropping onto a stool. The copper sword in her other hand clattered to the floor. Her head lolled back and her eyes closed.

"Iselde!" Koriolis dropped to his knees beside her. He examined the long gash running down her upper arm. Jumping to his feet, he tore open cabinets and rummaged through shelves and found nothing useful. Cursing, he cast his consciousness deep beneath the floor into the earth, searching for a ley line he could tap. He found one, but touching its power delivered a terrible shock. He doubled over and vomited. Spitting the vile residue, he lurched to his feet, picking up the copper sword as he stood. He shoved the sword under his belt, angling it so the blade wouldn't get in the way when he stooped to gather Iselde in his arms.

He carried her from the building, away from the stench of demons and blood and offal, scanning the buildings he passed. He saw the sign for an apothecary and rushed over. The door was closed. With both arms filled, he kicked the door. No one answered. He kicked it harder and shouted, "Open up!"

Still, no one answered.

Running on the fumes of frustration and rage, he kicked the door in and entered that building. The thump of feet hitting the floor above them preceded an angry shout of outrage.

"Get out! What are you doing? Get out! I am closed!"

"My mate needs help!" he yelled over the proprietor's shouts.

"Then find a physician!"

Koriolis' black eyes pulsed with a red glow, and several glass bottles on a shelf exploded. The apothecary shrieked and waved his hands.

"Begone! Leave!"

Koriolis directed his fulminating glare at the apothecary. "I need clean water, healing salve, and bandages. Fetch them!"

A few more bottles exploded. The apothecary shrieked again. "*Now!*"

The apothecary fled and reappeared a moment later with a jug of water, a tin of salve, and rolls of linen. He slammed them on the counter. "Here! Take them and go! Never come here again!"

Koriolis bared his teeth at the man and hissed, "Go back upstairs."

"You owe me!"

Koriolis snarled. More bottles exploded.

"Enough, beloved," Iselde whispered, the noise rousing her from the stupor of blood loss and exhaustion.

"I need a chair," he snapped at the apothecary who yet lingered to make sure the intruders left the premises.

The man sighed, realizing that no amount of shouting would deter the black-eyed demon from his goal or evict him from his shop. Muttering deprecations and complaining about the economic loss of his wares and supplies, he retreated to the back of the shop and returned carrying a stool. He set it down and headed back to return with a bowl for the water water and a clean rag. Setting them on the nearby counter, he said, "Here. Do what you need, then *go*."

"Thank you," Koriolis replied with grudging civility. He used his foot to move the stool to a better place then lowered Iselde onto it. She leaned against the shelves behind her. With tender care belying his recent violence, he cleaned her arm, smeared ointment over the laceration, and bound the wound shut, wishing he had silk and a silver needle to stitch the wound closed.

"It will heal soon," she whispered, blinking slowly.

"You're weakened," he stated.

"I am fatigued," she admitted, wanting to release her hold on the glass dome, the pool of water, and the flow of air she was forcing through the dome's ventilation system.

Koriolis glared at the apothecary who stood nearby and glared at them. "Where is the nearest inn?"

"Do I look like a guide?" the apothecary sneered.

"Shall I burn down your home?" Koriolis snapped. Flames popped into existence and danced on the countertop.

The djinn gasped and tried to wrest control over the fire, but could not break his unwanted customer's command. "Have mercy, my lord!"

"Where's the nearest inn?" Koriolis repeated through gritted teeth.

The apothecary raised a trembling hand and pointed. "Go that way, four blocks, then turn right and go another three blocks."

"Thank you," Koriolis forced himself to say.

"Are you going to pay for the damage you've done?" the apothecary demanded.

Koriolis growled and stiffened at the demand, but the shards and splinters of glass scattered throughout the shop flew through the air to collect in a pile on the floor. The pile turned viscous and fluid, quivering in an array of iridescent colors until it began to sink and flatten. As the molten glass oozed into a shallow puddle, it turned yellow and steamed as it hardened and transmogrified into metal: *gold*.

"When it cools, it's yours," Koriolis said. He wiped the sweat from his forehead.

I didn't know you could do that.

Koriolis' lips peeled back from his teeth as he smoothed back his mate's hair. *Neither did I.*

The apothecary's red eyes gleamed with avarice. Upper lip lifted in a sneer, he hissed, "Get out."

Koriolis left and hoped he could get a room at the inn without resorting to violence. *That would make for a nice change of pace.*

CHAPTER 27

ENSCONCED BETWEEN CLEAN, IF THREADBARE, blankets on a lumpy mattress, Iselde dozed. The imperative of upholding her promise to Indra and staying aware of her surroundings prevented her from drifting off into a deep, restful, healing sleep. She lay, eyes closed, with her arm cleaned, bandaged, and throbbing with pain, while Koriolis paced the small room.

"Go," she muttered.

He paused midstep. "What?"

"I can feel your hunger. Go."

"I cannot leave you."

"Have I given you the impression I cannot care for myself?" she shot back, opening those cobalt eyes.

He shook his head. "No, of course not. But this is Djaria, a land where every djinn would kill his mother to capture a high fae such as you."

"No djinn with any intelligence would dare touch me," she said.

He gave her a small smile, offering a glimpse of his fangs. "Ah, beloved, that's where your optimism puts you in danger, crediting these greedy djinn with a modicum of intelligence."

She snorted. It was a weak snort. She repeated, "I can feel your hunger."

Koriolis practically vibrated where he stood. "Now that it's been … *activated* … it's … it's a compulsion most difficult to deny. Not a hunger, exactly."

Her gaze sharpened. "A compulsion?"

"It's not so much an urge to fill my belly, but to *kill*."

Iselde probed further. "A general urge to kill?"

"An overpowering urge to kill demons," he admitted. "It's as if I cannot rest—will not be able to rest—until I have eliminated the presence of demons from all of Djaria."

Iselde pursed her lips and pondered his admission. "It's not *as if*." She scooted into a sitting position. "What you described is *exactly it*. The unicorns laid a compulsion upon you."

Koriolis' nostrils flared.

"I knew a fae who was similarly bespelled. He nearly depopulated the Quol."

"The Quol?" His eyebrows lifted. "Few fae even dare step foot in there, but to go in and hunt its native population?" He shook his head at the sheer folly or hubris of such a mission.

She nodded. "I was impressed, to be honest, but dared say nothing of the kind at the time. He was cocky, prideful."

"And what happened?"

"With the Quoli nearly exterminated, Uncle Uberon was able to push back the Quol's encroaching boundaries."

"He never mentioned …" Koriolis muttered under his breath. Shaking himself, he asked, "Has the desert been spreading?"

Iselde blinked in surprise. "I haven't paid any attention as to whether Djaria has been expanding its boundaries. That would explain the unicorns' urgency, especially if they've been losing ground to both djinns and demons."

"Something to consider," he agreed and glanced at the darkness beyond the room's small window.

"Go," she said. "You will know no peace until you have completed your task."

"I cannot leave you." She opened her mouth to object again, but he forestalled her. Raising his hand, he said, "You are exhausted and injured. Until you are healed, I will resist this compulsion."

"Tomorrow morning then," she relented. "Tomorrow morning I will let the desert return to its natural state and free Indra's people. Then I shall heal quickly."

"Not until I get some food into you," he said.

"Have you coin?"

Koriolis tugged at the gold armband wrapped around one bicep. She noticed the other was missing. "I have this. It will be sufficient to overcome the innkeeper's reluctance to host two fae."

"You already gave him one?"

"I did."

"Greedy."

He nodded. "We've little recourse, though. At least Indra thought to ensure we were appropriately accessorized."

Iselde looked at the gold bracelets circling her wrists. "Good point. I would, however, prefer more practical clothing."

"As would I. Tomorrow we'll go shopping."

"Assuming we find a shopkeeper willing to transact business with us," she pointed out.

"Assuming that, yes. Otherwise, I may need you to draw gold from the earth—"

She interrupted, "Or you may need to impose your own alchemy upon broken glass."

He gave her a sharp-toothed grin. "Or that."

"Go," she said once more. "Procure food and drink for us both. And bathwater if there's any to be had."

He nodded and crossed the room to stand beside the bed. He pulled the copper sword free and set it beside her. "Just in case."

She nodded and lay her hand over the hilt.

He moved to the door and wrapped a hand around the doorknob. Meeting her tired gaze, he cautioned, "Let no one in."

She gave him a small smile. "Of course not, beloved."

With another nod, he let himself out of the room. Iselde sighed and resisted the urge to fling off the covers and go prowling. She knew her body and knew herself to be dangerously exhausted. If any djinn intruded, she'd be hard pressed to defend herself with any efficacy. Her empty belly growled. She hoped Koriolis would return soon.

Long minutes passed with Iselde's belly protesting its empty state with growing vigor. Her breath caught in her chest as heavy footsteps slowed and paused outside the door. Koriolis moved like a cat, so she knew it wasn't him. Drawing on the fumes of her power, she thickened the air between the door and the bed. The thickened air would serve as a temporary hold, an unexpected obstacle to delay whoever might dare to invade her privacy long enough for her to take decisive action.

The footsteps did not resume. Her focus sharpened.

Air the consistency of water rippled when a djinn apparated between the door and the bed. Iselde flung back the covers and reached for the copper sword. Disoriented by the trap and floundering in the congealed air, the djinn still managed to apparate out of the room before the keen blade pierced his flesh.

"Damn it," Iselde hissed. She wiped her forearm across her forehead. It came away wet with sudden sweat. Her arms trembled with exhaustion. She panted from exertion as though she'd run a hundred leagues. Her weakness infuriated her. "Damn it."

Come back soon, beloved.

After a hissed argument and an appeal to the innkeeper's avarice, Koriolis parted with the other armband and a jeweled ring before the innkeeper agreed to provide food, drink, water for washing, soap, and linens and dispatched a servant to fetch everything. Fuming at the usury, he stalked after the servant to ensure he got his money's worth. Entering the kitchen incited another argument with him having to justify his presence and threatening the cook with violence before he would agree to fill a tray with food and drink. Bearing the tray, he again followed the servant to ensure that person fetched clean water, clean linens, and a small tin of soft soap.

It all took far too long for his peace of mind.

Disturbance rippled across the matebond. Koriolis urged the lazy servant to move faster. The servant gave him a resentful glare over his shoulder and continued at the same plodding pace. Finally—*finally!*—they stood at the door to the room he had rented for the night.

"Beloved," he called out. "I am here."

"Come," her muffled reply filtered through the door.

"Will you open the door?"

His keen ears heard a whisper of power sliding away followed by the light thump of her feet on the wooden floor. She shuffled across the floor, the slow scuff of her footsteps telling him more loudly than words of her perilous exhaustion. A long moment later, the lock turned and the door opened.

"Set the bucket on the floor under the window," he instructed the servant as they entered the room.

The servant did as he was ordered, letting the bucket land hard on the floor so the water slopped over the brim. Koriolis growled and raised his hand to reprimand the resentful djinn, but Iselde set her hand on his other arm.

"No," she said. "It's not worth it."

He lowered his hand. As the servant passed by on his way out the door, Koriolis grabbed his arm. Yanking him close, he snarled in a low, menacing voice, "Bring up another bucket of water immediately or I'll hunt … you … down."

The djinn's red eyes widened in terror, realizing he'd antagonized the fae-looking demon a little too much. "My lord fae."

Koriolis released him, and the djinn scurried from the room and its dangerous occupant. He filled a plate with food and handed it to Iselde, clenching his jaw when he saw the way her hands trembled beneath the weight of the loaded plate. He steadied the plate and helped her lower it to her lap without spilling. He handed her a fork. "What happened while I was out?"

Iselde stabbed a morsel of meat and brought it to her mouth. Spicy flavor exploded on her tongue. She chewed, swallowed, and finally deigned to answer him. Koriolis' jaw remained clenched throughout the brief recounting. When she finished, he growled, "I'll kill him."

Iselde shook her head. "No. I am weak now, but will heal and be restored to my usual strength by this time tomorrow."

"That does not matter. He attempted to—"

"Whatever the djinn attempted to do, he did not succeed." She sighed. "I doubt he'll try again."

Koriolis rubbed the back of his neck, clearly uneasy with her dismissal of the danger she'd successfully thwarted.

"I will not leave your side until you are restored," he vowed.

"But the compulsion?"

His upper lip lifted in a snarl. "I am no puppet to dance to any unicorn's strings."

She nodded, a single dip of her chin. "Eat, beloved. You must remain strong for me."

He sighed, filled a plate, and ate.

CHAPTER 28

BEAMS OF SUNSHINE STREAMED THROUGH THE room's small window, brightening the room sufficiently to wake Iselde from a deep slumber. Blinking her eyes against the early morning light, she sighed from her position within the shelter of her mate's embrace and released her hold on the protective dome shielding Indra's conquered people. She let her hold on the pond dissolve, and the water quickly drained through the porous sand. The ventilation tunnels collapsed, though the wind still blew above the ground. The relief from the constant strain of retaining that power and control made her sigh.

"Is it done?" Koriolis murmured from behind her.

"Aye."

He rolled aside and sat up. "Let me check your arm."

She obeyed, holding her arm out for his inspection. He grunted in dismay that the wound had not yet healed.

"A bit more time," she said. "With proper nourishment and a little time, I shall be fine."

Koriolis looked at the remains of their supper. They'd eaten their fill the night before and little remained of the small feast.

"We need not stay here," Iselde said. "And I doubt the inn-keeper will allow us to spend another night here."

"Given enough gold he would," Koriolis commented, his expression sour.

"Given their greed, djinns are not so different from humans," Iselde remarked.

"I do not think any race is exempt from greed."

"No, probably not." She kept a neutral tone. "But I'd prefer not to stay here anyway."

Koriolis concurred. "Then we shall leave." He rose and fetched the buckets of remaining water, soap, and linens. They washed and dressed in the outlandish clothing in which Indra had garbed them. Iselde was tempted to draw upon the power of the ley lines running far below the earth's surface to man-ifest new clothes, but Koriolis forestalled her: "At least wait until your strength is restored. Please."

She consented to wait. After all, he'd said *please*.

They gathered their few possessions and headed out. The innkeeper sneered at them as they went out the door and called, "And don't come back!"

Their outlandish clothing and distinctively fae looks garnered gasps of outrage, looks of contempt, and muttered imprecations as they walked through Arigoz's busy streets and pedestrian thoroughfares. Merchants, seeing the fae wore no slave collars, refused to serve them. A few even brandished weapons and uttered threats to make them depart from their stores.

"I'm of half a mind to let Indra deal with these people and leave them to the predation of demons," Koriolis said when they seated themselves on a park bench so Iselde could rest.

"Did you not have dealings with djinns before your exile?" Iselde inquired.

"No," he replied. "I had little reason to venture beyond the Seelie or Unseelie Courts—not that I was ever welcome in the Seelie Court."

"The djinn used to be more accepting of the different races, but that was millennia ago." She shrugged. "I'm not entirely sure when that changed. I was content—happy even—in the northern wastes far from here." She huffed a small laugh of self-deprecation. "I have never even visited Uberon at his new castle."

"New castle?" Koriolis echoed, his interest piqued by the comment.

"Oh, you probably don't know," she said. "After Mogren conquered the Unseelie Court and Uberon's castle collapsed, he moved north. There's a northern town by the name of Donshae where he raised a new castle and established a new court and took his new bride."

"New bride? I have a stepmother?"

"Yes, and siblings." Her lips curled in a small smile. "I hear Uberon is a doting father."

Koriolis snorted. "Doting" was the last word he would have used to describe the powerful, but cold and ruthless, Unseelie King.

"The gargoyles serve him," she added.

Incredulous, he turned to face her. "The gargoyles? They *serve* him?"

She nodded.

"Gargoyles serve no one."

She smiled again. "They deemed him worthy of their service, and by all accounts, he is a fair and wise king."

Koriolis shook his head again in disbelief. "That does not sound like the Unseelie King I knew."

"Perhaps he recognized where he erred and sought to avoid making those mistakes again."

"My father—the male I knew—never admitted to any error and never considered that he might even be in error."

Iselde shrugged. "It appears we both find fault with our parents."

Koriolis thought of having the enigmatic oracle as a parent and repressed a shudder of distaste. Another thought struck him: "Who is your father, Iselde?"

She pursed her lips for a moment then gave him the same answer she'd given him before: "I do not know."

He took her hand—cool and dry despite the desert heat—in his and gave it a light squeeze. "You are no hybrid of fae and something else."

She shook her head. "No, I am fully fae." Raising her other hand, she traced her fingertips over the jewels and silver tracery embedded in her skin, the outward sign of a truly mated fae. She let her hand fall to her lap and sighed. "It does not matter."

Koriolis disagreed. At least in the Djarian Empire, bloodlines did matter. He wished Indra good luck in subduing the empire's population and bringing them to heel.

"There they are!"

Koriolis and Iselde looked up, their gazes arrowing in on the shout. A group of belligerent-looking djinns headed their way. They carried knives and cudgels. Koriolis glanced at his mate's face. Her expression of dull resignation sent hot fury sizzling through his veins. They stood and positioned themselves back to back. Koriolis released her hand.

"They're behind us, too," Iselde said, pitching her voice low.

Koriolis' lips peeled back from his teeth as he drew Asi. "Can you fight?"

Iselde rolled her shoulders. "I am much recovered."

He understood that to mean she hadn't fully recovered, but felt sufficiently well to slaughter some stupid djinns. "Open the bond." An instant later he felt the connection between them pulse. "Use my strength as you must."

The connection pulsed again, a sign of her acceptance, although she said, "This is dangerous."

"You are my beloved," he replied as she lifted the copper sword.

"And you are mine," she replied, her voice a soft whisper. "And I find I thirst to spill djinni blood."

"Then let us drink." Koriolis lunged, attacking the nearest djinn.

With ululating war cries, the djinns leaped forward. Iselde gritted her teeth as she called upon every drop of strength, speed, and agility she possessed to meet the attack. Her copper sword glinted like fire as it slashed and struck. She hissed whenever one of the mob got in a lucky swipe or stab. Her skin sizzled wherever a ferrous blade touched.

Iselde began to falter, then felt a bright, icy swell of strength pour into her through the matebond. She gasped as it flooded her body and soul, igniting a strange hunger that made her want to wallow in its cold brilliance and absorb it until she had drained its source. With adamantine control, she clamped down on the flow, squeezing it to a trickle sufficient to energize and strengthen her while she defended herself and her mate's back even as he defended himself and her back.

"Well, we cannot undo that," she said as the last djinn fell to the ground, sliding off her blade with a grotesque sucking noise.

"No," he agreed, understanding she meant the intimate connection between them, the strength they now shared. He wiped his bloody sword on one of the fallen attacker's clothing. He sheathed the weapon and crouched down to rummage through the djinn's pockets and clothing for any valuables. He found a few silver coins and moved to the next dead djinn.

Pragmatic, Iselde did the same, quickly looting the bodies while passersby gaped in horror and appalled fury. One young brave approached, fists clenched.

"Come no closer, or you'll join them," she warned.

The young tough paused, red eyes widening. "Murderer!"

She said nothing and pocketed the coins she'd managed to lift from the fresh corpse.

"How do you feel?" Koriolis inquired.

"Hungry."

He bared his teeth. "Let's go hunting."

Iselde tore the bandage off her arm, the wound had scarred over. Baring her teeth at the growing crowd, she fell into step beside Koriolis. Before she'd gone a handful of steps, the small hairs at the back of her neck prickled in warning. She swiveled on one heel, sword drawn. The djinn who apparated right behind them swung his knife downward, but not soon enough to avoid being skewered by Iselde's copper sword. With a groan and a gurgle of blood that dribbled down his bearded chin, the djinn crumpled.

"Idiot," she sneered. Koriolis touched her hand. She glanced at him. "Yes?"

"That way," he murmured and veered in another direction.

She followed close behind, trusting his leadership. When he sprang into a run, she kept pace, her strides long and her footsteps light. His hunting instinct and the compulsion that ruled him aimed true. They crashed through a door where yet another nest of demons made their home. Startled by the attack, the demons soon fell to the fae warriors who preyed upon them. Before the last one fell, however, Koriolis bit deeply into the demon's neck, piercing the carotid artery. He drank in greedy gulps as the demon's blood and its power flooded into him and, by connection, through the matebond into Iselde. She cried out at the sudden influx of the fiery, corrosive power.

When he had drained the demon nearly to death, Koriolis dropped the limp body and wiped his mouth. He plunged Asi into the nearly dead djinn's soft belly. Within moments, the demon's carcass flared, burned, charred, and disintegrated into greasy ashes. He smiled, eyes blazing. "*That* felt good."

Iselde couldn't really say the same, but she agreed that the surge of energy was welcome. "Is your thirst satisfied?"

He took a breath and considered her question. "Not quite."

"Then we continue to hunt."

CHAPTER 29

THEY SWEPT THROUGH ARIGOZ LIKE A PLAGUE, calling upon their stolen power to sustain them, heal them, and boost their strength, speed, and prowess as they exterminated demons and demon hybrids. In the fulfillment of Koriolis' mission, they liberated fewer captives than anticipated, for the demons had quickly taken to feasting on their prey rather than rationing themselves to avoid detection and capture by local authorities more concerned with recovering stolen property than compassion for the demons' victims.

Word of the two fae spread throughout the city. Those captives freed from predation fled from them as though they, too, feared to come beneath the sharp blades that slaughtered their demon captors. One merchant whose two sons had been captured by demons—although only one was freed—showed his gratitude for the boy's liberation by outfitting the two fae in garb less outlandish (and cleaner) than what they wore. Iselde and Koriolis thanked him with grave formality then killed his half-demon concubine, destroying any gratitude he might have held for them.

As Iselde and Koriolis hunted the Djarian capital, they caught glimpses of the new emperor's soldiers patrolling the streets and beating down rebellious djinns in skirmishes erupting throughout the city. The soldiers loyal to the usurper were distinguished by the Gupta-era clothing Indra had them wear. They avoided any engagement with the two fae. Iselde presumed they were under Indra's orders not to engage with them. After several weeks of successful hunting that both depopulated the city of demons and spared the very djinns who hated them, Iselde and Koriolis returned to the palace.

A new major domo gaped in astonishment as they passed through the imposing portal. Servants and guards scattered as they prowled through the grand corridor. Sycophant nobles raised an outcry at the faes' presence. From his golden throne where he held a daily audience, Indra grinned.

"Welcome back!"

Koriolis bowed and asked, "How goes the hostile takeover?"

"Pretty much as I would expect," Indra replied and gestured for a servant to offer them wine. "I'm winning."

"I never doubted it," Koriolis replied, his tone bland. He accepted a goblet and took a sip. "Not bad."

"Eh, not as good as the 1982 Château Mouton Rothschild." He smacked his lips in memory. "Now *that* was a truly excellent vintage."

"We are here—"

"I know why you're here," Indra interrupted. "You'll feast with me this evening and take a well-deserved rest in the palace tonight. Tomorrow morning, off you go to eradicate demons from *my* empire."

"Thank you." Koriolis bowed with all the courtly elegance of a crown prince.

"Oh, and I've set up an account for you both."

"An account?"

"Well, not really an account. More like a large chest. It's half-full already."

"A large chest?" Koriolis echoed.

"Well, you don't think I'm the sort of god-king who lets such exemplary service go unrewarded, do you?"

"We hadn't thought about it," Iselde replied and took a sip of wine. Koriolis was right; it wasn't a bad vintage at all. *The unicorns don't normally offer rewards for jobs well done.*

Koriolis caught the cynical thought and replied mind-to-mind, *Indra's got a history of generosity. We should have expected this.*

"Of course, not. That's why I like you: you're so admirably selfless." Indra took a long gulp from his large goblet. "Anyway, when you finish clearing Djaria of this pestilence, there will be a vast fortune waiting for you. You'll have the wherewithal to go anywhere, buy damned near anything, and still have funds left over. I might even appoint you as a governor of one of my country's regions. You could even build a castle!"

"Your generosity is appreciated," Koriolis said.

"I've assigned a small caravan to accompany you on your journey," Indra said. "In addition to the usual beasts of burden and supplies and servants to tend the beasts and cook and whatnot, you'll have a guide and an armed escort."

"We do not need an armed escort," Iselde said.

Indra chuckled. "No, *you* do not need an armed escort, but the caravan and everything that goes with it does."

Iselde responded, "We will travel faster—"

Indra raised his hand. "Ah, ah, ah! I will not tolerate refusal of my generosity."

Accepting the inevitable, Koriolis bowed again and said, "We are honored to accept, Your Majesty."

Satisfaction oozed from Indra's broad smile. He gestured and said, "Bashim will guide you to your room where you may bathe, rest, and refresh yourselves before tonight's feast. I'll have some suitable garments sent to your quarters." A servant scuttled from an out-of-the-way corner to stand beside the two fae. Indra continued, "Now don't be late to dinner. Punctuality is a virtue, especially for the guests of honor."

Indra clapped his hands, and the servant beckoned to the fae to follow him.

In all her long, long life, Iselde had never endured being bathed by servants. However, the giggling djinni women assigned to her would not be deterred. She shifted uncomfortably as feminine hands touched her where none but her mates and she herself had touched her body since she'd graduated from diapers and learned to perform her own personal hygiene.

She didn't like it.

However, Iselde endured the groping intimacy and ignored the whispered comments regarding the hairless state of her body and the sharp claws curving over the tips of her fingers and toes. The servants chattered among themselves in their native language, perhaps not realizing the fae in their care could understand them. They exclaimed at her long, white hair, the silver tracery and blue jewels emblazoned upon her skin, and the long, slender, muscled length of her limbs. Djinni women, Iselde realized, tended toward short stature with full bosoms, rounded limbs, and wide hips. Those bodies, she decided, were meant for bearing and nurturing young. Her body, instead, was built like a weapon, sharp and keen.

When the giggling servants finally departed, Iselde looked at herself in the generously sized mirror. Her hair had been washed, carefully combed and oiled, then coiled and braided and twisted in a complicated arrangement that only the most indolent and pampered of aristocratic ladies would ever contemplate wearing. Djinni ladies, she decided, had abandoned all sense of practicality.

"This is ridiculous," she muttered under her breath as she wiped a hand over the front of her layered skirts. The tip of a claw snagged on the filmy fabric. She carefully worked it free so as not to tear the delicate cloth.

Iselde crossed the room, the many layers of her skirts swishing and softly hissing as the fabric fluttered and floated around her legs. She gently knocked on the door separating her room from Koriolis'. The low murmur of masculine voices filtered through the wooden door.

"Enter," Koriolis called.

She opened the door as the male servants put the finishing touches on Koriolis' djinni finery. She met his eyes and shook her head. "We look ridiculous."

He ignored the departing servants and replied in the fae tongue, "Indeed we do." He shrugged. "We can endure this for one evening."

"Ugh."

"The color suits you," he complimented.

She looked at the pale salmon colored froth of silk and ivory lace draped over her body and grimaced. "Not really suitable for the fearsome Ice Queen."

"Do you really want Indra's guests knowing exactly who you are?"

She scoffed. "Most of Fé-Ree doesn't know I exist. I prefer it that way."

"My point exactly, beloved. The Unseelie King leaves a wake of trembling sycophants wherever he goes. The Erlking is even worse: people *faint* from dread when he crosses their path."

Iselde's head tilted as she considered his words. "I've always rather liked Ishjarta, though."

"I remember him."

"I didn't know you'd met."

He shrugged again. "When Ishjarta and I met, we were more alike than not. We both thought Erlking a self-righteous prick."

"Perhaps."

He redirected the conversation. "Word among the servants is that Ishjarta is a king. I think you mentioned that before. He rules separately from the Erlking?"

She nodded. "He does. Do you remember the kingdom of Fyrgia?"

He rummaged through his memories. "Vaguely. I believe King Mogren carved out a portion of the Seelie Court for the humans arriving into Fé-Ree. There seemed to be a steady trickle of them washing up on shore at that time. They had nowhere to go, so he thought to give them their own territory, if I recall correctly." He shrugged. "I lived in the Unseelie Court and had little to do with humans. It is a human kingdom, right?"

"Yes." Iselde kept the story short: "Fyrgia caused mortal offense. The Erlking took exception. Ishjarta assumed the throne."

He raised an eyebrow. "I'm sure there's a bit more to the story than that."

She shrugged. "I wasn't part of it." She didn't mention she'd learned of what happened from the Archivist during one of his rare visits to the frozen north. Iselde looked out a window. "The worries and tribulations of Fé-Ree generally don't affect me in the northern wastes."

"You prefer it there."

She said, "It is a peaceful place. Clean."

"I wouldn't have considered the northern wastes as *peaceful.*"

She amended her statement, "It is peaceful if you know how to survive."

Koriolis stated the obvious, "And you do." She did not reply, so after a pause, he extended his hand and said, "Then let us survive this filthy threat. Our victory will see you returned to your home, unicorns be damned."

"Perhaps," she murmured and placed her palm in his. "I still do not know how much time has passed. When Mother sent me to the mortal realm, Ishjarta had been king of Fyrgia for perhaps a few decades. It's entirely possible that we have returned to Fé-Ree centuries or even millennia later—or earlier—and he still rules. Besides, the unicorns—"

"Damn the unicorns. They do not decide what you may or may not do." Koriolis, however, acknowledged the possibility that much time had passed, particularly since his own banishment. "When you left, did Mogren still rule the Seelie Court?"

She nodded. "And Thelan still served as the captain of his palace guard."

"He kept his moon-born then?"

"The one you attempted to take from him?" She ignored his wince. "Yes. She has earned great respect among the Seelie Court, and Uncle Enders mated her daughter."

"The *Archivist*? Mated?" Koriolis shook his head. "I never thought I'd see that day."

"Oh, there was much rejoicing. The celebrations went on for weeks."

"I assume you attended?"

"Briefly," she admitted. "It was nice to see him again when he wasn't focusing on me."

Koriolis chuckled. "I can imagine."

"*You* try being his pupil for millennia." Iselde grimaced.

"It couldn't have been any worse than studying under the hand of the Unseelie King," he countered and shook his head again.

A servant sidled into the room and bowed. "Honored fae."

They turned to acknowledge the man's presence. His complexion turned ashen when they leveled their haughty gazes upon him.

"Honored fae," he repeated and bowed again. "I am to escort you to the dining hall."

"Dinnertime," Koriolis murmured and tucked his mate's hand into the crook of his elbow.

"We mustn't be late," she replied sotto voce.

They followed the servant down long corridors and two flights of stairs to the extravagantly appointed dining hall. A small orchestra of sixteen musicians played in one far corner of the immense room, the skirling music sounding like cats screeching to Iselde's ears. Aristocratic guests eager to curry favor with their new king whispered, gossiped, and schemed among themselves while pouring flattery and false promises into his ears. Indra's sly wink at Iselde and Koriolis let them in on the joke: he knew what they were doing and was enjoying their machinations. Servants wandered about, pouring wine and clearing small plates of sweetmeats and other small morsels designed to whet the appetite.

Resplendent in Mughal period glory, Indra rose from his towering, throne-like chair at their approach, and the music and conversations stopped. The tall blue feather attached to his turban, pinned in place behind a ruby the size of a chicken's egg, fluttered in a current of overheated air. Raising his arms as though to draw them into his embrace, he called out, "Welcome! Welcome!"

The servant escorting the two fae bowed and scurried away. Koriolis and Iselde bowed to show their respect.

Indra tilted his head to one side. "No curtsey?"

Iselde flashed her serrated smile at him and replied, "I don't curtsey."

A collective hiss of indrawn breath followed, the crowd of noble guests anticipating their new king's eruption of wrath. Instead, after a pause, Indra grinned then laughed.

"You, my lovely Iselde, are a breath of fresh air!" He chuckled and gestured toward the empty seats at the head table. "Come, sit! Sit! Join me in this wondrous feast to celebrate the eradication of demons from Arigoz!"

Iselde and Koriolis climbed to the dais and took their seats, Koriolis sitting to Indra's right and Iselde in the chair adjacent.

"Music!" Indra commanded. "Let us have music and cheer!"

At his command, servants began circulating among the tables, carrying in platters piled high with steaming meats, fragrant breads, shining fruits, and more. Other servants brought in pitchers of wine in an endless stream of fruity vintages.

"I thought you preferred Gupta-era rainment," Koriolis commented under his breath.

Indra grinned that manic grin. "Nothing beats the Mughals for grandiosity when it comes to fashion." He lifted a goblet and drank. "And nothing impresses the djinns more than grandiosity."

"Whatever happened to the cohort who followed you here?" Iselde inquired in an undertone pitched to avoid djinni ears.

Indra tilted his head toward Koriolis and replied, "Who else do you think have settled into all those dwellings vacated by the demons you slew?"

Chapter 30

"LET'S NEVER DO THAT AGAIN," ISELDE SAID AS SHE rubbed her temples and began removing the jeweled pins from her hair.

Koriolis muffled a burp behind his hand and groaned in agreement. He sat on the bed and leaned back until he lay flat, his booted feet remaining on the floor. "I haven't eaten like that in forever."

She gave him a side-eyed look. "It's good to know you can still eat food, though."

He grunted. "I can, but I still crave blood. Demon blood." He shuddered. "There's nothing quite like it, the way it effervesces on my tongue, the way it warms my veins, the *power* it radiates."

"That sounds addictive," she said, remembering another fae whose addiction had posed grave danger to others and turned him into a cold, unfeeling monster.

"It *feels* addictive," he admitted. "Nonetheless, I need it. I need the power it gives me until I have fulfilled this compulsion laid upon me by the swifts."

"And we will fulfill that mission," she promised and hoped that, when that happened, the bloodlust would fade.

"Come, beloved," Koriolis said, holding out his hand.

She finished removing the hairpins and ran her fingers through the long platinum tresses. She looked at him, cobalt eyes meeting black as heated lust poured through the matebond.

"You are so beautiful," he crooned. "Starlight to my darkness."

Slowly, slowly, she crossed the room as molten desire filled her veins. Iselde positioned herself between his knees. She raked her fingertips down the length of his muscled thighs. He shivered, and the fabric stretching across his groin began to bulge.

"We leave at dawn tomorrow," she said. "It is already late."

"I don't care," he murmured, his voice going guttural. "It has been *ages* since I feasted upon you and you delighted in me. We are *mates*, and I am powerfully desirous of mating with you."

Iselde sank into a low squat. With gentle efficiency, she removed his boots, then the silk stockings encasing his feet. He moaned softly as she traced the strong arch of one pale foot. Fabric rustled.

"Come to me," he urged, his voice low and thick.

She looked up to see he had risen to a sitting position. The bulge between his legs had expanded and pressed against the fabric containing him. With a delicate touch, Iselde unfastened the fall of his breeches to expose the thick tumescence of his desire. She glanced up, meeting his heated gaze for a second before lowering her mouth over him. He hissed, then groaned as she fluttered her tongue along the underside of his swollen cock. He felt her hand wrap around the throbbing stalk. Her other hand, claws partially extended, traced his heavy balls with careful delicacy as she licked his length. He sighed at the pleasure of her oral ministration, then groaned deeply when she began to suck.

Keenly observant, she read his physical and verbal reactions, adjusting for maximum effect until he trembled beneath her. Iselde's sensitive hearing caught the hitch in his breathing that indicated imminent release. She gently scraped her sharp teeth over his cock and just as carefully pricked his balls with her claws. The precise delivery of just a hint of pain catapulted him over the precipice of pleasure. Clenching his hands in her hair, he cried out and grunted as she milked him with tongue and lips and hollowed cheeks.

When he subsided with shuddering breaths and his hands relaxed, she pulled away, pressing a moist, sweet kiss to the sensitive tip. Koriolis took a deep breath and growled. He shoved down his trews and tore off his sash, tunic, and shirt, tossing the garments aside without heeding where they landed.

"Take it off or let me shred it," he snarled as she watched him, eyes glinting with amusement.

Taking him at his word, she unfastened the layered skirt and shimmied as she worked it over her hips to let it puddle on the floor. She stepped out of her shoes, kicking them away. A moment later her bodice joined the puddle of fabric. Moonlight beamed through the window, limning her pale glory.

"So beautiful," Koriolis breathed in genuine admiration. "And *mine.*"

"Yours," Iselde agreed and stepped into his open arms.

Those muscled arms closed around her and pulled her down on top of him as he lay back. One hand traced the delicate line of her spine, skimmed over the sweet curve of her ass, then delved into the slick evidence of arousal between her thighs. She purred at his intimate touch and moved against his hand.

"And you are mine," she whispered as he stroked her.

"Always," he promised and angled his head to kiss her. Their tongues twined and tasted. Pulling away, he whispered, "Forever."

She sighed into his mouth as he kissed her again and chuckled when he rolled them over, placing himself between her splayed legs. His hand swept over her body, and she responded in kind, both of them drawing moans and sighs and shivers of pleasure from each other. She hummed low in her throat when he sank into her body, the thickness of him filling the unexpected hollowness of her as her flesh yielded to him.

"So good," he murmured as he moved in long, slow thrusts that she met with rolls of her hips. "So beautiful."

Iselde did not mind the repetition of his words because her own tongue had lost its command of language. They rolled over, still joined, and she rode him until she cried out as pleasure shattered in a million sparks of brilliant light. He gave her no surcease as he rolled them over again, holding her leg over his hip as he plunged in and out of her body. She flew over the precipice again and again until she found herself on all fours, her long hair wrapped around his hand and his other hand wrapped around her throat as his hips pounded against the bouncing flesh of her ass, his balls slapping her clit. She crested once more with a hoarse scream that he matched in a guttural shout of release as they found ultimate joy together.

Dropping to the mattress, now bared of its blankets, Koriolis drew a sheet over their sweating bodies and gathered her close, his slowly softening cock still buried inside her.

They slept until a servant woke them with a tray of food and the delivery of practical garb for travel.

Iselde looked over her shoulder at their entourage and pursed her lips in dismay. The number of warriors guarding their small caravan exceeded any expectation of need to merely guard it. Koriolis saw her expression, interpreted it correctly, and said, "Ignore them."

"This is absurd," she complained. "We'd get to the Uhltar faster and be more efficient in clearing out the demons without them."

He agreed. "Unfortunately, that's not all Indra expects of us. We're the vanguard for quelling any uprisings." He glanced at the warriors following them. "They'll not be involved in hunting demons with us."

She sighed and rolled her shoulders, stiff from hours of sitting in the saddle. She would rather have walked. "I dislike the subterfuge."

Koriolis chuckled. "That makes you unique among fae, beloved. We are renowned throughout all the realms for being addicted to subterfuge and scheming."

"Bah." She waved her hand in dismissal. "All this skullduggery reminds me of my mother's machinations."

He chuckled again. "A caravan isn't exactly skullduggery. We're not playing cloak and dagger games among the shadows."

Iselde raised her face to the sky, closing her eyes against the fierce sun. "No. Few shadows here."

Conversation lapsed into an easy silence both were comfortable maintaining for the next several leagues. The soft footfalls of an approaching riding beast roused their attention.

"Lord Fae," the caravan master hailed.

"I hate when they call me that," Koriolis muttered under his breath. "Would they like it if I called them Lord or Lady Djinn?"

"They don't think us worthy of actual names, but they give us the honor of address due to Indra's favor," Iselde explained. She frowned, "But I'll be damned if I call him or any djinn master."

Koriolis turned in the saddle and said, "Burrudi?"

Frowning at not being accorded the title "Master," the caravan master pulled down the veil covering the lower half of his face, protecting it from abrasive dust and scorching sun. "Once we crest the next dune, we will stop for the night."

"What's over the next dune?" Koriolis asked, knowing the perpetually frowning djinn would not answer any question Iselde asked. The caravan master preferred to ignore her entirely.

"Sand," came the terse reply. "The sun will set soon, and we must set up camp."

"All right," Koriolis replied with a curt nod.

The caravan master raised his veil to cover the lower half of his face and hauled on the riding beast's reins to turn it around. The beast grunted when Burrudi jabbed his heels into its side and took off at an ungainly gallop back to the caravan.

Iselde and Koriolis crested the next dune and rode their lurching beasts to the base where shadows had already begun to stretch beneath the late afternoon sun. When their beasts halted, Iselde swung her leg over the animal's back and slid down, knees bending to absorb the shock of hitting the ground. Dust puffed around her lower legs. She patted the patient beast and led it to the other side of the small valley between the towering dunes.

Koriolis followed suit. Catching up with his mate, he commented, "You do know you're supposed to cue the beast to cush before you dismount?"

She shrugged and shook a leg to ease the stiffness. "I'm sure the beast prefers I get off its back sooner rather than later, regardless of how I get off."

"Probably," he agreed and looked back to watch the caravan gingerly creep down the dune's steep side. "Burrudi was right. The shadows grow long here quickly."

"Oh, I doubt he'd shed a tear if we were to disappear and relieve him of the responsibility of escorting us safely to our next destination."

"He wouldn't. But that doesn't make his advice wrong," Koriolis pointed out.

Iselde shrugged and patted the ugly beast again and watched as the caravan reached the valley floor. Under the caravan master's orders, the group quickly partitioned the camping area into sections: one for the livestock, one for sleeping tents, and another for the burdens the beasts carried. Some of the guards were put to work unloading the beasts, and others were stationed at key points around the campsite.

By unspoken agreement, Iselde and Koriolis led their beasts to the campsite and relieved them of their furnishings. Koriolis' beast immediately dropped to the ground and rolled, kicking its legs and padded feet with ungainly enthusiasm and several grunts of satisfied pleasure. The beast rolled to its feet and heaved itself upright and shook, sending a thick cloud of dust billowing into the air.

Koriolis and Iselde joined the warriors who had begun to pour water into buckets and pull feed from barrels to share in the labor. Their presence garnered dark looks but no comments, clearly indicating without words they were not wanted, their presence was resented, and were the guards not bound by their vows to Indra, they would either be dead or enslaved.

"Cheerful bunch," Iselde commented under her breath.

Her mate snorted. Looking over the quickly erected camp, he took her hand and led her to the cookfire where the caravan master's personal cook was busy at work.

A bleating goat's noise ceased from the decisive chop of a cleaver, and its blood spilled into the sand. With the economy of long practice, the cook rigged a tripod and hooked the goat's carcass to the top. Brutally efficient, he sliced open the goat's belly and pulled out the innards, sweeping them onto a square of canvas old and stiff from innumerable kills. A guard folded the stiff canvas over and hauled the offal away, apparating out of sight to the other side of the dune where he dumped it for desert predators and scavengers to consume. A moment later, he returned and handed the soaked cloth back to the cook. The cook used the cleaver to cut through the hide at strategic places before pulling the edges of the severed skin and peeling it downward. He sliced through the connective membrane and detached the skin from the carcass.

While the cook butchered that evening's meat, another guard built a fire with wood carried across the desert, for there were neither trees nor bushes nor any fuel to be seen among the barren dunes. The fire built, the guard lugged a large iron pot over it and uncorked a water barrel to fill the pot. With the pot filled, Koriolis assisted the guard in carrying the barrel to the livestock to fill buckets for the thirsty animals. Iselde followed and assisted with distribution of feed to the beasts.

"Not like camels then," he remarked as he watched a riding beast raise its head from a bucket, slobbering.

"Camels?" Iselde queried.

"On Earth, they're called ships of the desert," he explained. "They're both beasts of burden and beasts for riding. A camel can store sufficient energy in the humps on its back to go for several days without being fed or watered."

She tilted her head, trying to imagine such a beast and failing. "What do these animals look like?"

A small smile curled Koriolis' lips. "A horse designed by committee."

She shook her head. "That makes no sense."

"It's a cynical joke mortals use."

She shrugged. "If you say so." She glanced at the beasts and pushed a wayward lock of hair behind her pointed ear. "If I must ride, I prefer horses."

"Most do," he agreed in a mild tone, not mentioning the one time he rode an orca in the ocean. That had been an amazing experience. He looked at the guard who waited with ill-concealed impatience for them to stop talking. Pointing at the now empty bucket, he said to the guard, "Shall we take the barrel back to the cook?"

The guard nodded, and the two males picked up the nearly empty and cumbersome barrel. They returned it to the cook-fire and dipped the last measures of water for consumption by the caravan employees, the guards, and their two fae guests.

"Are you sure we have enough water?" Koriolis asked the caravan master.

"If all goes well," the caravan master said, "we will have sufficient feed and water to get us to Uhltar. We have sufficient to sustain us through a delay of up to three days."

"Sandstorms?" Koriolis said.

"Among other dangers."

CHAPTER 31

THE CARAVAN MASTER BOWED TOWARD THE setting sun and gave thanks to the djinni gods that they had reached their destination without needing to shelter against a sandstorm or other disaster. Iselde and Koriolis waited impatiently as he recited long prayers of gratitude and hardly noticed when he added a muttered request to be spared from the taint of the fae in future travels. After a long journey filled with suspicious glares and muttered deprecations, they'd grown surprisingly inured to the simmering hostility aimed at them.

When the caravan master had finished, they thanked him for his escort and hospitality and proceeded on foot to the gates of Uhltar. A small contingent of the caravan guards hurried to catch up and form a vanguard. The ranking warrior presented a scroll to the sentry at the gate. The sentry read the scroll and frowned.

"So, it's true then? Djaria has a new emperor?"

The warrior nodded. "Yes, it is true. Emperor Indra sends these two fae to Uhltar to rid the city of demons."

The sentry glanced at the two fae and sneered. "Fae? And one is a female?"

The djinni warrior nodded. "I have witnessed them myself. They are … surprisingly effective."

The sentry grunted and handed the scroll back to the warrior. "Proceed then, and let the rat catchers do their job—if they aren't captured first."

Iselde bared her pointed teeth at him. The djinn snarled back at her.

"Don't allow them to provoke you, beloved," Koriolis murmured, stroking a hand down her back. He inhaled and his eyes widened. "I can smell them."

"It is said that Uhltar is *infested* with demons," the warrior volunteered.

Koriolis nodded. "We'll find a place to rest for tonight and start hunting tomorrow."

The warrior nodded and barked a command at his subordinates who arranged themselves in protective formation around the two fae. "They will stay with you while I procure accommodations."

Koriolis opened his mouth to object.

"Emperor's orders," the warrior added.

"So be it," Koriolis replied.

"No one will rent rooms to you here," he said.

"Xenophobic bigots," Iselde muttered under her breath.

Koriolis stifled a guffaw. The ranking warrior excused himself and headed out to procure overnight lodging. The group shuffled aside, remaining near the thick, mud brick wall towering above them as the passage of travelers, merchants, and others dwindled and the sun cast long shadows as it descended. Before darkness enveloped the city and the city gates closed, the ranking guard returned to escort them to their temporary home.

"Do the gates keep danger out or people in?" Iselde wondered aloud.

"Danger roams the desert at night," the guard said. "We were fortunate not to have encountered anything more dangerous than scorpions on our journey."

"What kind of dangers?"

"Brigands. Nightsuckers. Sand devils." The guard paused, then added, "It's possible we were spared such danger due to your presence."

"You mean our presence deterred them?"

"It's possible. I've never made the journey so far without encountering something."

"Then perhaps you should bear that in mind," Iselde suggested. "If fearsome brigands, nightsuckers, and sand devils avoid us, then perhaps it's because we're the greater danger."

The guard's red eyes met her gaze. "I make no mistake, Lady Fae, that you and your lord are very, very dangerous."

"But that doesn't mean he likes us, my dear," Koriolis murmured and enjoyed Iselde's soft snort in response.

"No, I do not like the fae," the warrior replied with blunt honesty. "But I am honorable and will fulfill my emperor's commands."

"I almost like him," Iselde commented.

The guard shuddered in distaste. "We are not friends, Lady Fae."

"Moons forbid," she replied. She wrinkled her nose and sneezed. "I'll be glad to leave all this filthy sand and dust behind."

"Djaria will be grateful to see you go," the guard said, red eyes narrowed in distaste.

"Nice to know we can come to an agreement."

The guard did not mistake Iselde's bared teeth for a smile.

They arrived at the inn where the proprietor gaped in outrage as the emperor's guards escorted two of the reviled fae into his establishment. However, he refrained from objecting, intimidated by the blatant threat of each guard setting his hand on the hilt of his weapon and bribed by the promise of the new emperor's gold.

"You didn't tell him you were escorting two fae," Koriolis commented.

"I did not, else he would have refused to rent us rooms," the guard confirmed.

Koriolis sighed. *I get weary of this bigotry.*

So compel the next innkeeper, Iselde replied, mind to mind. *You do not find compulsion distasteful?*

Normally, yes. But I prefer expedience here and am not inclined to cater to the delicate sensibilities of djinns, especially when they would happily bind me with iron as a slave.

He acknowledged her point.

Their escort stopped. The ranking guard gestured to a door. "This room is yours."

"Thank you," Koriolis replied and opened the door.

"Do not leave your room this night, Lord Fae."

"I assume one of you will be bringing us meals and water for washing?"

The guard nodded. "And a guard will be stationed at your door until morning."

"Do you really think we need such protection?"

The guard shrugged.

Koriolis and Iselde entered the room and closed the door behind them. They dumped their packs on the floor and explored the small space, noting the tiny window placed high near the ceiling. An iron grate covered the opening.

"Someone doesn't trust us," Iselde pointed out in a tone as dry as the desert through which they'd just traveled.

Koriolis pinched the bridge of his nose to ward off a headache. "How many cities does Djaria have?"

She shrugged. "I haven't been here millennia." She seated herself on the edge of the narrow bed. "If I recollect correctly, Djaria has four, perhaps five, large cities, urban centers sufficient to sustain a thriving population of demons."

"And villages?"

She shrugged again. "Innumerable, most little more than an extended family or three scratching out an existence in the sand and protecting their one well." She paused then added, "They tend to be rather inbred."

Koriolis sat beside her and pulled off a boot. "Perhaps the djinn have good reason not to like the fae."

Iselde blinked at what she perceived as an attack. "I've been rescuing slaves from the djinn for centuries, millennia even."

"There was a time when we fae considered them dirt beneath our feet."

She sniffed, a haughty sound. "They are."

"Antipathy met with animosity makes no friends, beloved. Perhaps fae and djinn are both at fault."

Since when had Marog, also known as Koriolis Valchik Dra'Acul and a near-demon who had ruled his vampires with an iron-shod control, become the voice of peace and compassion? Affronted, she sniffed again. "Their desert encroaches upon fae territory. We do not prey upon their people, yet they prey upon ours. I see no comparison."

Koriolis pressed his lips together and decided not to speak further on the matter. Iselde wouldn't be changing her derogatory opinion of the djinn anytime soon, especially since she had personal reasons to detest them. Catching the drift of her thoughts, he, too, wondered at this unwonted softness. Demon lord or fae warrior, one did not survive or thrive through gentleness without the ability and willingness to exert harsh force and unflinching will. He decided that being mated had somehow twisted his nature into something he wasn't sure he approved—something soft, mild, and gentle. With a grunt of self-loathing, he finished undressing and lay on the bed.

"Wake me in the morning, beloved."

She looked at him. "Do you not care to eat?"

He flashed her a savage smile. "I'll drink of demon blood tomorrow."

She nodded.

CHAPTER 32

MORNING ARRIVED WITHOUT INCIDENT. NO ONE attempted to gain entry into the faes' room. No one attacked the guard stationed outside the door. Night passed in surprising peace.

Koriolis did not eat when breakfast was brought to their room, merely reiterating he would dine on his prey. Iselde accepted his declaration and ate her fill, not knowing when she'd get her next meal.

When they emerged from their room, their ranking guard informed them he would seek longer term accommodation, as the inn's proprietor insisted they depart from the premises and never darken his door again. Koriolis nodded gravely in comprehension, and Iselde sneered.

Stepping outside the inn's door, the scent of demon pricked Koriolis' attention. He paused and inhaled deeply, discerning the mixture of scents in the air to determine the closest demon. Finally, he said, "This way."

With focused determination, he threaded a path through the city's early morning traffic. Pedestrians, mainly servants, and a handful of wagons pulled by the same beasts of burden used to cross the desert. The drivers either stared in offense at the presence of the fae in their midst or sidled away to avoid him and his mate. Fairly quivering in eagerness, Koriolis followed his nose to a mud brick house.

"Here," he said, then kicked the door open. He rushed inside to encounter its startled residents, logy after having feasted upon their prey the night before. He tore into them, claws, fangs, and flashing blade. Iselde caught those who managed to squeeze past him and incapacitated them long enough for her mate to clear the small building's two stories and return to drink deeply of their blood before plunging Asi into their flesh and turning them to greasy piles of charred ash.

Eye blazing with fervor and the corrupted power he'd ingested, Koriolis stepped outside the building and paused long enough to catch the scent of another nest of demons. Methodically, he swept through the city, decimating every demon having the misfortune to be found. Yet the city was large, and word of the murderous fae spread quickly.

One of their guards found them and informed them that alternate lodging had been secured. Then he added, "Demons are at the city gates trying to flee."

"Then we go after them," Koriolis said and headed toward the city gates.

"The imuda has ordered the gates closed to prevent their escape," the guard announced what the Djarian city's equivalent of a mayor had done. "He knows why you are here and wants to avoid offending the new emperor."

"You mean he wants us to rid his city of the demon infestation for him," Koriolis said. His teeth gleamed in a feral smile.

The guard nodded. "Emperor Indra has promised swift and lethal reprisal against any who defy him. The imuda wishes to keep his exalted position as the city's governing official."

"Ah, the beauty of self-interest," Iselde murmured under her breath and rolled her eyes.

Koriolis snorted and his black eyes practically glowed. "Then pest control I shall be." He extended his hand toward his mate. "Come, beloved, we have demons to kill."

Before he could tug her away, Iselde asked the guard, "Why has the imuda not already exterminated these demons? Is he not a djinn with power?"

The guard pursed his lips and averted his gaze while he pondered an answer. Finally, he admitted, "We djinns have no advantage over them. The demons here used to be djinns."

"Therefore, many of your people have allied with them," Iselde accused.

The guard's expression soured.

"Which explains why the Djarian desert is expanding," she added, thinking of how the boundaries of the Quol expanded and retracted as did the population of the Quoli. "What do you think will happen when the demons are exterminated?"

"We djinns will be free of their foul contamination, and Djaria will be returned wholly to its true people," the guard replied. Hope glinted in his red eyes. "Do you really think you can eliminate all demons from Djaria?"

"No, I don't think that will happen," she replied with blunt honesty. "However, I do believe we can reduce their numbers enough for you djinns to control their population."

"Come, beloved," Koriolis repeated.

She took his head and let him lead her away.

"Why does it not surprise me that the djinns are colluding with the demons?" Iselde muttered.

"It may simply boil down to collaboration in the name of preservation," he replied as he wove through the teeming streets and pulled her along behind him. "We don't know if they even realize the desert has been expanding, encroaching on fae borders."

"Well, we were charged with exterminating the demons so the Great Forest can regain its lost territory and, perhaps, even expand."

Koriolis came to a sudden stop and paused, sniffing at the air like a scent hound. "I do not recall the fae pushing at the borders of other nations."

"We never needed to," she replied, her tone crisp with haughty pride. "They always knew better than to encroach upon what is ours, well, except the humans."

"I remember when they first arrived in our realm." He turned his head, a slow side to side scan of scents.

"As do I."

Iselde pursed her lips in thought then said, "And, what is interesting is that a fae king now rules over a human kingdom. Fyrgia. Corta, however, remains a firmly human province. They are most hostile toward the fae, canidae, felidae, and other species."

"Back in the mortal realm, humans are hostile toward others of their own species for even more superficial differences," he commented. His nostrils flared. "Ah! That way."

Still grasping her hand, he took off, Iselde easily keeping up with his quick pace.

As before, Koriolis' nose did not lead him astray. They soon found another nest populated by a group of demons hiding from the bright sunshine amid the gory remains of the previous day's feast. After drawing Asi, he kicked in the door and charged. Iselde followed, staying close as she unleashed her claws, the frigid ice of her fury, and her copper sword.

As before, they found a locked room where a captive waited in terror. Iselde noticed the slave collar around the captive's neck, the wide brown eyes, and the rounded ears. "Human."

Demon blood dripping down his chin, Koriolis snapped the iron collar and hissed, "*Go.*"

The slave scurried away, not needing to be told a second time to bolt for freedom.

From there the two fae proceeded to the next nest and the next and the next, hunting until sunset when Indra's guards finally caught up with them.

"Come, Lord Fae, we have secured accommodations, meals, baths, and fresh clothing for you," one of the guards said. "It is best to hunt them down during the day when they're at their weakest."

Iselde and Koriolis meekly fell into step with the escort, the latter fairly humming with the power acquired through the consumption of demon blood. Again they found themselves in a small attic room with a tiny window tucked beneath the eaves. However, the bath was hot, the soap plentiful, and the portions of food generous. Koriolis wasn't hungry, but he ate anyway to keep his flesh tethered to mundane nourishment rather than risk addiction to demon blood.

"I do not like being cooped up in these small rooms," Iselde complained, pitching her voice low so as not to be over-heard by the guard posted outside the door to their room.

Koriolis pulled her closer to his body, tucking her against his hard, muscled length. "Nor do I, but hunting nests during the day is more ... efficient."

She sighed. "We might save more lives ..."

"Doubtful," he said, gently interrupting. Pressing a kiss to her neck, he added, "And do you truly want to save more djinni lives?"

She hummed low in her throat, a noncommittal sound. After a moment, she turned her head as though to look at him over her shoulder. "Have you noticed we have not found any demon children? Do demons even have young?"

With slow words, he replied, "They are much like vampires—*made*—not born. Vampires sire humans, turning their victims into fledgling vampires. Demons, at least those originating from Fé-Ree, are former fae, djinns, or other magical beings who kill their victims by drinking their blood. Demons not originating from this realm... I do not know. Strange as it may seem, I encountered few demons in the human realm and killed them without thinking to question their origins."

"The main difference is the magic," Iselde mused. "Humans are without magic and, so, must be turned by a vampire to become a vampire. Perhaps the races with magic turn demon without needing to be sired?"

Koriolis sighed and admitted. "I've never bothered to con-template the differences. They were immaterial. I never cared."

"That makes two of us." She sighed and rubbed her cheek against the pillow's rough linen surface. Another thought struck her. "Do you think that the djinns rebelling against Indra might ally with demons to retake their country?"

Familiar with the machinations and scheming of vampires, Koriolis shrugged. "It's possible, probably even likely." He stroked a hand over her hair, and her lips curled in a small smile. "Sleep, beloved. We hunt again tomorrow."

She sighed and closed her eyes, for at dawn they would again awaken to embark upon a new day of slaughter.

CHAPTER 33

ON THE EIGHTH DAY OF THEIR HUNTING EXPEDITION in Uhltar, Koriolis tracked a nest to the palace occupied by the city's chief governing official, the imuda. Accompanied by their company of guards, he demanded entrance into the palace. The guard at the palace gate denied them entrance: "No."

"There are demons in there," he said. "I can smell them."

The palace guard stationed at the tall iron gate ignored him.

The imperial guard commanding the small company assigned to the fae demon hunter positioned himself in front of Koriolis and said, "I am Captain Ibi Abdil of the Djarian Royal Guard. You will open this gate and admit us."

The palace guard's eyes widened. He spat a wad of phlegm on the ground, narrowing missing the captain's booted foot. "You serve a usurper."

"I serve the empire, regardless of who wears the crown," the captain replied. "Open this gate or I will have you flogged."

"Why don't you just apparate?" Iselde wondered aloud.

"The palace is warded against it," another guard replied under his breath.

"Oh, really?" Her lips peeled back to reveal her serrated smile. "Perhaps it's time we reminded Djaria that the fae are peaceful, not harmless."

"There is no difference," the guard muttered, his expression souring with disgust.

"Oh, but there is," she replied, aware Koriolis watched her from the periphery of his vision. "You see, one who is dangerous can choose violence, force, or peace. One who is harmless has no choice."

The guard shrugged.

"Why do you confine us behind a locked and guarded door every night?" she asked. "You have seen our work. Do you think we meekly accept such confinement because we must?"

"Because you and the fae lord …" His voice died away as he realized that insulting the deadly fae standing with him might not be the best idea.

"Exactly," she said. Extending her senses, she sought and found the tricky wards enveloping the palace grounds and the ley lines of power flowing deep beneath the surface. Using herself as a conduit, she channeled her will and that power into the network of wards. Sparks of energy flared and sizzled as the surge of power overwhelmed the wards and burned them to a crisp.

"Well, that was easy," she said, releasing the connection to the ley lines.

Koriolis looked at the palace guard who stared open-mouthed as the last remaining sparks drifted to the ground. Claws extended, he rested a hand against the iron gate. "Open the gate."

The guard hefted his spear. His voice squeaked as he answered, "No."

Captain Ibi Abdil kicked the gate open and charged through, the rest of his small company following, swords drawn.

"This is an outrage!" the guard shouted and lunged at the nearest warrior.

Koriolis and Iselde watched dispassionately as the imperial guards quickly immobilized the palace guard and divested him of his weapons.

"There will be a whipping post in the palace courtyard. Take him there," the captain ordered two of his men as he turned to face a contingent of palace guards hurtling toward them and yelling their ululating battle cry. "Twenty lashes. Make them count."

The other guards positioned themselves to meet the onslaught. Koriolis drew Asi and Iselde her copper sword.

"I never thought I'd be fighting alongside djinns," she commented.

Koriolis flashed a bloodthirsty grin at her.

The palace guards crashed into the royal guard and the two fae. The battle was quick, vicious, and bloody. Victorious, Indra's royal guard and the two fae marched across the grand approach to the imuda's palace, up the wide, shallow stairs, and into the imuda's luxurious, sprawling residence. Servants and slaves scattered.

"Where are they?" Captain Ibi Abdil asked.

Koriolis took a deep sniff and analyzed the scents, isolating the telltale stench of demon. With a more delicate inhalation, he determined their direction. Gesturing with his cleft chin, he said, "That way."

The imperial guard followed the fae lord, efficiently dispatching the few city guards who attempted to forestall the invasion.

"They're not well-trained," Iselde commented. "Disgraceful."

The captain gave her a pained look. "I'll inform the emperor."

She grinned. "Oh, I'd love to see his face when he gets the news that the second largest city in Djaria fell to a handful of imperial guards. How embarrassing!"

He threw her a pained look again.

"Shall I recommend you for the honor of training Uhltar's new guard?"

"Don't jest, Lady Fae."

She chuckled. "Even better, maybe I should recommend you to replace the current imuda."

"Please don't."

Koriolis' unerring sense of smell led them through the warren of corridors and rooms and galleries to a door deep within the center of the sprawling edifice, a place overlooking a central courtyard where the uncooperative guard had been tied to the whipping post. The imuda's guard screamed as a whip sliced through fabric and skin.

"Ward the room," Koriolis ordered.

Iselde exerted her will and sealed the room to prevent any djinn from apparating in or out of the space.

"Thank you, beloved."

The door to the room disintegrated in a hail of smoke and ash. The royal guards and two fae entered. Iselde noted thick, dark cloths covering the courtyard-facing windows so no sunlight spilled into the room. Torches burned in sconces on the walls and candles illuminated the maps on the table. The imuda, his cabinet, and a half dozen demons rose from their chairs to confront the invaders.

"Well, isn't this interesting?" Koriolis said as he took in the tableau. He tilted his head with the predatory curiosity of a prowling dragon. "Planning a rebellion, are we?"

"And colluding with the enemy, too," Iselde added in a bright, hungry voice. "What shall we do, my love?"

"Kill them, of course."

The imuda blathered in protest, blustering a series of non-sensical syllables.

"We should question him first," Koriolis said.

"That, Lady Fae, would be *my* prerogative," the captain said. Sword still drawn, he advanced toward the city's leader. He leveled his sword at the large bulge of the imuda's belly. "Imuda Wajav, why do you conspire with demons?"

I think we know why, Iselde remarked mind to mind with Koriolis. *I'd like to know what he has over them to remain safe in their presence.*

Koriolis, not inclined to observe the niceties of privacy in such a situation, slid into the imuda's mind like a hot knife plunging into a tub of butter. The city's chief official cried out and clutched his head as pain pierced his brain.

The captain lowered his sword and shot a disapproving glare at Koriolis. "Well?"

Well, that wasn't very nice.

I don't care.

Iselde shrugged and waited while Koriolis riffled through the imuda's mind, heedless of any damage he caused in the search for answers. After a moment, blood trickled from the moaning djinn's nose. A bit later, his breathing thinned to a labored wheeze. His complexion paled to an ashen gray. Koriolis withdrew, having found the information he sought. His victim drew a long, slow breath, and his knees buckled. The captain let him crumple to the floor where he whined and wept and drooled into his lap.

"Well?" the captain prompted.

Koriolis answered, "They serve as his assassins and warriors. He protects them from persecution and supplies them with … meat."

"No wonder the palace guards are so poorly trained," Iselde murmured.

Again, the captain threw her a pained look.

"I think you broke him," she commented.

Koriolis shrugged and pointed Asi toward the nearest demon. "Captain, perhaps you and your guards should depart from the room for a moment."

The captain looked at the six demons who watched them with expressions varying from cold hatred to keen hunger. "Leave one alive and coherent for *me* to interrogate."

"Consider it a gift," the fae lord replied.

The palace guards backed out of the room, none of them daring to turn their backs to the demons or the fae. When the last had passed through the doorway, the opening flashed and filled with what appeared to be a solid panel of sunlight. The demons cringed.

"After you, beloved." Koriolis gestured with his free hand.

Claws extended, Iselde pointed at the group and began to recite a children's rhyme, her fingertip moving with each sing-song syllable to point at a different demon. On the last syllable, she darted forward, sword drawn. Koriolis darted in another direction to catch those demons who scrambled away from his mate. Once again, they worked with brutal efficiency and coordination as if they'd been fighting together for millennia.

True to his promise, Koriolis spared one demon for the captain to interrogate.

CHAPTER 34

THEY COLLAPSED ON A LARGE BED SITUATED within a vacant, spacious bedchamber and ignored the frightened servants who scuttled back and forth carrying buckets of hot water which they poured into large copper tubs. A couple of other servants brought trays of food and wine, setting them on nearby tables.

"It looks like we're confined to quarters again," Iselde murmured, then heaved a deep breath as she straightened herself into a sitting position.

Koriolis grunted.

"You'd think they'd trust us by now."

He grunted again. *Like they would trust a wild lion.*

She levered herself onto her feet and stripped, not caring whether the servants saw her nude form. With a sigh, she eased into the hot water and ordered, "Soap."

A servant scurried to obey, gingerly placing a crystal jar of soft soap onto a palm crusted with blood. Gobbets of gore clung to Iselde's claws. The feared Ice Queen of the northern wastes sank down in the water until her head was submerged. A few seconds passed while servants continued to dump a few more bucketsful of water into the tub, filling it until the liquid's surface rose nearly to the brim. Difficult to see against the tub's copper, the water turned pink with the initial dissolution of blood.

Iselde lifted the metal lid off the crystal jar and set it aside. She dipped two fingers into sticky paste which smelled sharply of herbs. Setting the jar aside, she dipped her empty hand into the water and smeared some into the palm of her other hand. She rubbed her hands together to work up a thick, creamy lather. First, she tackled her hair, scrubbing at her itchy scalp and making sure the long, white strands were cleaned free of blood and gore. After rinsing, she turned her attention to scrubbing her face and body, using a small brush to clean the filth of death from beneath her claws.

The water was filthy when she finally stepped from the tub.

"This way, Lady Fae, to rinse," a female servant whispered and gestured toward a trough.

Iselde stepped into the trough and stood still while the servant poured a few more buckets of tepid water over her body, sluicing off any remnants of the soap. As she wrung out her hair, servants emptied the tub and refilled it with fresh water.

The servant attending Iselde handed her a small bottle with instructions to use a few drops to oil her hair. Iselde sniffed the hair oil which smelled of sweet lemon, complementing the lingering scent of the soap. She poured a small amount into her palm and rubbed her hands together, then rubbed her hands and fingers through the wet, tangled tresses. Such was the thickness and length of her hair that she needed several more drops to spread the hair oil evenly throughout her hair.

The servant handed her a long length of linen which she used to dry herself, then she wrapped it around her body. She followed the servant to a stool placed before a vanity boasting a large mirror. Iselde blinked at her reflection as the servant began to comb her hair. *I look thin.*

By then, the servants had emptied the copper tub and refilled it. Koriolis climbed in and began scrubbing himself. He glanced up, gaze scanning her lean form. *You have expended much energy and eaten little.*

She turned her head just a smidgen to look at Koriolis who was still engaged in scrubbing himself.

You're looking a bit gaunt yourself.

His lips curled in a small smile. *We shall dine well tonight.*

She glanced at the trays of food delivered while she bathed: cured meats, cheeses, fresh fruits, breads and pastries, at least four different wines, olives and pickled vegetables, and more. *The imuda did not sacrifice his own appetite, did he?* She felt his cynical amusement waft through her mind. *I hope they have something else for us to wear. I, for one, am weary of Indra's sartorial choices.*

You have but to ask, he replied.

Ah, yes, I should *do that.* Aloud she said to the servant working on combing her hair, "Find me something suitable for a warrior to wear."

The servant gasped, eyes wide. Her hands stilled.

"And burn my other clothing—just the clothing. It's beyond cleaning."

The servant glanced at the pile of clothes on the floor, wet with blood and fresh gore, crusted and stiff with dried blood and gore, and reeking of decay, dirt, and sweat.

"His, too," Iselde added. "We both need garb better suited for battle in this climate."

"Of course, Lady Fae," the servant whispered and audibly swallowed her disapproval of a female wielding a sword. Her hands resumed their delicate work of untangling the female fae's long, white tresses.

"Don't touch the weapons."

"No, Lady Fae."

By the time Iselde's hair was combed through and tangle-free, Koriolis had finished bathing and was dressed in a long, flowing banyan belted at the waist. She paused to admire him and said, "That color looks well on you."

Grinning, he turned around to model the robe. "Sapphire was always one of my favorite colors."

She snorted and accepted the long, nearly transparent robe the maidservant handed to her. She fingered the filmy fabric, so impractical in its delicacy as to be useless, careful not to snag her claws. Her upper lip curled in disgust. "Pink."

"It looks lovely on you," Koriolis complimented, unable to prevent his gaze from lingering on the darker shade of her nipples and areolas pressed against the flimsy fabric which barely concealed the shadowed juncture of her thighs. His cock twitched with burgeoning interest and began to swell. Ignoring its demand, he held out his hand. "Come and eat. You are famished."

Iselde yawned and rolled her shoulders even as her belly gurgled with hunger. "Aye, I am hungry." Worried, she asked, "Are you?"

"Not particularly," he admitted. "I drank deeply of demon blood today. Regardless, I will eat some mortal food to anchor me. I feel I will turn fully demon if I rely solely on blood for sustenance. I do not wish that, especially since the swifts restored much of my original fae nature."

Iselde approved. She took his hand and permitted him to guide her to a large cushion. She sat with a graceful economy of motion that indicated limber strength. Koriolis padded barefoot to the cushion across the low table from her and gestured for service. A manservant snapped to attention and began setting plates before them.

Iselde ate until her belly felt full to bursting. Koriolis did the same, eating little, although he drank more deeply of the wine than did his mate. They dined in companionable silence as palace servants efficiently removed the dirty bathwater, tub, rinsing troughs, and discarded clothes. Yawning, they slipped off their robes and climbed into the bed. The last two servants departed, carrying away trays of leftover food, wine, and dishes. They ignored the click of a lock when the room was empty but for the two of them.

"Do they really think the locks would keep us in if we wished to leave?" Iselde muttered as her eyes drifted shut.

"Who cares?" Koriolis replied, gathering her close, nestling her body against his. His aching erection found a comfortable place between her buttocks. He felt his tension ease and his tight muscles relax at the press of her body against his. He sighed at the welcome relief and felt her relax within the shelter of his embrace. Slumber descended upon them.

With a nearly inaudible *click*, the door unlocked but did not open. Bellies full, bodies clean, and feeling safe and comfortable, they ignored the soft sound and slept unmolested until dawn when a disturbance in the air awakened them. Eyes slitted open, Koriolis watched as two soft-footed servants entered the room. From the way they moved, he quickly realized the two males who entered weren't servants. He took a deep breath, inhaling the faded scents of lemon and herbs and smelled instead the natural fragrance of his mate: pine and ice. Against his naked thigh, he felt the prick of her claws and realized Iselde was aware of the intruders, too.

As the ersatz servants crept closer, one drew a dagger from a hidden sheath. Koriolis subtly shifted, but the poke of her claws stayed him.

Allow me.

He felt the pressure of power gathering, being held, confined, and molded by his mate's formidable will. A second later, she released it with a whispered word. Arctic blue light flared above the bed and sprayed deadly shards of ice. The two intruders cried out as the blades of ice shredded them.

"Messy but effective," Koriolis said as he sat up, letting the covers fall to his lap. He glanced at the door. "One of the servants must have unlocked the door for them."

Having come to the same conclusion, Iselde, too, sat up and swiveled to dangle her legs over the edge of the tall bed. "We're leaving."

"And where shall we go?" he asked as he collected the banyan that had been draped over the foot of the bed the night before. "We are not finished here."

"Away from Djaria. Away from *this*," she said, her voice flat. "We do not belong here, and I do not like it here."

"We have not finished our task," he reminded her again.

Her eyes narrowed. "Then we'll slaughter every last demon we encounter on our way *out* of the desert."

Koriolis opened his mouth to remind her a third time of the charge placed upon them by the unicorns, then thought better of it.

She sighed. "I weary of dancing to the tunes of others. I found the djinns who took my daughters. I killed them and their accomplices. I may detest djinns, but I have no desire to go to war against an entire race."

"And demons?" he prompted.

Every inch the legendary Ice Queen, she met his gaze, hers unflinching. "I will kill any demon hunting in *my* demesne."

He picked up her hand and kissed the palm, noting the calluses acquired through many, many centuries of hard work and the wielding of weaponry. Anew he realized his mate was no pampered female, no indolent aristocrat, but a fierce warrior who had eked out a harsh living from the unforgiving and hostile arctic lands far north and protected her clan while doing so. He understood this fiercely independent fae chafed at the manipulations of the oracle and the swifts.

He kissed her palm again and gave her hand a light squeeze. "Then we shall travel along the coast where the largest cities of Djaria are and slaughter every demon along the way. I will see you returned home where you belong and hope that I may stay with you."

She snorted. "Of course, you must stay with me. We are true mates never to be parted. And if you are unhappy in the northern wastes, we will go elsewhere—just not back to this infernal desert. Indra may have it." The tension left her shoulders. She nodded and squeezed his hand and glanced around the room. The servants had not brought them the requested garments. She reached for her own flimsy robe and shrugged it on. "First we find proper garb. I could weave us clothing from naught but light and air, but maintaining it would require a constant draw of power."

"Best to remain unencumbered," Koriolis agreed. "Stay here. I'll infiltrate the quartermaster's office and find what we need."

Iselde nodded then said, "I'll take care of this mess."

Koriolis wondered how she would do that, but decided to leave that task in her capable hands. He brushed his lips over hers, wrapped himself in shadows, and hastened away, employing the supreme stealth he'd developed over millennia as a demon in the human realm, a stealth particularly useful when hunting unruly vampires to either dispatch them or bring them under his rule.

When the door closed behind her mate, Iselde looked at the carcasses on the floor. Her upper lip lifted in a sneer as she examined them. Their clothing was nondescript and concealing, offering no clues to their identities beyond the distinctive features of their race. *Djinns.* She doubted Indra had sent them. *Perhaps they're loyalists to the old king or the imuda.* Regardless of their loyalties, it didn't matter. She didn't care who had hired the two assassins or even who had unlocked the door to their room to let them sneak in. *At least whoever hired them didn't entirely underestimate us by sending just one assassin.*

Edging past the splatters of blood, she crossed the room and flung open the shutters to let in the early morning light. She raised her hand to snatch a beam of golden light and rolled it between her palms to create a thin, nearly solid laser beam of heat. She focused her will and power and aimed the molten beam at the carcasses. Still warm flesh sizzled for a few seconds. With a flash, the light expanded, enveloping the dead men. A moment later, the vaporized bodies had been reduced to small piles of oily dust. The sweet, putrid stench of charred flesh hung in the air.

Iselde released the light and heat she'd drawn from the sun and summoned a gust of wind. Currents of air swirled and lifted the dust and carried it and the stink out the window into the courtyard. She decided to cover the small scorch marks burned into the stone floor by dragging a small rug over them. The servants would no doubt notice, but they wouldn't question the rearrangement until after she and Koriolis left.

I am weary, Mother, of dancing to your schemes.

You can only evade your destiny for so long, daughter. Without my scheming, as you put it, you would not now be so well mated.

Iselde snorted. *Nor would I have been assigned the task of exterminating demons.*

You don't know that. The demon infestation would have spread even into the northern wastes. By then, there would be no recovering from the blight.

And now?

The Great Forest has already begun to reclaim territory ceded to the demons and the desert.

The djinns won't like that.

The djinns don't realize they exist here at fae sufferance.

And yet they and the demons with whom they ally had the power to repel and push back the Great Forest. They are stronger than they know.

And you and your mate are stronger yet.

Thus far we've been a surprise weapon, but I am sure word has spread. Both demons and djinns will be ready for us, prepared to fight us sooner rather than later.

That is so.

Consider this my resignation from your service. If you wish me to survive, then set your scheming to favor fae victory as Koriolis and I work our way north.

Daughter, no one is truly exempt from fate. Not even you. Especially not you.

Iselde's mental shields slammed down, cutting off the mind-to-mind link with her mother. Voice hissing, she whispered, "I am not your puppet."

The door opened. Iselde swiveled on her heel, claws unsheathed. A servant entered and skittered to a halt.

"Lady Fae!"

"Bring me food," she ordered, claws retracting. "Now."

Blanching in terror, the servant nodded, bowed, and rushed back out the door. As Iselde still stood by the window, she leaned out and scanned the pretty courtyard festooned with flowering vines, pebbled paths neatly raked, large urns overflowing with plants, and marble benches placed near a central fountain that gurgled with musical cheer. The bed-chamber had no door exiting to the courtyard, which was probably one reason why the leader of their military escort had assigned them that room: fewer opportunities to escape while still maintaining the fiction they were honored guests.

"Honored guests. Hah." Her upper lip curled in a sneer.

A current of air curled around her, ruffling the lightweight fabric of her robe. Frowning, she pressed her hand against the wall and waited.

"Are you sentient?"

Iselde had known sentient castles. Both the Erlking and the Unseelie King lived in such formidable edifices. So did the Seelie King, but she had only met King Mogren once, which was sufficient for her. She'd not liked the way he eyed her, thinking to take her as his mate and to sire powerful, royal sons upon her.

The palace did not respond to her query. She sent out a thin tentacle of power, using it to sense the existence of another power, but she felt nothing. Either the palace was sentient and ignoring her, or something else had sent that current of air in acknowledgement of her bitter words.

"This is Djaria which has no love for the fae, yet *we* are the ones who are ridding *your* land and *your* people of demon pes-tilence," she said, her tone acid. "Perhaps you might consider helping us."

The air pressure in the room increased, squeezing her a moment. She withstood the pressure without wincing, eyes blazing with sudden ire. Her power flared, a nimbus of white light enveloping her. The scent of ice and pine filled the room, an olfactory manifestation of her powerful presence. The clash of powers lasted but a moment, but the air pressure eased. Iselde nodded and the light dissolved.

"As soon as Koriolis acquires what we need, we'll depart and leave you in peace," she whispered. "We don't want to be here as much as you don't want us here."

Another curl of warm air brushed her cheek in approval.

CHAPTER 35

THE REMNANTS OF EXPENDED POWER IN THE ROOM made Koriolis' skin prickle when he returned with the ill-gotten gains of his visit to the quartermaster's office. "What happened?" he asked as he dumped the contents he carried onto the bed.

Iselde looked through the garments and replied, "The palace and I came to an understanding."

"The palace?" He looked around. "Is it sentient?"

"To a degree," she said. "It doesn't want us here."

"Well, we don't want to be here, so we're in agreement."

"I told you so."

Koriolis opened his mouth to speak then realized she was addressing the building, not him. Instead, he sorted through the pile of garments and dressed, cursing under his breath about the djinns' general lack of height. It had been difficult to find garments long enough for him.

"These are clean and in good repair," Iselde commented as she buckled a belt around her waist to keep the trews from falling off.

"Unfortunately, everything is emblazoned with the imuda's crest." He tugged on the cuff of one sleeve, but no amount of tugging would lengthen it sufficiently to cover his wrists. The breadth of his shoulders strained the seams of the shirt he'd filched.

"I'll bet Indra would find that interesting." She pulled on a shirt that hung loosely over her lean frame.

Koriolis fastened his belt. "The imuda doesn't really care, not anymore."

"Reduced him to a drooling imbecile, did you?" Iselde sat and pulled on some stockings.

He shrugged and pulled on a boot. "I was careless." He pulled on a second boot and brushed his hands across his thighs. "Are we ready?"

"Let's blow this popsicle stand," she replied.

Koriolis' eyebrows rose. "And where did you hear that expression?"

"It's something Zarafille said. I liked the sound of it."

He grinned at her adoption of the modern American idiom. They grabbed cloaks, checked to make sure their weaponry was in place, and turned to leave. The door swung open. They paused, but no one entered. They approached the doorway and peered through. No one lingered in the corridor.

"You're right. The palace wants us to leave," Koriolis whispered.

"And it's willing to show us the way," Iselde said as another door down the corridor swung open on silent hinges. "Thank you."

They raced to the other open door and passed through. With the preternatural speed of their kind, their roundabout route through the palace flitted them undetected past sleepy guards and servants, including one headed toward their room and carrying a large tray of food and drink. They did not stop moving until they stood outside the wall surrounding the palace grounds.

"Where to first?" Iselde wondered.

"Uhltar sits near the coast. We head toward water, then turn north."

"We'll hit the main trade road."

"Exactly."

In the pearly light of a lingering dawn, they ran through the city to find a row of wharfs where sailors were already loading and unloading ships.

"We could get passage aboard a ship," Iselde suggested.

Koriolis opened his mouth to agree, but the words stuck in his throat even as his feet refused to advance one more step. Swallowing them, he rasped, "We can't. *I* can't."

Iselde muttered a curse involving her mother's name then said, "The oracle is playing with us again. I'm sure it's her. All right, we'll head north over land."

Koriolis sighed as the tightness of his throat eased and the weird pressure immobilizing his legs and feet dissolved. He took two steps north, proving the oracle was indeed meddling. "I do *not* like your mother."

"No one does, my dearest. No one does." She took a deep breath as she scanned the tall masts and the flags flying from them. "Bide a moment."

Koriolis had no time to respond; she'd already run. He scanned the wharf and whispered, "No."

He turned toward the wharf, toward the ship he was certain she'd run to, but his feet would not take one step in that direction. His throat clogged with something he'd seldom experienced: fear. Unable to go after her, he waited, a solitary figure standing amid the growing bustle of a busy port.

Koriolis' eyes widened as his mate strolled toward him, her white braid like a line of light against the browns of her mismatched clothing. So garbed, she would fade into the background of the desert terrain as well as the tangle of mud brick dwellings of any Djarian city.

Next to Iselde walked the mighty king of the Unseelie Court. His silver eyes flashed in the early morning sunlight, and his raven hair flew behind him like a banner of ill omen. Koriolis swallowed hard when Iselde smiled up at the tall, imposing male. They stopped and Iselde took her place by her mate's side.

"Of all the places I thought I might see you again, Djaria isn't it," the Unseelie King greeted his oldest child, the one whom he'd banished so long ago to the mortal realm rather than see him crushed by an outraged castle to the death he deserved.

"Coming here wasn't really my idea," Koriolis replied, easily following his father's lead, including the absence of a normal greeting.

"We seek passage north," Iselde said.

The Unseelie King leveled a narrow-eyed look at his oldest son, the former crown prince. After a few uncomfortable seconds during which Koriolis fought the urge to squirm like an errant child, he nodded. "Come and meet your stepmother, my own beloved mate, and your siblings."

Koriolis bowed. "I am … sorry, Father."

"It's a bit late for that, boy," Uberon said, every icy syllable clipped. "I'd smite you where you stand, but for Iselde's sake, I will spare your miserable life."

Jealousy flared within him. "What is she to you?"

Cold silver eyes met his black ones without flinching, implacable as fae steel and just as sharp. "Iselde has always been like a daughter to me, and now she *is* my daughter through her mating to you."

Koriolis bowed again then tried to take a step toward the wharf where the Unseelie Court's ship was moored, but again his legs wouldn't move. Frustration, embarrassment, and shame washed over him. "I … I can't."

Uberon raised an eyebrow in silent query, or perhaps silent condemnation.

"Mother," Iselde explained in a low voice.

Uberon sighed. Aloud, although quietly, he said, "Cease your interference, Bathasul."

The unseen force preventing Koriolis from going where he willed grudgingly faded. He breathed a sigh of relief, finally realizing how Iselde must have felt all those millennia under the oracle's paw. Looking at his father, he added, "It is not only the oracle's machinations that bring us here."

"Ah, the swifts."

Iselde nodded. "Indeed."

"They're probably responsible for allowing that upstart god here, too."

"You know about Indra?"

The Unseelie King leveled his steely gaze at her. "Child, Gus and I know *everything*."

She nodded, accepting the explanation. Changing the topic, she asked about the Erlking, "So, how is Uncle Gus?"

The Unseelie King, before whom entire worlds tremble in terror, grinned, an expression Koriolis could not remember ever seeing on his father's face. "He is well, a doting papa. Oriole had twins, both daughters." He paused, then commanded, "Come. And be prepared to work for your passage."

"Yes, Father." Koriolis fell into step behind the Unseelie King.

"My sailors are not all fae. Those who are will not welcome you."

Koriolis understood the warning. "I will not give them trouble."

"Good."

They accompanied Uberon aboard the sleek, four-masted clipper that was the pride of his fleet. A black pennant with a silver crescent moon snapped in the stiff sea breeze. The sailors halted in their work to watch who boarded the ship. Those who realized the male's identity glowered. Uberon led them to the upper deck and stopped to face his crew. A tall, slender female with red-gold hair and ivory skin stood nearby, her hands resting protectively on the shoulders of two children. She appeared to know who Koriolis was, too, and did not approve of his proximity to her family.

The Unseelie King spoke, "This is Marog. Some of you know of him. He has returned to Fé-Ree. Accord him the respect and courtesy he earns."

"I am now called Koriolis Valchik Dra'Acul," Koriolis interjected in a loud voice, noticing and not resenting that his father had not included the title of prince. "Marog is *no more*."

"Not Tepes then?" Uberon murmured under his breath.

Koriolis stifled a sigh. "No, not him."

"Good to know."

Uberon gestured toward the tall, thin female standing on Koriolis' other side. "And this is his beloved mate, Iselde. You will accord her all the respect due to any daughter of mine."

The breeze caught someone's whisper of "Ice Queen" and flung it about the ship. Iselde's slitted cobalt gaze met each sailor's with icy confidence and queenly arrogance.

"Allow me to introduce you to my family," Uberon said in a conversational tone to his newest crew members. He turned to join the red-haired female and the two black-haired children. Sliding a hand around the female's slender waist, he pressed a kiss to her bright hair. "This is Corinne, my beloved, and these two are Garim and Marisala."

Iselde favored them with a small smile and a regal bow. Corinne held out her hand and Iselde clasped it. After a second of uncertainty, they shook briefly. Iselde pitched her voice to soft warmth and looked into the Unseelie Queen's emerald eyes. "I am pleased to meet you. Thank you for allowing us to share your ship."

When Iselde stepped back, Koriolis stepped forward. A hard glare from his father prevented him from taking another step. He retreated, bowed, and said, "I am grateful for your generosity."

The Unseelie Queen tilted her head, her expression of polite welcome turning cold and predatory. "I've heard about you. Stay away from my children."

He felt the throb of her power and knew his father had found a mate who was his match. He nodded and replied in a grave tone, "They are safe from me."

Iselde's hand slid into his, a silent gesture of support. Koriolis knew he had much to atone for and that atonement would be long in coming if he ever managed to achieve it at all. After millennia of living in urban locations, the idea of residing where there were few people who knew of his transgressions and fewer to sneer at him appealed. *Perhaps the northern wastes will be my home after all, despite what the swifts said.*

A snap of air announced the apparition of Captain Ibi Abdil. The Unseelie King turned to him, his expression icy and forbidding. The captain nodded to him and faced Koriolis and Iselde. "I did not give you leave to depart."

"We are not under your command," Koriolis replied in an even tone.

"Nor Indra's," Iselde added.

"You will return to the palace immediately," the captain ordered.

Uberon's softly spoken baritone carried clearly across the ship: "You are not welcome aboard my ship. Depart. Now."

The captain looked over his shoulder at the tall fae male who commanded him to leave and sneered, "And who are you to order me, fae?"

Uberon's lips pulled back to reveal his own serrated smile. Power throbbed in the air. With quiet satisfaction, Iselde answered the djinn warrior's question, "The Unseelie King."

The captain's dusky skin turned ashen. "King Indra shall hear of this."

Koriolis replied with studied nonchalance, "We don't care."

CHAPTER 36

THEY SAILED FOR THREE DAYS BEFORE PULLING into port in Tunus, one of Djaria's ancient port cities. As Koriolis expected, the crew put him to the most miserable tasks aboard the ship, a measure to humble him and remind him of their antipathy. He did not complain, but performed each task with quiet competence. He'd lived long enough to know this trial, too, would pass. The crew treated Iselde with chilly deference and respect, having no grudge against the fabled Ice Queen of the northern wastes. They all wondered how the Unseelie King's disgraced and exiled son had managed to capture her and take her to mate. Although disinclined to engage in friendly chatter with the sailors, she offered them no insult and worked as hard as any of them, despite her lack of familiarity with the workings of a sailing ship.

In Tunus, everyone took shifts to disembark and mingle with other crews and merchants at taverns and restaurants and various shops. Beyond the natural inclination to enjoy their free time, Uberon's sailors used the opportunity to collect news and gossip. Bloodthirst gnawing at him, Koriolis went hunting when he was given leave to go to shore. Once sated and having turned his drained prey into ashes with Asi, he sat in a tavern to wash the taste of blood and power from his mouth and to listen to the gossip.

"Did you hear?" one barmaid said with salacious glee. "Every demon—every single one—in Uhltar was found dead two days ago! No one knows what killed them."

Another serving wench added her bit of gossip, "I heard that demons are dying in huge numbers as though from some pestilence that only affects them. Perhaps there's some contagious disease that only demons get?"

"Well, good riddance to them," the barmaid said, snapping her rag then wringing it out. "One of my sisters was eaten by demons, filthy, vile abominations."

Sitting at the bar, Koriolis finished his beer and set the mug on the bar. He rose from the stool and left the building, returning to the ship to meet Iselde. She brought him a bucket of water, soap, and a rag to clean himself of demon blood and any lingering bits of gore while they discussed the gossip.

"I wonder if it's the imuda's palace's doing?" she wondered.

"What do you mean?"

She related the rather one-sided exchange she'd had with the palace. "The building is married to the earth. It could very well have sent the command throughout Djaria into the land itself to kill the demons."

He frowned. "I'm not sure how the palace could do that."

She shrugged. "It's not necessary to know *how*. What I do know is that the palace is very, very old. Ancient things acquire power and knowledge."

"So?"

"The palace didn't want us there and was happy to help us leave. I'm going to guess it doesn't want the demons there either and is happy to somehow kill them off, since the demons *won't* leave."

"Then why didn't it act earlier?" he asked, pointing out the illogic.

"Sentient buildings tend not to be creative. Their sentience is meant to serve their occupants, not necessarily the greater good," she explained. "Did not the Unseelie Court's fortress serve you?"

He nodded in dim recollection. "It did, but more to the point, it served my father." He paused. "But cities beyond Uhltar?"

"Many of Djaria's cities are ancient. They arose because they offer sustainable sources for water and agriculture and remain because, for all their faults, the djinns aren't stupid. They know their homeland offers few places amenable to life." She tapped her bottom lip with an index finger as she pondered the matter. A moment later, she resumed speaking. "It's not beyond possibility that these ancient sites found connection through the ley lines."

"You loathe the djinns."

She blinked at the non sequitur. "I do. But that doesn't mean they aren't smart or adaptable. It also doesn't mean I am not happy to leave them to their beloved desert."

"You are a contradiction."

She shook her head and shrugged. "Perhaps. Mostly, I'm tolerant. I do not bother those who do not bother me." She flashed her pointed teeth. "Back home, I am seldom bothered."

He accepted that argument. "Who would dare venture into the northern wastes to accost you?"

She smiled at him. "Only the stupid, and they never make that mistake again."

Koriolis didn't ask whether she killed those fools.

A few hours later, Iselde disembarked for her shift on shore. As had her mate, she brought back news. "There is word from Djaria's northern border that the desert is retreating. The Great Forest is reclaiming lost territory."

That was fast. Koriolis mused aloud, "I wonder if this has anything to do with the deaths of the demons?"

"Of course, it does," she replied. "The swifts told us it was the presence—the taint—of demonkind that allowed the desert to expand. The swifts themselves could not venture into the desert."

"Then I'd say we've done our job," Koriolis said. "I grow weary of the constant slaughter and would enjoy some peace."

Iselde nodded, worrying that his powerful thirst for demon blood was more of an addiction. "Perhaps not quite in the manner the swifts anticipated, but the means don't matter so much as the end result." She leaned her head back, raising her face to the clear sky above. With a sigh, she said, "I cannot wait to return home."

Koriolis looked at the latest blister on his palm at the base of his thumb and agreed, "I cannot wait to make the northern wastes my home."

After taking on additional cargo, the ship returned to sea for two weeks before stopping at the next port where Uberon himself conducted business rather than leaving negotiations and transactions to the ship's captain. Goods were unloaded and more merchandise and supplies taken aboard over two days in port. On shore leave, Koriolis assuaged his ravening thirst for demon blood, efficiently hunting and killing every demon within the small city. Iselde did not remark upon his brutal efficiency and worried when he returned, his hunger unsatisfied. She also noticed the Unseelie King's assessing, silver gaze following her mate, but Koriolis controlled himself and displayed no aggression toward anyone aboard the ship beyond the occasional baring of pointed teeth.

Then they set sail again and headed for the open sea. Noticing a change in direction and the drain of power as they neared an archipelago weeks later, Iselde asked the captain where they were headed.

"There's an island where the gargoyles have made their home," the captain replied. "You'll find no magic there, not a single spark."

Iselde's face lit with curiosity.

"You truly don't want to visit there, my lady. Them gargoyles is *hungry*."

"My captain speaks truly," Uberon said, approaching silently from behind. "None but I am permitted to step foot upon their shores uninvited. All others they kill."

Iselde wanted to protest for the sake of her warrior pride, but knew that Uberon would not deceive her. Bereft of her formidable magic, she was little better than a weak human and no match for a large, ferocious predator such as a gargoyle. *How will Koriolis deal with his bloodthirst?*

"Spend time with Corinne," he suggested. "She would like to know you better."

Iselde nodded. "I'll do that." *Corinne might need someone to fend off Koriolis if he cannot control his bloodlust.*

Uberon nodded his dismissal of her and faced the ship's captain. Iselde returned to her duties and pondered what she would discuss with the Unseelie Queen. They had little in common.

When the crew gathered for their midday meal, Iselde found herself sitting between the bosun and another sailor. Both made very certain neither touched her. She appreciated their restraint, for the close quarters made her feel jittery. She realized the only male whose proximity she welcomed was her mate's—and he would definitely and violently object were any other male to touch her.

They do well not to touch you. I would kill them otherwise.
That wouldn't exactly endear you to them or to your father.
Father would understand.

She didn't argue that point. Uberon was protective to the point of obsession regarding his mate and their children. She finished her meal and headed back to work, still glad to have something to do that didn't involve killing. Feeling the echo of strain as her mate controlled his craving for demon blood, she turned her face to the warm, tropical wind and inhaled deeply of the ocean's scents of salt and fish and seaweed and the musky odor of the wooden ship. She listened to the gentle creak of wood, the quiet rattle of blocks and tackles, and the snap of black canvas sails. The journey thus far had been strangely peaceful, but she knew that, just like the northern wastes, the ocean could turn against them at any moment.

I detect no power, but do you think your father is influencing the weather? It's been strangely cooperative.

Of course, he is. Uberon leaves nothing to chance. He'll have reset the patterns of winds and currents weeks ago to ensure we're not caught in a storm within the time allotted for this journey.

Of course, I did. I do not risk my beloved mate or our children.

Iselde blinked in surprise, not having expected the Unseelie King to intercept her mind-to-mind conversation with Koriolis and inject himself into it.

You've grown lax with your mental shields, Uberon pointed out.

Indeed.

Iselde put more effort and attention into raising and maintaining strong mental shields, although doing so got harder and harder as they sailed closer to the archipelago where the gargoyles made their home.

After another two weeks of steady winds that kept the clipper skimming across the ocean's surface, the ship sailed into a small cove as close to shore as it could get without running aground in the shallow water. At the captain's signal, the first mate put a horn to his mouth and announced their arrival. The shrill sound sliced through the gentle breeze.

Hulking, unmistakably male figures bulging with muscles, adorned with curling horns and fearsome claws and bearing large leathery wings, gathered at the shoreline. As the ship lowered a fully loaded longboat, three of the gargoyles waded into the surf until they were waist deep in the water.

From his position in the boat, Uberon tossed a coil of rope to them. They caught it and began hauling the boat to shore. Iselde, Koriolis, Corinne, the children, and the crew watched as Uberon hailed them and spoke with them. Iselde called to the wind, hoping to summon a sprite, but nothing answered her summons.

"There's no magic here," Koriolis whispered, seeing the puzzled expression on her face. He rubbed his flat stomach, pressing the heel of his hand into the taut muscle as pain twinged. "None whatsoever."

"It's worse than the mortal realm," she said. *At least there I could access power.*

"I fret for him every time he comes here," Corinne confessed, overhearing Koriolis' words. "The gargoyles, however, are devoted to him. They have been good friends to me. But here, where there is no magic to sustain them in stone, they … change. They *hunger*. I worry their hunger will overcome their respect for Uberon."

"You are right to worry," Iselde replied, her voice quiet and somber. She touched the other female's hand, offering comfort. "Come, let's not borrow ill tidings. Tell me why Uberon brought you and the children on this journey."

Corinne sighed and let the other fae female lead her to the captain's quarters which Uberon had commandeered. The captain, in turn, had claimed the first mate's quarters for his own use. They stopped by the galley to request tea and sandwiches from the ship's cook. Koriolis joined them in the galley and simply stated, "I'm hungry."

Corinne sighed again when they took their seats in the cabin. Koriolis stationed himself outside the cabin door. The Unseelie Queen greeted both children with hugs and kisses as though they'd been parted for days rather than minutes. Looking at Iselde, she admitted, "I wanted to see for myself."

Iselde understood what the other female did not voice. "And now you have."

Corinne nodded and leaned forward. "So, tell me about yourself. I did not even know you existed, that the oracle had a daughter."

"Few people remember the oracle has a daughter," Iselde confided. "I prefer it that way."

"That means Enders is your uncle."

"It does."

"I imagine you have gone on wonderful adventures with Enders."

Iselde snorted. "Not so much. I'm not the scholar he wished to make me."

Corinne chuckled. "Few are. Did Uberon tell you how he had me learn about the Unseelie Court?"

"No."

The queen shook her head. "He had me record court proceedings. My hands would cramp terribly from all that writing!"

"Does Uberon still hold daily audiences?"

"When he's home, yes. He's a good king, a fair ruler."

"Yes." Iselde tilted her head, pondering what being a good and fair ruler required. "That is why Enders does not claim a court for himself. He would not be a good king."

Corinne blinked. "You know, I hadn't considered that, but you make sense. He prefers to manipulate from behind the throne."

"He's much like my mother in that sense. They're twins, you know."

At a knock on the door, Corinne sent one of the children to answer it. The cook's assistant entered with a loaded tray.

"Ah, lunch!" Corinne exclaimed.

CHAPTER 37

THE UNSEELIE KING STAYED ON THE GARGOYLE'S island for four days, returning to the ship with four gargoyles who flew him, his queen, and their children, to the island for an overnight visit while livestock and other goods were unloaded and transported to the island under the the captain's strict supervision. No one dared wander off to explore the island after unloading crates and cages on the narrow beach. Koriolis and Iselde did not accompany the king, his family, or the sailors.

Instead, Koriolis collapsed in his bunk, shivering and sweating with an uncontrollable craving that neither food nor water could satiate. He vomited what was given to him and cried out in delirium while Iselde tended to him as best she could with the crude implements available: a wet rag, a bowl of cool water, small cups of broth, and bits of bread provided by the ship's cook.

"I seen a man like that once," one of the sailors, a canidae, commented, pausing to help Iselde restrain the male's thrashing limbs. "It weren't the ague, but the red tar that held him in its thrall. He were dependent on it, and when the supply stopped …"

Iselde sighed and nodded. "I agree with you. Koriolis is suffering the absence of his addiction."

The sailor frowned. "Addiction to what, though? I ain't never seen him nor you chew the red tar or nothin' like that."

She gave him a small, sad smile. "It's an insatiable hunger for demon's blood imposed upon him. He did not choose it, but it was a condition of his return to Fé-Ree."

The sailor grunted as he wrestled Koriolis' lower half, finally draping himself over the male's kicking legs to hold them still. "Should've stayed where he was then."

Koriolis groaned and twisted, causing his shirt to pull away and reveal the jeweled silver band emblazoned across his chest. He flung an arm, nearly catching his mate upside the head. Iselde ducked and seized the limb and tried to anchor it beneath her body. Breathing heavily and sweating, she glanced at Koriolis' sweat-drenched face and replied, "Then I would have died."

The sailor grunted again and pressed down on an ankle, carefully avoiding the sharp claws extending from Koriolis' toes. "Almost makes me glad I'm not mate-bound."

With a loud, incoherent cry, her mate bucked beneath them before subsiding with a deep groan and a whimper of distress.

"Thank you," Iselde said with true gratitude as she drew back, carefully releasing her hold on him. "He should be quiet for a while now."

The sailor pushed himself off the bunk and stood. With a nod of respect, he left them to return to his duties.

A day later, loud thumps above deck announced the return of the gargoyles and Uberon's family. A shadow filled the hatch, the light streaming through momentarily blocked by the Unseelie King's tall, broad figure as he climbed down into the crew quarters. He strode to Koriolis' bunk and looked at the sweating, wretched male to whom Iselde was mated.

"How is he doing?"

She turned her face up to glare at him. "You did this on purpose."

"I did," he replied, his tone cool. "I know what the swifts did to him."

"This is cruel to make him suffer so."

"Perhaps, but I took a chance that the absence of magic would force his body to withdraw from the addiction imposed upon him."

She shook her head. "He would have weaned himself off the demon's blood."

"Ah, but we can't truly know that. In this place without magic, the swifts cannot influence him, although your mother … well, I have spoken with her," he countered. "Marog—"

"Koriolis," she corrected.

"—was bolstering his resistance with his own innate power, but only a true break, a *severing* if you will, would free him of this addiction."

"I have seen addiction before," she reminded him.

He nodded. "You have, but you have not been involved with it."

"And you have?" she challenged.

"Aye." He did not offer an explanation, and she knew better than to ask. "I'll have the cook send ginger water down to you. We'll stay here another day to make sure the compulsion is fully severed." His flashing silver gaze met hers. "He is still my son, Iselde."

Iselde sighed and shook her head, cobalt eyes brimming with unshed tears of frustration, anger, and grief.

"You'll thank me later," he promised.

"I doubt it."

"Then he will," Uberon said. He took a step back then paused. "Though he is no longer the crown prince of the Unseelie Court and no longer acknowledged as my heir, I do still love my son."

"Though you would kill him if you deemed it necessary."

"Aye."

Iselde bowed her head, wrung out the water-soaked rag, and dabbed at Koriolis' forehead. Voice thin and weak, she admitted, "As would I." She took a deep breath. "But first I want him to live as he was meant to do."

"The oracle's daughter believing in fate?" Uberon chuckled. "I never thought I'd see that day."

"You're just as manipulative as she is," Iselde accused. She dipped the rag in the bowl again.

"I believe in redemption," he said, then turned on his heel and headed back up. "I was a poor father to him, but I received the chance to do better with Corinne and our children. Mar— Koriolis deserves the opportunity to redeem himself."

Iselde squeezed most of the water from the rag and applied it to Koriolis' feverish brow again. Still unconscious, he moaned.

A collective sigh of relief rose from the crew when the ship finally sailed from the small cove and headed back out to sea. More sighs of relief accompanied nervous, over-the-shoulder glances as the island receded in the growing distance and no gargoyles flew after the ship. Within two days of departing the island, the crew had returned to their normal routines. Within five days, weak and disoriented, Koriolis rose trembling from his bunk. Iselde gently guided him to the weather deck where he found a coil of rope on which to sit and soak up the tropical sunshine. Iselde retrieved a jug of ginger water, some bread, and a small dish of herb-infused oil which he consumed with slow, cautious care.

Iselde tended to him as he recuperated, a dedicated helpmeet assiduous in her efforts to restore her mate to health. The energy he'd burned, combined with his inability to retain food or water, had reduced him to skin and bones. Generous portions of fish caught by sailors made their way down his gullet after passing through the galley for seasoning and cooking. Iselde made sure to thank the cook and crew for their generosity.

"He's become one of us," the bosun replied with simple honesty. "He's worked hard and not complained. We respect that."

By the end of that week, Koriolis insisted on returning to work, carrying out light duty with a peaceful calm that sat oddly upon his shoulders. As Iselde kept a wary eye on him, she noticed that those broad shoulders, now bony beneath the ragged state of his shirt, no longer held the stiff tension of power, restrained violence, and gnawing addiction. She wondered if his connection to his magic had been irrevocably sundered. Even the connection of the mate bond felt diminished, almost ethereal.

Koriolis said nothing about his loss of power.

Weeks passed in relative calm with Uberon ensuring the weather remained cooperative. The ship anchored in several more ports, continuing the exchange of merchandise that made the captain's eyes light up with mercenary satisfaction. Koriolis did not disembark, and Asi hung unused over his bunk.

The ship finally floated into the harbor of the Unseelie Kingdom's capital. Standing at the rail or perched among the sails, everyone aboard could see Uberon's towering fortress looming over the city like a harbinger of doom and threatening any ill-intentioned invader with lethal retaliation. Gargoyles flew up from the gray crenelated walls, their wings carrying them over the city and the water to alight with delicate precision aboard the ship. After a short, quiet word with the gargoyles, Uberon handed his mate and two children to the hulking, winged protectors who transported them safely back to the fortress.

"Captain, the ship is yours," Uberon called out. With a curt wave of his hand, he summoned Iselde and Koriolis. "Come with me."

They fell into step behind him as he walked down the gangway and up the pier to shore. They followed him through the surprisingly orderly arrangement of offices, warehouses, shops, restaurants, inns, and residences to climb the steep hills and traverse the narrow lanes leading to the castle.

"It looks like the Amalfi Coast," Koriolis commented, his voice pitched under the soft soughing of the ocean breeze.

Uberon heard it anyway. "But not as infested with tourists and better organized."

"You're familiar with it?" Koriolis panted. Sweat soaked through his clothes. His heart pounded, and his muscles ached from the exertion of climbing to the castle.

Uberon snorted. "You'll spend a few days enjoying my hospitality before you resume your journey. It will take great strength and perseverance to cross the Quol on your way to the northern wastes."

"Thank you."

"We'll travel slowly," Iselde said, "so that you will have fully recovered your strength before we venture into the Quol."

Koriolis barked a harsh laugh. "I do not know that I shall ever fully recover my strength."

"Then I shall protect you," she said.

He turned his bleak gaze to her. "I cannot even feel the magic anymore."

She patted his arm. "It is early days yet. You are fae, and we fae are creatures of magic."

He shook his head, lank sweaty locks swinging. "And when bereft of magic, we become as weak and mortal as any human."

"Then I'll have to find a vampire to turn you," she retorted.

"No."

"No?"

"No." He panted several breaths before being able to continue speaking. "I will not accept any master in exchange for immortality."

"You would rather die?"

"Than be eternally bound to a vampire who sires me? Yes."

Iselde swallowed her horror at his willingness to accept mortality and death, his willingness to abandon her and relinquish the mate bond. She'd endured two mates who died, one from his own foolishness and the other from old age. (She didn't count the one whom she'd killed.) She did not know whether she could endure a third such loss, especially since

Koriolis was her true mate, the true match for her soul. Taking a deep breath, she vowed, "Then it shall not come to that."

Silently, she decided to seek the assistance of the unicorns to restore her mate. *If only they ventured into the northern wastes.*

They certainly would not venture into the Quol, still a vast, hostile jungle despite having been contained and much of its territory reclaimed by the Unseelie King and his allies.

CHAPTER 38

ON THE THIRD DAY OF THEIR STAY IN THE UNSEELIE Court, a servant entered the drawing room where Koriolis sat reading a book and Iselde sat cleaning her copper sword.

"You have a caller, my lord."

They exchanged glances, neither having expected anyone to call upon them, especially not there.

"Who is it?" Iselde inquired.

"Don't bother to announce me," a familiar voice called out. The servant stepped aside as Indra swept past him into the room. He struck a pose, fists resting on his hips and one foot tapping. The god-king of Djaria leveled a hard look at Koriolis and demanded, "Give it back."

"You mean Asi?" Koriolis prompted, not bothering to rise.

Indra frowned at the disrespect. "Of course, I mean Asi. It was never yours to keep—and you're not even using it to kill demons anymore."

"The last we heard," Iselde said, interjecting herself into the conversation, "demons were dropping dead en masse."

"They were in the major cities," Indra confirmed. He frowned. "I don't know how you managed that."

"I didn't," Koriolis said. He gestured toward his mate. "She did."

Indra shook his head. "Don't bother to explain. *I* have to pick up where you left off."

"Did you bring our blood money?" Iselde asked, her tone and pose the essence of aristocratic nonchalance.

"Your what?"

She raised her eyebrows. "The wages you promised us for slaughtering demons in Djaria."

"You didn't kill them *all,* so, no, I didn't."

"But we did kill many," she pointed out. "And you promised compensation for our work."

"You mercenary little—"

"Don't," Koriolis warned, his voice a low growl.

Indra glared at him.

"A promise is sacred in Fé-Ree," Iselde said.

"Says who?" Indra glared at her. "I thought fae couldn't lie."

"Lying has nothing to do with breaking a promise," she pointed out.

"Sophistry." Indra's upper lip lifted in a sneer. Instead of continuing the argument with Iselde, he returned his attention to Koriolis. "Give it back."

Koriolis looked at Iselde. She shrugged and said, "We're not using it, and it won't have any effect on the Quoli beyond any other sharp blade."

Koriolis nodded. He set the book aside and rose. "I'll return shortly."

Indra glowered at him as he departed. Returning his attention to Iselde, he complained, "Your hospitality leaves much to be desired."

"We didn't invite you here," she said. "And it's not *my* hospitality."

He waved his hand. "Yes, yes, I know. This pile of stones belongs to the Unseelie King."

"And have you met him?"

"Who? The Unseelie King? What use have I for a prancing faerie princeling?"

"Don't let him hear you say that," she warned, amusement glinting in her cobalt eyes.

"I'm a *god*."

"In Fé-Ree, one might call him the same."

Indra sighed. "Iselde, I helped you. I treated you and Koriolis well, yet you abandoned your task. All I require now is that you return what I loaned you: Asi."

She nodded, a regal dip of her chin. "And we are happy to return the sword to you, but you may find it … changed."

Indra frowned again. "Changed? How?"

She explained, "We visited an island where there is no magic, none at all. The absence of power affected Koriolis, as you can very well see. He's not drawn Asi since before then—and you know I cannot wield it—so, we do not know whether those days spent without magic have affected the sword."

The god-king of Djaria brushed her concern aside. "If nothing else, I can restore it."

"Good to know," she replied and reached over to tug on the bell pull. A servant responded within seconds. She ordered a tray of refreshments be brought up.

"That's more like it," Indra grumbled as he took a seat. He leaned forward, bracing his elbows on his knees. "What happened to Koriolis?"

"He lost his magic."

Indra considered the statement. "Did he lose his magic, or did he lose his *connection* to magic?"

"I hadn't thought of that. He's not been able to sense power at all, not even the mate bond."

Indra pondered the matter. "You do realize I'm still available … and powerful? You could throw him over and accept my offer, be my queen."

"I am not so fickle," she replied, her tone prim.

Indra shrugged. "Ah, well, I'll have to try again later when the honeymoon's over."

Iselde frowned, not understanding the reference.

A servant arrived bearing a tray laden with delicacies and a pot of tea. Iselde poured. Indra took an appreciative sniff of the steaming brew then delicately sipped.

"Ahh, that's delightful. It tastes exactly like Darjeeling."

"It probably is Darjeeling," she replied, drizzling some honey into her cup. "Corinne likes it, and whatever Corinne likes Uberon makes sure she has."

"You fae are disgustingly indulgent," he commented and took another long sip. "But in this case, I can't complain. I've missed good tea."

"You could always return to the mortal realm."

He shuddered. "And once again be resigned to being nothing more than a rain god?" He shuddered again. "Perish the thought. I'll stay in Djaria. It's good to be king."

"As you wish," she replied mildly and took a slow sip from her own cup. "You should try those little cakes. They're wonderful."

Indra obliged and popped one in his mouth. He chewed, swallowed, and grinned. "You're right. I may have to steal your father-in-law's chef."

Iselde looked at him, not quite able to detect whether he was joking. Koriolis returned with Asi, saving her from the obligation to respond to the god's comment. He presented the sword, still sheathed in its scabbard, and said, "As requested."

Indra set aside his cup and saucer and stood. He took Asi and drew it, the soft hiss of the metal gliding through the scabbard filling the room. He ran his gaze over the blade, noting every tiny nick and a few spots of rust. Leveling a reproachful look at Koriolis, he said, "You didn't take very good care of it."

Koriolis shrugged. "I haven't been able to draw it since … since …"

"Since you lost your magic," Indra filled in. He sheathed the sword, the practiced move efficient and smooth. He approached, one hand outstretched. "May I?"

Koriolis nodded.

"What are you going to do?" Iselde asked, blinking at the god's mercurial change of attitude.

"Fix what's broken," Indra replied. "I tear down and rebuild worlds. This shouldn't be difficult."

"I won't have you tearing him down," Iselde objected.

"It looks like you or someone else has already torn him down." Indra stepped closer and placed his hand on Koriolis' head. He took a long breath and closed his eyes. "Interesting."

"What is it?" Iselde asked, worry quickly morphing into panic.

"Nothing I can't handle," Indra replied. He took another breath and concentrated his will.

Iselde heard the distant roar of power and felt it thrum in the core of her being. Koriolis closed his eyes against the surge of agony that whipped through him, mind and body. His legs buckled, and he began to convulse. His jaw locked in a rictus and foam gathered in his mouth and spilled over his chin. Keeping his hand on the male's head, Indra crouched down beside him. Korolis gurgled, a terrible, disturbing sound. Iselde shot to her feet with a wordless shriek of outrage.

"Bide a moment," a cool command from the doorway locked her in place.

She looked to the doorway where Uberon stood, his attitude watchful but not threatening. She looked back at her mate who shuddered weakly and sagged, his strength drained.

"I'll keep my gold," Indra said as he withdrew his hand from Koriolis' sweat-soaked crown. "Consider this payment in full."

The god-king of Djaria rose and glanced at the door. "So, you're Uberon."

The Unseelie King raised an eyebrow. "And you're Indra."

Indra flashed a tight smile at him. "Nice to make your acquaintance. I'd stay, but I've got some demons to kill in Djaria."

"Your kingdom, your rules," Uberon replied with a grave nod.

"Exactly."

Indra swept past Uberon who followed him with that inscrutable silver gaze. A moment later he stepped into the room and kneeled beside his oldest son. He pressed his palm against Koriolis' forehead and looked at Iselde, a small smile curling his lips.

"Indra probably doesn't realize what he just did," he said.

Iselde averted her eyes to stare at her unconscious mate. His lungs did not draw air. Tears gathered in her eyes and dripped to the floor, hardening into tiny white stones that pattered upon landing. "What did he do, exactly?"

"He conveyed a good bit of his essence into Marog."

"Koriolis," she corrected.

"Koriolis," he repeated. "Interesting. A fae turned nearly demon restored to mostly fae then drained to mortality and … well, *restored* isn't quite the right word … but *transformed* into what might be called a demigod. I've never seen quite the like happen before."

Iselde spread her hand across her mate's still chest and felt no heartbeat. Fury ignited in her gut, and she hissed, "He killed Koriolis!"

Uberon wrapped a hand around her upper arm. "Be at peace, daughter. That piece of himself—the power—that Indra gave to Koriolis he will not recoup. Indra may not yet realize he has, of his own free will, diminished himself. From here on, he will remain in Fé-Ree."

"As king of Djaria?" Iselde scoffed. "So what? My mate is dead."

"Not dead, not really," Uberon insisted. He blinked his silver eyes. "Give him time to return. Use the mate bond to call him back to himself and to you."

Iselde blinked, releasing more tears that hardened and pattered on the floor. She looked within herself and found the mate bond, lately having dwindled to a thin shadow of itself, once again burning brightly, although still threadlike. She grasped it with metaphysical hands and called her mate's name, sending her love and worry and desire for him across the connection between their souls. She did not notice Uberon rise and leave.

Iselde remained kneeling beside her mate as the hours passed. Servants brought trays of food and drink which she ignored. Corinne entered the room to check on her, but Iselde ignored her, too. Then, as the twin moons rose high in the night sky, she heard the ring of a unicorn's hoof on the stone terrace outside the drawing room. The terrace doors swung open and the dawn swift minced inside the room.

"Interesting," the beast commented after dipping its head and sniffing Koriolis' gaunt body. Iselde leaned aside to avoid being swiped by the spiral horn. The unicorn touched the tip of its spiral horn, then raised its head and tilted it to one side, meeting her gaze with one gimlet eye. "We did not foresee this."

She blinked and wiped away a tear. "Will you restore him?"

The unicorn snorted softly. "Oh, that's not possible. Not now." The horn dipped and touched her on the shoulder. "Take heart, daughter. All is not lost."

Iselde bowed her head and sniffled. The unicorn minced from the room back out to the terrace and disappeared as though it became one with the beams of moonlight. She leaned down and pressed her cheek to Koriolis' heart and listened to the silence beneath his skin. And she continued to call him, both with her voice and through the mate bond, soul to soul.

Night passed and gave way to the pearly light of dawn. When the golden beams of sunlight pierced the open windows and arrowed straight to Koriolis' face, his mouth gaped open and his chest expanded in a sudden and deep inhalation of breath. Iselde jerked back with a gasp, and tears welled anew when his eyes snapped open.

They were gold.

CHAPTER 39

NORMALLY QUIET, THE CASTLE SUDDENLY SWARMED with activity. A gargoyle scooped Koriolis off the floor and carried him to a bedchamber. A servant rushed into the room, bearing a tray with a pot of hot tea and a pitcher of cool water. Iselde followed close behind the gargoyle, not caring about the small fortune in fae tears she left scattered on the floor. She refused to allow her mate out of her sight. Gently placed on a bed, Koriolis sighed but said nothing. His golden eyes blinked slowly but did not appear to see.

"What is wrong?" she whispered to the Unseelie King who stood just inside the doorway. His queen stood with him, clasping his hand. "How do I fix him?"

"I don't know," he admitted.

Iselde's hands curled into fists as she took a deep breath to compose herself. With careful grace, she seated herself on the edge of the bed. She opened one hand and set it gently on his arm.

"*Kiya hawa?*" he whispered, his voice rasping as if coming though rusted vocal cords.

Iselde shook her head, not understanding the words.

He tried again. "*Enna natantatu?*"

Again she did not understand. He blinked rapidly as he seemed to sort through a vast repository of memories until he spoke a third time in the fae High Tongue: "What happened?"

Iselde's shoulders sagged with relief. Clasping his hand between both of hers, she asked, "Do you know who I am?"

He paused, again rifling through his memories for the answer. Slowly, it came: "Mate."

"Yes," she replied. "I am Iselde, your mate."

"What happened?" he repeated.

She shook her head. "I'm not entirely sure, but Uncle Uberon says you're a demigod now." She paused as he frowned, taking in her words. Then she said, "Rest now. We are finished hunting demons."

"Demons?" he rasped, the hand clasped between hers twitching.

She pressed it more firmly between her palms. "I'll tell you everything after you get some rest and eat."

"Hungry," he murmured, closing his eyes.

"That's a good sign," Corinne commented with a small smile from where she stood in the doorway. Uberon stood behind her, his hands resting on her shoulders.

Iselde stiffened, but did not turn to face the other female. Instead she replied just as quietly while she sat by his side and listened to him breathe, "As long as he's not hungry for demon blood."

She did not notice the Unseelie King and Queen leave. She paid no attention to the servants who shuffled in and left food and drink. She waited in stillness with the expertise of a skilled predator, ready to pounce on any disturbance or anomaly.

As Koriolis slept, she vowed never to return to Djaria. Indra could have that desert and its detested people with her blessing. She wondered if he realized that annihilating the demon population would result in shrinking the desert's expanse, that the Great Forest would push against the retreat of hot djinni and demon magic and fill the space with its own verdant power. She also wondered if he realized he was now trapped in the fae realm. If he didn't, she certainly wasn't going to inform him.

Under Iselde's careful watch, Koriolis ate and drank of foods harvested from his host's extensive gardens, orchards, dairy, and coop. She did not wish to trigger his bloodlust by feeding him flesh, however well-cooked that might have been.

"I want protein," Koriolis grumbled after swallowing the last bit of a boiled egg. He leveled a hard look at his mate and specified, "Meat."

Iselde stifled a sigh and nodded. "I'll see what the kitchen is preparing."

Nodding graciously, he replied, "Thank you."

That evening, she brought him a tray laden with vegetables, fruit, cheese, and bread—and a plate of delicately prepared fish.

"Don't think I don't know what you're doing," he commented as he dug into his supper.

She raised her eyebrows in a silent prompt.

He took a breath and gathered his thoughts. After a moment during which he consumed two healthy mouthfuls of food, he resumed speaking. "The bloodthirst is gone."

"You're certain?"

"I am." He leaned his head back against the headboard and sighed. "I'm as weak as a newborn kitten, but there's no craving for blood, demon or otherwise."

Hope ignited in her heart. A slow smile of relief spread across her face. She sighed then said, "That is good news."

"Perhaps tomorrow you'll allow me to rise from bed and work on regaining my strength?"

Cobalt eyes gleaming, she nodded. "Of course. I fear we're wearing out our welcome."

"I'm surprised His Majesty has accommodated us for this long," came the dry response. He paused, then asked, "How long has it been, exactly?"

A light knock on the bedchamber door halted whatever Iselde would have replied. Instead she called out, "Enter!"

The door swung open, and an old female entered, her step firm if slow. Koriolis stopped chewing and lowered his hands to the tray on his lap. Iselde's eyes widened in surprise.

"Mother? What are you doing here?"

The oracle stopped in the middle of the room and tilted her head. One hand clasped the white pendant dangling between her breasts. "How did you do it?"

"Do what?" Iselde asked, instantly wary, for her mother *never* left her humble cottage.

"You evaded your destiny. *Again.*"

"Do you mean the destiny of slaughtering demons in Djaria?"

"Yes. I meant for *you* to rule Djaria. You would save the djinns from the demons and set yourselves up as their new king and queen. *That* was your destiny."

"Despite all your machinations, Mother, I still have free will," Iselde reminded her. "Besides, I don't want to rule Djaria."

"No, that pesky god, Indra, upset my plans." The oracle glared at her only child. "Why did you not send him back to the mortal realm?"

Iselde shrugged, knowing no answer she offered would satisfy her mother.

"Please turn your focus elsewhere," Koriolis said, interjecting himself into the conversation. "You achieved one ambition: mating your daughter to me. Let that be sufficient."

The oracle raised her hand and pointed at him. "You. You were meant to *control* my wayward daughter."

Koriolis chuckled. "Iselde is my mate, my *perfect match*, not someone I would—or even want to—control."

Bathasul frowned, her milky eyes glowing with fury. "That is not what you intended when I brought you two together."

"No, it wasn't," he admitted as the oracle lowered her hand. "I did not comprehend how the mate bond worked, how it would alter me so thoroughly and completely. Because of it, I am a better male."

Iselde unlocked her tongue. "Mother, did you let Uberon know you were coming?"

The oracle turned to face her and frowned.

"Uberon won't appreciate the intrusion."

"She's right, Bathasul. I don't," the Unseelie King said from the doorway where he lurked like a menacing shadow. "It's most discourteous to simply enter where you have not been invited."

The old female straightened her spine and sniffed, a haughty sound, in defiance.

Uberon stepped into the room. "Don't ignore me, Bathasul. Pretending I don't exist won't do you any favors."

"And you think I need to curry favor with *you*?" she sneered. She raised her claw-like hand again and pointed toward him. "*I* know what's best for my daughter!"

"You are not infallible, sister," another deep voice interjected, the diction crisp and cutting.

"Uncle Enders?" Iselde blinked in surprise as the enigmatic Archivist appeared in the doorway and entered the room. She rose from where she'd been seated on the edge of the bed and took a step toward the tall, imposing male who'd served as a father figure alongside the Unseelie King and Erlking.

He ignored her and continued to speak to his sister. "Losing your mate damaged you terribly."

"You knew my father?" Iselde whispered. She glanced between her mother and uncle. "Who was he? What happened to him?"

"You were confined to your home for a reason, Bathasul," Uberon said as he moved aside to make room for the Archivist. "You knew what would happen if you broke that confinement."

The female's voice trembled as she shouted, "You have no authority over me! I am the oracle!"

"Oh, but we do," came the Erlking's silky reply as he, too, entered the room. Clad in black, scalelike armor with his red hair dancing like flames, he matched the other ancient males in height and breadth. He took his place beside the Archivist. Somewhere outside, perhaps in one of the fortress' courtyards, the Erlking's hellhounds bayed.

Iselde pressed her lips together in an effort not to gape. Until that moment, she'd never seen all three males standing together. Their resemblance to one another was undeniable. She wondered how she had never noticed it before. She glanced at the doorway and wondered if the unicorns would put in an appearance, too.

Finally looking at her, Enders said, "The light of your soul has redeemed Marog—"

"Koriolis," Iselde corrected.

"—but" —he glared at the oracle and continued to speak as though Iselde had said nothing— "Bathasul, you go too far."

"Did she reject her mate?" the oracle spat. "Does she deny her happiness with him?"

"That's not the meddling of which I speak," Enders said.

"It is *your* decision to decide the fate of an entire people, an entire species," the Erlking added.

"It is *my* decision, *my* power!"

The three males moved to surround the ancient oracle who turned slowly to glare at each in turn with those eerie, opalescent eyes.

"Please, don't kill her," Iselde whispered, eyes glowing with fury. "Her death belongs to *me*."

The Erlking met her gaze and gave her a small smile as he joined hands with his brothers, the three most ancient males of their race, and closed a circle around the oracle. "We'll not kill her, and neither will you."

Uberon's silver eyes met hers. "But we will bind her."

"Again," Enders added. "She will interfere in your life no more, except by your request."

"She owes me blood!" Iselde insisted. Her fists clenched.

The Erlking leveled a cool glare of reproach at her. "I am the hand of justice, not you, my dear. Forget your blood oath for vengeance; it holds no power. We will exact justice, not you."

The oracle screeched in fury as power exploded in the room, a deafening, blinding burst of white light. It pulsed once, twice, three times, and disappeared as suddenly as it had erupted. Iselde's ears rang, though she could have sworn no words of power had been spoken and the eruption of power had not actually had any sound. She felt pressure on one hand and looked at it to see it enveloped by her mate's large hand. Somehow he had set aside the tray and moved to steady her—and she had not noticed. She met his tired gaze with a worried look then looked at the three most powerful fae in all the realms. They no longer clasped hands. The oracle was gone.

"What did you do?" she asked.

"We sent her back home," the Archivist said. "She'll only exercise her power to aid those who seek her out."

"As Thelan and Ishjarta did," the Erlking added.

"No longer will she impose her will to arrange others' fates to suit her whims and ambitions," Uberon added.

"You always were an advocate of free will," Koriolis murmured, looking at his father.

The Unseelie King nodded and said, "You will leave tomorrow."

Iselde opened her mouth to protest the decree, to state that her mate was as yet not strong enough to endure the long and arduous journey to the northern wastes. However, Koriolis' light squeeze of her hand stopped the words from pouring forth.

"Thank you for your hospitality, Your Majesty."

CHAPTER 40

THEY WERE READY TO GO AT DAWN. WITH LITTLE more than the hastily acquired clothes they wore—provided to them courtesy of Uberon and Corinne—they waited in the barbican to bid a formal goodbye to their host and hostess. Corinne took Iselde's hands in hers and said, "From one queen to another, I hope you will visit again. I can always use a friend."

Iselde privately admitted that having a friend would be ... nice. She'd never really had an actual friend. She answered with a regal nod and replied, "Once I reestablish myself among my tribe, you are welcome to visit."

Corinne shivered and shook her head. "I'm afraid arctic weather isn't on my to-do list. I don't do cold very well."

Iselde paused to discern the Unseelie Queen's meaning before speaking. She offered a small smile, forgiving the queen her reluctance to endure even a few days of the northern waste's bitter cold and cutting winds. She turned to Koriolis who spoke quietly with his father. "Are you ready, beloved?"

His face drawn with weariness and pallid with weakness, he nodded and took a deep breath to fortify himself for the journey.

"Let's go then," she said and offered her arm to steady him.

"Bide a moment," Uberon interrupted.

She looked over her shoulder at the Unseelie King. He met her questioning gaze then looked upward. With astonishing lightness and agility, two gargoyles alighted on the gravel drive leading to the barbican. They tucked their wings behind them and focused blank, stone eyes at their king's departing visitors. The gravel crunched beneath their immense weight as the gargoyles approached.

"You shall be spared the arduous journey through the Quol to the northern wastes," Uberon said. He gestured toward the gargoyles. "They have agreed to fly you home."

Koriolis acknowledged the gift of a speedy flight with a faint air of surprise. Through the connection of the mate bond, Iselde realized his surprise arose from the association of "home" with the northern wastes. He did not consider that bleak territory his home, and though she missed it, she wondered if he ever would. Koriolis bowed his head and murmured his gratitude.

"Though the northern wastes are forbidding and hostile, the people who live there offer warmth and hospitality," she assured him. "You will find welcome among them."

His golden gaze conveyed doubt, though no words left his lips.

She looked at the gargoyle standing closest to her. "Do you know where my tribe is?"

"I do, my lady."

"Then bear us there, please," she replied.

The gargoyle's wings snapped out, extending wide. The hulking male squatted and wrapped his arms around her, gently cradling her against a body of living stone. The other gargoyle did the same, tucking Koriolis close. With a powerful thrust, each gargoyle leaped into the air. Their wings flapped hard, gaining them fast altitude. Koriolis looked down. His father and stepmother had already disappeared inside the castle.

Warm, humid air soon gave way to hot, humid air as the gargoyles soared north and approached the tropical latitudes where the Quol seethed behind the boundaries Uberon enforced to keep it contained. The equatorial sun warmed the gargoyles through as they flew day and night with steady purpose, unflagging strength, and astonishing speed—and without stopping, for living stone needed neither rest nor food nor drink.

The direct route took them over land and water, both freshwater and saltwater, with the topography rising and falling and eventually leveling to a vast, windswept plain that Iselde recognized as the northern steppes. Grass bent beneath cold winds carrying the bite of an oncoming winter, a season which came early and stayed long. She spied the yurts and grazing herds of a few nomadic clans which inhabited the seemingly endless grasslands.

Koriolis shivered within the gargoyle's embrace as hunger, thirst, and cold weakened him further. He'd lost count of the days they traveled, the nights he slept within the gargoyle's stony embrace, yet he refused to beg the gargoyle to stop to allow him true respite. Eventually, he stopped shivering and wondered if this time he truly would die.

You shall not die, Iselde declared through their shared bond. A pulse of warmth and energy flowed through the mate bond into him.

I cannot take your life force.

You are not taking it; I am giving it.

He had not the strength to refuse.

The gargoyles descended with targeted precision and landed on a wind-scraped stretch of bare rock. Iselde's legs trembled as she slowly scanned the bluffs overlooking the rolling surf of a dark, turbulent sea. She knew this area well. Sea birds screeched overhead, their cries mingling with the noise of the unceasing wind and crashing waves. Far below and in the distance, the low calls of seals reverberated. When the wind changed, she knew it would carry their stench inland.

"Will you take us into the encampment?" she asked, looking toward the valley on the other side of the bluffs.

The gargoyle did not answer, but merely released his hold on her and stepped away. The other gargoyle did the same, ignoring the way Koriolis crumpled to the ice-cold rock. Without a word, both gargoyles leaped into the sky and soon disappeared. Iselde stumbled to her mate and sank to the ground beside him. She wrapped her arms around his shivering body and said, "I recognize this valley and the tipis of my people. They will have seen us. They will come."

He nodded and said nothing.

They waited. Eventually, a vanguard of four warriors approached with caution, for a lack of caution in the northern wastes led to swift and painful death. She met the faded blue gaze of the nearest warrior.

"Matriarch?"

"Guorik?" she called out.

He rushed toward her, calling out to his comrades. Upon reaching her, he pulled off his cloak and wrapped it around her. "Where have you been?"

Another warrior pulled off his cloak and wrapped it around Koriolis. He looked at her, his eyes a faded moss green. "Another refugee, Matriarch?"

"My mate," she replied with blunt candor. While the warriors exchanged surprised glances, she added, "We are weak and need help to reach shelter."

"The maidens' tipi is empty," another warrior said.

"The girls have all mated?" Her cobalt eyes widened in surprise.

"Aye, Matriarch," Guorik replied. "We kept it ready for you."

She shook her head. "It is long past the time when the tribe should have moved to new hunting grounds."

"The sea is bountiful. Let us get you and your mate to shelter," Guorik said. "You shall eat and rest before telling us of your adventures."

A weary but appreciative smile spread across Iselde's face. Bowing her head, she said, "Aye."

Two warriors supported her, slinging one of her arms over the shoulder of each. They did the same with Koriolis who had yet to speak to them. With their assistance, Iselde and Koriolis descended into the valley and entered the tipi where a bevy of females busied themselves with the homely activities of hospitality: hot food, comfortable bedding, and warm welcome. Iselde thanked them and gratefully accepted the bowls of fish stew and jugs of water.

They ate and took their rest, sleeping soundly despite the howl of the arctic wind rushing between the tipis up the valley slope across the bluffs and out to sea. The next morning, Koriolis appeared much improved, if not fully recovered. He awoke hours after his mate had risen and rested quietly while she tended to his needs.

"Will you be ready to speak to my people today?" she asked after he handed her his empty bowl, scraped clean of its hearty, nourishing contents.

"I will," he promised.

She stared at him as though trying to see all his secrets, then said, "There is a longhouse we maintain here for tribal meetings. We will gather there after supper."

"What time is it?" he asked.

"Midday. You slept long and well."

He sighed.

"You needed it."

He pressed his lips together as though to hold back words refuting her statement. Opening them, he sighed again. "I grow weary of this weakness."

"You will grow strong again," she assured him. "This is not a gentle land. It will forge you as humans forge steel."

"But with cold rather than heat."

She nodded. "I have duties to attend to, but will return soon. Rest more while you can."

A gust of cold air burst into the tipi as she exited, making him shiver. It took several minutes before he regained comfort, although he huddled close to the firepit. Belly full and finally warm, he again slipped into slumber only to be awakened hours later when Iselde returned with more food and water. Two of her people followed her into the tipi, each bearing bundles of clothing better suited to the frigid weather than what they wore. After eating, they changed into their new clothes.

Iselde ran her hand over the finely tanned fur draped around her shoulders and trimming the tall shafts of her boots. "Ashkele has a fine hand with leather." She looked at Koriolis who yet struggled with the unfamiliar garb. "Here, let me help you."

He nodded acceptance of her offer and soon found himself properly accoutered for life in the northern wastes. "I'm surprised they had anything extra to provide."

"These clothes are hastily made," she confided. "Come summer, we will have time for finer work."

His anticipatory silence spurred further explanation.

"Though we live in a land of black and white, rock and snow, and outwardly, we appear just as harsh and dreary, we are a folk who love color and artistry, music and warmth. The hostile climate of the northern wastes protects us from the predation of other folk who would otherwise settle here. We thrive in this land where no one else cares to live. You shall see the best of us this evening."

He nodded and followed her from the tipi. She took his hand in hers and guided him through the winter darkness to the well-insulated longhouse. Stepping inside the structure, he noticed the brightness of fires burning in a line of pits down the center of the building. Adults and children of varying heritages and ages conversed and sang and laughed. The gust of cold air that accompanied their entrance into the building swept over the tribe like a herald's cry. They quickly quieted and watched in silent anticipation as the Ice Queen and her mate walked to an open spot at the center of one long wall. Iselde laid a folded blanket on the floor and sat. Koriolis carefully lowered himself to sit beside her. She offered no assistance so he would show less weakness.

One of the males rose to his feet and approached them. He bowed and held out a long stick, intricately carved and painted in primary colors. Feathers and small bells made from bone dangled from leather thongs attached to one end of the stick. Raising the stick so all could see it, he spoke, "We welcome your return, Matriarch, and would hear of your adventures."

He lowered the stick and angled it toward her. She took it in her hand and turned it over, the small bells jingling with the stick's rotation. With a gracious nod, she thanked him. The male returned to his seat beside a female who, Koriolis noticed, had red djinni eyes. Others had the feline eyes of the fae. Still others had human eyes. Few in the tribe, he realized, were pure blooded, except perhaps the two felidae who sat with another small family.

"It is good to be back among my beloved people," Iselde said, her voice clear and low, carrying easily to the ears of all who listened. She did not ask how long she'd been absent, for the passage of time meant little to an immortal. Also, time did not march in lockstep between realms. "I have missed you all." She ran her gaze over all assembled in the longhouse. "Some of you I do not know. Present yourselves."

The two felidae rose and approached, their steps careful and controlled. The male's face was bisected by a long, deep scar and one ear was torn. They nodded respectfully, for felidae bowed to no one.

"Matriarch," the male said. "I am Mroo-kral-an. This is my mate, Mroo sha-grik."

Iselde nodded. "Be welcome. What brings you to my people?"

"A djinni raid," the male replied. "They took our cubs and us into slavery and sold us."

"Your cubs?" she prompted.

"Two males, two females."

"Do you know where they are?"

Both felidae shook their heads. "We do not."

"And what boon do you ask of me?"

The female spoke, her lips peeling back to reveal her fangs. "If you could find out where our cubs are, we will retrieve them and bring them here to serve as warriors and hunters for your tribe."

"Would you swear fealty to me and my mate?"

"We are not canidae," the male growled. "We offer gratitude, service, and loyalty, but we do not offer obedience."

"Your offer is acceptable," Iselde said. She extended her hand. "I need a taste of blood from each of you."

Suspicious, the female asked, "And what does this taste do? What will be our obligation?"

Rather than take offense as Koriolis stiffened at her side, Iselde favored the felidae with a small smile. "You are wise to ask, for this is no small request. I will taste your blood, scent it, and trace it to the cubs who are the product of your combined essences. As you request, I will discover where they are. As you have not requested, I will help you liberate them. And, as you offered, I will expect you and them to serve my people as warriors and hunters."

The male brought his hand to his mouth and bit down on the fleshy base of his thumb. He held his bleeding palm over hers and let his blood drip into her hand. When he finished, his mate did the same.

"Be welcome, Mroo-kral-an and Mroo-sha-grik," Iselde said with another regal nod. She held up her blood-filled palm and inhaled. After a deep breath, she lapped at the fluid, a single, delicate dip of her tongue. She held out her cupped hand to Koriolis and said, "Scent and taste." He bent over her hand and did as she bade him.

His eyes widened at the musky scent. The distinctive qualities of the felidae blood bloomed on his tongue as he analyzed it and processed what he learned. To his surprise and relief, the smell and taste of their blood did not trigger a craving for more. He felt the invisible relaxation of his mate beside him as she realized the same absence of craving in him.

"Do you have it?" she asked.

He mulled over the blood on his tongue a moment longer before nodding. After swallowing, he said, "I will recognize the cubs."

The two felidae sighed in relief.

Once again, Iselde said, "Be welcome."

The two felidae accepted the dismissal and returned to their seats. Iselde called upon the next new member of the tribe to present himself to her. Tall and gangly, the adolescent Third House fae approached, a thin band of copper encircling his throat. He gazed with fear upon the bejeweled silver filigree showing above the collar of her tunic.

"Be at ease," she said. "What is your name?"

"Ludo," he replied.

"And your family?"

"Mel Ursai."

"Formerly subject to the House of Lahn Ursai?"

He nodded.

"What brings you here?"

The boy squeezed his copper-colored eyes tightly shut. He took a shuddering breath. Then he replied, "The Quol. It … it ate my family."

Koriolis felt Iselde's internal wince, although she displayed no dismay as she asked, "And did not King Mogren offer you a place in the Seelie Court?"

"I-I could do that?" he blurted. "King Mogren would give me a place in his court?"

"He can. He might. You would have to ask him, present yourself to him," she replied. "Or you may stay here and serve."

The boy shivered and hung his head in shame. "I do not wish to be ungrateful …"

She gave him a small smile. "The northern wastes are not for everyone. If you wish to leave to seek your fortune in the Seelie Court, then we will direct your path, but we will not not lead you there."

He pondered that for a moment, then replied with grave maturity, "It is winter and I will not survive on my own in the northern wastes. I will serve you until summer with gratitude, then find my way south."

"Be welcome, Ludo," Iselde replied.

Ludo returned to his seat with the family who had taken him into their care. Iselde called the next person and proceeded through six more. Three had already found mates among her tribe. Once the introductions were completed, one member of the tribe launched into song. Voices low and thrumming entwined with voices high and lilting in complicated melodies and harmonies that wove a warm, soothing magic of welcome and acceptance and protection. Koriolis had never experienced the like.

"You have a true community here," he whispered when the song ended, leaning close to her so his lips brushed her delicately pointed ear.

"We all serve the good of our tribe, but not to the detriment of any one person," she replied. "None here call me queen."

"No," he said, realizing the essence of what her people did call her: *Matriarch*. "What are we going to do about the cubs?"

She gave him a flinty smile. "We're going to liberate them."

He nodded, not looking forward to returning to Djaria.

"This is what I do," she explained. "This is what I have done for millennia. My tribe is descended from refugees, and occasionally we add to our number with fresh blood."

"Something Mogren would never do."

She shook her head. "No, he would not. I am not certain he will welcome Ludo."

"Third House fae have little power and less to offer," he said, understanding that if Ludo were refused a home within the Seelie Court and returned to the northern wastes, then Iselde would welcome him as a permanent addition to her tribe.

"Your prejudice is showing."

Chastised as he had never been, Koriolis blushed.

A heavily pregnant female approached.

"Yes, Ashkele?" Iselde prompted.

The female gave her a shy smile and said, "We would hear of your adventures, Matriarch."

Iselde's lips split in a wide smile. She looked at her people assembled around her in the longhouse and eagerly awaiting her story. "Of course, child. My story belongs to all of you."

Koriolis stiffened beside her in preparation for their condemnation. Iselde placed her hand lightly on his leg in silent reassurance. *We are fair-minded folk. They will accept you, and you will have a true home with us.*

He sent a pulse of love and gratitude to her through the mate bond.

Then she told them, and they *listened*.

CHAPTER 41

WHILE KORIOLIS ATE, RESTED, AND RECUPERATED, Iselde bent her magic to tracing the combined essence of the two felidae who yearned to be reunited with their children. Blood being powerful in itself, she exploited the connection and practically seethed with triumph when she located them. To her great relief and the relief of the cubs' parents, the four children yet lived.

"They have been separated, sold to different owners," she explained. "That will make retrieving them difficult."

The felidae male and his mate nodded, the male rubbing the scar on his face in memory of his own suffering. "We are strong and determined. We will do whatever is necessary."

"Good," Iselde said. "You'll have to."

She summoned a group of her most experienced warriors to her and gave them each cub's location, transferring the blood-link in her mind directly to theirs by pricking each warrior's finger and touching the bleeding fingertip to her own bleeding thumb. She used the blood-to-blood connection to strengthen the bond. After the warriors retrieved supplies and weapons, she split their number into groups, a trio focused on finding and retrieving each cub. The felidae mates she paired with her own grandson who frequently received the honor of such missions.

"Though felidae are not obedient subjects, you *will* obey him," she said to the parents whose children she had vowed to retrieve.

Tall, imposing, and every inch a fearsome warrior, the fae male leveled cobalt eyes at them.

"There is none better than the blood of my blood to help you," she added. Subdued, they nodded. She looked at her grandson. "Do what you must. Spare no effort. Waste no blood."

He locked gazes with her then bowed and pressed a light kiss to her cheek. "I accept nothing less than victory, Matriarch."

She lay a palm against his cheek and looked into his cobalt gaze, as hard and icy as hers. "I know your heart and you know mine. Go with my blessing." She looked up and faced the entire group and raised both hands. Balefire sprayed from her fingertips in a shower of blue sparks. She repeated, "Go with my blessing and return victorious."

Koriolis had never seen the like. As the group quickly departed across the bleak winter landscape at uncanny speed, he asked, "What did you do?"

"I gave them a boost," she replied.

He noticed her pallor. "You gave them *yourself*."

"Aye," she said, the sound more of an exhaled breath than an actual vocal expression.

She closed her eyes and wobbled. Koriolis moved to steady her, drawing her close to his body and giving her support. Through the mate bond he sent her a pulse of power. She gasped as it sizzled through her body, imparting heated strength and fiery love.

"Come," he said. "You no longer rule your people alone."

"I do not *rule* them," she replied, her tone peevish as he walked her back to the tipi they shared.

He chuckled. "You are the Ice Queen. Of course, you rule them."

"I am the Matriarch."

"You are," he easily agreed. Glancing at the icy expanse spreading around them, he said, "I once had ambitions of ruling the Unseelie Court, then I wrested the power to coerce New Orleans to yield to my rule. But you … you did not ask to rule, and yet your people willingly and gladly give you their trust and service. You are like no other royal I have ever witnessed."

She shrugged. "My empire is vast and largely unpopulated. Were there cities and large groups of people, my 'rule' would be none so easy." She gestured toward the collection of tipis and her people going about their business. "We are a family, if you will, and I am the head of this family. What affects one of us affects us all."

Koriolis opened the flap to their tipi and accompanied her inside. "The small number of your people enables you to govern with gentleness."

"It does," she replied, glad of his comprehension. "If I sought a 'real' kingdom, I would have complied with my mother's ambitions for a fate as Djaria's queen. I do not share her ambition." She paused. "And I hate the desert."

He grinned. "I rather think I will enjoy supporting the queen who sits on the throne rather than sitting on it myself."

She raised an eyebrow. "You think you're going to fade into the woodwork?"

He glanced around the tipi. "I see no woodwork."

Iselde shook her head. "You know what I mean."

Koriolis chuckled. "I do. And what I have witnessed here inspires me. Our children will know liberty as well as responsibility."

Her expression sobered. "This is a harsh land. It does not allow for an easy life."

"I do not wish our children to have an easy life. I wish them strength, resourcefulness, and resilience."

"And happiness," she added softly. "I wish them happiness."

"Aye," he agreed. "And what else did you give the retrieval party beyond a strong measure of your own strength, spirit, and power?"

Iselde's lips peeled back in a serrated smile. "I had a conversation with my mother."

"Oh?" He picked up a jug, poured some water into a small bowl carved from stone, and handed it to her.

"I convinced her to manipulate fate." She drank the bowl dry in just a few gulps. "She owes me one."

At least one. He raised an eyebrow and poured himself a bowl of water.

She added, "They *will* return, *all* of them, with their cubs."

Koriolis took a sip and said, "I don't know how you managed to do that, nor do I care. But good. *Good.*"

Iselde nodded. "She owes *us* that much."

Koriolis rather thought the oracle didn't owe him at all. The oracle had brought him his beloved mate, so perhaps he owed her.

Nah.

He sent a thought of gratitude toward the heavens. He'd returned to the fae realm, been relieved of his demonic affliction, and now had a true mate who was his match if not his better and who somehow managed to love him despite his past sins. Iselde, as ancient as she was, represented the best of the fae and, he believed, their future.

About the Author

Holly Bargo is a freelance writer and editor who lives on a southwestern Ohio hobby farm with her husband and their menagerie of cats, dogs, horses, and chickens. She has been writing stories since childhood and published her first novel in 2014.

Holly welcomes new clients for editing, ghostwriting, and book design. If you are seeking those services, contact her through the Hen House Publishing website, henhousepublishing.com.

As with all Holly's books in any series she writes, *Light of the Twin Moons* may be read as a stand-alone novel. Holly detests cliffhangers and will not inflict them upon her readers. This book is dedicated to the author's first grandchild, Evelyn Grace.

THANK YOU!

I deeply appreciate your support in purchasing this book. As you may already know, indie authors crave reader reviews. I hope you will take a moment of your time to leave a review on this book's Amazon page.

BOOKS
BY HOLLY BARGO

Series

Each book in any series written by Holly Bargo may be read as a stand-alone novel. Holly detests cliffhangers and won't inflict them on her readers. However, for the most enjoyment, it's advised to read the books in each series in order.

The Bounty (published by 0-0-8 Studios)

Book 1: *The Bounty: Jones*
Book 2: *The Bounty: Gerlaugh*

Twin Moons Saga

Book 1: *Daughter of the Twin Moons*
Book 2: *Daughter of the Deepwood*
Book 3: *Daughter of the Dark Moon*
Book 4: *Knight of the Twin Moons*
Book 5: *Champion of the Twin Moons*
Book 6: *Light of the Twin Moons*

Triune Alliance Brides

Book 1: *Triple Burn*
Book 2: *Double Cut*
Book 3: *Single Stroke*

Russian Love

Book 1: *Russian Lullaby*
Book 2: *Russian Gold*
Book 3: *Russian Dawn*
Book 4: *Russian Pride*
Book 5: *Russian Revival*

Immortal Shifters
Books 1 & 2: *The Barbary Lion & Tiger in the Snow* (duet)
Book 3: *Bear of the Midnight Sun*
Book 4: *The Eagle at Dawn*

Tree of Life
Book 1: *Rowan*
Book 2: *Cassia*
Book 3: *Willow*

Stand-Alone Titles

FOCUS
Hogtied
Shot from the Hip
Satin Boots
The Falcon of Imenotash
Ulfbehrt's Legacy
The Diamond Gate
Pure Iron
The Mighty Finn
Six Shots Each Gun (with Russ Towne)
The Dragon Wore a Kilt

Short Stories

Skeins of Gold: Rumpelstiltskin Retold
By Water Reborn